Secrets of the Trees

Secrets of the Trees

Alissa Lukara

Homestead Lighthouse Press
Grants Pass, Oregon

FIRST EDITION

Book cover and interior design by Ray Rhamey
Author photo by George Rubaloff

Library of Congress Cataloging in Publication Data:
20199440516

ISBN: 978-1-950475-03-2

To my ancestors

Chapter 1

2003

Nikkie had been running all her life. Running towards her dream of being a soloist with a well-known dance company. Running in circles when the path she had chosen to study and dance in New York left her feeling empty inside. Running away from that longtime dream.

Toward a new one. Sean and his indie rock band Stone Tara had asked her to be their dancer, and the band's career had taken off. All because of a song Sean wrote that ended up in an Academy Award-nominated documentary about the environment.

No more running toward or away from. Tonight, the band and I have arrived, Nikkie thought, electric heat surging through her. In a few minutes, she and the band would perform the song at the Planet Aid Concert for the Environment at the Hollywood Bowl. *I can't believe everything that had to come together for the band to be here because of one song—and for them to include me, a dancer, not a musician. It has to be the same odds as winning a lottery.*

Nikkie inhaled deeply, catching the scent of eucalyptus trees around the Bowl. Her breath reached down through her feet into the earth, pulling up its balance and grounding. She connected it to the expanse of the sky, felt the rhythmic pulsing of both as she drew them into her heart. The beat linked her to the lives of the audience.

Seventeen thousand five hundred lives to be exact. A lot to take in for any dancer. From her off stage vantage point, Nikkie watched the mass of bodies bobbing up and down before her, back and forth, barely visible in the half dark beyond the glare of the stage lights.

Indistinct, yet teeming with life, they bobbed on the ground, up the stadium seating. Sitting. Picnicking. Dancing. Some of the audience swayed in trees, their outlines barely visible against the rolling Hollywood hills behind them. They drank wine, smoked a bit of weed. All people did to celebrate the environment at this concert while they watched the likes of Paul McCartney, k.d. lang, Jackson Brown, Sheryl Crow and now, Stone Tara.

The audience looked like a mix of sea anemones and other sea creatures, tossing in a giant tide pool as the ocean brought them their nourishment. Tonight, she and the other performers were that ocean. Dancing for this sea organism would change her life even more than it had already changed.

In a few minutes, she would do the dramatic whirling dance she performed whenever the band played *Climatica*. Nikkie closed her eyes, tapped the rush of gratitude for being here, for the miracle of it. But along with these thoughts, self-doubt crept in. *What if I blow this chance? What if no one likes my dancing?*

Breathe in, out. Nikkie willed herself to drop through the tumult of sound, energy and backstage activity swirling around her, dropped through her own fear mixed with excitement to search for the still point within she connected to before each performance. Instead, waves of electric energy from the audience and performers already on stage, unlike anything she had experienced, coursed through her.

No stillness to be found here. No familiar ground. If she opened herself to the energy, she felt it would overwhelm her, leave her unable to perform. She felt nauseous and something she rarely experienced despite spinning during each dance—dizziness.

Just go with it, Nikkie said to herself. *Be in the moment.* Who was she kidding? Her vertigo worsened.

She turned her focus to the people she knew supported her. Her mother, Ellie, had come to L.A. to see her perform—one person amongst the seventeen thousand five hundred she knew would love her dancing. But concentrating on Ellie did not help.

Nikkie thought about her father, Peter, a dancer himself, who had died fifteen years earlier. She called on his spirit for strength and inspiration but came up blank. Perhaps he would have instead agreed with her teachers at Julliard—that leaving her dreams of joining a New York modern dance company behind to perform with Stone Tara was a mistake.

Anxiety two-stepped its way toward panic. *Stop doing this to yourself,* she told herself. But she could not.

What would Tom, her twin brother and manager, tell her, she wondered? And in that instant, as if he could read her mind, which he sometimes seemed to do in that telepathic twin way, he was at her side. All six foot two inches of him.

Tom grinned at her with the half-smile of his that seemed to express both the irony of life and some profound wisdom beyond anything the twins had lived. Nikkie loved that smile, felt a tad calmer looking at it and Tom's angular face.

"I can't make any sense of this," Nikkie said, sweeping her arm across the breadth of the audience and the stage.

"No one can. Don't try," Tom said. "This concert is bigger than anything you know. I mean, what's the largest crowd any of those indie festivals Stone Tara performed at ever had. Eight hundred? One thousand people?"

Nikkie nodded. "But what I'm experiencing is beyond stage fright. It's stage terror."

"Call it what you like, but I see it as fire for your performance. I can feel the fire you have inside you, see it shining in your eyes. It's fantastic. Like those bonfires we used to burn as teenagers that sparked and danced and lit up the night sky. That fire is your friend. Just what you need. Let it blaze. Don't be afraid of it."

"How can you be so sure?"

"Come on, Nik, I bet you've never heard of one instance of a performer internally combusting and exploding on stage." Tom ran his hand through his blond hair, cropped short at his neck, a little long on top, to slick back a strand falling over his forehead. He put his arm around Nikkie's waist, squeezed her tight for a moment.

"The fire is your friend," he said. "Remember that."

"Fire is my friend. I like that. Thanks." She rested her head against Tom's shoulder, kept repeating the phrase, "Fire is my friend. Fire is my friend," She envisioned herself as a bonfire radiating heat and light.

The fire in Nikkie's belly rose, surged through her torso, arms, legs and out through the top of her head. It created an explosion inside of her that matched the vibrant red of her dress and nails now, which triggered a new concern.

The red dress had been a last-minute addition by Ron, Stone Tara's new manager, replacing the white one Nikkie usually wore to dance. She had only found out about it that afternoon when it arrived in a clothing bag, along with a makeup artist and a hair stylist to curl and style her usually straight blond hair.

"I'm still worried this new dress won't move well, especially when I do the spin."

"Remember that Ron's got the experience with venues like this," Tom said. "What's important is it will look great projected on the screens, and the audience can notice the dress—and you performing in it—all the way to the cheap seats."

With Tom's encouragement, Nikkie willed herself to let her clothing concerns go. "All right. I'm accepting the dress and nails and hair. All of it." Giving the best performance she could, opening to this opportunity for her and Tom was what mattered, not how she looked. "The fire *is* my friend."

"That's the spirit," Tom turned to Nikkie, still holding her gently at the waist. "No more indie fests, where before you went onstage, you could run a brush through your hair and throw on whatever hippy, gypsy, flowy thing wasn't too wrinkled from living out of a tent and being on the road. We've moved on."

Nikkie smiled, rolled her eyes.

"Take it from me," Tom said. "You look gorgeous, and you and the band are going to rock the house, excuse me, amphi-theater. L.A. won't know what hit them." He hugged her, then leaned back. "Seriously, you're going to do great. You're an amazing dancer. And I can't wait to see the climax shot of you holding the earth."

In one of the visual impact moments at the Planet Aid con-cert, Nikkie would look like she held the world in her hands while dancing the signature move she did every time the band performed *Climatica*—the whirl.

The camera had been set up to create the illusion of her spinning while holding the earth in its delicate balance in space. That image would be projected on the screens behind her and Stone Tara. At this moment, Nikkie felt like she stood vibrating at the speed of light in the center of that world.

"It's time," Tom said.

The act performing before Stone Tara ended. Sean and the rest of the band were heading to the stage. She had to admit they looked better wearing the black leather pants and multi-colored silk shirts Ron had brought them. Sean's deep red one echoed Nikkie's dress.

Nikkie moved to her mark. *Fire is my friend*, she re-minded herself. Showtime. She knew the routine she had choreographed. She hoped she would also be able to let the spirit and the improvisational sparks that created the magic and uniqueness of each of her dances shine through the fire.

Fire is my friend, she repeated. Time to dance from that fire with all her heart and soul.

Waiting for the song to start, Nikkie focused on the spin in her dance. She had been whirling since she knew she wanted to be a dancer at seven years of age. Nikkie linked her own version of the spin to the long tradition of whirling dervishes, poets and spiritual masters, like Rumi and Hafiz, and other sacred dancers, who spun to connect heaven and earth, to embody spirit.

The blaze in Nikkie's belly, the wild beating of her heart was joined by a roar in her ears. Through that inner rumbling, Nikkie heard Sean's voice introduce their song and acknowledge the documentary and environmental movement.

Glancing at the wings of the stage, she made out Tom's face in the dim lights. He smiled, gave her a thumbs -up.

The music started, the natural rise and fall of the guitar and Sean's voice that she loved so. Something unknown inside her began to move, and she followed the prompting. Perhaps the fire was dancing her. She became aware not only of her own center but of all those in her environment. The band members. The audience bobbing and weaving. Tom. The stagehands watching the show. Camera crew motioning with their arms. A camera person holding a Steadicam crisscrossing the stage.

Nikkie brought her focus to her breath and movement. Instead of feeling enlivened, inspired, one dance step building on the other, like she usually did, she felt the fire, the vitality she was counting on, drain from her. It fanned out onto the stage like her dress fanned around her legs. Vertigo and nausea returned, stronger this time. A shudder she had never experienced vibrated through her body.

Soft focus. Let go, she told herself, recalling the words she used to remind herself how not to get dizzy while she spun. This action, so natural to her, had not needed words for years.

The time arrived in the song for her to spin. She checked to make sure she danced on her mark on stage. Hands at her heart, she turned to the right. Both her arms swept up simultaneously, first out to the side like wings, then up into a V above her head, palms facing each other. The movement was automatic like some internal force lifted them. She could barely hear the music. *Throw your head back. Look up at the camera. Smile. Dance.*

Nikkie twirled but felt like she was following orders she no longer knew or comprehended. She glanced down and was grateful to see the dress flaring. Did she appear to hold the image of the world as planned too? Arms wide enough? Head back enough? She had forgotten everything she had rehearsed, how to move, what step to take next.

The lightheadedness intensified. Fear of falling gripped her belly. *Come on, Nikkie. Be a pro,* she told herself and willed herself to keep turning. She wanted to close her eyes, to lie down, to sleep, to forget. What was happening? *Don't blow this. For yourself. For Tom. For the band. Don't blow it.* She let the rising emotion come through her, not clear she was dancing anymore.

She seemed to be traveling, traveling, the sounds around her being pulled out and away, the roar inside rising. When she brought her eyes to where the stage was supposed to be, it was gone. She was in the middle of a forest, a place she had been in once before when she was a child. A place outside of time.

Unease seeped through her. But she kept dancing, turning.

No. Not now. Not again.

In the area of the wings where Tom had been, a little girl, her long hair in two braids, stood in a clearing surrounded by trees. With her were a man, a woman, her parents perhaps, and other people as well.

Some were dressed in simple clothing, white cotton blouses, and grey and brown wool skirts and pants, of another era, like old family photos she had seen of the 1930s and '40s. Their hairstyles were also from that era. The scene looked like a WWII movie set. The girl wore a nightgown, held her mother's hand with one hand and a doll with the other. Her eyes locked on Nikkie. Some of the tall, thin trees had white skin, black markings—birch. Others were pine.

Nikkie wanted to run, run, run off the stage, hide, but she could not. She needed to perform, keep performing.

As she spun, she wanted to look anywhere but at the people in the scene. Screenshot one, two, three, their faces streamed by. But with each turn, for a moment, a flash, she saw them distinctly, imprinted every detail, texture. And then their bodies were in front of her, their faces in shock. The woman tried to get the child behind her. People began dropping, one after another, each one floating down to the ground. From left to right. Arms flew up in front of their bodies as if to protect. The father. The mother. The little girl. Dropping. The doll fell. Eyes. Open. Staring at Nikkie. Inside her, a scream rose, and stunning pain ripped through Nikkie's arms, the right side of her head and ear. The roar inside. Nikkie longed to drop her own arms, to fall as well, to crumple to the earth.

All she could focus on was that child, her connection to that little one. The girl appeared to lay dead in this forest of birch trees that stretched to the sky, rooted in the earth, surrounded the bodies like witnesses.

Nikkie tore her eyes away from the girl now, focused on the beauty, the magnificence of the trees. Their grace and strength kept Nikkie dancing in the spin, hoping, wanting, desperate to stop and spin in reverse, rewind the image she had seen, undo the scene that played out in front of her. The only ones who remained upright in her vision now were men in uniforms. Their guns extended, then dropped to their sides, the men ran, ran through the trees away from the scene.

The roaring in Nikkie's head stopped cold, and a new man appeared, tall, angular face, blond hair. He looked out of place, wearing black jeans and a white shirt. Startled, he ran to the bodies, knelt down and picked the girl up onto his knee. He held her, stroking her hair.

His head rose, and his eyes fastened on Nikkie's. Her body continued to whirl, but she was outside of the spin as well, standing still, staring at this man and he at her, surprised to see each other.

And this yearning intensified in her. A knowing. Like she knew this man. She noted that same recognition in him. He beckoned her with his eyes, mouthed something to her as he held the girl. And she heard in her head as distinct as if he was standing next to her, words she did not comprehend. Foreign words.

"*Palīdz man,*" he said. The words reverberated in her mind.

A tunnel of energy pulled Nikkie backward. The music on stage ended, and the vision disappeared. Just like that. Nikkie stood upright on stage surrounded by the night sky, the audience, Stone Tara.

Instead of ending her dance in a flourish, with her arms still extended in a "V" overhead, back arched, like the victory stance of a winning Olympic athlete, as she had intended, her arms had collapsed to her sides. Stunned, she felt frozen, unable to move. Like she was in a bad dream and could not wake up.

Bile ripped up her throat, into her mouth. She felt like she might fall.

Keep standing. Don't throw up. Don't throw up on stage, Nikkie repeated to herself as Sean extended a hand to her to join the band members. She linked arms with him and the band, took a bow. Then Sean bowed. Instead of bowing on her own as planned, she was swept again in a bow with all the band members, then Sean alone again.

The band members headed off stage, arms around each other's shoulders, but left Nikkie separate, broken off of the lined chain. Couldn't Sean see? See her distress? No one noticed her at all.

I can make it, she repeated, like a mantra, and walked off stage alone. Tom appeared next to her, his arm around her, holding her up.

"Steady girl," he said like she was a horse needing handling. And she did. Her head kept spinning, and she was falling, and somewhere, somewhere, the dead lay waiting.

CHAPTER 2

"Nikkie. Nik. Wake up."

Tom's voice filtered in through the blue and red lights flashing behind Nikkie's closed eyes. The right side of her head throbbed, pulsing like the beat of a drum.

She didn't want to open her eyes, wanted to watch the light show in her mind.

"Wake up." Tom's voice reached out to her again through the spectacle. His hand touched her own, warm, gentle. She wanted to obey her brother, but she wanted the lights more. A deep shade of sparkly blue. Red. Like the dress she wore when she danced.

Dance? *Oh, my goddess.* Had she slept through her cue? She had to get up, get on stage. No, she had already danced. The vision of the dead in the forest passed through Nikkie like the shudder of a ghost.

She wanted to groan but could not move her mouth. She wished she could take a pill to knock herself out further, anything to follow those flashing lights, already receding, anything to get her head to stop spinning and eradicate the vision.

"Is she okay? Nikkie, it's me, your mom," Ellie said. "What happened? Did she fall? Everything's going to be okay, precious girl."

The smell of ammonia hit Nikkie's nose like adrenaline. Smelling salts.

"Her eyes are fluttering." The mother voice again. "Nikkie. It's okay. We're here."

Nikkie opened her eyes. The lights receded, but not the spinning.

"What happened?" Nikkie tried to stand up but couldn't. The room turned before her. She fell back down onto something soft. So soft. She wanted to sink and disappear into the softness.

"Hold on. Don't try to get up," Tom said. "You fainted. Outside the dressing room. I carried you in."

Nikkie felt the velvet with her hands, recognized the burgundy velvet couch up against the wall of the dressing room. "I think I'm going to throw up," she said.

Tom slid the wastebasket over beside her. "Just in case."

Nikkie leaned over, put her head over the pail, but nausea that had come on like a wave receded like one too.

"I'll get some paper towels," Ellie said. "So you don't mess up your dress."

Dress. Nikkie became more aware of the mirrors, the makeup tables, the beige walls. The dressing room was empty. Where was everyone?

Performing, she realized. "I've got to pull it together. Is everyone on stage for the finale? Help me get out there." She started to get up again.

"Nik. Lie still," Tom said, a look of concern in his eyes. No smile. No ironic twist. "You're not going on stage. You might pass out again and hurt yourself. Besides, only Sean has to be there. He's the one who sings."

"But..."

"No buts, Nikkie; Tom's right," Ellie said. "Stay down. And if I remember my first aid for fainting, we need to put a pillow under your legs, so they are higher than your heart."

A new wave of queasiness joined Nikkie's frustration as Ellie raised Nikkie's legs and placed one of the couch pillows under them. She had never reneged on professional responsibilities, had always pulled herself together, even if she had a cold or the flu. But on the night it mattered most, even if she could manage to stay upright through the finale, she could not carry a wastebasket on stage in case she needed to vomit. And what if the vision came back? She sighed.

"Tom, would you go tell Sean? So he doesn't think I am not showing up without reason. Tell him I'll be fine by tomorrow," Nikkie said, hoping she would be.

"And while you're out, get Nikkie a ginger ale," Ellie said. "It might help settle her stomach."

"I'm on it," Tom said over his shoulder as he walked out the door.

Ellie pulled her chair nearer to Nikkie and placed her daughter's hand in hers. "It'll be okay. You're probably exhausted. Have you eaten anything today?"

"Not much. I was too nervous."

Through her still foggy brain, Nikkie wished what had happened on stage was that simple. She knew she had to tell Ellie and Tom about it but not now.

She was worried about her performance. She did not know if she had pulled off the special effect of holding the spinning earth or if her dancing during the vision had been a disaster. Maybe that was why Sean and the band had walked off stage without her.

Nothing had gone as she had hoped. For days, Nikkie had imagined her feelings of joy during and after the concert, spending an evening where she, Tom and Stone Tara could let down and take in their professional leap. Now, instead of celebrating with a cornucopia of celebrities, she was lying on a dressing room couch, reeling with self-doubt.

The months she had been with the band flashed through her mind. Not one of them could have predicted their success when *Climatica* had been included in the low budget documentary. Six weeks earlier, they had still been playing at indie music festivals. But after the film was nominated for the Academy Award, *Climatica* became an anthem for the environmental movement. A mainstream record label and a new manager signed the band. Now, Stone Tara and she had performed at the Hollywood Bowl. And in two days, she would have her own contract with the group to choreograph and dance its international tour and music videos.

She hoped Sean was not having second thoughts. She closed her eyes. Dealing with the vision would have to wait. Finding out about her dancing that night and whether she still had a career was all she could handle.

In a few minutes, Tom returned carrying the bottle of ginger ale, handed it to Nikkie. She took a sip.

"What did Sean say?" Nikkie asked.

"He's sorry you're not feeling well. Says to rest up. Speaking of which, are you feeling any better?"

"I'm starting to. The ginger ale is working, and my head has stopped turning.

"I felt dizzy and nauseous like I've never felt when I was spinning. I'm afraid I messed up my performance. So be honest. I want to know what Sean said about it—and what you thought." Nikkie looked from Tom to her mother. "Did I blow it?"

"Nik, you were terrific," Tom said. "Especially considering the technical problem. Sean felt bad, said it must have been tough to adjust. He emphasized that you handled it like a pro."

"Like a pro? What are you talking about?"

"The whole thing was disorienting," Tom said. "No wonder you got dizzy. All those different colors swirling on the screens while you danced instead of you holding the earth? Greens, yellows, oranges, reds."

"Colors on the screens?"

"Yes. Like a moving rainbow. I'm so sorry. I thought you knew. Your shot with the earth. It never happened."

"The earth wasn't there?"

Tom shook his head.

Nikkie thought her vision of a forest had been so strong it had blocked out the earth. "What was I holding?" she asked.

"Nada," Tom said. "There was a last-minute camera malfunction. The cameraman couldn't get the close up of your spinning and projection of the earth on the screens. They didn't project you at all. The swirling colors were their backup plan."

"No pictures of the earth—or me?" Nikkie asked.

Tom nodded. Nikkie's heart began to pound. "Why didn't someone tell me?"

"You were already on stage when the camera went dead. One minute it was working, the next, it didn't."

"Couldn't they replace it?" Nikkie asked.

"Not enough time. A crew member told me what was going on during your routine. There was no way to let you know, other than run out on stage while you were dancing."

"I'm amazed I stayed upright," Nikkie said.

"I could see in your face you were aware something was off," said Tom. "I thought it was because you were adapting to the new images. But the audience still loved you and the band. Didn't you hear the applause?"

Nikkie shook her head. She had barely heard anything above the roar in her ears and voices in her own head willing her to bow and get off the stage.

"That shot was going to be a highpoint for our number—and for the concert," Nikkie said, disappointment pricking at her.

"It was a highpoint for you," Tom said. "A spotlight was shining on you. You looked like you were spinning in sunbeams. It was beautiful."

"I agree," said Ellie. "Your dress caught the light and shadow onstage and rippled around you like it was alive. It added to your dancing."

"But I had wanted tonight to be perfect," said Nikkie. "Now, it's a mess."

"Don't talk like that," Tom said. "Your performance may not have looked like you thought it would, but despite technical issues, you danced superbly. And you're part of a hot new group that's about to go on tour and release a bunch of music videos."

Ellie chimed in her agreement. "The audience never knew anything was off, and neither did I. I could not wait to get backstage and tell you how great you were. I'm so proud of both of you." Nikkie let her mother's words sink into her heart, appreciating how she had always encouraged Nikkie to pursue her dancing.

"Okay. I'll take both your words for it. And I can find out more about what Sean thought at tomorrow's choreography meeting."

"About that. I almost forgot. New plan," Tom said. "You're not meeting. Sean's going to look at recording studios. Instead, the band's lawyer is messengering over some paperwork for you to the hotel tomorrow morning. A few final details to go over."

"Did Sean set up another meeting time?" Nikkie asked.

"He only said not to worry, to take the time to recoup. He'll be in touch."

Nikkie's stomach tightened. Sean's new plan did not sit right with her, passed over like a shadow.

"I don't know, Tom. I'm surprised. Considering what happened, it's weird Sean hasn't come to check on me himself."

Chapter 3

"So, what's with the dead people?" Tom sat in a plush white leather armchair in their boutique hotel suite in Santa Monica. Nikkie and Ellie half-reclined opposite him, curled up, one on each end of a white leather sofa. A mix of aromas from the mugs of steaming hot peppermint tea and cappuccino they held drifted through the living area.

A shudder rippled down Nikkie's body. She looked at Tom, sat up straight, put her bare feet on the carpeted floor. "But how did…?"

"You think you can see a vision like that and not have me know?"

Damn twin telepathy. Nikkie should have suspected. Ever since childhood, when they were in trouble, their sixth sense about each other became heightened.

Nikkie put her mug of tea down on the coffee table next to a breakfast platter of bagels, lox, cream cheese, tomatoes, capers and onions.

"Sometimes, I hate being a twin." Nikkie felt unnerved that Tom had tapped into any part of her experience onstage. "What do you think you saw?"

"Listen, I know you don't like me mucking about in your head," Tom said. "I don't like it much either. That said, I couldn't help but sense your distress while you were dancing. I thought it was because of the camera malfunction. Then, without trying to, I flashed on the images you were seeing. A forest. People falling to the ground. A girl with braids. I marveled at your ability to finish your performance. I knew it had to be even more disconcerting than the technical issues."

"Why didn't you tell me this last night?"

"I could ask you the same thing. But we both know we had more pressing things going on, like you fainting. Come on, Nik. Tell me now."

"Hey, remember I'm here too," Ellie said, straightening up and turning her gaze back and forth between the twins. "Will you clue me in on what you're talking about?"

"Isn't it enough this morning that I am no longer nauseous and dizzy?" Nikkie asked. "Can't I do this in my own time?"

Tom and Ellie waited in silence, giving Nikkie space. Tom sipped his cappuccino, then made a bagel piled high with the works and offered it to Nikkie. "If you're not going to talk, at least eat something. Not New York deli, but damned good."

"I'm not quite ready for the works." Nikkie put up her hand to block Tom's offering. Instead, she reached over and spread a light coating of cream cheese on a whole wheat bagel. She took a small bite.

Bursts of images in the forest broke through like shock waves to her system. During the night while she had tried to sleep, they had floated by her like a chill whisper on the wind. She attempted to will them away, temper them.

"One of you say something," Ellie said.

Nikkie sighed. "Okay. I know I need to tell you."

Tom sat forward at attention.

"It came back," Nikkie said.

"What?"

"The vision I had in the forest in Oregon. When you and I were ten," Nikkie said. She looked from Tom to Ellie. "The one that freaked me out so much. Remember?"

Ellie looked at her with the caring Nikkie knew she could count on, touched Nikkie's arm. "Of course. We all stood in the forest afterward, told the spirits to go away."

"Yes. And they did. Until now. On stage. Here I was at the most important event of my career. When I started to whirl, everything around me seemed to drop away, slow down. I saw a forest of tall, thin birch trees." Nikkie's head began to spin again as she recounted the images.

"Maybe I can't handle the pressure of the band," Nikkie said. "I'm going crazy and hallucinating."

"Come on," Ellie said. "You may be sensitive, but you're not crazy."

"Not any more nuts than usual," Tom said.

"You probably opened up to another dimension of reality," Ellie said.

When Nikkie and Tom were growing up, Ellie had taught them that different levels and dimensions of existence were as real as the three dimensions most human beings acknowledged. She believed people and spirits could move between the dimensions, and experiences of the kind many considered paranormal were natural, nothing to fear.

Nikkie had always felt in her belly that her mother spoke the truth. Tom remained skeptical but respectful of her and her mother's beliefs and experiences.

"Having a vision in Oregon was one thing," Nikkie said, touching her mother's arm. "But it was another to encounter it in front of a huge audience. It feels like some sort of cruel cosmic joke."

"What I don't understand is why the Hollywood Bowl?" Tom said. "It doesn't make sense. You performed so many times in real forests at indie music festivals. Those events seemed much more conducive to a vision than this one."

"I sure don't have an answer," Nikkie said. "I was having a hard enough time dealing with performing at the Bowl.

I could barely hold it together." Nikkie moved closer to her mother, put her head on her shoulder.

"Maybe it's as simple as that," Tom said. "The heightened stress of performing there triggered it."

Nikkie shrugged her shoulders and sighed.

"I had a thought," Ellie said. "You have always said your whirling joins earth to heaven and other dimensions and when you're most aligned, body and soul, your hope is for the audience to experience that connection too. Maybe in front of such a large audience, you were especially open. But instead of only linking to the audience, you somehow also reconnected to those spirits from the past."

Tom rolled his eyes.

"That first vision happened so long ago," Nikkie said. "Why would it repeat? It doesn't make sense."

"Not to our rational minds," Ellie said. "But those spirits could be caught in a dimension between life and death."

"If you're right, I don't understand why they're coming to *me*," Nikkie said, a hint of the queasiness returning. "I've got enough to deal with, things I'd rather deal with, like my whole career. I'm not a medium who connects with the dead. I am a dancer and choreographer. That's what I love. Period."

Nikkie turned her head and gazed out the floor to ceiling window over the clear ocean horizon. No confusing forests and dead people here. She felt the momentary relief of the expanse of water and sky unimpeded by visions of another time. The only people below her were very much alive, skating, running, power walking on the path between her and the ocean.

She took a deep breath and continued. "This vision was more disturbing than when I was a child."

"How?" Tom asked.

Nikkie explained how the spirits had started falling, dying, shot by soldiers, including the young girl. Her first vision had dissipated before the shootings.

"That must have been hard to witness," Ellie said.

"I'm friggin' amazed I didn't fall. And here's where it gets weirder. A new man appeared who wasn't in the first vision. One second, he wasn't there, the next he was. Tall. Blond. Good-looking."

"What was weird about him?" Tom asked.

"He seemed out of place like he was from present day," Nikkie said. "He was wearing jeans, and his hair had a modern style and cut. The others were wearing clothing like they came from the 1940s, World War II, the same as last time. And the new man looked as stunned to be there as I felt. I don't remember him from my childhood vision. He knelt down, picked up the girl and stroked her hair."

Nikkie felt her mother tense up. "Mom, is this too much?"

Ellie shook her head. "I'm fine," she said, though tension remained around her mouth. "It's a lot to take in. Please, go on."

"That man looked right at me like he could see me." Nikkie paused and felt her chest tighten against rising grief. "There was an urgency to the scene I don't recall as a child. Like I had to do something. Back then my biggest urgency was to make it go away. I'd still rather make it go away. What am I saying? I need to make it go away."

Remembering the man and the scene of death again made Nikkie's pulse quicken. The left side of her neck started to ache, and she instinctively massaged it, as if to comfort herself.

"As horrified as I felt, he and I seemed to be connecting," Nikkie said.

"Did he say anything?" Tom asked.

Nikkie nodded. "Words that sounded foreign or like gibberish."

"What?" he asked.

"I keep hearing it repeated in my head. *Palīdz man*, he said. *Palīdz man*."

Tom's mouth fell open in shock, and Ellie reacted like she had taken a sucker punch.

"What's wrong?" Nikkie asked. "You two are scaring me." The more Nikkie had talked, Nikkie noticed, the more Ellie seemed like an animal trapped in a closed space wanting to bolt.

"The words. They're not gibberish," Tom said. "They're Latvian. The man said, 'Help me.' In Latvian. Right?" He turned to Ellie.

"Yes," Ellie said. "*Palīdz man* means help me in Latvian."

The twins' grandmother, Indra, had grown up in Latvia before World War II, and Ellie, who was born in the U.S., had learned English and Latvian simultaneously. Peter, their father, was a Latvian dancer Ellie had an affair with while he was touring in the U.S. with the Nijinsky Ballet from Moscow.

"See, Nik. You may have opted to go to dance camp, but those years I spent learning Latvian and going to Latvian summer camp paid off," Tom said.

Nikkie rolled her eyes. "Come on, Tom. This is serious."

"All right, all right," Tom said. "I was trying to lighten up the conversation. So *seriously*, I did have another thought. You said the forest in your vision had birch trees? That could be Latvia. It's full of birch forests. Maybe the people you saw were Latvians."

"I don't care what or where they were; I want them to go away," Nikkie, who believed everything happened for a reason, to learn and grow from, had to admit she had no desire to learn and grow from this.

"Let's do a ritual, like the first time," Ellie said. "We can call on the spirits and tell them to go away. It worked then."

"But it didn't. They came back." Tom said. "In front of seventeen thousand five hundred people no less. What if this starts happening every time you perform, Nik? The pressure's not going anywhere with all the large venues on the band's tour."

Nikkie felt prickles climb up her spine. "It's not going to happen," Nikkie shook her head as if shaking the idea of it away. "The vision did go away for twelve years. I'd settle for that. I think Ellie's idea is good. And Tom, even though I know you're not one for ritual, I would appreciate having you with Ellie and me like the last time. 'Where two or more are gathered,' strength in numbers, and all that."

Tom sighed. "If you think it might help, I'm in."

"It has to help. I don't want us to worry every time I perform." Nikkie turned to Ellie. "I bet you have some good ideas for a ritual. We could find a park around here that has some trees. Or we could do it in the hotel room. I brought sage we could burn."

Ellie did not answer, seemed to be staring off at some point beyond Nikkie. When she did turn back to Nikkie and Tom, she opened her mouth, but no words came out. Then their mother, the woman who had been their rock all their lives, bent forward, her arms wrapped around her gut. Her face contorted. "I... I…can't do it," she said. "I can't."

Chapter 4

Ellie walked over to her suitcase in the corner of the living room, while the twins sat in stunned silence. She pulled out an eight by ten black and white photograph, handed it to Nikkie.

In it stood a tall, blond man, linked arm in arm with a line of men up against a barricade in what looked like the Old Town of a European city. It was winter, and the men were wearing coats, caps, gloves. All except one. The tall, blond man in the center, who looked like he was in his thirties, had no hat, gazed directly at the camera.

"But how did you get this? Who is he?" Nikkie said, heat rising up her chest and face. "It's the man from my vision."

Tom jumped up, came around to her side to see. "Are you sure? What's this about, Ell? How did you know?"

"From what you were saying, Nikkie, I thought it might be," Ellie said. "It was too much of a coincidence." She paused, breathed deeply. "The man in the center is Peter. Your father."

Tom and Nikkie turned from Ellie and the photo to each other. Tom sat down hard on the arm of the couch, grabbed Nikkie's hand as if he was holding on to keep from falling off the side of a building.

"You're saying my dead father came to me in a vision?" Nikkie said, looking back at her mother. "All these years, even when he was alive, I never saw him in a dream, and now you're saying he showed up in a vision that doesn't seem to have any-thing to do with him. Why?"

"I don't know," Ellie said. "But there's something else. This photo was taken three years after we were told he was dead. He was not dead. He was one of the men creating the barricade against the Soviet attempt to regain control of Latvia in 1991, a few months after Latvians had declared their freedom."

"Where did you get this?" Tom asked, his face as solemn as Nikkie had ever seen it.

"Your grandmother was at the opening of a new museum in Riga about the history of the barricades. One of the displays listed all the men and women who had participated. She saw Peter's name on a list, checked with the research staff there to make sure it was the same Peter. He had been one of the free-dom fighters."

"How could she be so sure?" Tom asked.

"She researched the archived photographs and old news-paper reports at the museum and found this one," Ellie said, her tears and tension seeming to ease as she spoke. "She called from Riga to tell me, then scanned and emailed me the photo. It's definitely him. Even though he's older, I'd know that look anywhere. Peter's not dead. He's alive. At least he was in 1991. But now with your vision, I don't know anymore. And here's what is also strange. I don't know if there's a connection, but that's also the same year you had the first vision."

Nikkie sat stunned. This image was of the father she had grieved when they thought he was dead. Nikkie had mourned the loss of him, as well as the possibility of meeting and get-ting to know him. The twins had never even seen a photo of him. Ellie had not had one, had not taken any of him the few days she had known Peter.

When they were six and had first asked who their father was, Peter had still been alive. But Ellie explained that writing or calling to tell him about the twins was dangerous. Under

Communism, the Soviets read and censored every letter that came in or out of the country and had wiretaps on every phone. Peter and his family might have been interrogated, arrested. He could have lost his career. "But we loved each other," Ellie told them then. "And he would have loved you."

The next year in 1988, during Glasnost, when travel to and from Communist countries became less burdensome, and Gorbachev began allowing more freedoms, Ellie had taken a chance and called the ballet to find out how to contact Peter. She planned to travel to the U.S.S.R. and tell him about the twins. If he were receptive, she would bring the twins over to meet him. Instead, she was told Peter was no longer with the ballet.

"But you told us the people at the Nijinsky Ballet said he had died," Tom said.

Ellie let out a long sigh. She nodded. "That's right."

"So, they lied?" Tom said.

"They must have."

"Why would someone do that?"

"I don't know," Ellie said, shaking her head. "I'm sorry." Tears welled up in her eyes. "I probably should have checked more, but it was such a shock. I never expected someone could lie to me about Peter dying."

"When did you find out about the photo?" Nikkie asked, emerging from her initial surprise enough to speak again.

"The day before your performance," Ellie said. "I didn't tell you right away because I knew it would be a shock, and I wanted to tell you both something this important in person. I still can't believe it. I had already planned to come to L.A. So, I decided to wait until after you performed and tell you when the focus could be on this."

"I appreciate that," Nikkie said. "Only now we don't know for sure if he's alive or he showed up in the vision because he really is dead. This is so confusing."

Nikkie remembered Peter's stunned expression in the vision, his plea for help. Was the appeal for himself? Maybe he had died in some shocking way and was now a wandering spirit, too, caught between realms with the dead in the forest she had seen. She felt a stab in her heart thinking of the possibility.

Ellie's shoulders began to shake, and her eyes overflowed with tears. "The truth is I've been crying on and off since I heard. I was happy, but I'm also sad this mix up robbed you of years of a possible relationship with him."

The twins listened, remained silent. Nikkie's stomach churned.

Ellie looked away from them and out the window until her tears stopped, turned back and took a napkin from the table to blow her nose and wipe her eyes and face.

"At least your grandmother found the photo now. She also called the ballet again to make doubly certain. This time, she was told that Peter had not left the ballet because he died. He had only quit. They refused to tell her why."

"It's still hard to believe someone would have lied like that," Tom said. "Did she find out where he went after he quit?"

Ellie shook her head. "They refused to give her a forwarding address. As a precaution to protect their dancers, they explained, they won't give out personal information.

"In hindsight, I wish I would have gone to Moscow in 1988 to find out more about his supposed death, but I did the best I could back then," Ellie said. "My responsibility was to you two. I was a single mother with two children and a pottery business to run. I couldn't drop everything and fly to Moscow. And since it was still under Communist rule, I doubt anyone would have talked to me about him anyway."

"I can understand it was a tough spot back then," Tom said. "But now I want to find out where Peter is and why he showed up in Nikkie's vision. Are you going to Latvia to look for him?"

"One step at a time," Ellie said. "First, I needed to tell you."

"Well, I'm going," Tom said.

"I want to go too, Tom, but neither one of us can now with a thirty-date tour coming up," Nikkie said, surprised he would even consider it. "I can't do this by myself. I need your help."

Tom sighed. His shoulders dropped. "Come on, Nik. Somewhere in this mess of a schedule, you can let go of me for one week to try to find our father. Have a little leeway. It's not all about you."

"It's never been all about me," Nikkie said. "But what's going on is also your career and opportunity. You want to chance messing it up by leaving? We only have six weeks before we hit the road."

"So, the best time for me to go to Latvia would be now, before the tour," Tom said.

"You know it's more complicated than that," Nikkie said. "Besides, we need a plan. If Peter is alive, which he seems to be, discovering he's the father of grown-up twins from the U.S. is going to be a shock. Who knows how he'll react? People change in years. Or he could already have kids and a wife who might not be thrilled if you pop up to tell him about us."

Hey, don't you two argue," Ellie said. "It's not helpful."

Nikkie had to admit her mother was right. She sighed, let her anger recede.

"The truth is I'm scared," Nikkie said. "We have so much going on already. And now you are dangling this hope in front of us. I'm used to thinking of Peter as dead. I've even been calling on his spirit to help me when I'm dancing, have imagined him watching over me, when he wasn't dead at all. He was alive. And the whole forest vision. I'm so confused as to why Peter was there. Peter and the dead. It sounds like the start of a horror film."

"Maybe it is some kind of clue as to where he is," Tom said.

"You think he's lost in a forest in Latvia?"

"Not in the forest, but somehow that vision is linked to him. Who knows? He could be living near the forest. God knows from what I've learned about Latvia's geography, there's enough forests. Even within commuting distance to Riga."

"Or if you found the forest first before we tracked down Peter, it could show you the next step you needed to take," Ellie said. "You know what? I had a thought. The family farmland your grandmother reclaimed after freedom was declared has forest on it. Maybe some of it is birch. I don't know why Peter would show up in a vision of that forest, but I agree with Tom. It's a place to explore. Besides, your grandmother has been after the three of us to come to Latvia for years, especially now that she has moved there." Ellie's mother had bought and renovated an apartment in Riga and moved there in the fall of 2002.

"But you seem to forget the tour," Nikkie said. "I can't go to Latvia. And wherever that forest is, it's not only a link to Peter, but also to all those spirits. I want to get away from them, not seek them out. We need to find another way."

"The other way is me right now," Tom said. "I agree you can't go, and I can understand why you don't want to dredge up the dead. But I could go to Moscow and Riga, places we know Peter lived. Ellie, do you remember if he had family anywhere else? Were they all from Riga?"

Ellie shook her head. "He mentioned Riga and Moscow. Wait, he did mention he had a relative in Kurzeme, an uncle I think, but not a specific place. Mostly, we talked about our own dreams for our lives, not about our pasts or our parents. I was only twenty-one. Peter did meet Indra though. I introduced her backstage after she and I went to the ballet's performance."

"Let me remind everyone about our own dreams," Nikkie asked. "It's a crucial time. And when we search for Peter, I'd like to be part of it. We should put it off until after the tour, go in September."

"Are you listening to yourself?" Tom said. "Do you really think now that we know Peter could be alive, either one of us will be happy sitting on that bomb for two months. If anything, it would sabotage your ability to put full attention on your dancing."

For the first time, Nikkie knew in her heart what Tom was saying was true. She would be obsessing about Peter, her focus split. They all would.

"And dreams aren't just about career," he said. "Meeting our father has been both of our dreams. Remember how we used to act out what we imagined would happen when he found out about us, what it would be like to have a father. How he would find a way to defect and come live with us?"

"You're making it sound like it's a done deal, and I don't have any say in this," Nikkie said, beginning to sound lame even to herself. She thought back to those imaginings. In them, Peter and Ellie would fall in love all over again and get married, and Nikkie and Tom would be the center of their lives. She let out a deep breath.

"Maybe with all the extra people around us from the label and Ron's managing company to help, you could go for a few days," Nikkie said. "But you have to promise to stay in touch.

"That's the spirit," Tom said. And of course, I'll stay in touch. I'll have my cell and my laptop. I could still handle any emergencies you have here from there. But in Latvia, I could at least get started with the tangible parts of the search.

"You have to promise you'll also call every day, so I don't feel left out," Nikkie said.

"I will stay until you sign the contract," Tom said. Then, you'll be busy with choreography and music videos. Ron's handling the tour logistics, so you don't need me for that. I can go then. Who knows? Maybe Indra will have found Peter by then, and we can both go." He looked at Ellie. "Is she still looking for him?"

Ellie nodded.

"I'll plan to go for one week. Ten days at the most. That's not overly long. You're not going to crash and burn without me in that time."

"I wouldn't be so sure," Nikkie said. Tom ignored her.

"Ellie, I'd love if you would come as well, so we could branch out and have more of us looking," Tom said. Nikkie watched as Tom's manager side emerged. He was already taking charge of the search, like a police detective searching for a missing person. She began to relent.

"And if, no, *when* we find him, we'll call right away before any of us tells him we're his long, lost family. That way, you can fly over, even if it's for a couple days. We tell him who we are, and you and I meet him together."

Nikkie sighed. "Okay, Tom. I don't like it, but I can see you're determined. And you're right. It's not all about our careers. I don't want to wait any longer either. I've got to know if Peter's alive and where he is. It's been twelve years since that barricade photo was taken. When you find him, promise me, I'll fly over."

"And who knows, my dear girl?" Ellie said. "Your vision may have only come back to corroborate and emphasize that Peter is still alive, and it's time to find him. Once you do, it may never return."

Nikkie felt a squiggle in her belly in response to what her mother was saying. *Peter may well be alive,* she thought. *But if that's all the vision had been, why had the spirits come again, and why had Peter kneeled in their midst, holding the girl, asking for my help?*

CHAPTER 5

"Send him up," Tom said, hanging up the phone and turning to Nikkie. "It's the messenger."

Nikkie felt relief. Legal paperwork concerning their new life. Something tangible to grab onto after the chaos of dealing with the vision of death and a father risen from it.

But when Tom opened the manila envelope the messenger brought, instead of the contract they were expecting, he removed two letter size envelopes. The messenger also left a large poster size package.

"These letters are both addressed to you, Nikkie" he said. "One from Stone Tara's lawyer. The other looks like it's from Sean. The package is for you too."

"You open the lawyer one and read it," she said.

Tom sat back down on the white armchair and read. By the time he raised his head, his face was ashen, a shade Nikkie could never remember seeing it, not even at his worst after a flu or a hangover.

"You need to look at this yourself," Tom said.

Nikkie's heart began to pound. She shook her head. "No. I don't want to. You tell me."

"I can't believe it," Tom said. "It's a bunch of legalese that says Stone Tara no longer requires your services as a dancer and choreographer." Tom paused as he scanned the letter again, shaking his head. He looked up at Nikkie. "It all comes down to one thing. The band is not giving you a contract. They've fired you. I'm so sorry."

Stunned, Nikkie grabbed the edge of the couch to steady herself. Shock and anger collided and flared in her belly. She could barely breathe. "It has to be a mistake," she said, her words catching in her throat. "Sean and I had an agreement."

"Agreement or not, this is no mistake," Tom said.

"Give me the letter from Sean," Nikkie said. She ripped it open and took out Sean's letter, handwritten on stationery from the Chateau Marmont in West Hollywood, a chic celebrity hotel where the band was staying. She read it to herself first, her jaw clenching. The room seemed to close in on her despite the expanse of sun and sky and ocean shining through the windows.

"What's it say?" Tom asked, leaning forward in his chair.

"Sean says the band—and the label—want to make their performance only about the music, rely on the strength of their songs. That's what sells. They're not going to use my dancing anymore."

"So, Sean supports what the lawyer wrote?" Ellie asked.

Nikkie nodded, felt her lower lip begin to tremble. "When Sean invited me to join Stone Tara, he told me I was his muse. My dancing inspired him to write *Climatica* and the new songs the label loved." She wanted to rip the letter up and throw it out the window. "I never expected he would drop me. Is this because of what happened at the Bowl? Are you sure this isn't about my performance?"

"This has the label written all over it," Tom said. "You did fine last night. It has nothing to do with your dancing at the Bowl."

"Doesn't it? Fine is not good enough when you're going on tour to perform for mainstream audiences," Nikkie said. "I wouldn't expect the label to want to keep me. Bands and music are what they are about, not dancers. But why wouldn't Sean himself fight to use me? I don't understand how he could send a letter and not talk to me in person, try to work it out."

Nikkie felt so many conflicting emotions—rage, sadness, fear, she was having difficulty relating to what she was reading. She handed Tom Sean's letter. "You read the rest of this yourself. Tell Ellie what it says."

Tom reached over and took the letter from Nikkie, scanned it, sighed. "Sean writes, the band has been working hard towards an opportunity like this for years." Tom smashed the letter with his fist on his lap. "*They* worked hard? Your whole life has been about dance. And with Stone Tara, you gave one hundred percent of your talent."

"Absolutely," Ellie agreed.

"How could I be giving 100 percent last night when I was having a vision and not even sure I was dancing anymore?" Nikkie asked. "Damn it. Right at the moment I most needed to succeed. Sean and the band got that when the pressure was on, I could barely stay on my own two feet—or appeal to a mainstream audience."

"You're being unnecessarily hard on yourself," Ellie said.

"Ellie's right," Tom said. "The truth is even if you think you blew it, you kept dancing full out, regardless of what you were experiencing."

"But it was the Bowl, Tom. The Bowl. I could not afford to have anything go wrong."

"This has to feel devastating," Ellie said.

"Or maybe the malfunction was a sign from the universe telling me I did not belong in the spotlight," Nikkie said. "Given what happened, I can't rely on myself as a performer. Not until I figure out why the vision of the dead returned and how I can stop it—for good. Otherwise, I have no guarantees the spirits won't keep on appearing."

"You'll figure it out," Tom said. "And you will dance and perform again. In an even better situation. In the meantime, we're here for you, and we know you're an awesome dancer."

Ellie nodded. "Is there anything else in Sean's letter, Tom?"

Tom lifted the letter off his lap, straightened it out. "A reminder that the band and Nikkie never had a written agreement, and they would not be continuing with her. He thanked her, told her what a talented dancer she is, wishes her much success. Signs it simply, Sean.

"No written agreement. Over." Grief stabbed repeatedly at Nikkie's heart as she spoke each word, her voice trembling. "Just like that." She snapped her fingers, then her hand dropped to her lap. "And he could not face me to tell me in person."

Tom put the wrinkled letter down on the coffee table, shook his head.

Nikkie felt like she was falling backward with nothing to grab onto. The tears she was fighting welled up. But she had one more piece of unfinished business.

"Open it," she said, pointing to a large poster-size package that had arrived with the letters. "Let's get this over with," already knowing in her heart what was inside.

Tom ripped away the outer packaging and bubble wrap to reveal a framed poster-size photo. The image was of Nikkie, taken by the well-known photographer who had been hired to shoot the publicity and CD cover shots of the band one week earlier. After the photographer had completed the shoot, she had told Nikkie how much her spinning had inspired her. She had asked Nikkie if she'd be willing to try an artistic shot after the band left. For fun.

In the framed photo, Nikkie was spinning, her arms lifted up in a "V" to the heavens. She was in her soft white dress that flared out in a circle as she whirled against a white background. White on white. Her face and body had been captured in a clear focus, but she had been shot in such a way that her arms were repeated, as if she had hundreds of appendages, raised up.

The photo was black and white, the only colors from an image of the earth. Nikkie's arms were holding it. An artistic rendition of what was supposed to have happened on the Hollywood Bowl stage during Nikkie's dance. She could see the image's brilliance, but now it felt like yet another slap in the face, a reminder of her failure, of Sean's betrayal, a taunt of what might have been.

No one said a word. Tom leaned the photo against the wall, moved over to Nikkie's side of the couch, squeezed in beside her and sandwiched her between him and Ellie. They put their arms around Nikkie. She closed her eyes and cried what seemed like waves of tears.

She cried for the lost dreams of success with Stone Tara. About knowing she had lost the opportunity to know her father all these years. She cried for all the work she had put into honing her artistry as a dancer to come to this.

She had been fired, left behind. She, the one who had always gone before this. She had chosen to leave Julliard. The New York dance world. Because she wanted to follow her own artistic vision rather than fit into that of an established dance company.

And where had those creative instincts led her? They opened her to re-experience the dead and resulted in the debacle at the Bowl. They led her to a band that had sacked her. How could she trust those instincts?

She felt dead inside like the dead who had appeared to her, who had lost all opportunity to fulfill whatever dreams they had cherished for their lives. Years of dancing and studying dance without stopping, years of running toward her aspirations as a dancer, the fiasco onstage and with the band, caught up with her all at once and left her feeling drained, knocked out, devoid of creativity, ideas and self-confidence. As devoid of color as she was in the photo.

And then she felt drained of tears. Drained of her very life waters. Like she had transformed from human to desert, and her portion of the seventy percent of all humans that was water had been used up, sucked dry, turned to sand that left her vulnerable to dispersal by any whim of the wind.

Tom and Ellie held on tighter. Her breath echoed through the hollowness of her.

"What do I do now?" she said in a voice that escaped from her desert depth. She opened her eyes, forced her gaze away from the photo and toward her brother. He sat up straight beside her, looked into her eyes, his arms still around her.

"Well, I can think of one thing," Tom said.

"What's that?" she said.

"We can go to Latvia to search for Peter."

Tom freed his arms holding her and got up to retrieve another piece of paper taped to the photo. "And this will finance the trip." He flashed a piece of paper in front of her eyes. It was a check for twenty-five thousand dollars signed by Sean. "I only noticed it taped to the corner of the photo after you started crying." In the "For" section, Sean had written simply, "Good luck."

Chapter 6

For the first time since she could remember, Nikkie couldn't dance. Didn't dance. Couldn't feel anything inside her to dance from, to dance about, not even the pain of not dancing.

Since she had become a dancer, she had experienced times, days, the occasional week when she stopped performing to recuperate from an injury or illness. Sprained ankles. Twisted knee. Childhood flu. But even though she wasn't moving her body, the dance lived on inside her. Her heart, her imagination danced. When she closed her eyes, she was in motion.

The first couple of days following the Hollywood Bowl debacle as Nikkie recouped in Oregon at her mother's home, she tried to start her day with a warm-up. It was what dancers did. The impulse to practice as part of her art flowed as naturally as breathing. Now, doing it felt like she was forcing her legs, arms and torso into a vise. She stopped.

Instead, she lay curved over the plush lilac couch in Ellie's living room in Ashland. She padded herself front and back with cushions. Her eyes were closed, her mind blank. No thoughts. No images. Not in a peaceful, meditative way. More like numbness tinged with exhaustion.

Nikkie had lost her drive. To dance. To prepare for the upcoming trip to Europe and the possibility of meeting her father. To deal with the vision. To care what Tom was doing in

Los Angeles to wrap up business matters. No desire to leave the house. One day when Ellie walked in at three o'clock after work at her pottery business, Nikkie was still lying around in her pajamas.

After one week though, Nikkie woke up on the same lilac couch, a quilt wrapped tight around her. She felt different somehow. No more easing into the familiar numbness of each day. An undeniable urge had slipped inside her in the night. She bolted upright, pulled the quilt up to her chin as she realized what it was. Nikkie was filled with a compulsion to return to the forest where she first had the vision of the dead as a ten-year-old. The urge did not come complete with ideas about what to do when she got there, but she had to go.

By the time Ellie emerged from her bedroom a few minutes later, Nikkie was already dressed in jeans, hiking boots and a teal long sleeve top. She stood at the kitchen counter boiling water for tea. She told Ellie her plan, then asked if she could borrow Ellie's car for the day.

"If you have such a strong feeling, you need to follow it," Ellie said. "Of course, you can borrow the car. But are you sure you want to go there alone? I'd be happy to go with you."

A striking woman, Ellie stood out in a lace-edged lilac tank top over a flowing wine-colored skirt and purple hand-crafted sandals. A circle of garnets set in a silver Latvian sun symbol hung from her neck. Her arm and shoulder muscles were gracefully defined from years of crafting pottery, working in the artist community's garden and doing yoga.

Nikkie had always appreciated her mother's aesthetic. "How I dress is one way I transcend whatever I'm facing in my life," Ellie told her once. "The way the colors, textures and materials go together remind me of who I am."

Today, Nikkie knew she, too, needed to be reminded of who she was—but how she dressed had nothing to do with that journey. "Thanks, mom, but I need to go by myself,"

Nikkie said. "I'll be fine." Inside, though, she wondered if she would be able to find the spot where she had experienced the vision again. And what *would* she do if the spirits reappeared?

"Do you want to talk about what you might do if you have another vision while you're there?" Ellie asked as if she had picked up Nikkie's thought.

"Part of me still wants to tell them to go away and leave me alone like we did the first time," Nikkie said. "Because I certainly do not want them to show up if I start performing again. But now that the vision seems linked to my father, I can't bring myself to do that. 'Help me,' he said. But I don't know how or what he meant."

"Maybe going back will give you some answers," Ellie said.

Nikkie nodded. "I hope so. Because when we go to Latvia, the prospect of finding and meeting Peter seems daunting enough, let alone figuring that out too."

"I agree," Ellie said. She put her arms around Nikkie and gave her a hug. "Now can I at least fix you some breakfast before you head off?"

While Ellie made them garden omelets, Nikkie poured them cups of green tea and set the table. She pieced together a lunch for herself of cheese, baguette, an apple and enough water for the day and put everything in a daypack.

"Take your cell phone," Ellie said when they finished eating.

"I will, mom, but I doubt I'll have any reception out there."

As they walked to the car, Ellie gave Nikkie one more hug, then waved her off from the driveway as Nikkie drove away. Ellie usually only did that when Nikkie was going back to her own home.

In a way she was. She was headed back to the wilderness area trail that bordered the land in the Applegate Valley her family had lived on. Back to the madrone tree there that would serve as the reference point to get her to the clearing where she had had the vision.

Stepping onto the trail, any nervousness that remained flowed out Nikkie's feet into the earth, and the peace of knowing she was doing what she needed to be doing, no matter what happened, replaced it. She felt relieved to find the madrone still stood, that it had survived age, fire, disease, lightning and high winds. The tree still bore their mark.

Nikkie and Tom had been ten when they carved their names into the smooth orange wood of the madrone tree, where the outer bark had peeled away—the same day she had the first vision. Twelve years later in 2003, their names remained; dark scars healed, the jagged edges of the cuts rounded with time.

Nikkie could still hear Tom's prodding. "Let's pretend we're lost," he had said. "We'll write our names in the tree. Someone will see them and know to look for us."

Well, I don't have to pretend anymore. Nikki ran her fingers over the letters of their names, savoring each one. Today, she did feel lost. Here in these woods she and Tom had explored as children, she was questioning the meaning of the vision and the next steps for her life. *Ironic that until I got fired, I believed I had a clear direction.*

She drifted back again in her mind to the day she had had the vision. Once Tom had carved his name into the tree with a pocket knife, she had begun to cut hers. But after three letters N-I-K, when the pocket knife had pierced the skin of the tree, she had heard it scream in pain inside her head. Her arms weakened and fell to her sides. She let the knife drop to the ground. She refused to cut anymore.

"The madrone told me it hurts," Nikkie said, her voice firm. She had straightened up to her full height, a good quarter head taller than Tom, pulled her shoulders back and down like her ballet teacher had taught.

"Nikkie, trees don't talk. You're making that up."

"Yes, they do, too, talk," Nikkie said. "This one showed me that cutting her feels like cutting my name into my own arm. And look who's talking about making things up. We're not lost. You want me to hurt a tree for a make-believe story."

Nikkie had asked the tree's forgiveness that long-ago day and tenderness filled her that told her it had. Now, touching the madrone all these years later, she felt like she was greeting an old friend she had not seen in a long time.

She could still hear her child self call out to Tom, "I know how we can really get lost." She had shoved Tom back into the underbrush, then run off the trail into the woods on her own. That was when she had the vision.

Now Nikkie oriented herself in the same direction she had run as a child and stepped off the trail into the forest. This time she walked, let her intuition guide her past madrones, cedars, oaks, ferns, and underbrush back to the clearing, amazed at how easily she found it again.

Nikkie sat down cross-legged on the ground, looked around her at the trees that remained. They had witnessed her first vision, she realized.

The setting seemed so peaceful, so quiet. Dappled sunlight streamed in through the thick of the forest like it had the first time she came here.

"It happened again," she said to the trees, believing they were listening. "The dead. I saw them. And my father was there this time. But turns out he's alive. Alive. Can you help me figure out what it all means?

Funny, Nikkie thought, how she found talking to trees easier sometimes than to people. Trees seemed to listen without their own agendas clouding what they heard, without judgment or opinion, without interruption. But this time they did not offer her any answers like she had hoped.

As a child, being in these woods in tune with nature and her deepest impulses, Nikkie had lived unburdened by the desire to be anything but herself living in the moment. This ability had taken root like these trees. She had been able to tap into it after she had the first vision, after she had left this place of her rural upbringing and ventured forth into the world. It had helped her maintain her balance even when she whirled—until now.

Since she had lost her opportunity with Stone Tara, she didn't have to spin while she danced to feel off balance. Nothing made sense. She was floating through her life groundless, uprooted.

Sitting on the forest floor, Nikkie could feel the roughness of the earth, twigs, dead leaves, mulch, the familiar texture under her hands as she leaned back on them for support. She drank in the sweet, refreshing scent of fir and musk of compost. *Okay. What can I do at this moment to deal with the visions of the dead?*

She concentrated on the impulse that had brought her here and sensed she needed to start back at the beginning. Perhaps if she could recollect her first vision in as much detail as possible, she might get some clue or insight about it, trigger something she had not recalled either the first time as a child or at the Hollywood Bowl.

Breathe, Nikkie said to herself. *Nothing can harm you here.* She let herself focus on the long-ago day that had changed her perception of life.

She remembered how she had begun to whirl in the light of this clearing, imagining every tree was a person come to see her dance. The more she had spun, the more the trees and woods had lost their distinctive forms and become one mass of swirling green and brown colors.

Back then, she had begun to feel the world inside her, like she was each tree. She was each bird and its song. And this exquisite love like the hum of a hummingbird had filled her up and lifted her out of her body to meet and become the air, the wind, the sky.

When she had felt dizzy, she had dropped onto the leaves and grasses covering the earth. For the first time, she had heard the trees' song, the note of each tree sounding like a chorus of love and life force energy that filled her. Her heart had brimmed with tender gratitude.

She had heard the faint crackling of leaves and branches in the trees nearby. *It must be Tom,* she thought, *or a squirrel or bird.* Instead, when Nikkie opened her eyes to look, she had seen the girl with the long blond braids. The sounds had come from her. The girl was crying.

Nikkie had also seen the men and women from another time and place. At first, she thought they were live people play-acting in the woods. But none of them were solid. She could see the outline of the real forest of madrones, cedars and fir trees behind them.

Are they ghosts? Nikkie had wondered and felt her belly tighten. At that very moment, the young girl had looked right at Nikkie, seemed to see her, to plead to her for help. But Nikkie's intuition had said to turn away from the scene unfolding in the spirit world, to run from the pain and confusion she saw in that girl's eyes and the distress she sensed in the adults. So she had.

She had rushed back to Tom and the madrone and their game of make-believing they were lost. She ran to the life she knew, to the brother and mother she loved.

She had told Ellie and Tom about the vision. "How can I make sure I don't see them again?" Ellie had held and comforted her.

"Let's go back to the clearing and do a ritual," Ellie had suggested, and the next morning they did. Nikkie had worn her favorite pink t-shirt and purple jeans to help her feel stronger. She walked between Ellie and Tom, holding their hands, her heart pounding as they got closer to the clearing. All three were relieved to find it peaceful; the spirits had gone.

"Yesterday your intuition told you to run away," Ellie had said. "What does it tell you will help to keep the spirits away now?"

Nikkie thought for a moment. "I want for all three of us together to tell the spirits to stay away. Loud. I want us to yell it." She felt a fluttering of rightness in her belly.

"Great idea," Ellie said. "Let's do it." And the three had made kind of a game of the ritual with Nikkie yelling and Ellie yelling and Tom too. "Go away, spirits," Nikkie had shouted. "And don't come back."

"Don't come near my sister again," Tom screamed.

By the end, they were roaring like the mountain lions who graced Southern Oregon, laughing and feeling powerful.

Next, Nikkie lit the bundle of sage Ellie had brought with them to smudge the clearing with the smoke. Ellie had taught the twins the Native American tradition, which would help transform negative energies in a place back to positive ones. Nikkie had first smudged her mother, Tom and herself with the smoke, holding a large abalone shell under the sage to make sure no sparks fell to the forest floor. She fanned the smoke with her hand all around the clearing and the trees, walking with confidence now through the area where she had seen the spirits.

"How do you feel?" Ellie had asked Nikkie when she finished.

"Better. The spirits are gone," Nikkie had said with certainty.

And afterward, the forest had remained as it was. No more dead spirits. Only trees. Birds. Sunlight. Shadows. Bugs. And three live humans.

Or so Nikkie had thought. Now, the dead had returned to her again, albeit twelve years later and at the Hollywood Bowl instead of in this forest.

Nikkie opened her eyes, bringing herself back more fully into the present day. Letting out a deep sigh, she unfolded her legs, feeling the earth beneath them, then got up and stretched. Coming back to this place where she had seen the dead as a child had so far brought her no new information. No message. No visible spirits.

And why had a vision of her father appeared with them at the Hollywood Bowl? What did he have to do with these spirits? She did not remember seeing him when she was ten. But then, she realized, she had run away as a child before the full vision unfolded like it had at the Hollywood Bowl.

She asked the spirits now, "Who are you? How are you linked to my father and to Latvia? Why did you come to me again—and why at the Bowl?" A fresh wave of pain washed over and through her as she flashed on that performance and its aftermath.

"What do you want from me?" she cried out once more into the open space. Nothing.

"*Palīdz man.*" Help me, her father had said in her vision at the Hollywood Bowl. But did that mean he was asking Nikkie to help him with the girl and the other spirits? What could she and Peter do to help in any case? Or was Peter himself in trouble?

Then there were the not so little obstacles to finding Peter in the first place and telling him she and Tom were his children. He might not want anything to do with them. And if she followed that zinger up by mentioning seeing him in a vision of the dead, he would most likely think she was insane.

She heard a woodpecker nearby, hammering at a tree like she was hammering at herself. Only the woodpecker was doing something useful, hunting for food. *Stop being so hard on yourself. Don't bang your head against a closed door,* she heard Tom and Ellie telling her. She sighed and took some deep breaths to quiet her mind and ground herself. She tried to bring herself back to the present by centering her attention on the trees, on the woodpecker's rhythmic beat and single-minded purpose, on the familiar squawk of blue jays, the hum of insects, the coolness of the shade.

The sun threw its waning light through the trees. The whole day had passed. She had never touched her lunch, had barely taken a drink of water. Nikkie realized she needed to leave the clearing to get back to the trail and out of the woods before nightfall.

She had hoped that being here, connecting to the first day she had seen the dead would have perhaps resolved the vision or offered her a clue as to where she and Tom might begin the search for their father and what help he needed that was linked to the vision. But all she had were the same unanswered questions.

She got up too fast. Floaters swirled in front of her eyes, and her head began to reel. She stood, with her legs in a wide stance for balance, to allow her vertigo to dissipate.

But even as she regained her bearings, she felt a subtle shift in the atmosphere and a strong impulse to spin around again. But not whirling in her natural way as a professional or even as the girl of ten. Instead, now she took tiny steps running around in circles on the same spot, feeling the weight of her body moving into her feet. Her breath remained shallow, high up in her chest. Her heart began to pound. She got so dizzy she lost all sense of direction and crumbled to the forest floor.

There, in the still center of all that swirled around her dropped this notion. That night at the Hollywood Bowl, she had not arrived at all like she had been so confident she had. She had still been running from that vision of the dead. She had always been running from it. Her marathon race to outdistance the dead and the darkness and burden of lost lives and dreams that surrounded them had not worked.

She had not smudged and yelled them away with her mother and brother that day. The dead had remained, a breath behind her, matching her pace, her silent, invisible lifelong companions. At the Bowl, she had merely recognized what had been there all along.

A darkness seemed to emerge from the forest shadows now, wrap itself around her, sink its teeth into her neck. She felt its shudder move through her, could not stop what was happening, oddly, did not want to. This darkness—was it of the dead, she wondered—sucked out any remnants of faith, trust, and certainty in her, and replaced them with fear, anger, doubt. But instead of feeling alarm, she sensed in a bizarre, neutral way, this claiming of her was what she most needed.

She may not have been able to see the dead anymore, but she understood now that her energy had leaked out to them always, still did. A tiny, steady string of life force like the fine silk thread of a web that held her, wrapped around her like a spider with its prey. The dead had haunted her in that way her whole life, not in an in-your-face horror movie way, but in the way a rushing river wore down and carved a canyon.

"You are our destiny." She remembered now. The chorus of words rose up in her mind. The spirits had spoken them to her when she was a child, too, even though their lips had never moved, she realized. She had refused this fate that day, blocked the words, run from them, danced herself into a frenzy in the hopes of staying away from them. This was the only choice she could make to handle what she had seen back when she was a girl. But all the years she ran, she had also been running toward a past she did not know but carried in her bones.

This past had to do with the dead. It had to do with her father and with Latvia. Her only hope of unraveling its secrets was to go there and start where she could, by looking for her father. Maybe finding him would be enough to release her.

At that moment though, undeniable clarity pierced her like the woodpecker's beak drilling through the bark of the tree to get to insects. Or the sharp knife she had used to cut her own name into the madrone tree when she was a child. And what was exposed in the process was this. That besides searching for her father in Latvia, she also needed to seek out the dead at the source. The forest where they had lost their lives and their dreams for those lives.

"You are our destiny." She allowed herself to hear the chorus of the dead that spoke the words whose meaning was a mystery.

She heard a sound emanating from the trees as well, a droning incantation that sent silver shivers down her spine and legs and arms. "Seek them out," they seemed to chant, each word accentuated with the hammering of the woodpecker she still heard against the tree. "The. Key. Is. In. The. Forest." Nikkie felt the truth of this puncture its way into her.

Bowing to the trees and the woodpecker, she moved away from the clearing. Back at the trail, she nodded one more time to the madrone tree that bore her and her brother's name and left the forest.

The shadows of evening had spread and come up beside her by the time she reached the car. As she unlocked the door, they seemed to lean right into her, whisper to her. On the summer afternoon that she had seen the dead here, like a spider, she had begun to spin her own web, light as air, to catch herself.

Chapter 7

"Follow my lead," Tom said. He and Nikkie walked down the corridor to the offices of the Nijinsky Ballet Theater in Moscow. They had decided to start their search for their father at the ballet, hoping to discover why he had left and where he had gone. Nikkie breathed in the musty scent of this closed space and thought about Peter navigating this same hallway. She imagined she could hear his footsteps echoing along with their own. Photos of ballet dancers dancing and posing lined the walls.

"What does that mean?" Nikkie said. "You know what we're going to ask? What if the office staff doesn't speak English?"

"What if, what if. Do you hear yourself?" Tom said. "Have a little faith. I've got us covered."

"That's what worries me. I'm not sure I *can* follow you," Nikkie said. "I'm so nervous."

"Trust me. You'll like the surprise I have for you." Tom squeezed her hand, let it go and pushed open the heavy, dark wood door of the ballet's administrative offices. The small, windowless office was nondescript, beige walls lined with filing cabinets, not a piece of art or personal photo to be seen.

The secretary, a striking middle-aged woman sat at a massive dark wood desk, her hands folded. She had pale blond hair pulled back tight against her head and rolled into a braided bun at the nape of her neck. Given the style, Nikkie noted, the woman probably was or had been a dancer.

She immediately spoke English to Nikkie and Tom. *How did she know?* Nikkie found that ever since she landed in Moscow, the Russians sized her and Tom up in one second as Americans. A surprising number spoke passable English.

Nikkie had her own hair pulled back tight against her head as well, and clipped, but it lay loose on her back. That morning, she had started to put it into a bun, automatically without a thought, a reminder of how she and other students had worn their hair going to classes and performing at professional dance camps and at Julliard.

Tom asked the secretary her name, Natasha Petrov, and loaded on the charm, which he had in abundance. "My name is Tom Ozolins, and this is Nikkie Madrone, Ms. Petrov. We're writing a book on the featured secondary dancers of the great dance companies," Tom said, giving Nikkie a quick pinch in the arm. So, this was the surprise, Nikkie thought, trying to keep a straight face. "We have a contract with a publisher that has published several books on dance, Kirkland Press." He handed her a letter of introduction with official-looking letterhead signed by a senior editor.

"Please give access to author Tom Ozolins and his researcher/interviewer Nikkie Madrone," it read. Perfect. He had given her the fake last name of one of her favorite trees, the madrone. Tom presented Natasha with business cards from both of them. Then, he pulled out a box of fancy Godiva chocolates from a bag he had been carrying. "Our gratitude for any extra work our request might cause you."

So that's what he had been buying at Duty-Free in the airport on their way to Moscow, Nikkie thought.

"The book is going to be a behind the scenes look at the dancer's lives. We would like to interview several featured dancers from the Nijinsky Ballet." He rattled off a list of names.

When had Tom had the time in Los Angeles to do all this research? Nikkie was grateful he was adept at this kind of subterfuge. She would never have thought of it and hoped she could pull it off with him. Let Tom talk. Keep her mouth shut as much as possible.

"We chose a dancer or more from each decade since 1959," Tom went on. "Any background material you have about them would be helpful." He paused.

Her brother had been busy. How had he found out these dancer's names?

The Internet. Wikipedia. You should try it some time. Nikkie heard Tom's voice come through in her mind.

"If you could help us get started today even, say, with any background or contact information for one of the first dancers we would like to interview, you would be most helpful. We understand we may need to travel in Russia outside Moscow or to one of the neighboring countries that were part of the former USSR to meet with the dancers themselves."

He looked down, perused his list. "Let's make it easy and start at the beginning of our list. Peter Berzins."

Tom sounded so convincing, Nikkie wondered if he had rousted up a real contract to do a book in the two weeks that had passed since they lost their jobs with Stone Tara. He had been a creative writing major at Columbia focused on poetry who had stopped writing because he said he could not find what meaning or purpose his poetry served in the U.S. in an increasingly digital world. He had become Nikkie's manager instead.

Natasha's non-smiling face frowned. "Peter Berzins? He left the company years ago. I am sure we do not know where he went. I recommend you choose another dancer, Mr. Ozolins."

"Let me explain why we especially want to contact Mr. Berzins," Tom said. "We heard he had performed in an unusual

Pas de Deux for a modern ballet. One of the ballet's choreographers had specifically worked with Mr. Berzins and another male dancer to develop it. The collaboration involved their improvisation and was a unique approach. Sadly, the other dancer and the choreographer have passed away, so Mr. Berzins is our only hope of getting the story. It seems such an important part of your ballet company's history."

Where did Tom get this information? Was he making it up? Nikkie marveled at her brother's ability to dig deep and uproot facts to come up with this creative slant. She looked at Natasha Petrov, who was staring down at her desk, averting her eyes from Tom's.

"Can we see his file here then? I'm sure you have records of your dancers. And if you could, would it be possible for you to tell us your last known address for him?"

"File, yes. But address? No." Natasha said, looking up now. "It is against regulations to give out addresses for our dancers, even if they have left the ballet."

"Yes, but he was from the S.S.R. of Latvia, right? Perhaps you have his family's address there."

Nikkie noted Tom's diplomacy in not smearing in this woman's face the fact that Latvia was now independent.

Natasha paused for a moment, then nodded. "Why not check in Latvia? It's not such a big country."

"That is true," Tom said. "But if he's living there, well, Berzins is a common name in Latvia. Who knows how many people there have the same name? Please. I know it's asking a lot, but you could make a big difference."

Natasha sighed. In silence, she got up and walked to a file cabinet on a nearby wall. She bent over at the waist, back straight, pulled open a drawer and removed a large file. *Perfect forward bend,* Nikkie thought. *Definitely a dancer.* Then, Natasha walked over to another file cabinet further away and took out a three-ring binder filled with papers.

She opened the file first, removed the top sheet, turned it upside down and placed the file folder in front of Tom and Nikkie. "Berzins' records," she said. She flipped through the binder, then raised her head. "I looked at old addresses from before computers. Yes, we do have one for him, but we cannot give it to you. Regulations. I doubt he lives there anymore in any case."

"I understand. But Mr. Berzins' family still might, or a neighbor or apartment manager might know something," Tom said. "That address would be a place for us to begin. It's in Latvia, I assume."

"Not possible," she said. "Begin with the file. I take you to a room where you can look at it. I hope you read our language. Most is in Russian of course."

"Thank you. We will manage. Perhaps we can make copies?" Tom said, nodding toward the copy machine. "We will pay of course. And I do understand about the address. Regulations and all. We appreciate the help you are giving us. But might there be someone else we could also ask to see if the regulation, in this case, could be lifted? Since the book will benefit your ballet company and highlight the grand tradition of the Russian ballet the world so loves and wants to know about."

Natasha paused, opened the box of chocolates Tom had brought her, put one in her mouth, and chewed it slowly. "My superior might," Natasha said. "But he is out of the office for the next two days." She pulled open a file cabinet next to her desk, took out a sheet of paper. "Fill out this special request form and sign. Both of you. I will give it to him when he returns. We should have an answer for you," Natasha looked at the calendar, "in one week. Next week on Tuesday after thirteen o'clock." She pulled out several more forms. You will need to fill one out for each dancer you would like to contact. You might as well submit them all at once."

Nikkie kept quiet and smiled a lot.

❧

Natasha set them up in a conference room with a table and chairs where they could look at the materials. The file was thick. *Like a dossier,* Nikkie thought. The writing was in Russian. But it was also filled with photographs of Peter in various dances and rehearsals and newspaper clippings.

The grace of Peter's movement shone through. He might not have been the prima soloist, but he was a featured performer. He was tall, she noted. Like her and Tom. And had a leg extension in arabesque that seemed to reach for miles.

In one photo, he stood with another male dancer in a scene from what looked like a classical ballet. His arms formed a perfect Port de Bras.

Nikkie's chest tightened. He was so much younger in this photo than he had been in the one Ellie had shown them of him at the Barricades in Latvia. Tom looked like him. And she did, too. The same prominent cheekbones. His hair was straight, like theirs, and in the photo, it was chin length, swept back from his forehead.

Nikkie grasped Tom's hand, unable to look away or at each other.

"I wonder if this photo was taken before he met mom or afterward," Nikkie said in a low voice. "It might be from when mom was pregnant with us. Or after, when we had already been born, and he had no idea we existed."

"Careful, Nikkie. I'm not sure if these walls still have ears," Tom whispered.

Nikkie nodded her understanding, but whispered back, "I think you've been watching too many spy movies. The dissolution of the Soviet Union happened more than a decade ago."

What would her life have been like growing up with a dancer father, she wondered, unable to take her eyes off the photo. He might have understood her as an artist. But would he have supported her involvement with Stone Tara? It was not exactly classical ballet.

"I wish I could have talked to our father before I made a choice to leave New York," Nikkie whispered, ignoring Tom's admonitions about rooms being bugged. "Maybe with his advice, I would still be there and have a career with a major dance company."

"Nik, you forget how miserable you were," Tom whispered back. "You made the right choice, regardless of what he might have said."

Nikkie felt the truth of Tom's words, but also a fresh stab of pain in her chest like she was reading Sean's letter all over again.

"I know you're still hurting from what happened with Stone Tara, but just because that opportunity didn't go the way you wanted doesn't mean joining the group was a bad decision. You followed your heart. You took a risk. That's what art is all about. Peter would understand that."

Nikkie noted Tom referred to Peter by his first name just like Tom most often referred to Ellie by her name rather than their parental distinctions. "We're all equals," he said, and using names emphasized that to him.

But she liked thinking of Peter and Ellie as her father and mother. Most often, she called Ellie "mom" and referred to Peter as her "father," except when she thought of him as a dancer. Then, he was Peter to her.

She ran her finger over the matt finish of one of the close-up shots of Peter. It was like she could feel his face somehow, the warmth and animation of it. She imagined him supporting her artistic choices the way Tom had suggested, encouraging her to trust her instincts.

"Look, I found some things that aren't in Russian," Tom said at full volume now, holding up a piece of paper. "This one is a bio from when Peter toured in the United States. It's in English. It says he was 14 when he won the competition in Riga for a chance to study at the Nijinsky ballet school. That was when he moved to Moscow and lived in a dormitory with other dancers from various republics in the Soviet Union."

Peter had been a young dancer with dreams to follow in the tradition of the other great artists who had come from Riga and moved to Moscow to study, Nikkie thought. Like Mikhail Baryshnikov. And the Bolshoi star, Maris Liepa. Teenagers with talent and passion who left their families and countries to pursue a life of dance.

"I remember Ellie saying how Peter felt it was an honor to have been chosen," Nikkie said out loud now too. "But I know what a rigorous commitment that honor required from studying Russian dancers in my Dance History and Technique classes."

"What did that involve?" Tom asked.

"Peter would have had a grueling schedule, dancing all day every day and into the night, learning technique, choreography. Training like an Olympic athlete."

"I can't imagine it was any more dedication than you and your dancer friends in the U.S. had," Tom said.

"Maybe you're right." Nikkie thought back to the six to eight hours a day she had spent practicing and dancing for years, searched inside for a glimmer of the fire that had driven that passion for performing. She felt nothing and brought her attention back to her new focus—finding her father.

"But he also probably missed out on normal childhood or teenage activities, even dating. And his dedication to training and practice, like my own, continued when he became an adult. I'm sure he competed for his place in the ballet company."

"But the reward was worth it for him, right?" Tom said.

Nikkie nodded. "He must have known he wanted to dance from a young age, and despite not being a soloist, he was one of the select few to be chosen for one of the great dance companies of the world."

"Here's a review of the ballet in *The London Times* from a European tour in 1983 that mentions the Pas de Deux and its choreographer," Tom said.

"That must have been the year it premiered in Moscow too," Nikkie said.

Tom nodded. "That's what the review says."

"What does it say about Peter?"

"They don't mention him or his partner," Tom said. "Only that the choreographer used improvisation to develop it. The rest of the review is about the prima dancers and their numbers."

"Peter would not have been passed over by a reviewer like that if he was a soloist," Nikkie said. "I do wonder how he felt about never becoming a principal dancer. And why he never was? Was talent a factor? Or were internal or Communist party politics involved?"

"Hopefully, we'll get a chance to ask him," Tom said.

Nikkie wondered about all the pieces of Peter's life that weren't in the file or were unintelligible to them because they could not read Russian. She had so many questions, but she knew if she met Peter right now, she would forget every one of them.

"Are you finding any articles from Latvian newspapers?" Nikkie asked. "They might mention how Peter felt about leaving Riga and his family to dance. Or if he ever got married."

Tom flipped through the remaining papers and articles in the file. "None I can see. I imagine his feelings about missing his family and Latvia would have been taboo subjects to speak about. Latvian newspapers were also regulated by the Soviets."

"I guess you're right," Nikkie said. "But I already feel so much closer to him after seeing his photos and reading about him. I'm disappointed though that we haven't found any clues for how to find him."

"Let's look through the file again and make sure we didn't miss anything."

Nikkie and Tom perused the materials in silence but uncovered nothing new that might lead them to Peter.

Tom closed the file folder and laid his hand on top. "Okay, think for a moment about what we already know about him. We know from Ellie that Peter supposedly 'died' in 1988. Since he was twenty-two when he and Ellie met, he would have been thirty years old then. And that is the year he left the Nijinsky."

"Maybe his leaving was linked to his age," Nikkie said. "He and the company would likely have known by then he would never become a premier soloist. The company may have fired him to make way for younger, more promising dancers or ones who were also members of the Communist Party."

"That's a possibility. But there's the year itself," Tom said. "In 1988, the freedom movement in Latvia was revving up. Maybe he returned to take part in it."

"Or a personal reason that had nothing to do with politics or dance," Nikkie said.

Natasha came into the room. Nikkie hoped she had not heard any of what Tom or she had been saying.

"This file is so helpful," Tom said. "Thank you for letting us see it."

An unexpected smile broke out on Natasha's face "I remembered something I think you will find interesting for your research. Leave the file on the table. You can come back to it later." She motioned for them to follow her and led them to another room where a few chairs and a film projector and screen were set up. On the projector was a reel of film.

"Sit," she said, more like an order than a request. And they did.

Natasha flicked off the lights in this new beige room which was even starker than her office. While the walls of the conference room had been filled with blown-up photographs of the current dancers, here, the walls were bare. *Almost like it was an interrogation room*, Nikkie thought. *Stop being paranoid. It's an empty office.*

Natasha turned on the projector.

Nikkie and Tom gasped. In front of them was Peter, dancing what Nikkie assumed was the Pas de Deux with the other featured dancer. Seeing her father in a photograph had been emotional enough, but witnessing as he moved, twirled, turned, held the weight of his partner, Nikkie grasped Tom's hand and squeezed tight to keep from crying out.

Peter was beautiful. His dancing. The line of his muscles. The leaps and jumps. The pirouettes. A classically trained dancer. She couldn't look at her brother but kept her head turned toward the screen, or she knew she'd lose it.

"Beautiful, yes?" Natasha said.

"Yes," Tom and Nikkie chimed.

"This is incredible footage. Thank you," Tom said. And Natasha left them alone.

For the next two hours, Nikkie and Tom watched and re-watched the reels of film that included their father. Dancing in classical ballets. Swan Lake. And in modern choreography. In the corps de ballet. With other men. Lifting a ballerina.

Waves upon waves of elation at seeing Peter coupled with sadness at what she had missed in not knowing him as a child swept through Nikkie. She remembered her own experience of being lifted by male dancers at Julliard. She had always had a niggling fear one would drop her. And they had. In rehearsals, repeating a lift or a jump and catch again and again until she hovered over their heads held up by one or two hands. What would having her own father lift or catch her have been like, even as a child?

Later on, the reel was footage of a rehearsal, probably the Pas de Deux again. In the end, Peter and his dance partner came up to the choreographer and stood listening. They were speaking in Russian, but Nikkie assumed the choreographer was making suggestions on how to improve their performance and interpretation.

And there it was on Peter's face. The same half smile Tom had. What irony had Peter's smile carried, what emotions were hidden behind it?

"Do you see it?" Nikkie whispered. Tom looked at her quizzically. "The smile," Nikkie mouthed silently. "It's yours," and mimicked Tom's half smile. He looked at Peter more intently, let it sink in.

"We've got to find him," Tom said. "We've got to."

"Thank you again for all you've done to help us today," Tom said. "We'll call again when we need to see more files. Meanwhile, we'll fill out those request forms."

Natasha smiled, seemed more relaxed with them now.

Tom placed Peter's file back on Natasha's desk. On top of it was a single photo and underneath it, but half of it showing, a twenty-dollar bill. "But I did have one more thought," Tom said, pointing to the photo. It was of a group of dancers, Peter included, standing in front of an ornate building.

"I wonder, was there someplace, maybe even this building, where the dancers all lived together when they were studying and dancing here in Moscow? We would love to see the building if you could give us the address. Who knows, maybe someone still living there knew Peter and could tell us some dancing anecdotes. When he left the ballet in 1988 was not so very long ago."

"That's where you're wrong, Mr. Ozolins," Natasha said, the smile disappearing, stiffening up again. "It was a lifetime ago. We were still in Glasnost then. We were still the Soviet Union, the world's greatest superpower."

Oops. Nikkie realized that not all Russians welcomed Glasnost and the dissolution of the Soviet Empire.

"Oh, you are absolutely correct," Tom said. "How short-sighted and insensitive of me. I am sorry I offended you. I did not mean to. I cannot begin to imagine how challenging the changes have been for your country. And that's what I want to include as a backstory of this book. That kind of important information. How the changes affected the ballet. In fact, I'd like Nikkie to interview you for the book. I'm sure you could provide great insight into that historic moment in time."

Thanks a lot, Tom, Nikkie thought and stepped lightly on his foot. She was a dancer, not an interviewer. And they need-ed to keep moving, not spend time in Moscow interviewing former Communist secretaries.

But out loud, Nikkie heard herself saying, "Yes, I would like that. Your contribution would be integral to the tone of the book." *Now she was doing it.*

Natasha's mouth relaxed again. She reached over and took the photo. The twenty-dollar bill vanished as she glanced down at the image. "I would like to help in any way I can." She flipped through the three-ring binder again that held the dancer's addresses and was still on her desk. "Yes, Peter did live in an apartment building with all the dancers who came from outside Moscow."

As in wiretapped phones and furniture, walls, toilets even and probably a full-time KGB agent to monitor them from what Nikkie understood about the times.

"But he would not have been allowed to remain there af-ter he left the ballet," Natasha said.

"Could we see the building anyway?" Tom asked. "We'd like to photograph it for the book because I'm sure other dancers we interview will have lived there as well. And as

I mentioned, we'd like to talk to the dancers who live there today."

"I doubt anyone will talk to you, Mr. Ozolins. And we don't want you bothering the other dancers."

"We wouldn't want to do that," Tom said. "Well, to photograph it then."

Natasha sighed, looked him in the eye. Tom flashed his half smile, which was likely filled with the same kind of irony that was part of the consciousness of anybody who had grown up in the Soviet Union or one of its republics.

Natasha told him the address. "The ballet owns the building. You can photograph the outside, but you would need a permit and both the ballet administrator and the dancers' permission to photograph the inside or any of the apartments." She pulled out a desk drawer and brought out more forms. "Here's the paperwork you need to fill out to take photos. We will also need to approve of the photos before you use them. We will make the final choices of what you can and cannot use."

Nikkie's head was spinning with the bureaucracy.

"I understand," Tom said. "Right now, we are happy to see it, even from the outside."

Nikkie felt the walls closing in around Natasha's mind. *Time to go, Tom,* Nikkie thought.

CHAPTER 8

The apartment building where Peter had lived in Moscow was old and ornate with large windows and high gables. Being an artist in the U.S.S.R had come with its privileges, Nikkie thought. Living in this beautiful building had been one.

"Do you think the apartments are bugged?" Nikkie asked.

"Who knows? Maybe," Tom said. "But bugged or not, I doubt anyone is sitting around recording and listening to tapes or watching monitors anymore. Shall we try to go in?"

The twins walked up to the front doors. Locked. The intercom and buzzer set up listed apartment numbers, but no names. Tom randomly rang one. "Let's see what happens."

"Good idea," Nikkie said, eager to get inside the building.

Nothing. Tom went down the line, buzzed all twenty apartments. No response.

"Well, someone who lives here has to enter or exit sometime," he said, and sat down on the concrete steps leading up to the front door, motioning to Nikkie to join him. "We will wait."

And they did. For half an hour a series of nondescript people dressed in neutral gray and brown clothing not much different from the sidewalk, the building or the sky, walked past them down the street. Each time, they watched expectantly, hoping one would turn toward the apartment, but no one did. And not one looked remotely like a dancer.

"When someone does come, what are we going to say?" Nikkie asked.

"Did they know Peter? Or was anyone in the building with the ballet in 1988 who might have known him?" Tom said. "I don't know. We'll make it up as we go along. Like we did at the Nijinsky."

Nikkie felt the hard, cool surface of the concrete beneath her hands. "Hard to imagine our father walked up and down these stairs hundreds, if not thousands, of times over the years he was with the ballet," Nikkie said. "I wonder if he ever thought about Ellie while he was living here or what might have happened if he had defected."

"Maybe, but maybe he had also tucked his days with her away in his stash of tour memories and moved on with his life," Tom said. "I wish he had known about us and that Ellie had made more of an effort from the beginning to contact him, censorship issues or not, or had tried to find out more when the ballet office told her Peter was dead."

"But could she really have done that?" Nikkie said. "You saw how closed Natasha was to giving us information even years later. In the grand scheme of things now is when we are supposed to know he's alive and to have a chance to find him. Besides, mom's meeting us in Latvia now to help find him now. Let's just focus on the search."

Before Tom had a chance to answer, he and Nikkie looked up, their eyes drawn like magnets to metal to a woman walking toward their stoop. Dressed in a tight black dress that accentuated her full, voluptuous form and a modicum of cleavage, she stood out like a geyser on barren land. Her shoulder length wavy light blond hair framed her face and ruby red-lipped smile. She carried a black coat and red silk scarf on her arm and wore red heels with pointed toes.

Her gait spoke of elegance and confidence, her head held high, her hips swaying naturally. An artist. Had to be, Nikkie surmised. But a dancer at the Nijinsky? No. She looked to be in her late 40s, a little older than Peter would be.

The woman nodded and smiled at them as she moved by, greeted them in Russian. Nikkie felt drawn to talk to her, had been disappointed she had not turned to enter Peter's old apartment building. But at the very next apartment building, also ornate, she began the ascent up the stairs to the front door.

"Excuse me," Tom was on his feet first. "Pardon. Skuzi. Mademoiselle." Where was their Russian phrase book when they needed one? "May we speak with you for a moment?"

She stopped and looked over. "A—meh-ri-can?" she asked, emphasizing each syllable.

Nikkie nodded, stood up as well. "Yes. Do you speak English? Please excuse us that we do not speak Russian. We're writers from America. Journalists. Writing a book about the Nijinsky Ballet." Nikkie was amazed at how easily she had slipped into Tom's made up story.

"A-a-h-h-h," the woman said and reversed her steps down the stairs. She came over, offered the back of her hand as if for a kiss, instead of a handshake.

"May I?" Tom, ever the charmer, asked, taking her hand in his and lifting it towards his mouth.

The woman obliged willingly, holding her hand out farther, chuckling in delight when he bent forward and kissed it. "You want to speak to the dancers who live here?" she asked.

"Yes, but not ones who live here now," Nikkie said. "Ones from the 1970s and 1980s. The featured and partner dancers, not the premier dancer. By the way, my name is Nikkie um Madrone, and this is my bro…. partner, Tom, Tom Ozolins. We come from New York City." New York had in fact been the last place the twins had an actual pied-à-terre before they had gone on the road with Stone Tara.

"Ah, New York…. I love New York, USA. I traveled there many times to perform. My name is Alexandra Markova."

"Nikkie and I were commenting that from the way you looked you had to be an artist or performer," Tom said.

Alexandra's smile radiated even more. "Yes, I am a singer. Light opera. I sing with the Sokolov Operetta Theater. Also second. Not the lead. But in my own mind, I am the lead. Yes?" And she laughed, breathed in and extended her chest, flourishing her arm in front of the twins as if greeting her performing public, taking a slight bow, then curtsy. "We performed at Lincoln Center in the 1980s. In Chicago, Boston, Cleveland, Washington D.C. Now, we sing most often here and in Europe."

"We would love to hear about your experiences," Tom said. "Is your building where the opera singers live?"

She nodded.

"If you lived here in the 1980s, did you know any of the dancers in this building?" Nikkie asked.

"Yes," Alexandra said. "I knew them. We were friends, and I, how you say…. dated some of them. The dancers were much more handsome and had more beautiful bodies than the male opera singers with their…." She pointed to her stomach and made a round belly. She laughed. "Handsome like you." She nodded at Tom.

"Why, thank you," Tom said. "You are so kind. And Nikkie's right. May we hear some of your stories about the dancers you knew and your own as an artist in the Soviet Union? It would be such a help for our book."

"If you are willing, could we go someplace to talk?" Nikkie said. "Make an appointment for a more convenient time, or we're available now as well."

Before long, Nikkie and Tom found themselves entering a bustling café with subdued lighting and dark wood booths, not far from Alexandra's apartment. The walls were filled with photos, many autographed, of opera singers, painters, writers and artists of Russia. From Tolstoy to Gogol. Alexandra's signed photo was there, too, as she pointed out.

People began to nod at Alexandra. She may not have been the main diva, but she apparently had renown here. Several men, the bartender and waiter included came over and kissed her hand. They bowed their heads in her presence, each in their own way offering their obeisance. A couple in their twenties asked for her autograph. Alexandra graciously acknowledged each one of them, then directed Tom and Nikkie toward a booth at the back of the café that offered more privacy.

Alexandra focused her attention on Nikkie and Tom. For the first twenty minutes, she regaled them with stories of her performances and experiences at the Sokolov operetta theater. Nikkie listened and responded with interest, but inside, her heart was bursting with the central questions looming in her mind. *Did you know Peter Berzins? What was he like? Do you know what happened to him?*

She knew Tom's had to be as well. Or was it? He seemed genuinely interested, drawn into Alexandra's world, which Nikkie realized had been her father's world. The world of the artist in Soviet Russia.

"I love your stories, Mademoiselle Markova," Tom said.

"Please, call me Alexandra," she said.

"Alexandra, then. We're also trying to get a better sense of the changes that have taken place here. Background for the book, you understand. Nikkie and I would so appreciate your perspective."

Alexandra nodded. "Please go on."

"For example, how did you and the artists you knew feel when the time of Glasnost came, and you realized you might gain your freedom," Tom asked. "I'm asking because some of the dancers who defected to the U.S. before that time had said one of their main reasons was to gain artistic freedom."

Alexandra remained silent, her eyes for a few moments, like a wild animal, scanning the room for danger before moving out into an open field. She shook her head for a moment, focused back on Tom and Nikkie. "Excuse me. Even a decade later, I am not used to talking about such things in a public place. During Communism, we did not dare. But for years after the fall of the Soviet Union, I still did not talk about anything serious in a public place or in our apartments, afraid everything was still bugged. Many of us were like that, not knowing whom to trust in case our new government did not last. It's only now we are beginning to believe our new way of life will continue."

Alexandra took a deep breath, straightened up, her confident manner returning. "Yes, it is important to talk about these more serious matters. And I do not believe you are former KGB posing as American journalists."

Nikkie flinched inside at the word "posing," feeling a bit of guilt about lying to Alexandra.

"I will answer as best I can," Alexandra said. "In some ways, during Communism in Moscow, we as artists had more freedom than others. Yes, we were under constant scrutiny. But we were respected, had certain privileges, as long as we stayed within the bounds of censorship and performed state-approved operettas and musicals."

"What kind of privileges?" Tom asked.

"The main one was we singers got to perform, to do the thing we loved to do," Alexandra said. "We did not have to work in menial jobs like many of our friends and family, jobs that had nothing to do with their intelligence or skill. But our families did what they could to survive. We also had other privileges. We did not have to wait in long lines for hours to get our food or clothing like most people. We shopped in special stores, or others waited in lines for us. We had access to luxuries, hot water in our apartments, fresh meat, vegetables, fruit, good shoes, and clothing, as long as we did not step out of line. We could not question or criticize the government or anyone in the Communist Party."

Nikkie had never thought about her father living like that. Mostly, she had imagined him dancing. But as a performer, likely he had those privileges. Or on top of the rigors of dancing, did he also have to wait in line for food? She wondered about his family back in Latvia. Did privileges extend to them? What did they have to do for a living? She wanted to shift the conversation over to the dancers, but let Alexandra continue. Nikkie was learning so much she had never considered about what her father's life might have been like here.

"What about Glasnost?" Tom said. "What changed for the artists?"

"To be free …." Alexandra's voice trailed off, and she sat in silence, thinking before speaking. "During the change times, I did not know if I would survive to see our country free. If the artists I knew and I stepped out of line, we might still be arrested and shipped off to Siberia never to be heard of again. Or interrogated, tortured and locked away in prison somewhere. Some were exiled."

"Were artists you knew imprisoned?" Nikkie asked.

Alexandra's expression grew serious. "Some. Most we never heard from again. But the threat was constant for all. We had to be careful of what we said to whom and where."

"I can't imagine what it would have been like to live and perform under that kind of scrutiny," Nikkie said.

Alexandra gently stroked her left hand with her right as if to comfort herself. The three sat in silence for a moment.

This conversation was moving in unexpected directions. Alexandra seemed to need to talk, and she and Tom needed to listen, to find out more about what life had been like for Alexandra and their father.

But Nikkie felt like a fraud. *Here, this woman is entrusting us with her precious life stories thinking we are writers and she is contributing to a book,* she thought. *Our questions are stirring old, painful emotions and memories. And for what? Our gain, not hers.*

Their goal to find their father had clouded their judgment, Nikkie realized. Their well-intentioned plan to pose as journalists started as a game, but now was causing this woman pain. Nikkie wanted to blurt out right then and there who they were and what their real mission was.

At that moment, a waiter arrived. Alexandra sat back, seemed to compose herself, put on her public mask again. The waiter set down three pieces of vanilla torte topped with lemon cream icing, plus cappuccinos for Alexandra and Tom and a chamomile tea for Nikkie. Alexandra nodded to him and expressed her thanks but stopped talking until after he left.

Seriousness gone, Alexandra's eyes lit up, and she broke out into a big smile, flipping both hands palms up motioning toward the cakes. "Do you love cakes as much as I do?" she asked them. "When this was the Soviet Union, we would never have been able to buy pastries like these at a café or a store. Even with the privileges of being an artist. Cakes and pastries, chocolates were a luxury the rare times we got them. Good coffee. I savor each bite, each sip." She picked up her fork and used it to cut through the cake, put a piece in her mouth, chewed it slowly.

Nikkie, who like most dancers watched every calorie, dove into her piece without a second thought, hoping her own enjoyment of its sweetness and flavor would override the conflicting feelings inside her. "All the more delicious appreciating the symbol of freedom it represents," Nikkie said after a few bites, wiping a bit of frosting from the corner of her mouth with a napkin. Tom, who had never watched a calorie in his life and was still as slim as any dancer, agreed.

Alexandra nodded and smiled. "You know, I may not have been the diva. But I had a following here. I still do. Loyal admirers, who spend hard earned rubles and buy me flowers. Dinners. Write me letters. The people in Russia, our patrons, appreciate the arts and artists."

"I hope I do not presume too much in asking, you said you went to the U.S. and Europe on tour with the operetta company," Nikkie said. "Given the pressures of living in the Soviet Union, did you ever think about defecting? Or know performers who did?"

"I thought about it when I went to New York City. I did not have family here. No brothers and sisters. My parents had died. I had no husband, no children. I had not wanted to be tied down. To live in the man's shadow, as you say it. I was alone. So, what did it matter I thought to myself. Yet it did matter."

"How so?" Tom asked.

"My friends in the opera world and dance world had become my family. The audiences who adored us. Yes, I might have more artistic freedom in the USA. But I had never been the diva in Russia or on tour. I was not assured of having a career as a singer in your America like they would have been. And that is what I did have here. My singing."

"Did you know any opera singers—or dancers –who did defect or wanted to?" Nikkie asked, grateful Alexandra was eager to talk to them. She put both her hands around her cup of tea, wanted to hold something to steady her nerves as she attempted to steer the conversation to the dancers.

"I was afraid to talk to the other singers." Alexandra leaned forward and lowered her voice. "If one of them let slip that I had asked about defection, I might have been questioned by management or the KGB and lost my privilege to tour abroad. But when the big ballet stars defected. Nureyev. Baryshnikov. Godunov. It caused quite a stir amongst us. The dancers brought it up when we went out together."

"What did they say?" Tom asked.

"Like us, our dancer friends all understood the pull to artistic freedom in the West, though we had to denounce the defectors publicly. But like I said earlier, those dancers were stars already. Their fame, their jobs in the free world were guaranteed. For the rest of us, at least here we had jobs and were respected."

"I never thought of it in that way," Nikkie said. "But it's true. If any dancers who weren't already stars defected during Communism, I never read or heard about them." She considered Peter for a moment. Had he thought about defecting when he was with Ellie? Would he have been able to continue dancing with a renowned company if he did? Who knows if their relationship would have developed enough to withstand the rigors of that kind of major transition?

"I could also see in America that despite your freedom, the opera world, the dance world, they still had their own politics," Alexandra said. "Their own favorites."

I know all about that, Nikkie thought, remembering dance camp, Julliard and her experience with the band. She wished she could say it out loud.

"Here I knew what I was dealing with," Alexandra continued. "There.… I did not. Yes, I had my voice, my looks, my acting ability, but I did not know if I would have the chance to perform. I did wonder if I had made the right choice. I would have liked to have the courage to leave. But now, as we find our way to freedom in Russia, I am happy I stayed to take part in the changes."

"I'm glad that you continue to be able to sing here, too," Nikkie said. "I'm curious though. You said you knew many of the dancers and might be able to help us. I'd like to ask you some questions about them. Is that all right?"

"Yes, yes," Alexandra said, patting her heart, then extending her hand, palm up toward Nikkie and Tom. "I have been going on and on about myself. Please, I will tell you what I can about the dancers."

"Do not be concerned; we love hearing about your life here," Nikkie said. "It's a great help in understanding the life of an artist. But I'm wondering about one dancer, in particular, we're hoping to interview but have not been able to find. We know he lived in the building next to yours and left the ballet during Glasnost. He was a Latvian, who had toured in America, like you, in the early 1980s. New York. Chicago. His name is Peter Berzins. Did you ever meet him?

"Ah. Peter." Alexandra's face lit up, and she smiled. "Yes, I knew him. We were friends, went out together, a big group of us. I don't mean we were lovers, though I must admit I would have liked that. He was a handsome man. A good man. And talented."

She moved in closer, cocked her head and looked more closely at Tom's face as if examining a specimen. "I am wondering why you chose Peter."

At that moment, Nikkie wanted to tell Alexandra what their actual connection to Peter was, but as if Tom could read her mind, he squeezed Nikkie's hand firmly. "Nikkie and I both have Latvian ancestry, like Peter, even though we were born in the U.S.," he said. "It's one of the reasons we wanted to interview him."

That seemed to satisfy Alexandra, and she leaned back in her chair. "You Latvians with your blond hair and high cheekbones. Tall and good-looking. The other Latvian dancers with the ballet were the same way. You all look like you could be related." She nodded at Nikkie. "You also."

"Maybe we can interview those dancers, too, if they were secondary dancers," Tom said.

"But let's start with Peter now, especially given that you knew him, Alexandra," Nikkie said, turning to the singer. Her heart began to pound. This was the closest she had gotten to someone who had actually been her father's friend.

"We spent the afternoon at the Nijinsky Ballet looking at movies of him dancing the Pas de Deux," Tom said. "Did you ever see him perform it?"

"Yes, many times," Alexandra said. "Beautiful."

"Did he ever talk about that dance," Tom asked.

"Peter was nervous to do a good job always, but especially the first time for this dance. It was his opportunity. If he excelled and audiences liked it, he hoped to get out of the corps de ballet and second roles to become a principal dancer."

"Do you know how the dance was received?" Nikkie asked.

"Here, and in America on tour, the reviews for the Pas de Deux, for Peter, were good, excellent sometimes," Alexandra said. "He kept copies and read them to us when he returned. But at the Nijinsky? Succeeding at the ballet company, like at the opera, was always clouded over by internal politics."

"Did that impact Peter in any specific way?" Tom asked.

"I know he never got to be a lead dancer," Alexandra said. "Then, something happened with his partner."

"I did read that Peter's dance partner for the Pas de Deux died," Tom said.

Alexandra's smile shifted from radiant to wistful. Her expression turned solemn. "Peter's partner, Maxim was his name, did not just die. He was arrested. He had been a member of a group of musicians, dancers and writers who were against the regime and meeting to discuss ways to protest against it."

"Arrested?" Tom said. "I hadn't known that."

"It was during the early days of Glasnost, 1987," Alexandra said. "We never knew what the formal charges were. The next we heard was that Maxim was dead. Suicide, the paper said. He made a noose from his undershirt and hung himself in his cell from a hook. None of us believed that's what happened. We all thought he was murdered by the KGB."

"Was Peter suspected of feeling the same?" Nikkie asked, worried about what her father might have suffered as a result of his association with Maxim.

"He was brought in for questioning, not once, but several times," Alexandra said. "Many dancers were questioned.

Maxim had been part of our group of friends, so other singers and I were also questioned. They wanted us to say things that would build a case against him. For a time, we were afraid we might be arrested—guilt by association. Maxim had been an outgoing and friendly man. All of us liked him. We never knew what he had supposedly done that was so traitorous, only that he had been at times publicly critical of the regime."

Knowing this story, Nikkie was glad Ellie had not pushed her way through the obstacles she would have faced under Communism to let Peter know about the twins when they were young children.

What if he *had* been questioned, lost his job or worse, been arrested as a result of having any ongoing association with Americans, as Ellie had feared?

She remembered now what Indra told them about her first visits to Latvia in the early 1980s when the Soviets opened only Riga to visitors again. Any relative who had come to Riga to see her had been interrogated by the KGB afterward as to why they were visiting Americans, what Indra wanted with them, what they had told her.

Talking to Alexandra echoed what their grandmother had told them—that any associations with Americans were a problem. Who knew what impact his affair with Ellie would have had on his personal or professional life if anyone in charge at the ballet company had discovered Peter had fathered twins in America on tour?

"Fortunately, Peter was never arrested," Alexandra said. "But he knew his every move and conversation would be under greater scrutiny. Then, something else happened. The ballet officials took away Peter's Pas de Deux. Instead of giving him a new partner, they replaced Peter. They said they were giving new dancers a chance. But we all knew the real reason was his association with Maxim. The fact he had not been a member of the group of artists arrested did not matter to those in charge."

"He must have been devastated," Nikkie said, angry at the unfairness.

Alexandra nodded. "At first, yes. He knew any hope to be considered for principal roles or new secondary roles was over. He tried to have it be enough for him that he was still dancing in the ballet, as he had throughout his dance career. But later that year, when people were arrested in demonstrations with thousands of people in the Baltics, in Latvia, something snapped in him." Alexandra paused. "Are you sure you're interested in this? It's not all about dancing."

"Yes, yes," Nikkie said. "We want to know the full picture of Peter's life."

Alexandra seemed to settle again, released a rush of air through her nose as if blowing away any anxiety and continued. "Dance was no longer everything to Peter. The chance for freedom in Latvia and the rest of the Soviet Union began to pull him stronger than his dance. I don't know where the courage came from to do what he did, but he did what for many of us was unthinkable. Crazy. Professional suicide. He quit the ballet. He had intended to go back to Latvia. But I don't know if he ever made it."

"What an amazing story," Tom said. "But why do you think he might not have made it?"

"We had gone out one night, and Peter told me what he was going to do. He was the happiest I had seen him. But the next day, he was gone. Gone. I never saw him again. I hoped he had departed for Latvia, but who knew back then. Two men came and emptied out his apartment. I asked if they were going to ship Peter his things, and they told me to mind my own business. Which I did. Because that's what we still did in those days, or we would suffer the consequences. I wrote to Peter after the Soviet Union dissolved. But if he wrote back, I never received the letter."

"You wrote to him?" Tom said. He tensed, sat up straighter. "Do you happen to know an address for him in Latvia? It might help us find him."

"It was his parent's address," Alexandra said. "He gave it to me that last night I saw him. Yes. I do have it." She tapped her head. "Right here. I have what you call a photographic memory." She smiled broadly.

"That must be convenient," Nikkie said.

"Very convenient for remembering lyrics for opera," Alexandra said. "Also, in the Soviet Union when you do not want to put something in writing."

"So, Peter's parents' address?" Tom said. "What would that be? Unfortunately, I do need to write things down." He held up his notebook and pen.

"*Strēlnieku Iela*," Alexandra said. "11 *Strēlnieku Iela*. 'Iela' is the word for 'street' in Latvian in case you do not speak the language. It is one of the main streets in Riga, he told me. An apartment building. Maybe that will help."

"I'm sure it will," Tom said. "It gives us a starting point at least."

"One more thing," she said. "Peter's parents were in Riga. But he mentioned an uncle who lived in Kuldiga. A beautiful small old city, he said. On the Venta river. Nature all around. It was near the hill country, the little Alps, Latvians called it. It was a joke. There are no mountains in Latvia. So that's all I know. I was always sad not to know what happened to him. When you find him, would you write or call and tell me?"

"Yes," Nikkie said. "We would be happy to do that. You have been so helpful. It's the least we can do." Nikkie hesitated for a moment. "Would you mind if I asked you one more thing about Peter?"

"Of course not," Alexandra said. "I love this chance to talk about him.

"What do you remember about Peter's dancing itself?"

Nikkie asked. "Did you enjoy it? Did he ever talk with you about what it was like for him?"

Alexandra shrugged.

"What I do know is for years, dance was everything to him. Then, after Maxim, it wasn't anymore. As a dancer? In truth, the ballet had better dancers than him and worse dancers. Peter was a good dancer. You saw that in the film, yes?"

Nikkie and Tom nodded.

"But for me, he was something better than a good dancer," Alexandra said. "He was a great human being. He made everyone around him feel better like you were the best person alive. I always liked being around him. He cared. About people. His country, Latvia. Artistic expression. Went out of his way to help you.

"It was almost like he was too good for this earth. Too good for the Soviet Union, that's for sure. Please let me know what happened. It never made sense the way he disappeared. I was afraid he had been arrested, shipped off to the Gulag."

Tom and Nikkie reassured her again they would.

"And send me a copy of that book when it is published," Alexandra said, then leaned in closer to them. "So I can read about Peter."

Tom and Nikkie looked at each other for a moment, then down at the table. "Of course," Tom said.

"The book with the true story," Alexandra said.

Nikkie snapped to attention.

"You know. The one that tells me who you really are and who Peter is to you."

Alexandra leaned back again, smiled. "It is okay. This game you play. But I am not only a good singer, but a good actor and judge of people's character.

Nikkie felt the heat rise in her face as she blushed, reached over and touched Tom's hand. It jerked slightly under her fingers as if she had stung him.

"For many years, I studied human nature, paid attention to people's mannerisms, yes?" Alexandra said. "I learned so much to use in my performance and in life, to know whom to trust. I used to watch Peter when we would go out as a group or alone. He was so good looking. More than that, I loved the way he moved, with his whole body, even while he talked and was sitting down, which he had a hard time doing for long. Like you do." She looked directly at Nikkie.

"And his expressions. The way he used his mouth, the irony in it and in his eyes, the fiery spirit peeking out from behind it. The inflection of his voice." She turned to Tom and paused. "I felt deep inside me that I could trust Peter." She moved her gaze back and forth between the twins now. "I had the same feeling about you, even though I know there is more to the story here than you are telling me. You *writers* with Latvian ancestry in your blood."

Chapter 9

"Welcome to Latvia, your homeland," Indra said as she opened the heavy carved wooden doors to her apartment building on Krišjāņa Valdemāra street in Riga. She retrieved a bouquet of flowers from under her arm and extended it. "I'm so happy you have come."

Nikkie and Tom had not seen their grandmother since she had moved to Latvia three years earlier. Indra was five feet tall, shorter than Nikkie remembered, but she carried herself as if she was as tall as Nikkie and Tom. At 71, her perfectly made up face remained free of wrinkles, and her short, straight blond hair had been styled to reach above her chin. She wore a pair of well-tailored navy-blue slacks and a short-sleeved pale pink blouse that suited her coloring and paid homage to her career as a corporate executive.

"We're excited to be here," Tom said. "You look beautiful by the way."

"You do, *vecāmamma*, stylish as usual," Nikkie said, using the Latvian word for grandmother. "We've missed you."

The three embraced in a group hug, and for a moment, Nikkie felt like she was coming home after a trip instead of arriving in a place she had never been before.

"Did mom make it all right?" she asked.

Indra nodded. "Elīna is still sleeping." Indra, who still spoke English with a Latvian accent, used Ellie's full Latvian name when she referred to her daughter.

Entering the foyer of Indra's apartment cooperative, now inhabited by Latvian American expats, Nikkie felt like she was in a Cold War spy movie. In the center was an antique elevator, a cage with bars on the sides and top. Around the elevator swirled a spiral stone staircase with decorated wrought iron railings. The area smelled musty with age and was lit by natural light from a courtyard window.

"I'm on the third floor," Indra said, motioning them to put their suitcases in the cage while she got in. "You take the stairs. The elevator doesn't always work." She handed them her apartment keys. "In case I get stuck."

She pressed the third-floor button. Creaking and groaning, the cage moved up along exposed pulleys. The twins circled up the stairs, having no problem keeping pace with the elevator. At the third-floor landing, it stopped. Indra pressed a button several times, and the door jolted open.

"Made it." Indra stepped out, beaming with pleasure. "Each ride is an adventure." She reclaimed her keys and unlocked three sets of locks.

The door opened onto an expansive living area. While the furniture was modern, the high ceilings had cornice molding with ornate designs in each corner, and the floors were refurbished parquet. The street side wall was lined with tall windows. Light streamed in and created patterns on the floor.

"Wow, you scored on this place," Tom said, walking into the middle of the off-white living room. "I love the combination of old and modern."

Indra smiled. "For my first, and I hope my only renovation, I'm pleased with the way it turned out."

"Where's mom?" Nikkie asked. Indra motioned down the hall and to the right.

Without hesitation, the twins ran to the bedroom and jumped onto the bed on each side of Ellie's sleeping form, sandwiching her in a wake-up hug. "Sleeping during the day is bad for jetlag," Tom whispered. "We need to get you out in the sun."

Ellie rolled over onto her back and pulled them closer to her. "Glad to see you, too."

Soon, the family was seated around a round oak dining room table, eating Latvian rye bread, cheese and creamery butter from the farmers' market, and drinking tea. Tom and Nikkie updated Ellie and Indra about what they had discovered in Moscow.

"It gives me such hope we'll find him," Ellie said. "Do you know Strēlnieku Iela, mama?"

Indra nodded. "It's in the Jugendstihl section." She explained the area was famous for having some of the most excellent examples of art nouveau architecture in all Europe. The buildings had fallen into disrepair during the Soviet years, but several had already been renovated.

If Peter and his parents had lived at 11 Strēlnieku Iela, they no longer did. The five-story basic nineteenth century apartment was in the process of being converted into condos. Across the street stood two art nouveau buildings that had been renovated with stone goddesses, griffins, ancient symbols and other fantasy shapes protruding along the top floor and window frames.

So much for easy, Nikkie thought, despite feeling grateful to see the building her father had lived in. She had imagined it would still be occupied, and they could talk to a manager or tenant.

Tom found out from the workers that a Latvian-German firm now owned the location, but when he called its Latvian representative on his cell phone, he came up blank. No Berzins in the registry of occupants when the new owners bought the residence.

The next week's hunt for Peter did not reveal anything either. Even with Indra and Ellie helping, searches of the phone directory, the Latvian National Ballet, newspaper archives and the internet offered up no new information. He was not listed as a participant or one of the organizers of the upcoming song and dance festival.

Still, Nikkie could not have asked for anything more involving to transport her away from her dance-focused life in the States, away from the spotlight on fame she had lost.

They had not found Peter, but they were finding out about their ancestry and his and their culture. They were getting to know the influences Peter had grown up with and felt closer to him as a result.

Nikkie and Tom went to classical music concerts in thirteenth and eighteenth century churches and at the ornate Latvian National Opera House. They met Indra's friends, including a top choir director, Martin Zandbergs, whose choir had won gold medals in world competitions. He would be directing songs during the Song Festival's main concert as well as other events.

Indra and he had become friends when his choir performed in Chicago during Glasnost, and she had offered to take him on a shoe outlet shopping spree. At the time, Latvians in Soviet Latvia stood in line for hours to buy even a pair of ill-fitting shoes. Martin wept when they walked into the first store and saw the expanse of choices.

Now, he had that choice in Riga, too. He invited Indra and the family to a reception in an opulent hall at the opera house following a classical concert that the Latvian president, Vaira Vīķe–Freiberga, attended. She was a Canadian Latvian, a Ph.D. psychologist, who had returned to live in Latvia.

Martin wore a dark grey tunic over black slacks. His long blond hair was pulled back and held in place by a black leather tie. "In our president's speeches, she stresses Latvian's worth and implores us to allow ourselves to dream and go after what we want for ourselves and for Latvia," he said, as they watched her converse with a group of people across the hall. "In one well known speech during Riga's eight hundredth birthday celebration, she had us repeat the phrases 'We are strong. We are great. We are beautiful. We know what we want. And what we want, we can.'"

"I can certainly understand how living under Soviet occupation would have impacted anyone's ability to follow one's dreams," Nikkie said.

Martin concurred. "Her approach is a good boost even for me when I look for opportunities outside Latvia for my choir."

Walking through the city, talking to people Indra introduced them to, Nikkie had already noted what she sensed as an air of the sadness for dreams lost during the Occupation. It seemed to hover above the people walking Riga's streets, lived behind the brightness of their eyes. From some, flashes of grief thrust in past the words of hope and humor.

Navigating the streets, she was aware of the historic Old Town architecture that had been restored, given new life, and of the vibrancy of the city overall. But outside Old Town, she sensed those unrealized dreams clinging to the sides of sconces and some of the stone buildings that remained run down. Those lost dreams, the residue of years of blocked potential, seemed ready to drop from above or jump and grab on to passersby who lingered too near them. She marveled at how, in the midst of the repression, Peter had found the motivation and drive to follow his own dreams, hoped they would find him, and she would soon be able to talk to him about it in person.

She looked up and out at the people passing by. She and Tom sat at an outdoor bar and café in Old Town, like they did many afternoons and evenings in Riga. This one was on Dome Square—Doma Laukums. She imagined one of the multitude was Peter, and they would recognize him, even though he was more than a decade older than their photos of him.

They waited for Indra and Ellie, who were exploring the City of Riga Registry archives to see what they might uncover about Peter. The twins listened to a group of street musicians playing a jazz rendition of Sting's *Fragile*. A couple danced cheek to cheek. The expansive plaza, a hub for events and activity in Riga's Old Town, was named for the Doms Cathedral, the largest in the Baltics with one of the biggest pipe organs in Europe.

"Latvians don't seem to have any idea how cool they really are, and it is refreshing to be around that," Tom said, sipping his beer. "The people I've met seem to maintain a sense of self-effacement and irony even after they succeed. It's like they know how easily they could lose everything they gained or achieved."

"You're right," Nikkie said. "And yet they have achieved so much." She thought about Martin and other award-winning choirs and composers. Latvian opera stars graced the stage of every great opera house in the world. Mariss Jansons, a famous conductor, directed world renowned orchestras from London to the Royal Concert Hall Orchestra in Amsterdam.

And even though old forms and institutions, rundown buildings crumbled around them, new ones continued to emerge. Tom and Nikkie sensed a freshness here, of thought, of ideas, of entrepreneurial spirit. People had woken up after being asleep, after having to hide their feelings and their individual dreams for fifty years.

Walking the cobblestoned streets of Riga, traversing its plazas, Nikkie felt as if Latvia, the land beneath her feet, was seeping into her bones, like a magnet connected her to it. The earth exuded a palpable pull for her. She had come home in a way she had not experienced since she had first seen a contemporary dance company perform when she was 10. And Tom had come home, too.

"I feel like I found my people here," he said. "Latvians have wit and depth, but not in an 'I'm better than you' kind of way. They use their humor to find the larger perspective in life's challenges. I wonder if Peter has that element of cool mixed with humility, too."

"I hope whatever he's like, he likes us," Nikkie said.

At that moment, Indra and Ellie walked up to the twins' table with a sheet of paper held out in front of them and smiles on their faces. "We found something," Indra said and laid the piece of paper on the table in front of the twins. "It's Peter's birth certificate. We found it at the Registry Office."

Tom picked up the piece of paper and read. *"Dēls, Peters, dzimis 9 Aprili,1958. Tēvs un māte, Tālis and Anita Berzins."* "A son, Peter, born April 9, 1958. Father and Mother, Tālis and Anita Berzins," he translated for Nikkie.

She took the certificate from Tom and ran her fingers lightly over the paper, as if doing so would somehow bring her closer to Peter.

"This is amazing. Now we know our grandparents' names. Did you find anything else?" Tom asked.

"A death certificate for his parents. They died six months apart from each other in 1985. I couldn't find more about his family so far, but many records were lost during WWII and the Occupation when the Soviets destroyed the churches."

"I love seeing Peter's birth certificate," Tom said. "And I'm sad knowing about his parents." He paused, let out of sigh. "Thank you. It's a step. But it doesn't let us know what to do next."

Nikkie felt Tom's frustration herself. It brought her back from her and Tom's reveries about Latvia into the reality of the main reason they had come here. To find their father.

"Should we hire a detective?" Tom said. "Berzins seems too common a Latvian surname for us to search the whole country on our own. Especially given most Latvians use cell phones that aren't listed in phone directories. I feel like we've reached the proverbial dead end."

"Maybe he moved to another country to dance with a company after he left Moscow," Nikkie said, perusing the stream of people passing by. "If he was here, you'd think *vecāmamma* would have found some recent mention of him in the newspaper archives. Or he'd be associated with the Latvian National Ballet."

"I wouldn't give up on Latvia yet," Ellie said. "Peter came back to be part of the freedom movement. He would have wanted to be part of this country's rebuilding and renaissance. While we were together, he mentioned how much he missed his homeland, despite being grateful for the opportunity to dance."

"You're probably right." Tom said. "But what *do* we try? I hate to say this, but you don't think Peter's dead? Alexandra was concerned he never wrote to her."

Nikkie slapped his arm. "No. I don't think he is, and don't you think that way either. I don't care what Alexandra said."

Indra looked solemn. "I did check. I didn't find any death record. Even if he'd been arrested and died, I'm sure it would have been listed. I had already checked the newspaper archives to see if he had died in the confrontations with the Soviets during the barricades, and he had not. So, for the moment, I'd say for our Riga search, our next step might be the Song Festival. With so many performers and performances, it could offer up some clues. In the meantime, I suggest we take the search in another direction."

"What's that?" Tom asked.

"We have been so focused on Peter, we have neglected the second mystery that brought you here," Indra said.

"The vision," Nikkie said.

Indra nodded. Nikkie hesitated, felt her resistance rise like a stone wall, but knew the time had come to begin that search as well.

"I have a strong feeling about where to start—our land in Gulbene," Indra said. She had grown up on a farm in Vidzeme near Gulbene which the Soviets had taken over when her family escaped. She had reclaimed it after Latvia was freed. "What better place than our own forest."

"Ellie did mention part of our land was forested," Nikkie said.

"Yes, at least half the eighty-eight acres," Indra said.

Nikkie felt a rush of energy shoot from her legs to her gut. "The land has forty-four acres of forest?"

Indra nodded. "Besides, I want you to see where I grew up," Indra said. "You'll also get to meet relatives. Your second and third cousins. Perhaps they know stories about shootings in a forest—even our own. Who knows what happened after our family escaped?"

"That's a good point," Nikkie said, and her resistance to bringing to the forefront what she had tucked in the background in Riga began to crumble, breaking up like stones in a landslide.

"Not to mention, we could celebrate Jāņi the way it was meant to be celebrated," Indra said. Jāņi was Latvia's version of Summer Solstice and probably it's most important holiday, observed beginning the evening of June 23rd and officially on June 24. All businesses, most restaurants closed down. Latvians from Riga, other cities and rural areas, met at their ancestral country homes and lands, built bonfires, sang, danced and drank all night in celebration of the sun and the fertility of the land.

"I'm sure both of you would be encouraged to jump over the bonfires with the other young people," Indra said.

"Couples have also been known to go off into the woods to make love all night. Of course, I was too young for that sort of thing when I was on the farm."

Right, Nikkie imagined. *I go off to the woods and just when things are getting interesting, have a repeat of the vision.* She shuddered and turned her thoughts away from that image back to Peter. She wondered how he had participated in Jāņi. Had he jumped over bonfires and made love in the woods? Was he celebrating it now, perhaps with his own family? Going into the woods with a wife or lover, while his children sang and danced around the bonfire. Children he knew, unlike her and Tom.

Chapter 10

"Before we go to our land, I wanted to show you the train station," Indra said. They walked around a large two-story yellow stone building in Gulbene's center. "It was one of the largest in Latvia, an important junction."

It was also where all the Latvians arrested by the Russians on the night of June 13th and the morning of the 14th, 1941, were brought—more than fifteen thousand five hundred, Indra explained. From this platform, they were jammed into cattle cars and shipped to Siberia.

"It must have been chaos," Tom said. "The platform is big, but not that big." They imagined it and the station house crowded with people wrenched from homes and lives.

"My mother came to witness it," Indra said. "One of her sisters called to say her mother, brother and his three children were amongst the deportees. It was surreal. Unthinkable. My mother stayed up all night baking bread and brought it and the cheese she had been making for Jāņi, to the station. She hoped to give them to her mother but could not find her. She finally gave it all to a mother with a baby. When she got home, she refused to talk about what she had seen. But that night, in bed, I heard her crying."

They remained silent now. Nikkie imagined she heard the hint of voices, screams on the wind. Uncertainty hung dense like fog in the air. No matter what questions and lack of clarity she had about her future, none of them was like what these people had experienced. If she left home, it was by choice. If she never danced again, her life remained filled with possibility no matter how sad she might feel. Yes, fate was involved. But barring the unexpected of accidents or illness—or losing a job—that stripped a person's life of what had been, she still had herself. Tom had himself. And they were free.

And that was the perspective her grandmother had found as well. One of her favorite quotes was from Viktor Frankl, who had survived the concentration camps and written *Man's Search for Meaning*. "Everything can be taken from a man but one thing: the last of the human freedoms—to choose one's attitude in any given set of circumstances, to choose one's own way." Indra had told them how she and her parents had left everything they owned behind in Latvia to escape during World War II, but unlike those family members sent to Siberia, they were free to choose life, to begin again. And Indra lived life as if she was grateful every moment for that freedom.

"Mama, would you tell us more about what happened?" Ellie said, placing her arm around Indra's shoulder. "I know you don't like to talk about it. But why were our relatives arrested?"

Indra exhaled deeply.

Nikkie thought back. Yes, Ellie and Indra had mentioned the deportation. But that was all she knew. She felt a wave of sadness, then shame. In the flow of life that was Oregon and New York, that was the present moment, that was dancing, relatives sent to Siberia seemed like a distant past. She thought of herself as compassionate. But her own family's suffering had been reduced to a few sentences—until now.

"My uncle was a boy scout leader. Because of that he was considered an enemy of the state, a threat." Indra looked away for a moment.

"How can that be?" Tom asked.

"Absurd, right? During that occupation, anyone in a leadership position, many landowners, were arrested or shot. Their families. Wives. Children. None of it made sense. My grandmother was taken only because she lived with her son. The family was given a few minutes to gather belongings."

"That's crazy," Tom said.

"The men were separated; most never saw their families again. My uncle Janis was sent to a different gulag and died of pneumonia. My grandmother Karlīna and aunt Sandra stayed with the three children. Their names were Rudis, Harolds and Rita. One night, Rita– she was only two –wandered off while the others slept, her family guessed to find food. They were all starving. They never found her. My grandmother died soon after, most likely of a broken heart. She was seventy-two."

Nikkie imagined the compounded losses of all the families whose loved ones suffered and perished for no reason.

"After the first deportation, Germany pushed the Russians out of Latvia and occupied it for a time. But in 1944, the Russians invaded again. My father was a landowner, who had spoken out against the Russians, and was warned our family was on a list to be arrested. That's when we left our farm. After the war, in 1949, another mass deportation of more than forty-two thousand Latvians, mostly from the farming population, took place."

"I can't help but think about what would have happened if my grandparents had hesitated," Ellie said. "None of us would be here now. I am so grateful for our family's strength and courage."

Nikkie's thoughts wandered to Peter's family. Growing up, her focus remained on Peter himself. She and Tom would imagine what their lives would be like if their father had taken an active part in their upbringing. When they thought he died, she and Tom grieved the loss of him. But neither of them had considered the rest of his family. She knew nothing about their lives or deaths, their names, how they were impacted by the war or Occupation.

"Did any of our family in Siberia survive?" Tom asked.

"The majority of deportees died, my uncle's wife also. The two sons returned after seven years to live in the home we left behind in Gulbene until the Soviets destroyed it in 1967. Harolds, the older boy, died of alcoholism in his thirties. Rudis died last year, of cancer. His daughter and a few of her family still live in Gulbene. Others will come for Jāņi. We'll meet them."

Nikkie said a silent prayer for the peace of all these family members who had died, added one for Peter and his family as well, especially any who had been sent to Siberia—or shot in a forest. Apparently, every Latvian family sustained tragedies such as these.

"Thank you, mama," Ellie said. "It helps make what happened more real and offers us an opportunity to remember this part of our family. To acknowledge them for what they endured and for their inner fortitude in facing such challenges."

"It's time to go," Indra said. She, Ellie and the twins stood at the edge of their family's land in Gulbene, a field of grasses, weeds and wildflowers surrounded on all sides by forests stretching as far as they could see on both sides of a two-lane country highway. "That's what my father said to us the morning we departed, August 5, 1944. And just like that, we left our home."

Nikkie could only imagine what the scene had looked like. The buildings and orchards were gone now.

"Even then, we did not know the full ramification of his words. In our minds, leaving was temporary. We would be gone for a month or two. When the war ended, we would return."

"Where was your house?" Tom asked, putting his arm around Indra's shoulders.

"See the oak tree over there." Indra pointed at stately oak one hundred feet from the road. "The tree was already huge when I was a child. I bet it's three hundred years old. The house was built in its shade, the barn behind it." She motioned to a spot. "The *pirts*, our sauna … was there. In the winter after a sauna, we would roll in the snow to cool off and whack each other's skin with pine branches until it was red and tingling."

"What did you grow here?" Tom asked.

"Beyond the *pirts* were acres of crops, like wheat, rye and apple and pear and plum orchards. We had cows, pigs, sheep, horses, geese and chickens. We had a family garden, too, for vegetables, everything we needed to be self-sufficient. Living and playing in these fields and forests made for an idyllic childhood. And then the war started."

The more Indra talked, Nikkie found herself looking beyond the field toward the wall of trees surrounding them. She swept the expanse with her eyes. Could it have been here on her family's land that the scene from her vision had taken place? If so, she did not have a clue where. No intuitive flash pulled her this way or that. Without it, she could not imagine how long it would take her to search forty-four acres.

She would need to find a tactful way to ask her relatives if they had ever heard of people being shot in any forests in this area. But even if they had, there was no guarantee they would turn out to be the people from her vision. The more she heard about the war and occupation, it seemed Latvia's forests teemed with stories of people hiding or killed in forests by the Germans or Soviets. Shake a tree and skeletons fell out.

"Let's take photos," Tom said, pulling Nikkie out of her reverie. "Ell. *Vecāmamma*. Stand by the oak tree, please." While Tom might call Ellie and Peter by their first names, he rarely called their grandmother anything but the Latvian version, *vecāmamma*.

"Wait," Indra said and bent over to pick wildflowers and greenery for a bouquet. "There, I'm ready." She and Ellie walked over next to the tree. Indra held the bouquet up to her heart with her right hand and placed her left around Ellie's waist. "Today, I am happy. I have dreamt of the day you would all see where I spent my childhood."

Tom took some shots, then Indra gave Nikkie the bouquet, reached for the camera. "Now you and Tom." Nikkie situated herself next to the tree, rested her hand on it and felt a tiny shock shoot through her arm. She instinctively tried to pull it away but felt her hand magnetized to the tree.

"You might like to know the oak tree is associated with the Latvian goddess Māra," Ellie said. "Latvians would circle around the oak and call on Māra for aid. She was the Divine Mother, earth mother, right Indra?"

"Yes, the Mother of both life and death," Indra said. "Māra helps us through the ups and downs of life."

"Maybe through this oak, we should ask Māra for help in finding Peter and resolving the mystery of the vision," Ellie said. "And call in the Latvian goddess Laime, or Fate, as well. For certainly fate led the family away from this land in 1944, and fate has brought us back here today."

But as the family circled around the tree and Nikkie lay the flowers by the oak in an offering, the winds picked up, dispersing the blossoms in the grasses. And while Ellie rested her hands on the oak's trunk, leaned into it and asked for Māra's assistance, the clouds that had been threatening to unload on them for the last few minutes did.

The foursome ran back to the car. "I hope that wasn't Māra and Laime telling us to forget it," Nikkie said.

"Not a chance. If anything, the storm is a message of powerful forces at work guiding you to Peter and the vision," Ellie said.

"Let's see if we can wait the storm out so we can spend more time on the land," Tom said.

"If you like," Indra said.

"I know what I'd like," Tom said. "A longer story of how our family escaped the Russians. I've always hoped you'd tell us more."

"Me, too," Ellie said, and Nikkie agreed. "I know you have not wanted to talk about our family's escape much or burden us with stories of what our ancestors endured."

"Yes. Why dwell on what we can't change?" Indra said. "It was a painful time for our family."

"But we want to know," Nikkie said. It's our history, too. And we're here—at the home our family left."

And so, Indra did.

The day they left, she told them, her mother, Lilija, buried the silver under the grandmother oak tree, and put a bit of dirt in a pouch to take with them. The family—her own and her cousin's—packed up what belongings they could carry in three wagons pulled by horses and followed by a cow and a pig. Her father, Rudolf, rode a fourth horse, a black stallion. Indra was thirteen.

"It's time to go," Rudolf said. And Indra explained how they left the birch trees, ash, oak and pine, tall trees swaying in the summer wind. They left friends and neighbors and all that was known and secure and headed out to they knew not what or where.

All they knew was their lives were at risk. Even though they had everything they needed on the farm, even though they loved this land, to stay was death. The choice for life was to plunge into the unknown.

"I can't imagine it," Nikkie said. "The closest in my life would have been when I dropped out of the mainstream dance world. I felt like I would die inside if I didn't change my life, but it was never in danger. And I still have so much choice and freedom and comfort. You all had tremendous strength and courage to leave everything behind."

Indra nodded. "For my cousin, Liesma, and me, the journey started out like a game, a vacation. My parents must have been going through so much, but they hid their feelings.

"For the first days, we moved a few miles down the road and stayed at a friend's farm. One day, we rode bicycles back to our own farm and watched from the forest, unseen, as the Russians moved in and commandeered our house as their headquarters."

On the way back to the neighbor's, Indra related how she had seen a line of young people marching down the road, guarded by a Nazi soldier with a rifle. He had ordered her and Liesma to join those, who were being commandeered to build trenches for the ensuing battle.

These two thirteen-year-old girls were soon marching away from their families into who knew what future. But something in them balked. And on impulse, they jumped on their bikes and rode off as fast as they could.

"Halt," the soldier yelled. But they did not. "He fired a shot into the air. But we still did not stop. He could have shot us. I don't know why he didn't."

"What a brave thing to do," Tom said, turning from the driver's seat to look at Indra in the passenger seat. The car windows were fogging over on the inside, blocking off their vision of the land. The rain tapped against the roof of the car, having a hypnotic effect.

"I guess, though it didn't seem brave." Indra shrugged. "Liesma and I always egged each other on to take risks."

Then, with the Russians beating the Germans, the time came to go once more. The family traveled hundreds of kilometers to where her mother's remaining family lived, near the Baltic Sea, to the home in Kurzeme where her mother Lilija had been born. Indra told them how she and Liesma ran and walked alongside or behind the wagons, mostly barefoot. Their parents walked barefoot as well. "We had no hiking boots—no

REI then—and only had one pair of shoes. You need to save them for winter, my father told us.

"My father kept us safe, guided us over farm fields, dirt roads, through forests. Never on the main roads. That's where refugees were getting shot or bombed, he explained, and why we were staying out of the main line of sight. At night, we slept in the woods."

"How did he know where to go?" Ellie asked.

"I have no idea. We had no map. But your great grandfather had an uncanny sense of direction."

In Kurzeme, the family came to the Baltic Sea, and when the Russian front approached once more, they had nowhere left to escape on land, Indra told them. Her parents made the unthinkable decision—to leave Latvia.

With the land borders closed and guarded, they had one option. Take a boat to Germany. Ships were bringing in German soldiers, docking in Liepaja. They agreed to fill them up with Latvian refugees to take back to Danzig, which had been taken over by Germany. The ships were returning there for more soldiers. Thousands of Latvians waited at the docks, hoping to find space on a ship before the Russians came. Some had been waiting for weeks.

Indra's mother acted on instinct. "My mother, who spoke German, went to the boat carrying a bottle of vodka and a hefty slab of bacon. She proceeded to bribe the captain to take us to Germany."

The families could only bring what they could wear on the boat, no suitcases, so Indra explained how they piled on as many layers of clothing as they could. They filled pockets and sewed jewelry and things of monetary value into hems. Rudolfs hoisted a sack of flour on his back that would keep them from starving over the next weeks, gave the horses and the rest of their possessions to their relatives. They got on the boat to Germany. From one fire to another. Maybe death there too. But maybe life.

"It's time to go." And they went once more. All except for Indra and Liesma's paternal grandmother, Līze. This grandmother, who had lived with them, helped raise them, told them she was not coming. "*Vecāmamma* was kind and loving. And so soft," Indra said. "I loved to sit in her lap. Everything about her felt padded, and we would sink into that softness, her arms wrapped around us. I'm seventy-five years old, Līze told my father. I'll hold you back. I couldn't live with myself if something happened to you because I was with you."

And after much protestation, they left her behind. "I never had any idea how she made it back to Vidzeme. But she lived into her eighties."

"Talk about courage," Nikkie said from the passenger seat, the rain on the roof pounding stronger now. "What happened next?"

"Traveling away from Danzig and into Germany, the bombing was all around us, lighting the sky," Indra said. "We could hear it like fireworks in the distance. As refugees, we were put to work in the German countryside. Liesma and I worked in a factory, and my parents worked for a farmer. Eventually, we landed in a Displaced Person's camp in Würzburg, in Bavaria. But near the end of the war, Churchill and Roosevelt betrayed the Baltic nations and gave them to their allies, the Russians, during the Yalta Conference in 1945.

"We were part of the compromise," Indra said. "Not worthy of a fight. At one point, the American soldiers who managed our camp told us we were to be sent back to Latvia. No, we explained. If we return, we will be deported straight to Siberia. Finally, we were allowed to remain. Some Latvians at other camps were not so fortunate."

Indra related how she spent the rest of her teenage and high school years in the DP camp. All six members of her family lived cramped into a one-room cabin with three other families and two single people. Once a week, they waited in line for a ten-minute cold shower. Their mainstay diet was potatoes and a thin soup. But the adults were resourceful. Schools were opened for the children. Her mother sewed them winter coats out of the army issue green blankets and a traditional Latvian skirt and vest for herself from a roll of red cloth Indra and Liesma had taken from an abandoned factory.

"In the camps, the adults carried the responsibilities. We teenagers had fun no matter what. We dated. We organized dances. We found the good, the enjoyment in the life we had. I believe in staying positive."

Nikkie knew those qualities about her grandmother but could not help wondering how Indra's past still impacted her present or if it impacted her brother and her too? Perhaps that was one reason she experienced the vision in the forest that seemed linked to this war.

The more Indra talked though, the more Nikkie marveled at her family's resilience and ability to adapt to what many would have considered devastating circumstances, and to Latvian strength and adaptability in general. She wondered if Peter and his family had those qualities and hoped to tap more in herself.

Indra shared statistics Nikkie had never taken in before. Overall, Latvia lost one-third of its population in WWII, five hundred fifty thousand people from a country of two million people. More than one hundred thousand of those were soldiers. Seventy thousand were Latvian Jews murdered during the German occupation. The rest, civilians killed in the war or in Siberia. One hundred twenty-five thousand, like Indra, did not die, but fled Latvia.

When the time came to dismantle the camps, the refugees had to find a new home in a new land. "I hoped for Australia. Sunshine. Far from Europe and war. But my mother's father had escaped to America in the early twentieth century because he had spoken up against the Czar during the Russian Revolution.

He had died of pneumonia before he could send for his family. My mother wanted to fulfill his dream for his family to live in the U.S. A Lutheran minister from Sunbury, Pennsylvania sponsored us. So, we went in 1949."

For one year, Indra worked as a maid for a wealthy family and her parents worked as migrant farm workers at a local farm. Afterwards, they moved to Chicago, where Indra went to college, met and married Ellie's father, also a Latvian. Ellie's father, Nikkie knew, had died in an auto accident when Ellie was fifteen.

"More than thirty years passed before the U.S.S.R. opened the Latvian borders to foreign visitors in the 1980s," Indra said. "My parents had already died in Pennsylvania."

Once Latvia was freed in 1991, Indra fought to have the land returned to the family. "A lawyer got much of the original land and forest back for us and a portion of a property that had adjoined ours. Eighty-eight acres, Twenty-seven hectares. So now you know how deep your roots are here. Is it enough detail, Tom?"

"Yes," he said, smiling. "For now. Thank you."

But as the rain pelted the car, insisting it be heard, Nikkie remained silent. And at the moment, those roots, deep as they were, did not feel grounding to her at all. Not like when she did exercises imagining her own roots, like a tree's, extending into the earth's core. Instead, when she felt into them, they felt like chains, binding her to a distant past that was not her own. She felt closed in, wanted to jump out of the car and run. Run from the family stories. Run from all she had learned about Latvian history.

Yes, the stories taught her about Latvian endurance and courage. But they had also been a crash course in displacement, genocide and suffering. In Riga, she had discovered Latvia had been oppressed by other nations for seven hundred years. For hundreds, they had been serfs. But what did it all have to do with her life now?

The life that had been lived here by her family was gone. Annihilated by the whim of the Soviets. Indra's idyllic childhood vision wiped out. What grew here now were weeds. And none of them, including Indra, would want to come back here to revive the farmland. Even Indra, who felt so strongly about the land, had chosen to live in the city, not here.

Nikkie was glad they had come to see the land. But how was being here going to help her find Peter or resolve the mystery of the dead in the forest so she could get on with her life and dancing? Life in the present moment, not in some time warp of WWII and post-War occupation.

Indra saw the life lived on the farm like a technicolor movie on a blank screen. But all Nikkie saw was the blank screen. And right now, she wanted to get away. To go back to Riga and get on with the search for Peter. Maybe that's why the storm had come up. To cleanse away the past, to blow away what had been. And the family's attachment to it.

Perhaps it was telling them, Save yourselves. Get out of here. Let go. Do you really want to make this the story of your family's life? The "look at what we endured and how resilient we are in the face of devastation" story. Wasn't it time to rewrite the story? Their story. Her own story. Let go of the story. Eradicate it from her cells and most certainly, her DNA. Create a new story that left out the "see how much we suffered" past. A grand adventure story set outside of time and war and the horrors humans do to one another, one that focused on the good that could be done, that poured all the family's abundant strength into creating and living all of their heart and soul-based dreams rather than enduring the past.

Yes, it *is* time to go, Nikkie thought. Time to move on from this land and its memories. Like the young Latvians, the Latvians of all ages, who didn't want to dwell on the past, but who were dedicated to a new Latvia, to rebuilding, recreating, moving forward here or leaving the country altogether for opportunities elsewhere. At what point did dwelling on her family story, on Latvia's past, on telling and retelling it, turn toxic, like milk gone sour, meat become rank, turn to holding on to what needed to be let go so one could move on.

And then a new thought entered her heart like a one-two job. Was that what she was doing with Stone Tara? Was she wallowing in her own story, even as raw and recent as it seemed? Had the time come to stop grieving? Move on, whether she danced or not.

True, she had experienced a loss, though not on the same planet of loss as anyone who had truly been oppressed. These last weeks, she had let outer circumstances dictate her attitude. But today, for the first time, she wanted to let go of the sadness about her recent story, too, not mask it by filling her life with other activities. Even if doing so meant dangling in the dark, as groundless as air.

She could be like an empty pail waiting to be lowered into a well with the prospect of being filled to the brim and pulled out into the sun to share life-giving water. And sitting in this car, being in Latvia, she could feel some silky strand of connection to a more life-infused way, even if she did not know what had happened to Peter or feel inspired to dance yet.

Accepting her own loss more, she could take in more of what her grandmother was saying. Her feelings of overwhelm about Latvia and her family's story dissipated, and in its wake, her internal landscape shifted once again. Instead of pushing away the family story as she had only minutes earlier, it had now turned into something full-bodied, alive.

Before Indra had related more details, when she heard this story, it was a sound bite, like it had happened to some other family. But coming here, having Indra finally talk about it, made it real *to her*. And as she breathed through it, rested in the dark of it, she sensed not only a legacy of suffering and endurance, but something more. And if she did not exactly feel roots on this land yet, she did feel a deeper connection here. The experience was forming new muscles in her, a subtle core of strength outside of those which had taken years to build as a dancer. This strength had nothing to do with being physically fit. It had to do with hope. And it was rising, rising up in her.

Chapter 11

Tonight, we celebrate joy, Nikkie thought to herself. *Finally. We meet our family and experience Jāṇi, Latvia's sacred holiday. We dive into the ancient roots of this culture. And the song and dance of the land.*

The rain had stopped by the time they drove up to a traditional one-story stone farmhouse being decorated with tree branches and greenery. Women and children braided garlands of leaves and flowers to create crowns. Oak leaf crowns for men, Indra explained, and wild flower crowns for the women. The men stacked logs in a fire pit.

Two long picnic tables were covered with a feast's worth of food. Loaves of sliced rye bread. sausages. *Jāṇu siers,* a light cheese with caraway seeds, the traditional food most associated with Jāṇi. Tomato, cucumber and mixed green salads. Boiled potatoes with sprigs of dill. Creamery butter. Sour cream. Mustard, Indra warned, so strong it would clear their sinuses. Bowls of strawberries. Kegs of beer.

A tall, large-boned woman with short brown hair greeted them at the table with a Latvian hello, *"Sveiki,"* first hugging Indra, then welcoming each one of them.

"This is Silvija," Indra said in English. "Elīna's second cousin." Silvija, who seemed to be around Ellie's age, wore a long red wool traditional Latvian skirt tied with a woven belt of spring green and red and an embroidered white linen blouse.

"I am so pleased to meet you," she said, switching to English. She carried crowns for each of them and placed them on their heads, despite Tom's protestations against wearing a huge oak leaf creation.

"If only your friends in New York could see you now," Nikkie said, laughing.

"It's the tradition," Silvija said. "All the men wear them." She invited them to the table and told them to help themselves to food and drink. "You must be hungry after your travels."

"Everything looks delicious," Tom said, and the family chimed in their praises.

"It's all local," Silvija said. "We brewed the beer and bought the meats at a local butcher. A farmer drops the butter off fresh every week as well as the milk that we used to make the cheese. The tomatoes, lettuce and dill are from our greenhouse. You'll see our garden later."

"Thank you for going to so much trouble," Nikkie said, filling up her plate, and Indra laughed.

"You'll find Latvians go all out for their guests," Indra said. "No matter what time of day or night. Holiday or not."

"Yes." Silvija's face lit up. "It gives us great pleasure. And we've heard so much about you. We are excited you have come."

They went on to talk about their impressions of Latvia and meeting family for the first time. But Nikkie did not mention their search for Peter, realizing she had never asked Indra whether the family in Latvia knew about their father.

"Who else here is our family member?" Tom asked. They sat around a long picnic table with their food and mugs of beer.

Silvija called out to a young man and woman to join them and introduced them as Andris and Agrita, two of Silvija's three adult children who had come home for Jāņi. They were both in their early twenties, similar ages to Tom and Nikkie. Their sister, who was twenty-five, worked in the banking industry in Germany and could not get away from work.

"How are we related?" Tom asked.

"I was cousins with Silvija's father, Rudis, on my mother's side," Indra said.

Rudis. Nikkie felt a shiver of recognition. Silvija's father was the one who survived being sent to Siberia as a boy. This was his family. He who had seen so much death as a child, suffered so much hardship and starvation, had returned to Latvia, moved on, married, had a family. And now that family was here, celebrating, embracing freedom and new opportunity, choosing life. The circle of life continued.

"That makes Ellie Silvija's second cousin," Indra said. "You and Nikola are third cousins with Andris, Agrita and Rasma."

"*Es esmu priecīgs jūs visus satikt,*" Tom said. "I am happy to meet you all," he translated for Nikkie.

Silvija's face lit up. "Your accent is very good. Did your mother teach you?"

"Mostly my grandmother, and my mother spoke Latvian with me at home. I also went to Latvian camp, *Garezers*, for two summers."

"And you?" Silvija looked at Nikkie expectantly.

Nikkie shook her head. "A few words," she said, wishing she had taken more time to learn. In this moment, she hated being the typical American who only spoke English, while many Latvians also spoke English, Russian and German. Everyone had switched to English in order to include her in the conversation. "I'm learning while I'm here."

"Did you also go to Garezers?" Silvija asked.

"No." Nikkie took a deep breath. "I chose to go to professional dance camp one summer and to the summer dance intensive at Julliard in New York City the next. My goal was to get a degree in dance from Julliard."

"That is a high honor, yes?" Silvija asked.

"Yes," Nikkie said. "The admission was very competitive."

"Good for you," she said. "And your grandmother told us you both graduated from college. Where do you dance now?"

Nikkie felt the familiar tightening of the belly in response, reminding her that she danced nowhere. "Until recently, I danced with a music group, Stone Tara. But that job ended, and now, I am taking some time off to be here."

Yeah, right, she thought. But no need to drag her new family into her drama.

"Don't be so modest," Ellie said. "Only a couple months ago, Nikkie danced at the Hollywood Bowl, a famous outdoor venue in Los Angeles, California. She's a terrific dancer."

And then I got fired, Nikkie thought, but caught herself, reminded herself. *How many dancers even get that far?*

And Nikkie shifted once more, remembering her gratitude for the choices she had had growing up. That she had been able to do what she loved all these years both as a student of dance and a professional. She doubted Silvija had had the same options. And she knew Silvija's father Rudis had not. "I've been very fortunate to have skilled teachers and mentors."

"And your father is a dancer, too, Indra told us," Silvija said.

Nikkie felt relieved. *Oh good. She knows.*

"Yes," Ellie said. "A Latvian. Peter Berzins. He danced with the Nijinsky Ballet in Moscow but left the company in 1988 to return to Latvia. Do you know of him?"

Silvija thought she might have read an article about him in years past, but nothing specific. Andris and Anita did not know anything either.

The twins explained how they thought Peter had been dead, but they were now looking for him hoping to reconnect. But neither Silvija nor her children had any thoughts to add on how to find him other than what the twins had already done.

They also told her they were interested in World War II history of the area. "We're especially intrigued by incidents in the forests, including any shootings or arrests of local people there," Tom said. But Silvija had nothing specific to offer them. She talked some about her father's experience of being deported to Siberia as a child, but noted he, like many Latvians, never discussed it much, wanted to leave it behind and move on.

Tom asked Silvija to tell them more about Jāņi.

"Jāņi is about having fun and letting go of the cares of life," Silvija said. "For many of us, it's our most important holiday. It comes after the crops have been planted for the summer, and we want to celebrate fertility. Latvians gather in community all over the countryside. The crowns and garlands used as decoration ensure a successful harvest."

"How will we participate?" Ellie asked.

"We stay up until dawn—4:30 a.m.," Silvija said. We light the fires at a highpoint on our property after sunset—around 22:30 p.m. at this time of the longest day of the year. The fires are so huge, they light up the sky and can be seen all around. And we sing Līgo folk songs. Līgo means to sway. We sing and sway."

"Did you celebrate like this when the Soviets were in power?" Tom asked.

"It was forbidden," Silvija said. "But we always connected to the land regardless. We might not have been able to sing and dance openly, but we had 'barbecues.' We always knew what was most important. It's what linked us to being Latvian and to that spirit inside of ourselves."

"I'm amazed you could feel that connection living in fear of arrest," Tom said.

"How could we not?" Silvija said. "It inspired us to go on. My father taught me that. We could still let go of our troubles. Drink a little or a lot. Sing and dance. Even if we could not do it in large, public gatherings."

"I wish we could have met your father," Nikkie said.

"I do too," Silvija said. "He knew about you though your grandmother's letters and photos." Nikkie wondered if Rudis had sent photos of his family as well but did not remember Indra sharing them.

Silvija told them that one of her fondest memories with her father was when they took part together in the largest mass demonstration, the Baltic Way, of what became known as the Baltic countries' Singing Revolution. It took place on August 23, 1989, the fiftieth anniversary of the 1939 Molotov-Ribbentrop Pact, the non-aggression treaty between Berlin and Moscow that secretly divided the Baltic states into spheres of German and Soviet influence.

Two million people from Estonia, Latvia and Lithuania joined hands along the one road that linked the Baltic countries and sang together. They sang songs that had been forbidden by or disapproved of by the Soviets but had now been brought back into the expression from before the Soviet Occupation. Singing them, Latvians gained inner fortitude and resolve. Singing them in demonstrations and at the Song Festivals again helped them reaffirm the freedom Latvia had once enjoyed. The Baltic Way led to more mass singing demonstrations, and two years later, Latvia, Estonia and Lithuania declared their freedom. Without war and with relatively little violence, the U.S.S.R. and fifty years of oppression collapsed.

"Instead of meeting war with war and hate with hate, our people reached deep and countered it with truth, heart and soul through singing the songs that recalled a free Latvia and that they had not been able to sing for fear of arrest and imprisonment," Silvija said.

Nikkie felt a surge of pride that Peter, too, had taken part in that nonviolent call to freedom. Soon Nikkie, Indra, Ellie and Tom joined the circle of relatives, friends and neighbors and sang and swayed. That they did not know the words did not matter. They hummed the melody and joined in on the refrains of "Līgo," which peppered the lyrics.

> *Tumsas māte, miglas māte līgo, līgo*
> *Aiz ezera velējāsi līgo*
> *Dun bauzīte, čukst vālīte līgo, līgo*
> *Ievelk mani niedrājāi līgo*

Indra told them the translation.

> *Goddess of darkness, goddess of fog līgo, līgo*
> *Is being purified on the other side of the lake līgo*
> *Reeds are thundering, flowers whispering līgo, līgo*
> *Their voices tempt me into the shrubs and reeds by the lake, līgo*

And soon they danced. Circle dances everyone could dance together. To her surprise after months of not dancing, Nikkie's heart leapt forward into the circle and her body followed, lifted up in the spirit of celebration. Her feet followed the patterned steps of the Latvian folk dances. Her cousin and various young men spun her around. And instead of feeling the heaviness and distress of the last two months, she was swept up in the lightness and joy of the event. Nothing to prove. No one to impress. No pressure to perform. No one caring if she made mistakes. Least of all herself.

And she found herself smiling, then laughing and like Latvians, her ancestors—Rudis included—had done over centuries of oppression, she let go of the images of suffering and displacement that had filtered through the last two days. She let go of loss they and she had experienced. She let go of the disappointment around her career and not feeling any closer to finding her father or resolving the vision of the dead. She let the land beneath her feet take it. She let the air take it, the trees beyond the clearing.

The simple patterned dances spun the lethargy out of her and left her renewed, with a sense of ripening and possibility that she had some seed sprouting inside of her and pushing toward the sun.

And when the bonfire was lit, the men, including Tom, jumped and leapt over it, laughing and whooping. She also spontaneously joined in the line waiting to jump. She ran to gain momentum and leapt, her legs stretched out in front and behind her like the dancer she was, clearing the fire below her, feeling its heat, her hair streaming behind her. Participants clapping and calling out for her.

"Uu-rah! Uu-rah!"

She leapt for all the Latvians who had lived and died on this land. For Rudis and his family. She leapt for their courage and resilience—qualities she hoped were being awakened more in her. And she leapt for no reason at all, for the sheer joy of it, the "I am able to lift my body up and fly" majesty of it.

Afterwards, as she sat at the tables and replenished herself with a cold beer and some food, she noticed as a few couples made their way off into the night together and remembered what Indra had said about making love in the forest under the guise of searching for a rare fern that only flowered once a year on Jāņu nakts.

"I guess you and I are not meant to get 'lucky' tonight," Tom said, easing in beside her, filling up his own plate.

"I don't know about you, but I feel like I've gotten 'lucky' already," Nikkie said.

"That's right. Wasn't that you I saw...." Tom paused, "dancing out there?"

And the two broke into laughter and clinked together their beer mugs in a Latvian toast. *"Prosīt,"* they both said.

"Prosīt," Nikkie said one more time and swept her glass across the horizon to encompass all the people, imagined raising her glass to the Latvian gods and goddesses who were part of the

festivities. *"Paldies,"* she said. "Thank you," and let the gratitude rise up in her heart and spread out through her torso and limbs.

That gratitude remained through the rest of the shortest night and into the dawn when the celebration wound down. Nikkie, Ellie, Indra and Tom walked, arms linked, four across, singing Līgo songs Indra taught them, heading in to the country house to the beds Silvija had prepared for them.

Chapter 12

Unable to sleep after the excitement of Jāni, Nikkie retrieved the keys from Tom's pocket and went for a drive, drawn back to the family land. She wanted to explore it before they returned to Riga. Despite Silvija not knowing of any incidents in their forest, she wanted to go there and see if she could sense the dead from her vision.

In truth, she came back because she felt a yearning arise, a deep longing to touch the earth, to place her bare feet on its ground. She wanted to fill herself with the life lived and lost there.

The yearning Nikkie felt for this family land, the emotion that rose from her gut, her heart, that pulsed through her had no basis in any reality she knew. But it was alive. Palpable. Tinged with grief, joy, and most prevalent, love.

This morning, after all she had learned about her family, about Latvia, she had an irrational love for this place. Stepping onto the land her maternal ancestors had owned and farmed, she felt like she had come home. Arrived.

She could have thrown herself on the ground and kissed the earth, hugged the ancient oaks that had bordered the family farmhouse and barn for decades before the Soviets burned down the buildings and the farm's orchards. She wanted to bow to the acres of forest her family owned, the forest she would soon explore in hopes of finding the dead she had run from all her life.

And this time, instead of the wind rising, clouds and rain coming as she walked the land, the sun and sky welcomed her, the land accepted her.

Her family had lived here, she thought. They had sung here. Made love here. Borne children here. Danced here. Died here. Been oppressed here. Found the strength to persevere here.

Their blood was on the land. In this land. Their hands and backs and arms and legs had worked this soil. They had tilled the earth and planted crops and orchards—grown apples, berries, wheat, corn, tomatoes, greens. They had herded cattle and pigs and milked cows.

The women had shorn sheep and woven their own cloth and wool. Knitted and crocheted mittens and socks and sweaters, which had intricate symbols and colors and patterns. Every pattern in Latvia, Silvija told her, had an ancient meaning meant to give people strength and affirm life.

Her ancestors had enveloped and adorned their bodies with clothing and jewelry that highlighted and honored symbols of nature, the sun, thunder, moon, and of the Latvian gods and goddesses of destiny and good fortune. *Saule. Perkons. Meness. Māra. Laima.*

Her ancestors had known and lived the divine in all things here. In the flowers, the crops, the trees. They had given their pain to the trees and found comfort in the dark of the woods.

They had gotten drunk here, too, on life, to heighten life or run away from it. They drank to celebrate at weddings, births, funerals, or to gather courage to jump the bonfire on Jāņi. Her great-grandfather drank a shot of vodka in the dark of the morning, a jolt of liquid oomph and heat to brace himself against the freeze as he went out to tend the animals.

During the oppression years, hers and other families had drunk to stuff the pain of not being able to realize themselves or provide for loved ones, of losing freedom.

Still, nothing quelled the spark of light that shone in them. Theirs was the land where no matter what happened, her ancestors' souls were not crushed. They found laughter. They sang. Their spirits rose again and again.

Nikkie felt the earth under her feet, ambled forward to touch the grandmother oak where her great-grandmother had buried the silver before her relatives left everything behind to escape the Russians. They had gone even though they loved this place and each other. They had known who they were here, even when they had forgotten for a time. One tribe.

And now Nikkie loved it and sparked a glimmer of whom she might be here. Their yearning for their homeland had seeped into her bones.

As she strode now towards the forest, she called on the strength of her Latvian family, who had remained in Latvia, who had collectively longed for better lives even when all hope of those lives had been systematically and violently crushed daily.

She called on the potency they discovered when they came together as one during the song and dance festivals. During the Singing Revolution. When they rose above the fact that for decades, they couldn't choose to sing the songs they knew and loved and had to sing songs of Soviet propaganda. They learned the power of double entendre, double meanings and sang their freedom into being.

And the yearning, like hers, their own love of the land, each other, themselves, rose up en masse when they remembered the power and joy of their voices joined as one in song.

"It was like we were asleep, numb to our very beings," Silvija had told her last night as they sang Līgo songs. "But the song, singing together, joining as one, woke us up to ourselves and the potential for freedom."

And now that song, the music sung in song festivals and in song and dance collectives throughout the land by tens and hundreds of thousands of Latvians vibrated throughout the earth beneath Nikkie's feet. It lived there, she realized, just as her family had once lived on this land. Nikkie felt its resonance, its tingling reaching up through her feet and filling her body, calling her into the trees.

The leaves called to her. The grasses. The underbrush.

Nikkie felt the vibration not only of the song but how the stamping of the dancing feet of all Latvians who danced here continued to pulse, sent currents of energy shooting out over the land. It had reached out to her in New York and called her home to herself in ways that went beyond anything she thought she knew about herself, about dance, about life.

She prayed, prayed that when she walked into the forest before and around her that she would find the dead who had haunted her childhood. She prayed she would be led somehow to help them find the healing they needed, that the yearning she felt in them, would be fulfilled somehow.

She stood at the edge of the forest. Birch. Ash. Pine. Like in her vision.

There was a raw truth in Latvia, a raw truth she did not feel or know in the States. And she wanted to sob, to let her tears fall to the earth to mingle with the tears of centuries of ancestors who had hidden their pain in the trees, to blend with their blood and juices, their sweat and toil, their leaps and falls.

She wanted her tears to rise in joy for their lovemaking in the forests. Their celebration of the sun's rays shining through the darkness.

Latvians might not have been able to go to a market and buy a kiwi or anything else they had a whim for at four a.m. like she could when she had lived in New York, but they had soul. Depth. Poetry in their movement and expression, even when they were unaware of it.

This tiny country of two million people, the size of West Virginia, her family's homeland, was in the world's eyes, insignificant. Not worthy of saving, in a way. Not worthy.

When she had come to Latvia, she told herself she was going to a foreign country. She never much felt Latvian, even though her ancestors were Latvian. Then again, she never felt American though she loved that country. But she never felt America's soul like she felt the soul of this land. America's vastness, yes. Beauty, yes. Miraculous variety of landscape and people. Yes.

But she had felt displaced there, unsettled, never rooting, like an outsider. Now she realized the displacement had been passed down to her from the ancestors who left this land. Their yearning for home, for a sense of place, had become hers.

And yet, as she allowed the longing in, as she did not resist it, as she let herself dive into that yearning, that inexplicable and gorgeous yearning, it shouted, I am alive. I am alive. I am spirit and soul and heart. I have roots. I blossom. I sing. I am part of one voice. The collective. The connectedness. I am the unique expression but part of something larger than me as well. The whole, Nikkie thought. And that whole is joyful. A relief. A release.

To breathe as one. Sing as one. Dance as one. Be part of nature and the trees as one.

Standing at the edge of the woods, Nikkie felt so much a part of this land now, that when she looked down at her arms, she expected to see branches sprouting, leaves unfurling, roots growing deep into the earth and bark forming on her skin. She stepped into the dark of the forest.

Nothing. Nikkie felt nothing of the dead in her vision as she strode further into the woods. She knew in her belly now this was not the place to search. What she could sense was the hint of musk and earthiness, like the scent not only of the forest floor but of an old photo album depicting the lives of her family that had been lived there. Her grandmother and great-uncle and their friends as children playing there. Men hiding in the forest for months to avoid being shot. Her great grandparents and other ancestors hunting for mushrooms and wild animals or walking there connecting to their love for the trees.

And as she felt her own gratitude and love for the trees, what struck her most was that her ancestors seemed not only to be the people who had lived on this land but the trees themselves. They had cut a path through the four chambers of her heart and claimed their territory there. Their blood, their sap, had become her blood. And their resin, hardened into amber, which she hung around her neck, served as a reminder of their ancestral link.

"The key is in the forest" was the message the trees had incanted to Nikkie when she returned to the forest in Oregon where she had the original vision. She placed her hand now on the tree nearest to her, leaned into it, rested her cheek against its bark, sensed the connection of all the trees in this forest, root to root, branch to branch, lifeblood to lifeblood, forest to forest across Latvia. She spoke that message out loud once more and waited.

I thought I had a choice, she mused after a few minutes had passed. Instead, she saw that this mission to find and somehow bring healing to the dead in the forest had been growing in her for years, that it was her destiny seeding, taking root, sending out branches through all her veins and arteries, blossoming, leafing, reseeding. And that the forest where the dead were was no longer some unknown spot, but in some inexplicable way living inside her like her ancestors, like the forest on the family's land, lived inside her, growing, expanding, beginning to flourish as she sought it in tangible reality.

She mouthed the words again, "The key is in the forest,"

asked the trees, her family, to be shown more of what that meant. And what she heard in response came in a woman's voice that seemed to emanate like a whispered incantation spiraling around her through all the trees:

> The forest holds the song.
> The forest holds the breath.
> The forest holds the secrets.
> The forest holds the dark and the light.
> The forest holds the death.
> The forest holds the renewal.
> The forest holds the dance.
> And it's time for the forest to release them all.

And Nikkie envisaged the power of the forest to radiate out and create healing, shift imbalance to alignment, help those who were uprooted to find their roots again. She pictured its power to witness and honor suffering so wholly that its bearers felt seen, could release their grief, reclaim their lost innocence and move on. Beyond. Into a clearing where the sun warmed the forest canopy. Where leaves, blowing in the wind, rustled like satin skirts on a dance floor. And in the center, a light glowed.

"Focus on the light of what you seek," the woman's voice intoned one last time. "Not on the darkness there, but on the light."

Chapter 13

Ever since Nikkie had gone to Gulbene, she had been dreaming of war, of torture, of imprisonment. The last two nights, lying asleep in her grandmother's Riga apartment, the atrocities the land, the trees, the waters had witnessed spoke to her. She observed them through her own body.

The dreams sobered her. But at the same time, she felt more alive than she had in months. Having those traumatic images course through her system grounded her somehow.

Perhaps it was because she was viewing how others had suffered in a way she never had, acknowledging the darkness her own family had undergone. Or maybe the dreams were a sign she and Tom were getting closer to the dead and hopefully, to their father.

Whatever the case, she was grateful that for her and for her family, they were only that—dreams. Not real. Every morning or middle of the night she woke up and would say, "Thank God. It was only a dream."

Running down roads and through forests, being chased by soldiers ready to shoot and kill. Only a dream. Starvation. Only a dream. No chance to express opposition or truth without punishment. Only a dream. Imprisonment. Only a dream. Nearly beaten to death. Only a dream.

❧

"Elizabete?" The tall man with dark blond, shoulder-length hair and a tan camera bag slung over his shoulder said.

"Excuse me?" Nikkie replied.

"Are you Elizabete Riekstins, the writer for *National Geographic*? My name is Mikis Engelis. I'm the photographer." He spoke English without an accent.

"No, I'm Nikkie Ozolins. Not a writer. A dancer, albeit one on a bit of a break. My brother's the writer or was one, not me. We're traveling together. We live in America, but our ancestry is Latvian. It's our first visit. I'm supposed to meet him here."

Why was she babbling on like this, telling this stranger about herself when all the man wanted was to find a *National Geographic* writer? Well, he was attractive, with high cheekbones and an angular face. Listen to yourself, Nikkie said, feeling nonplussed around this man. It's not like she wasn't around tall, good-looking men all day long in Latvia. Baltic men and women were striking people, so much so that Tom had taken to calling Riga "Super Model Central."

They stood in Riga's best-known plaza at the entrance to Old Town in front of Latvia's Freedom Monument. When she had first visited it with Indra, she had learned it was built between World War I and World War II, when Latvia was declared a sovereign nation. The one hundred fifteen-foot high structure had miraculously withstood both the war and the Occupation. At the bottom, sculptures depicted Latvian history and folklore. On top, Mother Latvia, affectionately called Milda, held three stars, one for each of the main sections of Latvia, Courland representing both Kurzeme and Zemgale, Vidzeme and Latgale. The longer Nikkie was in Latvia, the more she appreciated how hard won the freedom it commemorated was.

"I was supposed to meet Elizabete in front of the Monument," Mikis said. "My editor told me to look for a tall, beautiful woman with long blond hair carrying a blue day pack." He pointed at Nikkie's blue day pack.

She felt her cheeks flush. He thought she was beautiful. "Are you doing an article on the song festival?"

Mikis nodded. "That and how Latvia is faring a decade-plus into its freedom, poised to join the European Union."

"That sounds intriguing," Nikkie said. "There is so much vibrancy and possibility here today and in Latvia's cultural heritage. Are you from the U.S.? You speak English impeccably."

"Portland. Although I'm traveling so much, I'm rarely there."

"Small world." Nikkie mentioned she was from Southern Oregon. "I'm based in New York now."

"Given we're practically neighbors, do you have a minute?" Mikis said. "With your permission, I'd love to photograph you at the monument."

Nikkie found herself saying yes—without hesitation.

While Mikis photographed Nikkie from a distance, Tom walked up, a full smile spread across his face, and gave Nikkie a big hug, oblivious of the photographer. He was holding a bouquet of flowers from one of the nearby flower vendors.

"For me?" Nikkie asked. "How lovely."

"Next time, Nik. This is for my other girl, the one behind you. Milda." He pointed at the monument's goddess of liberty. "Remember, it's customary to leave flowers."

"That's right." Mikis came up next to Nikkie, camera in hand. "Ever since the monument was erected in 1936. Except for during the Soviet Occupation. Then, if you left flowers, you could be arrested."

Mikis extended his hand to shake Tom's. "Mikis Engelis. I've been photographing Nikkie for an article for *National Geographic*."

"Tom Ozolins. The brother." Tom turned to his sister with a puzzled look. Nikkie smiled.

"Would you mind if I shot the two of you putting those flowers on the steps of the monument?" Mikis asked.

"It's okay with me if you're up for it, Tom," Nikkie said.

Tom, no longer smiling, turned back to Mikis. "No offense, man, but could I see some credentials?"

"None taken." Mikis let the camera hang from its strap around his neck and opened a side compartment of his camera bag. He pulled out his press card and a letter from an editor about his assignment.

"Looks legit, thanks. But do you mind if I talk to my sister alone first?"

"Go ahead," Mikis said. He walked away and started to photograph the flower vendors and plaza.

Tom put his arm around Nikkie and led her to the side of the plaza away from Mikis, shielding her in part with his jacket. "I think you should reconsider being photographed. Remember Moscow?"

Moscow. What the hell was Tom talking about?

"Alexandra? Remember?"

And then it hit her. Tom had forged their credentials.

"To what end?"

"I don't know. Maybe the man is recruiting for the sex trade. It's a problem here. Offer a beautiful young woman a chance to model or work as a teacher in another country, and before you know it, she's been kidnapped and put into prostitution. Did you ever think to ask for his credentials?

"No, though it would have been a good idea. But I do think Mikis is with the magazine."

"Maybe, but that's so conveniently cool. He's also into you. Or hadn't you noticed? Whatever his motives, you came here to find yourself away from all that glam cam stuff, remember. We're looking for our father, and it's like the man fell off the earth. You need to resolve your vision. Let's stay focused on that. With Mikis, it would be first he takes some photos for the magazine. Then you go out to dinner and a concert and before you know, well, you know."

"I'm sure he's only interested in photographing us. He started talking to me because he thought I was the reporter on the assignment, and then it turned out he's from Oregon."

"Yeah, right. I've heard of lines but…."

"Not everyone has an ulterior motive."

"True but remember why you are here."

"You know what. I'm not arguing. I hadn't thought it through. Even though Mikis is attractive and interesting, it's not why we're here. And we don't need to complicate things. On the other hand, maybe he and the reporter could help us find Peter."

"Your call," Tom said. "I'll go along with what you decide." They walked across the plaza now toward Mikis who was photographing a child and its mother laying flowers on the steps of the freedom monument. Nikkie felt a glimmer of disappointment Mikis had found other people to shoot.

At the moment they reached Mikis, a voice spoke behind them. "Mikis? Hi, I'm Elizabete Riekstins." Nikkie and Tom turned to see a tall, beautiful, blond woman dressed in black jeans and a royal blue shirt carrying a matching blue day pack, nearly identical to Nikkie's.

"Glad to meet you," Mikis said.

"Am I interrupting?" Elizabete glanced from Mikis to Nikkie and Tom.

"I've been taking shots while waiting for you," Mikis said.

"Sorry to be late, but I was setting up an interview with this amazing folk dance choreographer I heard about this morning. We need to go to her studio now."

"Great. What's our focus for the interview?" Mikis asked.

"She's a young dancer and choreographer, whose troupe

performs and competes internationally," Elizabete said. "Many are young women and men who came out of orphanages. It is an issue here, children ending up in orphanages because their parents became alcoholics and could no longer care for them. One had also escaped sex trafficking, a problem here."

See, Nikkie heard Tom's voice say in her head. *It is an issue.*

"Her name is Māra Berzins," Elizabete said. "Her troupe is Saulīte."

Māra Berzins? Nikkie and Tom looked at each other, flashing on the name. It was a stretch, but Māra was a dancer with the same last name as Peter. Maybe she was his daughter or otherwise related.

"How old is Māra?" Tom asked. Nikkie sensed he was following up on that possibility.

Elizabete raised her right eyebrow, cocked her head at him.

Tom extended his hand and introduced himself and Nikkie. "Sorry. We've been looking for Peters Berzins who was a dancer with the Nijinsky Ballet but have come up against a lot of dead ends. Māra has the same last name and is a dancer. Maybe she is related. He'd be in his 40s now."

Elizabete looked at Mikis. He nodded for her to continue.

"She's in her twenties, like you two. But you do know Berzins is a common surname?"

"Could we come along to meet her just in case?" Tom said. "Or could you please tell us how to get in touch with her? It's so important to us."

"I hope you understand. I'm not in the habit of showing up to interviews with an entourage or handing out source's phone numbers. It's hardly ethical."

"Of course," Nikkie said. She felt a need to tell Mikis and Elizabete the truth and heard the words coming out of her mouth about why she and Tom were looking for Peter. She could not lie anymore—to Mikis first and foremost.

And she could not live in the secrets of this place anymore and the story they had made up in Moscow to gather information. All the words and stories that people had stuffed or hidden to survive. All the creative expression that had been squelched. She needed to speak the truth in the light of day, especially in this spot with the symbol of freedom towering above them. Talking, she felt herself grow taller, embody the grace of her dancer stature. She saw compassion in Mikis' eyes, interest in Elizabete's.

"It's a stretch connecting Māra to Peter," Nikkie said. "But my brother and I both had a strong feeling when you said her name. And we want to follow every lead."

"If she is related, she would not know about us and most likely not about our mother and Peter's connection," Tom said. "We don't know if Peter would want to meet us, but we need to learn what we can about him and let him know we exist."

Elizabete was nodding ever so slightly as Tom spoke, Nikkie noticed and hoped it meant she would help.

"Peter quit dancing to be part of the freedom movement," Nikkie said. "We know he was at the barricades. But after that, nothing. All our leads, all our explorations of Latvia's classical dance community have led nowhere."

"What a great story," Elizabete said. "I could see including it in the *National Geographic* piece if you are willing. Regardless, I will help you. And I have an idea."

"What?" Tom asked.

"Why don't I tell Māra that Nikkie is a professional dancer from the U.S. with Latvian ancestry who would like to meet other dancers. And you are her brother and manager, which is true."

"I love that," Nikkie said. "Because I do want to meet dancers here. You might tell her I'm exploring collaborations with Latvian dancers." Nikkie felt an excitement rise in her, like a thousand butterflies taking flight, as she spoke about partnering with dancers who were part of the energy of possibility in this place, grateful for the opportunity to express freely now.

"We'll need to ease into mentioning Peter," Tom said. "Maybe you could ask if her parents were dancers."

"If her family comes up, I will do that," Elizabete said. "Meanwhile, Mikis and I need to go. But we can call you when we're done."

"If you don't mind, how about we walk with you to the studio?" Tom said.

"Are you worried we're going to blow you off?" Elizabete turned to Nikkie. "I like your brother. He covers all the bases."

Elizabete brought up the calendar on her cell phone and showed it to Tom. "I trust your discretion. Here's the address on Brīvības Iela—and my card with my phone number. We are staying at the Radi un Draugi Hotel in Old Town."

"Thanks," Tom said. "I apologize if I sounded pushy."

"No problem," she said and paused for a moment. "And you can walk along with us. But remember I've got a great motivator to keep in touch. I want to include your story in the article. Twins coming to find their heritage and father. Experiencing the festival."

Nikkie smiled. Tom seemed to have forgotten all he had suggested about Mikis taking them off course on their search.

"How long have you lived in Latvia?" Nikkie asked Elizabete.

"One year," she said. "I grew up in Chicago. My parents were both Latvian. But Latvia itself has called me since I was a teenager. We had traveled to Latvia three different times after it was freed. And I went to the Latvian camp Garezers in the States a couple times."

Tom and she discovered they had missed each other by one summer at Garezers. "I want to know your expat story," Tom said. "I could definitely see living here for a time—if I wasn't working with Nikkie."

They walked past Vērmanes Garden. Germanic and pre-war art nouveau buildings with modern storefronts lined Brīvības iela. Trolley wires crisscrossed the street above them. Tom walked next to Elizabete on the busy sidewalk, and Nikkie fell back into step with Mikis. She felt comfortable with this man, trusted him, even though she had no reason to. But she had no reason not to, either.

And, yes, there was a physical attraction. Yet how often had that taken her down a rosy, then muddy path? Nikkie and Mikis' eyes met, and she felt the electric charge run from her eyes to her toes. Trouble. She needed to follow Tom's advice and stick to the search. But how well was Tom avoiding complications himself? She had seen a few looks pass between him and Elizabete.

"Regardless of what happens, I'm excited to meet a dancer who uses folk dance to empower her dancers and to bring awareness to social issues," Nikkie said. "And as important as singing is in Latvian culture, folk dance seems important too. At the very least, it is a form of expression that uplifts the soul. And uplifting audiences, connecting people to their hearts and souls is what I love to do in dance as well." Nikkie was surprised to hear herself say that. It was the first time since being fired she had reconnected to this about herself.

"Wait until you see more than thirteen thousand dancers performing together at the festival," Elizabete said.

"I can only imagine," Nikkie said.

"Speaking of it, I'm not only writing the article, but I'm also singing," Elizabete said. "I'm part of Riga's expat choir. I've dreamt of doing it ever since my parents brought me to the 1993 song festival in Latvia, two years after the country was freed."

Mikis touched his camera. "I wish I had been here to photograph it."

"Talk about connecting to the soul of a people," Elizabete said. "That festival touched mine so profoundly I'm now living and writing here. And with every song we perform, I am acutely aware I am singing with thousands of people who know firsthand what it was like to be part of the Singing Revolution."

"I'd love to hear more about that," Tom said.

"Of course," Elizabete smiled. She paused as if searching for the right words. "Experiencing the aftermath of what happened here, I wanted to be part of this culture that chose peaceful dissent against a world superpower. Latvians made a conscious choice not to use violence against the Soviet Union, and, like Gandhi and Martin Luther King and all the other great proponents of nonviolence, had the crazy notion they could gain their freedom without violence. In Latvia's case, the demonstrators chose to sing."

Elizabete's voice vibrated with passion. "I mean, how does a nation of a couple million people choose singing over bombs and weapons and physical fighting?"

"I don't know," Tom said. "I'd like to think I'd pick nonviolence too. But I've never been tested."

"Exactly. What quality of character that shows," Elizabete said. "I'm not glossing over the problems here, which are considerable. But I also want to explore that choice for peace more fully and bring it out in the article. And I want to foster it in myself."

And our father was one of those people, Nikkie thought. She hoped Māra would now be the link that would lead them to him.

The paint-chipped walls in the lobby were antiseptic beige, but the ceilings were high with crown molding and corniches in the corners. The carved wood doorway was heavy and oversized.

Elizabete came down the stairs, shaking her head. "Māra didn't want to talk much about her past, but Peter is not her father. Her parents were alcoholics. She was in an orphanage for a while, then raised by an uncle in Kurzeme. She didn't say where. She wanted to focus on the positive that's happening for her troupe and for Latvia, not the difficulties of the past. 'If our people are to thrive,' she said, 'they need to let go of the sadness and difficulties of the past and move forward.'"

Nikkie felt an overwhelming desire to talk to Māra anyway. "Will she see us? I'd still love to talk to her about dance. I have a strong intuition we might inspire each other."

"Yes," Mikis said. "She can talk for a short while now and has invited you to stay for a rehearsal that starts in about an hour. I'm returning to photograph it."

"I do have one surprise for you," Elizabete said. "Māra's studio used to be where the Riga Ballet School students took classes. She went on about how it was the third most famous ballet school in the Soviet Union after the Kirov and the Bolshoi, and many of its students ended up at the famous Russian companies. I'm quite certain your father would have studied at it, perhaps in this very studio."

Chapter 14

Walking into Māra Berzins' spacious studio, Nikkie felt her skin tingle with a sense of rightness, of coming home. Three walls were painted a soothing sage green and lined with ballet barres. A mural of three trees reaching to a clear blue sky, their roots extending into the earth and the floor, graced the fourth. Each tree framed a window. The polished hardwood floor pulsed, alive, its planks breathing under her feet. She caught a whiff of musk and oak.

Nikkie imagined a young Peter at one of those ballet barres, the instructor barking warm up positions to him and other promising Riga Ballet School students. How many had been chosen to go to Moscow like Peter had? How many leaps and turns, realized and unrealized hopes and dreams remained suspended in the air in this room?

But Nikkie's feeling of what home meant had to do with more than the history of this room and the possibility their father had begun his dance career there. It also had to do with the present moment. The comely tall blond woman situated by the window might not be their sister, but she was a dancer nonetheless, and Nikkie felt that immediate connection and comradery she experienced with other dancers.

Māra wore a full, long, white skirt and white linen shirt with billowing embroidered sleeves. Tied around her waist was a Latvian belt woven with patterns in red, yellow and black. She walked, no, she flowed toward them as if sliding on air, crossing the expanse of the dance floor in a diagonal.

They introduced themselves, and Nikkie commented on the beauty of the space, asked about the mural. Māra's face filled with pride. "A gifted artist, a friend of mine, was generous enough to paint the mural for us when we moved into this space after the Riga Ballet leased it to us." She spoke English with a slight Latvian accent.

"Each tree is an image of an actual sacred tree in Latvia. The middle oak is the most personal. It is from the forest on my uncle Vilnis' land, and I danced around it when I was growing up. We associate it and oak trees in general with the Latvian goddess Māra, whom I was named after."

Nikkie thought back to the grandmother oak that held the stories of generations of her family on their land in Gulbene. It, too, had a feeling of the sacred about it.

"These trees and their roots hold and frame a window intentionally," Māra said. "We wanted to create the impression that the outer world, the busy-ness and development of Riga, lives inside each tree trunk. It symbolizes that all of us, the dancers, people walking by, Riga's buildings, the traffic are part of nature."

Māra crossed her hands over her heart, and Nikkie mirrored her. "Before we rehearse or perform, we honor our connection to nature and call on the spirits of the sacred trees and forests, on the Latvian gods and goddesses connected to them to inspire and motivate us."

"I can't believe those are actual trees and one comes from your family land," Tom said.

"Yes, Uncle Vilnis had a special connection to the trees in his forest and taught me to have one, too," Māra said.

"It's a beautiful mural," Nikkie said. "I can see how it would inspire you. I would love to dance and create in this space."

"Have either of you seen Latvian folk dancing before or danced yourselves?" Māra asked.

Tom told her about Garezers. "I learned dances there. But it was about having fun."

"I never did," Nikkie said. "But our grandmother took us to a Latvian song and dance festival in the U.S. when we were sixteen. The climax dance performance had five hundred dancers, nowhere near the number in Latvia's festival. But it was still moving."

"I'm astonished so many people participate in the traditional dances and singing here," Tom said, dropping his hands on the table as if for emphasis. "Forty thousand singers, dancers and wind musicians, right?"

Māra nodded.

"I can't imagine getting that many people to devote their time and energy to rehearse and perform on a national stage every five years," Tom said.

"Or to get a major television network to broadcast the events live, like Latvia does, so the whole country can watch," Nikkie said. "We'd be lucky if PBS covered just one event."

Māra smiled. "For us, it's part of our culture. We look forward to meeting weekly for those five years to prepare."

"That is a lot of dedication," Nikkie said.

"It is," Māra said. "And not everyone who prepares gets to sing and dance in Riga. Only the best groups are chosen. Thirteen thousand four hundred dancers will perform."

"It must be exciting for them," Tom said.

Māra nodded. "Yes, for some, coming to the festival represents their first time away from their rural communities. They stay in dormitories or with family here. They get to meet people from all over Latvia and the world. But I don't know why we're standing here. Please, come into our break room, where we can sit and talk."

She directed them to a smaller room with a couch and a few round wooden tables and motioned to Nikkie and Tom to sit. The off-white walls of the windowless room were lined with pictures of Saulīte performing and rehearsing, including in what looked like a clearing in a forest. She walked over to a small refrigerator and brought out an assortment of bottled waters and juices.

"Help yourself," Māra said, motioning to the drinks.

Nikkie and Tom each reached for waters and thanked Māra for meeting with them.

"It is my pleasure." Māra lowered her eyes.

"We would love to know more about Saulīte," Nikkie said.

"Saulīte is only two years old. But many of my dancers and I have been dancing the traditional dances since childhood. I have always been drawn to the cultural traditions, even when it was dangerous to be."

"Was that because of the Soviet occupation?" Tom asked, leaning back in his chair.

"Yes, the Soviets did not want us to have a Latvian identity. But since independence, we have the freedom to give our traditions breath and life and allow them to evolve."

"How so?" Nikkie asked.

"Culture is an organic thing," Māra said. "During the occupation, we held onto traditions in whatever ways we could, in small groups, in our homes. Now we begin with those, but we also let them take on new forms. It's an exciting time to be an artist here."

"How does that come into play at the song and dance festival?" Nikkie said.

"One way is we use not only traditional folk music but also songs composed today, some specifically for the song festival. And we give ancient music a modern twist. You probably know Riverdance, the popular Irish dancers."

Tom and Nikkie nodded.

"Like them, we build on traditional patterns and steps and add dramatic impact and high energy. In some dances, partners pair off and form circles of eight, but we also connect in larger rings, lines, and patterns on the floor. Staging, lighting, props all play factors."

"How do the organizers decide on dances?" Nikkie asked.

"The theme is based on nature and draws on ancient tribal traditions and sacred symbols," said Māra. "This performance, called 'My World,' celebrates the four elements—earth, fire, water, and air. It honors the divine in nature—not only life but also death, day and night, the expanse of the skies and heavens and the rootedness of trees." Māra swept her arm over her head as if through the heavens themselves, then bowed to the earth. "These elements came into being to support life in our world."

"That's beautiful," said Nikkie. She thought of the sacred dances from different cultures she had been drawn to study—Indian, Native American, Hawaiian.

"And poetic," said Tom. "It reminds me of Thoreau and Emerson, the American writers who wrote of the divine in nature."

"The patterns we create symbolize the sun, the moon, thunder, the Latvian gods and goddesses," Māra said. "When you watch us from above in the stadium, the dancers look like living organisms. They flow seamlessly from one dance, one symbol and pattern to another. For the first time, I am also choreographing one of the dances."

"What a wonderful acknowledgment of your creativity," Nikkie said.

Māra flushed with pride. "I've been preparing for this moment all my life. I started dancing when I was seven. When I turned eighteen, I joined one of the oldest folk dance groups, Līgo, and performed with them for three years before directing my own group."

"That is a lot of commitment," said Nikkie.

"Yes, I had to learn the dances and do the physical training to build stamina. I studied ballet and other dance forms to build technique. I was also fascinated by the folklore, which infused the movements with power and meaning. It's what led me to want to choreograph dances that would give an experience of the symbolism of nature."

Nikkie reflected on how much nature and the divine inspired her own dancing. But she had never connected that aspect of her creativity to her ancestral roots before. "Which element did you choreograph?"

"My dance honors the spirit of water, how it renews us and sustains life. The Water Mother is one of our goddesses who both creates and like a river, carries away. Water is perceived as our blood, and the rivers are our arteries."

"And you direct thirteen thousand dancers?" Tom said. "What a logistical nightmare."

Māra smiled. "Not a nightmare. A beautiful dream. But most dances do not use all the dancers. Mine has twelve hundred. All the dancers converge together on the dance floor at the end for a grand finale."

"I'm sure I'll be wishing I could be down there with them," Nikkie said.

"Maybe you will be someday." Māra's hand came up to rest on her heart. "Thinking about that moment always moves me. Our first festival after Latvia declared its freedom was especially poignant. We knew in our hearts what magic we had created in singing and dancing our way to freedom and were now creating for the audience. I cannot wait for you to experience your first time."

"Yes." Nikkie felt her heart open in response to Māra's enthusiasm. How long since she had felt that kind of connection to her dance? Well before Sean had fired her. Listening to Māra, she felt an inner stirring that what had started merely as an interest in traditional movement was feeding her creative soul. And she had not even seen the dances yet. Māra was as committed to folk dancing as Nikkie was to her forms.

"Māra, your passion makes the experience come alive," Nikkie said. "How long do you get to rehearse at the stadium itself?"

"Three days."

"That's it? It doesn't seem like enough time," Tom said. Nikkie nodded her agreement.

"It isn't. But we rehearse for many hours each of those three days. Otherwise, we could not create cohesiveness as we meld five hundred dance groups into one. Making certain the patterns are visible from above calls for tremendous precision. Dancers in the wrong place can destroy the symbolism we wish to convey."

"Do Saulīte and the other professional groups give individual performances?" Nikkie asked.

Māra looked puzzled. "For the main dance event, there are no professionals, only Latvians joining as one nation. Groups perform not to outshine each other but to blend and support each other to perform at their highest level. Throughout the week, though, dance troupes do compete with judges choosing the best ones and the best choreography."

"I have a question," Tom said. "Nik and I grew up near a forest in Southern Oregon. But it's difficult to maintain that connection to nature living in New York City. How do you keep it alive for yourself and your dancers in Riga?"

"It's a good question," Māra said. "Let me start by telling you a little about my background. My own parents were alcoholics who could not care for me and like many children of alcoholics in Latvia, I ended up in an orphanage."

"How challenging for you," Nikkie said, surprised this self-assured woman had come from that turbulent background.

Māra nodded. "But I was fortunate. My uncle Vilnis and his wife took me in and raised me in the countryside outside Kuldiga in Kurzeme. Not only did I dance in the forest on their land and learn to love the natural world from Vilnis, but he had been one of the first people who encouraged the fire for dance in me. He also suggested I use dancing and nature to heal my childhood memories. That early association between dance and nature and their power to heal helps me keep it alive now for myself and my troupe."

"And you started a company of dancers with similar backgrounds to your own," Nikkie said. "That's inspiring."

"I hope so," Māra said. "And I wanted the Saulīte dancers to experience that forest as well. So, for two weeks each summer, I take the group to Vilnis' land. We camp. We dance and rehearse in a clearing in the forest I danced in growing up. Recently, Vilnis helped me build an outdoor dance platform there from trees on the land.

"Dancing in that place today deepens the troupe's link to nature and our ancestral roots. It heals us and reminds us how precious our freedom is." Māra pointed out some photos of the dancers in a forest dancing on the platform. She also showed them a picture there of her and Vilnis, a slim, muscular man in his sixties, who looked at her with deep caring and pride, and the twins expressed how thankful they were Māra had that support.

"I danced in the forest too," Nikkie said. "When I was ten, I danced in a forest in Oregon that surrounded the land we lived on. I started spinning there and found my inspiration from the trees and earth. I call on them and the divine beings, who guide me when I dance or choreograph, even in New York. Being in Latvia, I am now drawn to the Latvian goddesses, Māra and Laima, and imagine I'll call on them for guidance and aid."

"We have a lot in common as dancers, Nikkie."

"Yes, like kindred spirits. I thought how I approached dancing was from my own connection to nature and the divine. I had no idea that part of me had deep ancestral roots from Latvia."

"And we're hoping to visit Kuldiga, too," Tom said. "We may have family there."

Māra's face brightened. "Maybe we're related."

Tom and Nikkie looked at each other. *If only,* Nikkie heard from Tom.

"Tell me more about your dance life, Nikkie," Māra said. "I've talked a lot. Elizabeta said you studied at Julliard and danced professionally with a band. It must have been exciting to be at the center of dance in New York."

How to tell Māra what it was like to be chosen for such an elite school, be primed by world-class dancers and instructors, then to turn away from the life it had prepared her for.

She thought how arrogant and unappreciative she must sound to Māra. "One day, I felt like the walls of the dance studio were closing in on me and I couldn't breathe. I couldn't fit into the formal structures anymore. I needed to learn to listen to myself, to how my body wanted to move. To find all I could be without formal direction regardless of the beauty and artistry that evolved from that mentorship."

She explained the external demands to push her body harder came up against an inner resistance, a need to stop forcing her body to reach for the impossible. She felt compelled to let go into spontaneity and what was sacred.

Nikkie felt Tom's presence next to her, grateful that at least he understood. She experienced difficulty looking at Māra as Nikkie spoke about diving into freeform dance, letting movement arise from what felt like the deepest part of her being, her authentic movement expression. "While our methods are different, I, like you, wanted to give audiences a meaningful, spiritual experience."

She worried about how she must sound like an American who took her freedom for granted and tossed away opportunity, but Māra looked at her without judgment, only curiosity. Nikkie relaxed.

She shared what had happened with Stone Tara and admitted, "I don't know what my next steps are, only that I am not motivated to return to New York or the U.S. and look for work with a dance company there, as astonishing as they are. Sometimes life has other plans for you than those you make. When I met Stone Tara, life invited me away from the direction I thought I was going. And now, one year later, I am on yet another new course."

"Thank you for telling me your story," Māra said. "I have many questions. Could we meet and talk again?"

"I would like that," Nikkie said.

"Right now, my dancers will be arriving for our afternoon rehearsal. I hope you will stay and watch."

"We would love to," Nikkie said.

Māra rose to her feet. "I'll see you back in the studio in about fifteen minutes? Mikis will be back too." Then, she spun on one foot to walk toward the door, her skirt flaring around her as she passed through the door. She turned back to face them. "I was going to wait to surprise you. But I want to make sure you stay for the whole rehearsal."

Nikkie did not know why, but her heart began to pound.

"I did not yet tell you about my other uncle, who also inspired my path as a dancer. He used to dance with the Nijinsky Ballet and started his own contemporary dance company in Riga this year. In an hour, he is coming to give us pointers on technique. He's a brilliant dancer who helped me lease this space."

Māra put her finger up to her lips as if shooshing them. "Don't let on you know anything to the other dancers. It's a surprise."

Nikkie felt the blood rise into her head. Tom's hand tightened around hers. The dizziness came on like a snake slithering up and tightening around her neck, so she could barely breathe. *Not now*, she willed her body. *Not now*.

CHAPTER 15

Tom and Nikkie froze in place. *Shit. Shit. Shit.* In one hour, a dancer, who might be their father, or who *knew* their father and where he might be now, would walk through that door.

"Are you okay? You look as stunned as I feel," Tom said.

"I am dizzy as hell. I can't move. Afraid you will tell me I hallucinated what I heard."

"In that case, let me assure you, you can move. If you did, I hallucinated the same thing, and I for one would like to move my butt over to the couch where it's more comfortable."

He helped her get up, and they collapsed together on the couch. The dark brown cushions were harder than Nikkie had imagined. The couch squeaked, and the pillows only gave way a little when they hit the surface.

Tom put his arm around Nikkie's shoulders, and Nikkie held his other hand in hers. Her head was swirling, and she felt a stabbing pain from behind her ear down her neck to her right shoulder, as if the snake wound around her neck was sinking its fangs into her. Goddess, I hope I do not have a heart attack."

"Courage, ma brave." Tom squeezed her closer to him. "Time to change gears. I have been so focused on the search for Peter, I wasn't prepared for what we would do when we found him."

"Let's not get our hopes up. Maybe it's not him."

"How many Latvians named Berzins do you think were in the Nijinsky Ballet company at once, Miss Normally Positive?" Tom said. "I'll be shocked if it's not him. But enough. We have fifteen minutes to pull it together. How about you do one of your grounding exercises? I don't want you fainting. Heck, it will help me."

Nikkie guided them to breathe deeply. "See ourselves like the trees in the mural, our roots extending deep into the center of the earth and our branches up to the heavens." Nikkie's own mind still raced. "Bring the energy of both into our hearts to create a vast pool of love and surrender any thoughts, any anxiety into that love. Breathe in that love. Breathe out that love. Be it, and feel it filling and surrounding every cell of your being."

Nikkie's thought-racing slowed. In the silence, the dizziness washed through her. Without resisting, she let go with a soft focus like she did when she whirled. Gentle tears filled her eyes. Tom's energy felt calmer as well. They rested that way for a few minutes, breathing deeply. In. Out.

"Better," Tom said, stretching his arms over his head and his long legs in front of him. "Hey, that stuff worked. How about for you?"

"Me, too, and the dizziness is gone." She extended her arms, her fingers interwoven to maximize the stretch. "I imagined it like the spin in my dance, and it disappeared." Nikkie wiped away the tears with her hand and reached into her daypack for Kleenex to blow her nose.

"How do I look?" She turned toward Tom. "I don't want to meet Māra's dancers or Peter with puffy eyes." She brushed her hair back from her cheeks and anchored it behind her ears.

"As if puffy mattered, gorgeous one," Tom wiped a tear from her cheek with his thumb. "And is it Peter you're worried about seeing you like that—or Mikis?"

Nikkie rolled her eyes.

"But let's get serious." Tom looked deep into her eyes. "How *are* we going to handle meeting Peter?"

"We can't exactly say, 'Hi, we're Nikkie and Tom Ozolins, the long-lost children you never knew you had.'"

"Right. You boinked our mother in Chicago in 1980. The artsy Latvian one? Tour? Remember?" Tom said. Nikkie chuckled, despite the butterflies in her belly.

"Why not go with what worked with Māra?" said Tom. "Ask if we could come to his studio and learn about his company."

"That sounds logical. And if it's not Peter, we can ask both Māra and her uncle if they know of a Peter Berzins from the Ballet."

"Okay, but it is Peter. It has to be." Tom rose up from the couch and extended his hand to pull Nikkie up. "Now, let's go do this thing."

Every movement Māra made was infused with grace and passion. Walking amongst the dancers, she held her head high, shoulders back exuding confidence. And that strength was mirrored in her dancers, who threw themselves into each step. The energy in the room was palpable. Men lifted knees high. The women floated on air. Each let out yelps as they leaped and swung each other around. Quick, sharp turns. Eye contact between the pairs and when the dancers passed each other.

This dance was about connection. Connection to self and to the other dancers. Connection to the earth. Air. Fire. Water. Spirit.

The music added to the experience. The singer's voices had an ancient droning quality and were accentuated by bagpipes, fiddles, low toned drumming.

The group ran through a couple of dances, so Nikkie and Tom, sitting in wooden chairs on the sidelines, could experience them, and Mikis could photograph them. Nikkie's heart flew into her throat. Their dancing filled her to overflowing.

Māra guided Saulīte's dancers with a flick of a finger here and a flourish of arm movements there, like a conductor conducting an orchestra, steering them with hand signals. Her arms circled like a waterspout, a geyser when she wanted more motion and energy, and her hands tapped downward like she was patting the earth when she wanted them to tone down.

While the dancers were fully engaged, they also remained attentive to her every move. They seemed not to notice Mikis who moved unobtrusively around the room, appeared not to be impeded by the traditional performance garments with their long magenta woolen skirts, white pants and vests, and white linen shirts they wore for the shoot.

Apparently, the dancers adored Māra and adored what they were doing. And even at a young age—Māra could not have been much older than Nikkie and Tom, she commanded respect.

Māra encouraged the dancers, helped them rise up to their full stature. The words she spoke. The way she looked at them, like a proud mother, but also a peer. Māra was a real mentor and guide, who felt the dance in her bones, her muscles, joints, breath.

She embodied dance. She embodied herself, earthy, grounded, yet light as air. And she embodied the spirit in her body, her soulfulness, even when she walked across the room. No matter what the rest of these dancer's days looked like, here in this room performing with Saulīte, they got to shine, to thrive, and Nikkie knew their experience could not help but spill over into other parts of their lives.

As distracted as Nikkie should have been waiting for the uncle who might be her father, as drawn to Mikis as she had been earlier, now she could not help but watch the dancers and Māra, spellbound. And while dancing at Jāṇi had been fun, now for the first time, Nikkie wanted to leap up and join these dancers, to be part of Māra's dance collective as opposite as it was to her improvisational style.

She wanted to be passionately engaged like them. Not apart from, alone on a stage, connecting from afar, but up close. Taking down the walls and barriers she had unwittingly erected around herself and her heart. Since when had they appeared, she wondered. This last year? After getting fired? Her whole life? How long since she had honestly, genuinely, ardently, intimately connected to her audience, to another dancer, another person one on one, other than her brother and mother?

She reached over and squeezed Tom's hand. And when she started to move it back to her lap, he grabbed it and held on.

Tom leaned over and whispered, "I could fall in love with this woman." Nikkie nodded and let the depth of what was happening in this room sink in. Being with Saulīte and Māra, she felt healing going on inside her. A vast and deep rip she did not know had existed in the fabric of her being was being mended by forces she did not understand, regardless of whether or not the man who walked through the door in a few minutes turned out to be their father.

Chapter 16

"My uncle Peter has been delayed and may not be able to come," Māra said.

Peter. It was the first time Māra said her uncle's name. *Peter.* How many Peters from Latvia could there have been in the Nijinsky Ballet? This was one more confirmation Māra's uncle was their father.

Disappointment edged its way in. Delayed or not coming. No. They were so close. Nikkie could feel it. If Peter was not helping Māra today, the twins had to ask Māra to get them invited to his studio. Nikkie's mind raced with possibilities. She barely registered what Māra was saying.

"I had already told the dancers I had a surprise for them. A gift," Māra said. "Would you be that gift, Nikkie—now that Peter can't come?"

What? Nikkie snapped back into focus.

"It makes perfect sense," Māra said. "Would you dance for us? One of your special dances that includes the spin. It's such a coincidence. I had wanted Peter to help us improve our turns. But here you show up—an expert in that, too, no?"

No, Nikkie wanted to scream. *I'm not an expert in turning. Not in anything. And not a gift.*

"Will you dance for us?"

"Yes," Nikkie said. "I will."

The words floated up unbidden, emerged from her throat and mouth as if she had no choice. She needed to say yes. If she let her "no" reign, it would grip her, clamp her down with such finality she might not rally the will to dance again. And she very much wanted to dance, especially for Māra.

A gift. I can be the gift. And as Nikkie said those words, a path opened up before her. She had no idea where it was leading, only that she was ready to take the first step.

Māra gave Nikkie time to warm up. She was already dressed in loose clothing. A pair of flowing black yoga pants and a pale blue fitted t-shirt.

"What about music?" Māra asked.

"I have an iPod with Nik's music on it," Tom said. "Do you have a dock?"

"Yes," Māra said. "Would you want to dance to the song you did at the Hollywood Bowl?"

Nikkie thought for a moment. Would she dare dance to *Climatica* here? No. She did not want this to be about facing down the Bowl experience and the time she had seen the vision of the dead. She wanted it to be about her source of inspiration, the same source that inspired Māra.

"Not that one. Put on *Spirits of the Forest* by Karunesh," Nikkie said. "From his *Way of the Heart* CD. Do you have it?"

Tom nodded. "I keep every song you've ever danced to or might want to dance to. Though after this visit, I have a feeling I'll be adding a lot more Latvian songs to the playlist."

Relief cascaded through her. This music connected her to her heart. In New York, dancing to this song honoring nature and trees had helped her find clarity of being as she traversed the noise and chaotic energy of the city and the demands of Julliard. It was the perfect song to honor this moment of desiring to dance again, of knowing she would meet her father soon, and of washing away the setbacks of the last months. The forest. She would focus on the forest, the trees, her Terpsichore, her muse, and dance for Māra.

Māra and thirty some dancers stood against the walls, surrounding her like the trees in the forest when she danced in the clearing as a girl. She started in stillness. Then the music spoke to her. The trees of the mural spoke to her. The forests that covered forty-two percent of Latvia spoke to her. The dance and choreography she had witnessed from Saulīte spoke to her.

She embodied that language of inspiration and imagined it like roots extending deep into the core of the earth and circling back up into her heart. Nikkie swayed and bent like a tree in the wind. She shimmered like leaves shining in the sun and rustling with the rhythm of a summer breeze. She moved from the energy coursing up and down and through her torso and limbs. Extending. Contracting. Rising. Falling. She danced. She followed an inner cadence and pulse that sang to her of tenderness, implored her to maintain a slowness of movement. Nowhere to rush, the internal notes sounded. No one to impress. She sensed the vibration of reentering the unknown with an open heart.

Then, arms flowing up in a V-shape, she turned slowly at first, envisioning herself like the rings in a tree trunk. One turn for each ring, one turn for each year, each moment, each lifetime.

And instead of turning counterclockwise in tune with the rotation of the planets like she usually did, she trusted and followed an inclination to spin clockwise, unwinding something deep inside her, rather than winding herself up. Gentle, slow, steady. Head back. Soft focus. Sensing the Dervishes, her mentors, helping her reorient, then whirling faster. It wasn't about holding onto one spot of focus. It was about giving up the need to focus at all, of feeling her feet sprout roots and reach deep into the earth, of letting go of the need to be upright and stationary. Then she could do it evenly and serenely over and over, turning and turning. Her own path. Her personal journey.

It was also beyond any one person. Sometimes, Nikkie could see others as she spun and come back to them again and again. But she was amazed at how little they interested her when she was in the spin, in the mode, the zone, the flow, outside the story of her life. Outside and inside at the same time.

She could have turned for hours. But the music was over, and the whirling stopped. Māra and her dancers broke into spontaneous applause, bringing her out of the reverie.

Had she danced well? She could not measure what had happened, did not want to. She had remained detached while she danced, surprising considering this was the first public dance she had improvised since Stone Tara. Throughout, she felt like she was in her body, but standing outside of her body at the same time. An in-and-out-of-body experience.

It was so soft and peaceful there in that space between time and place. She could see the world of time spinning around her. But in the spin, she created her own cocoon, her own outside of time, outside of space as she knew it. It was a new space. A sanctuary space. A created anew space, a place of Advaita.

What was most important was that she had broken the cycle. She had danced. She had whirled and hoped she had tapped enough to be useful to Māra and her dancers. She was glad Mikis had been there. Not so he could photograph her, but so he could get to know her both on a human level and on an artistic one.

She looked to him now, and he gave her a smile and a nod that filled her with a feeling of yellow daisies inside. Tom, who stood next to him, offered her a thumbs-up, and subtly pointed in the direction of Māra.

And then she saw him. The man in her vision, the man of the barricade photo Indra had found. How could she not have been aware when Peter, their father, had slipped into the room? How could she not have sensed the sheer electric force of this momentous event?

Had he seen her dance? She was glad she had not noticed when he arrived, or she would have become self-conscious. Instead, she could at least say she had followed what arose from inside her to dance, relaxed into the changes that were happening in her first personal dance since the Bowl.

After looking for Peter for so long, she felt like perhaps she had danced him into being. The Peter of her vision. Was he real? The Peter who stood before her looked like a dancer. He had an air of charm and depth around him. His blond hair was streaked by the sun and a little long. He wore black jeans and a white shirt just like he had been wearing in her vision. Underneath was a pale blue tank top, the same shade of blue as Nikkie's t-shirt, almost as if they had planned it. He moved with grace and strength.

Nikkie could see what had drawn her mother to him—his sensitive face had definition, exuded wisdom and power. She could guess what attracted him to her mother, beyond her physical beauty. His life and creativity had been more structured and contained at the ballet in the U.S.S.R, her mother's more open and free. Peter had found and followed a passion despite the oppression of his environment. Ellie, too, had carved her own path, uncovering what she wanted to express as a potter and built a livelihood around it. Both had rebelled against the status quo in their own way. And Tom and Nikkie shared that creative, rebellious impulse with their birth parents.

"Thank you, Nikkie." Māra walked over to her.

Nikkie jolted when Māra said her name.

"We all thank you." Māra swept her arm around the room to include her dancers, who were nodding their agreement and smiling. They clearly understood English, as many Latvians did.

Her eyes were drawn back to Peter. What was his face revealing as Māra asked her to expound on how she created her improvisations and what part turning played in them? His expression remained neutral, not giving away his thoughts. She still did not know if he had seen much of her performance.

"Improvising is like a continual freefall, a trust of some force larger than myself," Nikkie said. "It's a constant movement into the unknown, requiring presence and concentration. It means saying yes to that unknown and following what unfolds without questioning myself. I let the movement arise rather than forcing it or making something up to fill the empty space."

She spoke about how that day she had trusted her impulse to reverse her turn. "I did everything in the opposite direction I usually do. Instead of whirling counterclockwise toward my heart and like the planets orbit the sun, something inside prompted me to move clockwise. Instead of using my right foot to pivot around my left one, I used the left foot to pivot around the right. As I turned, I had this delicious feeling of unwinding.

"This turning wasn't crisp like in ballet or folk dancing, but more like the dance of the Sufis, the Whirling Dervishes. I offer it to you as an alternative approach. Improvising means trusting that inclination to do the unexpected, even when it seems like the crisper turns would be what you would more likely do in your dances."

She hoped she was making sense to the dancers and not sounding like a fool in front of Peter, Māra, and Mikis. She purposely avoided looking at Peter or at Mikis, as much as she wanted to stare and take in every expression. Instead, she let her gaze span the line of dancers along the walls, checking in to see if they looked interested or not. Their faces remained open. She paused at Tom, whom she could count on to send her support or let her know if she was losing the room. His face said, "You've got this. Keep going."

Nikkie explained she started with her hands crossed at her heart, then extended her arm, right palm up as if to receive divine energy, pass it through her body and the left palm down to act as a conduit to give the energy on to the earth. "That was the spiritual piece of it, what I learned from the Dervishes.

"On the practical level, you might be interested to know how I kept from getting dizzy." Several dancers and Māra nodded.

"When I turned, rather than focusing on one spot like dancers do in traditional form and turning my head around quickly back to that spot, I kept my eyes open and level, not focused on anything in particular. Until the end. Then, I stared at one spot on the floor. There." She pointed toward the center tree of the mural. "I picked a spot right in front of the sacred oak mural and looked at it when I stopped dancing until the room stopped seeming to swirl, and I knew I could move again without falling."

The dancers turned and looked at the spot as if Nikkie had placed a marker on the floor. She noticed Peter look, too, then at the watch on his arm.

"The 'why' behind what happened as I improvised in new ways might become evident later. Or it might not. Either way, I realize I am on a new course. A different direction. And being here with you today is part of it, inspired it."

Nikkie thanked everyone and was about to invite questions when Māra stepped forward and interrupted her.

"Thank you again, Nikkie. I'm sure many of us have questions, but I wanted to introduce you to my uncle, Peter." Māra extended her hand to him. "I invited him here, and he has informed me he has a limited amount of time. He wants to work with the dancers now and apologizes for cutting you short. Is that all right? We can do questions after if you can stay."

On the outside, Nikkie agreed, but inside, the open-hearted vulnerability she felt while sharing turned to self-consciousness. Peter stepped forward, made no comment on her dance or what she had said. Without smiling, he thanked her for understanding, shook her hand.

So much for the charm she thought she had seen. She barely had time to register this first physical contact. Then, he was off focusing on Saulīte, and the dancers moved their full attention from her to him. They rattled off words in Latvian, so Nikkie was cut off from understanding, would have to rely on Tom for a translation. Intentional or not, she felt like she had been flicked away like a fly.

What kind of person did that, Nikkie wondered. Cut a colleague off. Did he really think he was that important? Was what was going on with his own dance company so crucial that he could not have waited another few minutes for her to do Q&A and let her interaction with Saulīte end naturally? Or did he not like what she had done or said that and didn't care how disrespectful he was? Anger and shame claimed her.

She sensed Tom move closer to her. Next to her. Usually, this would comfort her, but when he reached over to touch her shoulder, she flinched. Tight. Every muscle in her neck and shoulders clenched in defensiveness, so even her brother's loving touch felt like a stab.

She made herself watch Peter demonstrate the "Nijinsky Ballet method" of turning. He worked with the dancers on perfecting their turns, their focus on one spot in the room. Quick. Efficient. Crisp. Over and over, he turned in place and then across the room. Arms and hands and legs in perfect positions. His technique was exquisite. One turn flowing into the next.

Then, the Saulīte dancers went through steps leading into turns, and Peter suggested improvements for individual dancers, moving an arm, a leg, a hand this way or that, straightening a back, lowering a shoulder. Nikkie lowered her own

shoulders which she noted were up against her ears, length-
ened her long neck.

Peter called out, and the dancers began to turn again as a
group. Māra had put on music, and Peter clapped along, one
clap per turn.

Nikkie flashed on all the classes she had ever taken in New
York. The calling out of instruction. The clapping in rhythm as
dancers pirouetted across the floor. All of them pushing themselves forward, pushing forward. Extend. Excel. Extend. Excel.
Improve. Improve. Never enough.

Why was she seething? Peter was only doing what Māra
asked, and Māra was listening intently, respectfully. Peter's
clapping speeded up. Shaking his head back and forth.

"Ne tā—ātrāk, ātrāk," he called out. Not like that. Faster.
Faster. She heard the translation in her head and flashed on
the scene in the movie, *The Red Shoes.* In it, the prima ballerina
is possessed by the red ballet shoes, pushed by the impresario
to put dance above all else in her life. She cannot stop dancing,
keeps dancing faster, faster until she collapses and dies.

And then Peter stopped the music and turned away from
the dancers towards her. He pointed at her, motioned to her.
He leaned into Māra for a moment, spoke to her.

Had he forgotten her name? Her name. That's it. He was
asking Māra for it. Then, he straightened up and said it.

"Nikkie," Peter said. "I understand you studied classical
dance in America, yes?

Yes, she said to herself. She gave him a fiery nod, felt her
breath hot. *Steady, girl,* she imagined Tom saying in her head
like he had the night at the Hollywood Bowl. Only this time,
instead of feeling dizzy, she felt like a horse pacing in a starting gate prepared to explode onto the race track. She stepped
forward.

"At Julliard, "she said. "I *graduated* from Julliard. And now
dance professionally."

Māra reminded Peter that Nikkie had danced at the Hollywood Bowl. He nodded, tipping his head side to side, impatience evident. Was he manic or rude? Nikkie stretched taller, sure that if they could be, her nostrils would be flaring.

"Is there something you would like?" Nikkie asked.

"Would you be willing to turn for us?" Peter asked. "Not like you did in your dance. But how you learned at Julliard. It would help me to show these dancers how to improve their technique."

How do you know which turning method will improve their technique? Nikkie asked in her head. *Maybe instead of forcing a stylized turn, they need to let loose, to let go and turn from their spirits.*

Without thinking, she exploded out of the starting gate, eyes blazing, arms finding their way automatically, thoughtfully after the hundreds, thousands of repetitions during her years of dance classes into as perfect positioning as she had ever positioned. It was as if she had been getting ready to turn like this for a hundred years and became the turn itself.

And so, she turned, spotting and positioning with perfection and ease. Once, twice, twenty times. Thirty. She could have gone on, but she sensed the moment in the turning zone pass and slowed to a stop.

"Now, that is a turn," he said, nodding to her in acknowledgment. "You *do* have the technique." He turned his attention to the dancers and spoke to them in English, Nikkie assumed to include her. "That's what can happen when you practice and turn so much it becomes part of you. Ballet or folk dance. You must realize and accept that folk dancing is its own form of high art and requires as much precision and exactitude, attention to detail, as the lead part in *Swan Lake*. See yourself as true artists like that. Know you are an artist whether you perform solo or in a group. Breathe that knowing. Live it. And most of all, dance it whether you are wearing the ballet shoes and tutus and leotards of a ballet dancer or the traditional woolen folk costumes and the leather slippers, *pastalas*, or boots of folk dancers."

Nikkie's heart pounded, split in two as to whether she was furious at Peter or if this had become the happiest moment in her life. Had Peter called her a true artist in his own way? Had he seen that in her when she turned in a classic style?

Peter thanked Nikkie, then asked if she would help him one more time. He extended his hand to her, bowed. He was asking her to dance. "First, let's turn together, simultaneously, side by side," he said. "Then, we'll turn as partners to dance the polka."

And she did, the two of them turning in sync, nailing it as if they had been dancing together for years. Like they were Ginger and Fred pretending they were meeting and dancing sensationally together for the first time in a movie. She and Peter followed each other diagonally across the floor, turns and lines in perfect sync. Then he was standing in front of her, facing her. She could smell the dampness of his skin. Feel the warmth of his hands as he placed one of hers in his and the other around her back. She felt his shoulder where she had put her other hand, could feel the taut fluidity of his muscles beneath her fingers.

He led. She followed. All the imaginings Nikkie had had about dancing with her father coalesced into this one moment, this one dance. She who rarely did partner dances was dancing this one with grace. Naturally leaning back against Peter's arm, trusting as he supported her back and turned with her faster and faster, both whipping around in the full energy of polka. And then, the song was over, and Peter was smiling and laughing. And she was too. Once again, he thanked her, bowed to the Saulīte dancers and motioned to her to join him and do the same. The dancers broke into whoops and applause. Māra clapped with the greatest enthusiasm of all.

"Paldies, Mīlš paldies jums abiem! Nu tas bija forši, vai nē?" She nodded at her dancers. *"Vai cik labi ka Nikkie bija te dejot ar Pēteri."*

"Thank you both. That was terrific, wasn't it," Tom translated for her. "It was good that Nikkie was here to dance with Peter."

More whoops of acknowledgment from the dancers. And Peter smiled full out, keeping his arm on Nikkie's upper back, giving it a pat. He released her now, moved away, back to the dancers.

"Now you turn again," he said to them. "Do it like we did. Like Julliard and Nijinsky Ballet. Yes. Couple by couple. Four turns to the right, then coming together and four complete turns in polka in groups of four. Diagonally across the floor, one after another, then around in a circle."

And they did. And this time Peter said, "Yes. Like that. Now you're getting it. Yes. Yes." With emphasis. Over and over, and they did get it. They had been fine before, but now they had caught the fire of Nikkie's flaring, of Peter stoking the flame.

"Fire is my friend," she mouthed under her breath, remembering the mantra Tom had given her at the Bowl. And today, here in Māra's studio meeting and dancing with her father for the first time, it was.

Chapter 17

Peter's studio was all white with high ceilings and elaborate crown molding, mirrors and ballet barres along the walls. His troupe gathered around him looking down at his right foot, which was extended out to the side, arched with an impossible arch, his toes pointed toward the floor. It was the kind of hyper-arch young ballet dancers, who were competing for a spot in the top companies' schools, forced by strapping their feet to wooden contraptions designed to push the foot structure past its natural curve. Nikkie wondered if Peter had used one, imagined the pain and discipline involved. "It looks like a device used to torture people in the Middle Ages," Tom had said when he saw one.

Peter's shoulders were down and back, his right arm extended in a semi-circle chest height in front of him, his left arm in another semi-circle down against his body. The hand placements thought out, engaged to the end of each finger and beyond. Deceptively simple. Infinitely exact. He seemed poised, momentum building to move.

This was *her* father. And she and Tom had come to his studio with the intention of revealing their identity. They had no idea when or how but trusted the perfect opportunity would unfold. They had decided they wanted to tell Peter who they were on their own, rather than with Ellie, but would let him know Ellie was in Latvia, too, and wanted to see him. Ellie had agreed.

Nikkie remembered how when she was seven, she first consciously realized that other children had fathers unique to them, while she and Tom did not. The twins had adult males in their lives, a godfather, "uncles," Ellie's friends and arts collective colleagues. Ellie made sure they had caring men in their lives.

Over the years, Ellie had the occasional long-term relationship, which sparked hope that her partner might translate into a father who loved them in the special way their mother loved them. But that never happened. The first time, she and Tom both opened their hearts to Ellie's boyfriend. Then, two years later, he went away. Not for a day or a week, but for good. He left Ellie—and them as well. That hurt. The second time, they grew warier. "Uncles," "godfathers," Ellie's friends were more reliable than boyfriends.

From the time at seven when they both became more curious about a father, she and Tom had longed to know who their real father was and had asked Ellie. To see this father who now graced them with such a flawless stance that Nikkie's heart ached with its beauty. "Some children have fathers who live with them, and many do not," Ellie had told them. "Yours lives in a country, the U.S.S.R, where the government does not allow him to visit us, and we cannot visit him yet. It would not be safe for him."

But even though Ellie and Peter had only spent a few days together, she emphasized they had loved each other. "You were brought into this world in love," she said. "And I know he would be so proud to have you both as his children."

Proud. A new longing for that acknowledgment rose from Nikkie's gut, but she willed herself not to succumb to it here in Riga. Would Peter be proud of them, of who they had become?

Ellie had explained more about why they could not contact Peter. But she suggested the twins write to him anyway, about anything they wanted him to know about themselves. She promised to save the letters. Hopefully, one day, when they were older, or the world changed, they could meet Peter and share those letters in person.

Soon after, when freedom became a possibility, Ellie had called the Nijinsky Ballet and been told that Peter was dead. *Why would someone lie to that extreme?* Nikkie wondered. Was it because Peter had quit dancing for a company no performer in their right mind would quit? Had he been arrested? Was the person who answered the phone a spurned lover? Or had it been a bad translation? "He is no longer here. He quit," might have been mistranslated as "He is no longer here. He is dead."

Nikkie started to feel panicky, light-headed, felt Tom's eyes on her. How were they going to get Peter alone, so they could tell him who they were? After a lifetime of waiting, Nikkie felt she could not wait another second. She wanted to run out on the dance floor and blurt it out.

"Are you okay? Do you need to sit down?" Tom whispered.

She shook her head "no" in Tom's direction. He moved closer beside her, put his arm around her waist, propped her up. She felt his strength, and centeredness rolled in to replace the nerves.

"How about you?" Nikkie whispered back to Tom. "Can you believe we are in our father's dance studio?"

"We've imagined this for so long," Tom whispered back. "But being here is a long way from when we used to play 'meeting our father' as kids."

That game, one of their favorites, had always included a joyful reunion as an ending. In one version, they were James Bond-like government spies who parachuted into the U.S.S.R and whisked their father across the border to freedom. In another, they met him while he was on tour with the ballet, told him who they were. He chose to defect; he and Ellie got married, and they all lived happily ever after.

Nikkie motioned to Tom she was going to lean back against the barre for support. He came with her. Then, she wondered what Peter with his perfect posture would think seeing her slouched against the barre, while all his dancers stood erect, mimicking Peter's lead, arching their feet, shaping their arms, pointing their toes. Nikkie recalled how she had once found comfort in controlled meticulousness but had come to resist it, how relieved she had been to give it up.

Still, leaning up against the barre now, like all those she had leaned on for support growing up, she did find comfort in its familiarity, in the memories associated with the hours she had spent at barres like this one. Throughout her dance life, barres had provided stability, an anchor to hold onto and help her reach for her dreams. Like a pianist playing the scales daily, she had taken class after class that involved the barre. Even when she was not studying, she practiced at it. She loved stretching on the barre, going through the exercises at it that built her strength and foundation, fine-tuned her dance movements.

She remembered leaning into it, touching it lightly, like a dance partner. She had often envisioned her father at a barre, and that image had motivated her to keep going, to move through pain, to move from the barre to the dance floor to the stage.

Peter broke out into laughter, bringing Nikkie out of her reverie. All the dancers laughed with him. "And that's what it was like day after day at the Nijinsky Ballet School," Peter said, speaking English so Nikkie could follow him, too. "This strictness around each movement, but also forcing the body past its natural limits. It was all part of preparing the mind and body, and it created great dancers. But at what cost? The spirit soared in the dance, but bones and muscles and ligaments screamed.

Knees, hips, tendons, joints, feet fell apart. Long term, it was not sustainable."

What? Tom and Nikkie looked at each other, questioning.

"So here, we look for our spirit in a way that sustains us, yes?" Peter continued. "We reach for the best in us, for the grace and beauty and meaning with movement that does not take such a toll on the individual." He walked back and forth moving his arms up over his chest and head as if calling on that best in each dancer to rise and overflow like a waterfall.

"Challenging, yes. And sometimes, our bodies still hurt. But we also rest so we can support ongoing performance. In this manner, when we keep our shoulders down and back, we are no longer forcing them into position. We do so because we know inside that this posture allows our body's poetry to bubble up and our hearts to bare themselves in our dancing. Shoulders up around the ears and forward cut you off from your body, the truth, and reveal fear."

Nikkie felt herself relaxing. She liked witnessing this encouraging Peter, the one with a sense of humor and drama. And so apparently did the dancers in his company. Their eyes and heads moved with him, seemed to soak in everything he said. "It's also why we add exercises like Pilates that develop the core and protect the body while we dance. And Yoga which taps the spirit. Then, together, we can create and convey the story we wish to tell in the dance. We can live and breathe rhythm and emotion."

Do I have a story I want to convey now in my life? Nikkie wondered. *What story moves me, fills me enough to embody it in dance?* What came to her was that the only story she wanted to dance, to speak, to scream at that moment was the "telling Peter who we are" story. Revealing, "Peter, we are your children. You are our father. Love and accept us. Care about us, and let us love you. Know you. Be part of your life. This life." This was the story that filled the space inside her.

"So now my dear collaborators, I would like you to experiment as we develop this piece," Peter said, pulling Nikkie back to Peter's process. "Which is why I asked you to wear your hair pulled or slicked tight back. Like in ballet. Come into the center of the room. Stand in the pose I showed you."

The dancers moved into position, feet extended and arched, arms in semi-circles.

"Now, with a flourish, one at a time, pull out what binds your hair. Start at the left. Ingrida, let your hair loose." A young woman undid the pins holding her hair, released the hair band, flicked her head.

"The rest remain in the pointe and etude. But the dancer who has freed her hair, begin to improvise movement. Feel what is inside you. Hair free. Relax the stomach muscles. Swing the hips back and forth, bend the knees slightly. Let the arms drop and sway in response to the body and hair. Then the next person does the same. That's right." The dancers released their hair one by one and joined in swaying and swinging.

"Start interacting with each other and each other's hair," Peter said. "Let's see what evolves. Good. Fantastic. Like that." The room filled with a sea of personalized movement that incorporated hair like a separate body part along with hips and knees, arms and torsos. A group dance began to evolve.

Nikkie was thrown back to her own experience of hair in ballet. Like most dancers, she had worn it pulled back in a bun. Smooth. All stray strands slicked down flat. The sense was that hair got in the way of movement, was individual. Buns blended.

When Nikkie had moved to improvisational solo dancing, her hair, like for Peter's dancers, had turned into an appendage with its own mind. It was no longer a wild child needing taming. It danced, shone as a separate shape, an extension of the truth that flowed inside her. It might start out resting against her back, its weight grounding her. But as she moved, the hair flew forward and back as she bent and arched. Freed up, it re-vealed spontaneity. The unexpected. It covered her face, then with a flick, it swung to the side or stretched out behind her. Like a wing. Like fire. Recalling her joy in that freedom, Nik-kie felt herself and her hair wanting to run into the middle of the dance floor and join Peter's dancers in their collaboration.

"Yes. I love it," Peter said, his face filled with color and joy. "Now try something a little different. Become looser still. Let yourself jerk, shake your body and your head. Imagine the release a duck uses when it has been in an altercation with an-other duck or has fled an eagle. Before the duck can return to its business of living, it first shakes off that encounter.

"Be that duck making the transition. Let yourselves vi-brate. Shake your heads and your hair. Move from rigid and frozen to shaking the encounter off, vibrating it off. Ripple the tension off your backs. Think of your own lives, how you or your families were when Latvia was being released from years of oppression. Let go of that oppression held in your bodies. That fear. Feel it. Be it. Let your bodies and your hair free to express that. That's it. Beautiful."

And as the dancers continued their exploration, in one un-expected motion, Peter turned away from them and toward Nikkie and Tom. He flashed them a smile that included them in this act of creation, in them witnessing it and his pleasure. He punctuated his motion with a quick nod and thumbs-up of acknowledgment as if he was colluding with them and they were creating along with him. Then, his focus returned to the collaboration on the floor, their connecting gaze following along with him. And with that short interlude, Nikkie recog-nized the gift Peter had given them, regardless of what hap-pened next. For one moment, Peter had taken them into his trusting, open heart.

She felt her yearning rise again, to have this man, this dancer, know and love her as his daughter, as she had loved him before she ever met him. That yearning was primal, a cry like a drop of rain sounding in emptiness as vast as Death Valley.

The yearning lived deep inside, had since childhood for both Tom and her. When they thought Peter had died and the desire would never be fulfilled, they were only seven years old. Ellie had led them in a ritual by a grandmother oak near a wilderness forest. Their name meant oak, she reminded them. Near the oak stood a birch tree. Berzins, like their father. They had buried acorns, leaves, and small branches from both trees.

Tom and she had also decided to bury the letters they had written to their father, in hopes they would find their way to Peter in the spirit world. "Are you sure you don't want to keep them?" Ellie had asked. Nikkie and Tom had rolled their eyes at each other and buried them. They had stacked a pile of stones, a cairn for his spirit like the Native Americans of the area used, to mark the spot.

She thought back to what she had written about to Peter in those letters—her love of dancing, how she wished they could dance together, what an inspiration he was. After that ritual, she had called on the impulse of what she imagined his ballet life had been like to keep studying and growing and to stretch past limits and fears. Out of love for him. In dedication to his memory. By the time she was ten, she knew dance was her life. "He would have wanted you to go on, to reach for the stars if you want," Ellie said, and Nikkie had done that. And now, even though Peter had no idea who they were, she was in his studio watching him in his own act of creation, reaching for the stars in a free country.

Chapter 18

Nikkie felt exposed, as she, Tom and Peter settled into an empty table near a window. *Not the place I would have chosen to tell him about us, but I'm ready. This is our moment.* Nikkie thought, but Tom's hand touched her arm as if the cautioning her at the crosswalk of an intersection, "Wait. Wait. Do not go. Wait."

"Please sit down. I will put in our order," Peter said. "This is on me, for my new American friends."

Nikkie ordered her usual chamomile tea to calm her. Tom chose a double espresso and a pastry.

"And I must apologize up front, but I need to cut our first meeting short," Peter said. "An unexpected opportunity has come up. But if you are willing, we can talk a bit now. Then, we can meet again in two days at my apartment. I could show you photos there of my years as a dancer, from the barricades and the Baltic Way."

After rehearsal, Peter had asked the twins to this coffee house outside of Old Town, modern with Swedish style blond wood furniture, all sleek lines and large glass windows streetside that invited the light to pour in.

"Let's tell him anyway," Nikkie insisted while they waited for Peter, feeling impatient and needing to free herself of the secret. Her heart resisted the logic of holding off until their next get-together when they would have less distraction.

"No," Tom resisted in turn. "What if he leaves in the middle of the conversation."

"We've waited long enough."

"Only two more days. Peter—and we –need the privacy to process his response."

Tom was right. But Nikkie's fears flared. Irrational or intuition warning her? What if Peter died or canceled between now and then? What if something happened to her or Tom? No time like the present.

"Let's not blow this when we're so close," Tom said. Nikkie sighed deep into the earth, hesitated, then squeezed Tom's hand, signaling reluctant agreement.

Nikkie brought herself to the present moment. They were going to have their first real no pressure conversation with their father. They would get to know him without the overlay of telling him who they were. It dissipated the strain of not telling him.

She admired Peter even more now that she had seen him in action with his dancers. She was already impressed by what he had accomplished as a dancer and a freedom fighter. Now, she was struck by how he had reinvented himself, risen like a phoenix, to lead his own dance company and support Māra's company.

Before Latvia became free, the U.S.S.R. mined many of the best and brightest young Latvian dancers, like Peter, as their own. But now, he was creating opportunities for those dancers in Latvia, she assumed to tempt them to stay or at least be known internationally as Latvians, like the renowned Latvian opera singers, conductors and classical musicians who graced the world's great stages from the Metropolitan to the Vienna Opera Houses.

"Peter, we would like to hear about your career, like what inspired you to leave the Nijinsky Ballet and return to Latvia," Tom said, opening the conversation.

Peter closed his eyes, let out a deep breath, as if sighing away a burden of a lifetime. "The chance to express my individual dance talent called me to Moscow as a boy. Being part of the ballet school and company was my chance to make a mark on the world, to become the best I could be at something I loved. But when I left Latvia, I also lost a part of my soul. A piece remained in the land and forests there.

Nikkie flashed on that piece awaiting Peter's return. It had lain on the ground in a Latvian forest covered in moss, guarded and nestled in a crook of an ancient oak.

"It was that and the united soul, the one heart of my country, that called me home in the late 1980s. And that soul was nowhere expressed as much as in Latvia's song and dance. The air was filled with the ringing of notes that came to be known as the Singing Revolution, our conscious nonviolent demonstration against the Communist dictatorship. Small groups, then tens of thousands, sometimes hundreds of thousands of people joined together in common purpose. To sing our way to freedom. We sang songs that had been banned.

"When I felt the collective awakening of my people, I woke up too. Latvia's freedom quest blasted through the wall around my heart. And I began to understand my true calling beckoned to something greater than being the best dancer at the ballet."

Nikkie thought back to her life during those years. She and Tom had been children, playing, expressing their creativity, exploring in beautiful Oregon. Latvia's freedom movement existed in the periphery of their lives as news their grandmother relayed to them during calls or visits. She participated in demonstrations and fundraising for it in Chicago, where she lived and worked then. "Growing up in the U.S., I've never been faced with choosing to fight for freedom," Nikkie said. "I assumed my one true calling was to dance. I have no idea how I would have responded faced with your circumstances."

"Sometimes, you have no choice. Peter nodded his head, motioned as if tipping his hat to them. "The impact of *Atmoda*, the Awakening, our term for what you might have known as Glasnost, stretched everywhere. In Latvia. The U.S.S.R. Even in the privilege of the Nijinsky Ballet. But so did repression. My partner in the Pas de Deux was arrested and died, was likely killed, in prison for his activities to free Russia. This radicalized me. It woke me out of a stupor. I realized I most needed to make my mark in my homeland. I needed to plant my feet on its earth once more even if those feet never danced again because of this choice. To reclaim my soul, I needed to join Latvians in their revolution.

"Before that, I thought dancing was everything, but this freedom was most important to me. This intangible that beckoned to my people and many nations still ruled by the Soviets."

"I'm almost ashamed to say freedom is something we've taken for granted," Tom said, and Nikkie agreed. "I'm beginning to understand what a privilege it's been, how fortunate we are."

"Yes. And worth every risk," Peter said. "I knew once I told the company I was leaving, I might be arrested. I might die. But I was ready to give it all up for a cause that was larger than me."

"What did happen?" Nikkie asked.

"I was fortunate," Peter said "I made up an excuse as to why I had to leave. What I said almost didn't matter. Hordes of younger dancers lined up ready to grab my vacated spot."

"Was giving up dancing difficult?" Nikkie asked. "Even in my situation, I feel quite lost without it."

"I was happy to be returning to Latvia," Peter said. "Yet in my choice, I cast myself adrift from the world that had been my chief focus since I was twelve years old, not to mention my cushion against the rigors of living in a Soviet-occupied country. At first, I felt like I was drowning. My heart would pound all night. I couldn't sleep. If I wasn't taking classes, rehearsing or performing, taking care of this body, who was I?"

"I can relate to that feeling less dramatically," Nikkie said. "I've been experiencing that sense of not knowing who I am since leaving Stone Tara and Julliard."

"But for me, I immediately had a purpose. I connected with those in the *Tautas Fronte*, the movement for independence in Latvia. I threw myself into that work with as much creativity, passion, and discipline as I had brought to dancing."

Not so different, Nikkie thought. She had an immediate purpose as well—to find the man now sitting in front of them and resolve the mystery of her vision.

"Then, I discovered the power of singing," Peter said. "I had always believed the arts, words, music, dance had the power to create a revolution for freedom. It is why artists are targeted and suppressed in dictatorships. As crazy as it seemed, the arts, especially singing songs that had been forbidden for decades, were what was driving change and the chance to be free in the Baltic nations. I threw myself into the mass singing, let myself, along with the populations of Latvia, Estonia and Lithuania, be buoyed by it, carried by it, like a wave rising to meet the shore."

"That's remarkable," Nikkie said. "Did you also have talent as a singer?"

Peter shook his head. "No more than the average person. Yet even today, when I hear one of our folk songs—we have more than one million, everything feels possible. When I open my mouth and sing with my countrymen and women, all is well."

"Over a million folk songs?" Tom said. "That's unbelievable. It's almost a song for every Latvian."

Peter nodded. "In 1989, whether or not Baltic people had singing ability, singing was not only in our soul, it was our soul. It still is. When I sang, I mattered. I'd venture to say most Latvians believed singing together mattered, especially the songs the Soviets had banned for so long."

"And whose voice excelled was insignificant," Tom said.

"That's right. Our collective voices exuded strength. And the way singing connected us to our common vision of freedom. It reminded us of our aliveness, brought us into the trees, the sun, the light. Our hearts and voices soared. Joining with Latvians, I sang for hope. I sang out my cares and sorrows. I sang my dreams. When hundreds of thousands, millions of voices in the Baltics sang as one, the experience was like chanting a common prayer."

Peter crossed his hands over his heart, then extended them, palms up, as if reaching out to the world. "We offered our songs, the melodies, to the heavens. We hoped God and the world could hear our collective voices. Our collective yearning and pain. Our collective joy."

"And the world did hear," Nikkie said, feeling her skin tingling as if the resonance of those historical voices still hung in the air around her.

"Yes, they did. Even if people in a distant land did not consciously know we were singing, I could sense our singing touched them. Maybe it opened their hearts for a moment, washed away their concerns, gave them hope. Perhaps even for you two."

"What a beautiful sentiment," Tom said.

"Singing was our choice to reawaken the feelings from a free Latvia," Peter said. "Our heart's work. Our sacrament. Our expression of love for the land beneath our feet. We would not have had a chance if we tried to use force or guns against the Soviet Union."

"I never thought of it that way," Tom said.

"Singing connected us to all peoples, including those who were our oppressors. It was the universal language. Energy beyond language. And we did it. On the Baltic Way, where we held hands across the three Baltic States; in the mass singing demonstrations in each country; in small gatherings of people in the countryside, in demonstrations of Latvia in the U.S. and other nations, we sang our way to freedom. When I helped build and protect the barricades against the Soviet's final takeover attempt of our government buildings, knowing the power of joining together in songs that we had been forbidden to sing for years gave me the courage to face Soviet tanks, guns and possible death."

Nikkie felt a quivering in her heart hearing about her father's participation in Latvia's freedom.

"After Latvia was freed, we felt so much excitement," Peter said. "But I did not know what to do next. I had, what you call 'burned my bridges' in Moscow. I was in my thirties. Relentless dancing had taken a toll on my body. Not dancing, for the first time since I was a child, my body was out of pain. I wanted to learn how to live outside of a dance studio, to find the balance in what had been an unbalanced life. Maybe you know this feeling, Nikkie? I am sure in New York, you did not have much time for the rest of life."

Nikkie nodded. "In ways, this trip to Latvia is the first time I have had away from dancing since childhood. I see how little I know of myself if I am not dancing."

"You understand then," Peter said. "But the big question for me in 1991– and for you now—was what to do next. Initially, I threw myself into the rebuilding of Latvia but found myself too exhausted to participate fully. I decided to explore what freedom meant. I rested. I traveled to Italy and France. I relearned how to enjoy life, free to go wherever I wanted. But once my body and heart healed, I missed dancing. I had changed though. My passion had turned from traditional to modern dance, like the Pas de Deux. I longed for its greater freedom and how it was not dependent on certain body types or how old or young the dancer was."

"I've always been drawn to contemporary forms," Nikkie said. "And improv, of course. How did you get started again?"

"I met Pina Hoffman, the German modern dance choreographer, performer and ballet director. She orchestrated elaborate collaborations with her performers. I joined her company."

"I know her work," Nikkie said. "But Tom and I never got to see her perform live."

"Yes, then after a couple years, I yearned for Latvia, wanted to bring more modern and contemporary dance forms here as part of the country's rebuilding. An old friend, Olga Vilks, started a contemporary dance company in Latvia in 1996. I joined it, taught, learned about raising money for the arts. Then with her encouragement, I formed my company. And who knows, Nikkie. Perhaps that is why we are meeting. You are at a crossroads. Perhaps it is time to collaborate with members of a company. You have much to offer. I go by my gut. I would like to invite you to dance with us here some time. You have a gift to share."

Nikkie felt her face flush. Dance with her father's company? How accurate was the old refrain that she wanted to be a solo act? She already felt drawn to Māra's company. Now, the thought of collaborating with her father filled her with possibility. The same sense of "everything is possible" that hung in the air in Riga. And that she had not felt around her dance in months.

"That's an interesting notion," Tom said.

"It's a generous offer," Nikkie said. "Thank you. I'm not sure I'm ready, but…" What was she thinking? This was her father. Her *father* had asked her to collaborate.

She had dreamt of this moment. Not ready? "…yes. Yes. I'd love to do that."

"*Forši*," he said. "That means 'great' in a 'cool' way in Latvian by the way. Let's talk more about it when you come to my apartment."

Peter looked for a moment at the clock on the wall. Nikkie's stomach fluttered. He would leave soon. She wanted to hold on somehow. To this moment. To this conversation.

"I wondered if I could squeeze in one more question," Tom said.

Peter looked at the clock again. "Please go on."

"I hope this is not overly forward, but in the Soviet days when you were touring, did you ever consider defecting? Clearly, you had strong feelings about freedom."

Peter stiffened, paused, then spoke. "Every dancer thought about it. And two dancers from Latvia, Baryshnikov and Godunov, had already done it. But you must excuse me. I must go now. Please, let us continue this talk. In two days, you come to my apartment where we have privacy. And *you* will come to dance with me." He tilted his head, looked at Nikkie, pulled his head back as if observing something he had not seen up until this point.

What was it she saw? Surprise? Concern? Fear? She started. It was the same look she had seen on his face in her vision. When he held the child. When he repeated the words, *"Palīdz man."* Did he need her help? And what about her? Did she need his? Right now, she would need help waiting two days until they met again.

He put his attention on Tom now. "And when you come, I will tell you about the one time I almost defected. In America. A woman was involved, of course." He put his thumb and index finger up close together, the smallest of spaces between them. "I came this close. But now I must go."

Chapter 19

To take the family's minds off the impending meeting with Peter, Indra suggested they take a day trip to visit the historic sites at Turaida Museum Reserve near Sigulda. Their first stop there was the grave of Turaida's Rose, who died in 1620. The Rose, a beautiful 19-year-old maiden had chosen to perish at the hand of a soldier, who wanted to force her to marry him, rather than deceive her fiancée and true love, a gardener. Her act became a symbol of eternal love and devotion, and newly-weds continued to come to her grave with the hopes it would bless their union.

Nikkie could not help but wonder if Ellie and Peter would have known that depth of love if their relationship had been given a chance to flourish—or if she or Tom would ever know anything like it. So far, she only felt that devotion for her dancing and needed more to reaffirm that vow than become involved with a man. She hoped dancing with Peter's company would help.

"Mom, I think this is a great spot for you to tell us your story of meeting Peter again," Nikkie said. "I don't know that Indra has ever heard it, and we were children the last time you told us. I'm sure you censored a lot."

Ellie smiled. "Sure. It's a good time to remember something positive." She paused, closed her eyes for a moment, opened them and began. "The first time I saw Peter, he was wearing nothing but pale green tights. He had this blond hair, long on top, that fell forward over his forehead like a wave. It crested above these pale blue eyes that exuded intensity, poetry and a spark of something—humor I'd say. He had a great build of course. It was pure luck I met him at all."

Ellie explained she had scored a temporary job at the Chicago Ballet Theater for the Nijinsky Ballet performances because the wife of a Latvian ceramicist with whom Ellie was interning that summer worked there.

"Peter noticed me too," Ellie said. "Part of my job was handing out costumes. I remember our eyes locked. I swear my heart beat faster. I was trying to look hip, wearing these cool, high top black shoes, a fitted black skirt and purple top. He smiled at me, the same half smile you have, Tom—like we were already sharing a private joke."

Nikkie ran her hand over the smooth surface of the stone on the bench they sat on. She relished hearing Ellie tell her love story now when she might learn details about her parents Nikkie had not known.

"My imagination must be on overdrive, I thought," Ellie said. "He most likely wants to cover up. It was air-conditioned—cold even for a Russian, or I knew he could have been one of the two Latvians in the ballet with his high cheekbones, blond hair, blue eyes, and the height.

"'He greeted me and asked for his costume in Latvian. I couldn't figure out how he knew I was Latvian until he picked up my hand and pointed to this ring." Ellie lifted her hand to show the twins the ring on her left ring finger. It was a traditional Latvian ring with dangles and ancient symbols that Indra had given her when she was fifteen. Nikkie had never known Ellie not to wear it.

"But my ring was not what I noticed as he held my hand." Ellie stroked her left hand with her right one. "When he touched me, my hand felt like it had been plugged into a socket. And what did I do? You'd think growing up in Chicago, I would have maintained a semblance of urban cool. But no. I giggled. I'm sure I grinned. And blushed. I remember rising heat in my face and neck." She blushed once more as she shared the memory.

Ellie had explained to Peter most of the costumes were late because they had not made it on the plane. The first shipment had arrived though, and she offered to look for the one in the pile with his name. "Peter Berzins," he said. He shared the same surname as one of her mother's second cousins, she noted, mentioned maybe they were related but inside, hoped they were not.

"He told me it was unlikely since it was a common name. He asked if mine was also Berzins. No birches in my immediate family, I answered. Only oaks. Elīna Ozolins, I said, then told him my nickname, Ellie."

Ellie's face lit up. "He said, I'm much happier to have you as a charming and beautiful new American friend than a cousin, Ellie."

At that moment, the dancer behind Peter poked him in the back and let out a stream of Russian words Ellie did not need a translator to understand. Some equivalent of, "Stop talking to the Latvian chick and move along. I'm freezing."

Peter shrugged, accepted his green sequined costume and thanked her. "*Es ceru ka mēs atkal satiksimies,*" he said in Latvian. "I hope we meet again."

"I hoped he meant it," Ellie said.

The next opportunity to talk to Peter came at a reception for the ballet, she explained. "I had already seen him dance. He seemed to shine on stage, stood out for me with his jumps and charisma. He performed in small groups of men or men and women. I couldn't take my eyes off him.

"When I saw him at the reception—this time he was wearing an open shirt with a black fitted suit jacket—I was a goner.

I wore a long dress cut low in front and back that I bought for the event. The two dancers with him seemed to fall away when Peter and I came together as if we created a magnetic field only we could enter.

"The first time we kissed was that night in the dressing room he shared with another dancer. A couple of days later, we made love and talked on the private rooftop garden patio of the small boutique hotel where the dancers were staying. The Chicago skyline served as our witness. It was a hot August night—a time out of time."

The couple felt a real heart connection and spent as much time together as possible for the next few days. Ellie imagined what might happen if he would defect but did not mention it. She also knew how unlikely that was. Ballet was his life. His company was one of the best in the world. Ellie, who had recently graduated from college, hoped to build a business as a potter and artist and had plans to join an arts collective in rural Oregon.

Before either of them voiced fantasies about a future to-gether, one of the principal male dancers did defect. The media descended. Security clamped down. And all private access to the touring dancers was cut off.

"I did not get to say good-bye alone," Ellie said. "Only in a crowd of people with the crew and guards present. I sensed sadness in his eyes. Perhaps it was my own sadness projected there. A few weeks later, after I moved to Oregon, I realized I was pregnant."

Ellie shifted on the bench, reached over and touched Nik-kie, who sat next to her, on the shoulder. "I was determined you would grow up free, unlike your father, and wanted to encourage you to believe in yourselves and your dreams. And now you've met him, and he'll soon know who you are. I just hope he won't be angry at me for keeping you a secret from him."

The plan was for Ellie to join the twins when they went to visit Peter at his apartment, and they would tell him who they were together.

"Who knows?" Ellie said. "Maybe Peter doesn't even remember me."

Not remember? Nikkie had not considered that possibility.

"I doubt that's true," Tom said. "I bet that the woman he said was a reason he almost defected was you."

Nikkie hoped what Tom said was true. Ellie had been one year younger than the twins when she met Peter—only two years older than Turaida's Rose at her death. Nikkie contemplated the thought of handling a similar situation. Would she make a choice to become a mother to one, let alone two, children, given her dreams of dancing?

But Ellie had not let the inevitable challenges deter her. Nikkie believed her choice revealed a courageous love and devotion the Rose of Turaida would have acknowledged and understood. Nikkie felt a renewed respect and gratitude for her mother.

The Folk Song and Sculpture Park's massive modern stone sculptures spread out on a grassy hillside above Turaida castle, which had been built from the 11th to 13th centuries. The snakelike Gauja River wound through lush green forests and parkland below it. There, Indra asked her family to talk about what they were feeling about their ancestral heritage now that they had spent some time in Latvia.

"Growing up, I was focused on dance, not my ancestry," Nikkie said. "Even my interest in my father was around dancing. But being here, experiencing Latvia's vitality, I wish I had learned more about it, especially how to speak the language."

Nikkie turned and admired the span of history surrounding her—from the hill fort to the modern sculptures. "I have also discovered here that so much of what's important to me—a love of nature, a connection to the spiritual in nature, creative expression, music, dance, the arts—has its roots in my Latvian heritage."

"It's true," Indra said. "And the Latvian folk songs celebrated here in these sculptures reflect what is important as well. Song is the constant for Latvians from birth to death. And our wisdom and values were passed on in an oral tradition through our songs."

She pointed to a sculpture, an oval gray stone with words carved in it. "This puts that idea into context. It translates, *I was born and raised singing.*" Further on, Indra pointed out the Krišjānis Barons trail to the Gauja River and explained that Barons, who lived in Turaida in the early twentieth century, collected two hundred thousand Latvian folk songs and was considered their father.

As the four walked, the sky clouded over, and Nikkie felt a chill in the breeze. She put on the light jacket she carried in her day pack. The changes in weather and temperature reminded her of Oregon where she always traveled with layers to add or discard.

"What about you, Elīna?" Indra asked. "Do you now appreciate more why I sent you to Latvian school on Saturdays when you were growing up to learn the language and culture?"

"I definitely feel more connected to the country and the land, and I've always loved its culture," Ellie said. "Growing up in America, I had wanted to assimilate, to be like my American friends. But, unlike me, most of the American friends knew little about the countries of their family lineage. I felt like something of an outsider, especially since there are so few Latvians. Now that I am here, I feel like I do belong. I see my face in the faces of the Latvians in Riga. It reminds me that I share an ancestral history not only in this country but with the Latvians I grew up around in the U.S. Like Indra, their parents and grandparents had almost all escaped Communism and Nazism and worked hard to create new lives in America."

"I would have liked to experience my culture more," Tom said. "I wished we had lived near a Latvian community. That's why I chose to go to Latvian camp."

Indra nodded approvingly. "As Latvian immigrants, we also knew it was up to us to make sure we kept our culture alive because the Soviets were trying to eradicate it in Latvia. That tradition of passing on the culture and language to our children in the U.S. continues even now that Latvia is free. The Latvian Saturday school in Chicago still has more than one hundred children."

"But growing up, I hated that sense of responsibility," Ellie said. "It felt like a guilt trip. Like if I didn't speak the language, learn folk songs and history, go to Latvian School, join Latvian Girl Scouts, marry a Latvian, the Soviets would succeed. The culture would die. And it would be my fault."

"Lucky for us though, you did manage to have Latvian children," Nikkie said, and her family laughed with her.

"My own resistance to that cultural responsibility growing up is why I never forced Latvian anything on you, Nikkie and Tom, but let you find your own way—according to your own interests," Ellie said.

"I did not have that same resistance," Tom said. "I loved coming from a country hardly anyone ever heard of. And speaking a language only a couple million people spoke was cool. When I told Americans where my family was from, they'd ask, 'Where's that?' They'd mispronounce it, call it something like 'Laff-ia.' LAT-vee-ya, I'd emphasize."

Ellie laughed. "I still find that all the time," and Nikkie and Indra agreed.

"What I remember most is you wanted us to be free of having to be identified by either culture," Nikkie said. "Not 'Ra Ra' America or 'Ra Ra' Latvia or 'Ra Ra' any nationality."

"You got it," Ellie said. "I didn't want you to deny your roots, but I suggested you look towards what I termed a heartland, rather than a homeland. I am against any notion that one country is worthier than another. It's led to many problems in the world. Wars and occupations."

"Yet Latvian identity is in all of our blood," Indra said.

"That it is," Ellie said.

"And I am proud of that identity," Indra said. "Latvians are everywhere, and we are being recognized, especially for our contributions in the world in music.

"As you should be proud, mama," Ellie said. "We all can be. And like Nikkie, being here, I'm understanding more and more what a huge influence Latvia has been in my life, not only positive though, challenging too. Which reminds me, have any of you heard about the field of epigenetics and the new research around it regarding trauma?" The twins and Indra shook their heads no.

"Indra's psychologist friend, Birute, had mentioned it to me when Indra and I had tea with her the day you went to Māra's studio, and I read more about it on the internet afterward," Ellie said. "I had wanted to get your take on what she said. What epigenetics shows is that ancestral trauma—including that from war and oppression—can be passed down through our DNA to the next generations."

Nikkie flashed back to the traumatic events in her visions of the dead in the Latvian forests, wondered if they were somehow linked to trauma passed down through her own family's DNA. "So, are you saying our family's trauma impacts us even though we did not experience a traumatic event ourselves?" Nikkie felt shivers of recognition running up and down her arms.

Ellie nodded. "Given the occupations and wars here, most Latvians, our family included, must carry ancestral trauma. And if we don't recognize that, epigenetics says it can unconsciously drive our actions—and be passed on to future generations."

"Post-traumatic stress disorder from the occupation and even the war does remain an issue for many here," Indra said. "And depression. Birute also mentioned she thinks it will take three generations to heal it more fully."

"So, how can we recognize the trauma—and not take it on?" Tom asked.

"I'm wondering if that's part of why I had the vision. It was certainly a traumatic situation," Nikkie added.

"That's an interesting idea, Nikkie," Ellie said. "It might well be. But to answer Tom's question, Birute also told us about a method people are using to heal family traumas. Have you heard about family constellation work developed by Bert Hellinger?"

The twins had not.

"It's a group process that highlights how we have unconsciously taken on suffering in a family. Participants sit in a circle. The person setting a constellation chooses which participants will represent both the family members involved in a particular family dynamic and other contributing factors or supportive influences like a country of family origin or an illness. Birute shared some about a series of constellations she took part in."

"Can you tell us any of what she experienced?" Tom asked.

"She could not share specifics," Ellie said. "But what she did say was the work shifts the imbalances created by old family traumas—like wars, deaths and illnesses—so love can flow through the family system again. The families can start to free themselves and their children from old family traumas. Latvia came up in her own constellation, she said. And she experienced both her Latvian ancestors' suffering and their strength. The constellation helped her more directly draw on that strength."

Nikkie imagined what ancestral strength might feel like in her life. For her, what seemed like dozens of invisible hands, Līze's hands, Karlīna's, Lilija's hands, known and unknown ancestors' hands, radiated healing and life force energy into her upper back. And to her surprise, as she opened to receive it, the grief she held surrounding the Hollywood Bowl and its aftermath, around her own family history, began to ease its grip on her heart.

Chapter 20

"I keep thinking about how mom has told us she and Peter were in love," Nikkie said. "I'm not sure I would be open to falling in love right now."

Nikkie and Tom sat on modern dark leather armchairs in an upscale Old Town bar that could have been in New York. After Turaida, Ellie and Indra had gone back to the apartment, and the twins had gone out on their own. The bar counter was sleek, shiny and black reflecting the overhead track lighting. Modern art in shades of black, white and red graced the walls, the color playing off white cushions on shiny metal bar stools.

"I love the idea of love," Nikkie said. "But isn't it weird I haven't ever been in love?"

"I wouldn't worry about it," Tom said. "We're only twenty-two. Besides, you do love dance. Now is your time to love it and shine. Better to channel your emotions and energy into knowing who you are as an artist, especially while you're at your physical peak. That won't last."

The air in the bar was scented with sweet and bitter—high-end cocktails and alcohol mingled with floral tones of red and white gladiolas and roses arranged in clear heavy glass containers. They reminded her of the flowers in a clear vase Sean kept on the coffee table in his New York loft, blood red roses or fiery dahlias.

"I may love dance, but does it love me? I don't exactly know who I am as a dancer at the moment—not since Stone Tara." Nikkie gazed at one of the modern paintings on the wall. The swirling shapes appeared to be in motion like she longed to be.

This bar might be in the land of her own ancestors, but it was not about the old. It was about moving on into the new. Like Latvia was doing. Like she needed to move on from Stone Tara.

"What about you?" Nikkie asked.

Tom smiled. "Love is not forefront in my mind."

"Not even potential love? Like with Elizabete?" Nikkie poked him in the side.

"Not even her, though I do like her," Tom said. "But I am thinking about what's next."

"Do you know what that is?"

Tom nodded. "It's this place. Latvia." He paused. "I want to move here."

Nikkie felt a bubble of energy burst in her belly, drain down and out her legs, taking her grounding with it.

"And why not move with me," Tom said. "I mean, how cool would it be to live in Europe, where dancers and singers and poets and artists are actually appreciated? Supported even. Much more so than in the U.S."

"But my opportunity to dance is there."

"Is it? You could dance here. With Peter, maybe on an ongoing basis. And thanks to me, we are dual citizens and could do it without any hassle."

When Latvia had been freed, it had opened up the opportunity for Latvians, who had escaped and not returned because of the Occupation, to become dual citizens. That extended to later generations, who had also been born in a foreign land. Tom had insisted Ellie go through the process, so he and Nikkie could get Latvian passports in addition to their U.S. ones. He had wanted the options dual citizenship afforded.

"Plus, it will be even cooler when Latvia votes to become part of the European Union," Tom said. "Then, we could live and travel and work anywhere in it, not only Latvia."

And where did Nikkie's own heart call her to be? A wave of panic bubbled up, no action seeming to help her feel stabilized. Was moving here what her dance—and life—needed?

"All I know is when I think about going back to New York or the States, I feel dead inside," Tom said, and Nikkie was surprised to discover that she did too. "Here, I sense so much possibility. I could start writing poetry again. I'm sure of it."

But you are my manager, my brother, my best friend—you can't leave, Nikkie wanted to scream, but did not. That was her own self-interest, not what was best for Tom.

Of course, he needed to write again. Poetry was his unique gift.

"It's a great idea," Nikkie forced herself to say. "Really. I'd be thrilled to see you someplace you're called to be—especially writing again." Despite her ambivalence, she did want the best for her brother.

"I read this cool quote from a German geographer and traveler, J.G. Khol, in one of *vecāmamma's* books. He said, 'Every Latvian is a born poet; they all compose verses and songs, and they can all sing these songs . . . They deserve to be called the nation of poets.'"

"That's so appropriate," Nikkie said. "And certainly, true of you."

"Thanks. I can't wait to explore that creative side of me again and see how it wants to express itself here."

"That sounds so right," Nikkie said. "I don't know about me moving here though. There's so much unknown right now, including Peter's response when he finds out who we are. But for you? I'm happy."

"Let's celebrate," Tom said.

Nikkie pushed aside the San Pellegrino sparkling water she had been drinking and ordered two glasses of Absolut vodka over ice.

Tom looked at her quizzically. "I didn't mean *you* should drink. Are you sure you want to?" He pointed to the glasses the bartender set in front of them.

"It's Swedish, right? I thought that was a good brand. I didn't feel right ordering a Russian one."

"Very funny." Tom picked up one of the glasses and raised it to her. "You know what I mean. You don't drink, remember? We need to be in good shape for Peter."

"Do we? I'm sick of needing to stay in good shape. I've held back from imbibing all my life to stay in shape for dancing. What better time to live a little? A few shots can't hurt. Maybe they're what I need to give me the extra courage to talk to Peter—and to make major life decisions, whether I make them with a hangover or not."

"Hangovers are not all that fun."

"Okay. Drink enough to relax then. How about I promise only to get half-loaded?" Nikkie grinned.

"Hey, you're an adult. It's time I back off and let you become a true Latvian. Trial by vodka. But since I'm the more experienced twin in this arena—well, the only one with experience—how about you let me be the designated cobblestone navigator and take my arm like a good sister on our way home."

"Done," Nikkie said, fear receding. She could do anything she pleased now that she didn't have commitments to a dance tour. Peter would accept or reject them as his children soon enough. And tonight, she couldn't do anything about hunting for the dead either.

She would fortify herself with a drink or two—or three. Like a warrior preparing for battle. She would relinquish years of dancer discipline in favor of a wilder, more fiery side of her. She would discover firsthand what Tom, the band, and so many others found unique about getting lit.

She held the cold glass in her hand filled with the clear iced liquid she pretended was spring water, lifted it to her lips and drank half the glass.

"Whoa, Nik. If you're going to do this, do it properly," Tom said. "Drink a full glass of water first and let me order us some food."

Nikkie rolled her eyes but accepted the water Tom offered and guzzled it. Then, before he could say another word, before she lost her nerve, before the bread and cheese he ordered arrived, she tossed back the rest of the vodka as well. It slithered down her throat, took her breath away, left heat in its icy wake. It filled her belly, rushed to her head as though she'd injected it.

But instead of bravado, instead of good feelings, deep insecurity flashed back to the surface. *What if I'm merely a loser,* she thought, munching on a piece of cheese, and realized that was what she had feared since the Stone Tara failure. But it was what she wanted to drown out with a drink, not invite in. *Maybe I need another,* she thought, put down the cheese, and ordered another round.

"I'm counting," Tom said, a bemused expression on his face.

Nikkie lifted her glass to him. "Count away." She toasted him. *"Prosīt."* Drinking again, she sought out the arms alcohol offered to hold her and numb her pain. A delicious haze permeated her consciousness, seeping in like smoke from a smoldering fire, spreading, burning up, smothering her brain function and thoughts of loser-dom.

Rock music played over the sound system now. The lyrics were in Latvian, she thought. Laughter. People, like her, out to have a good time. Their voices seemed to grow louder. They wanted release from the cares of the day. She aspired to escape too. Escape from the promise she'd made to dance with Peter's company, afraid she had nothing to express. Escape from the responsibility of revealing they were his children. Escape from the probability of Tom moving to Latvia and leaving her alone.

After their third round, Tom suggested she might have had enough, might want to take it easy. But what did he know? Maybe she would drink him under the table—wasn't that the expression? While she had been restraining, he had imbibed himself silly on numerous occasions. It never stopped him from doing it again.

She downed a fourth, let out a deep sigh. *I thought drinking was supposed to drown sorrows, not amplify them.* Nikkie felt increasingly mired in a cesspool of negativity.

"This sucks," Nikkie said out loud. "It's not fun at all. I'm out of here." She started impulsively walking, more like weaving her way to the door, as she had seen Tom, Sean and his bandmates, and other friends do on occasion. She turned back around and saw Tom walking toward her, arm extended.

"Come on, Nik. Remember our agreement. I'm the designated cobblestone navigator. I've got ya covered. Let's get you—and me—home while I can still walk. I may have celebrated a bit much myself." No judgment in his voice. Only love. The love she hoped to hear in Peter's voice the next day. The love she wanted to hear in her own voice when she talked to herself. The love of the audience when she danced. The love she did hope to hear from a beloved in the future. In the now, Tom's love bobbed toward her like a buoy in a rough sea, up and down, bouncing over the waves into her heart. She reached forward and slipped her arm through his.

"How many times did I lead you home after a night on the town?" Nikkie asked. "Mr. Navigator. It's about time you returned the favor." Did she speak that out loud or had she thought it, she wondered when Tom did not respond?

They walked out of the bar. Walking was an overstatement. Tom walked. Kind of. She alternately lurched. Wove.

Stumbled. The cobblestones and sidewalk were slick after a summer evening rain. She felt like the Leaning Tower of Pisa shifted off balance, ready to topple. Why the heck did she have to be so tall? She seemed to be on a moving walkway trying to balance on one leg.

"Take a breath, Nik," Tom said. "You're fine. I'm fine. I think. We'll get a cab at the edge of Old Town."

The distance between Nikkie's head and the sidewalk loomed monumentally. From the top of the "Leaning Tower of Nikkie" to the ground. Up to down, down, way down below. How had she gotten to this state? She who always seemed so sanguine in the face of challenge. Tom was the one with the edge. Until now, she had hopscotch skipped through life leaping over cobblestones and tall buildings, hitting the mark. Winning the game. A winner. Now she was no more than a tipsy tower on a tear, a bender. What if her father saw her now?

"Only a few more blocks," Tom said. "Keep focusing. One step at a time. You've done enough of that as a dancer."

And Nikkie cringed at the word. Dancer. Would she be that again with Peter? Or anywhere else? Why not start right here? Her alcohol bravado reared.

And with it, she released herself from Tom's hold on her arm and willed herself to turn. She may not be able to walk on water, but she could at least twirl on cobblestones. *Let Peter see me now.* And she pitched from one foot to the other, prodding her legs to cooperate and turn—Did she have three all of a sudden? She managed to extend her arms for balance.

Her bravado was short-lived. Negative Nikkie returned full force. If Peter and the twins' connection lasted and she was able to dance with his company, how was she going to live up to the standards of the mighty Nijinsky Ballet? Or the moral high road of a freedom fighter?

Soon he'd find out how talent-challenged and wimpy she was. She also was not up to the task of traipsing through the woodlands of Latvia in search of dead people who needed healing.

"Stop, Nik." She heard Tom's voice as if in a fog. "I'm having a hard enough time walking a straight line myself after those drinks, let alone taking care of newbie you. And stop beating yourself up. It hurts my head to hear it from you."

Nikkie cringed. She had not realized she was talking out loud. The self-negation stopped, replaced by amplification of head spinning. She stumbled, tumbled in earnest, headed down, down, down to the street. Weightless. Relax, her dancer training called out, and she did.

Tom reached for her, grabbed to take hold of her, catch her. But he lost his own balance in the process and fell, too. His head hit a pilaster first, bounced off a stone step like a rubber ball to the sidewalk—but not before making a sound, like a mallet smacking the ground. She should have taught him how to fall like a dancer, to be weightless. Like her. No substance. Letting go. Rolling away.

Voices shouted nearby, came closer.

Tom lay face to face with her, half splayed on the sidewalk, half on the street, warm liquid spread against her cheek. Had she vomited on herself? Purr-fect. Vision blurred. Why was Tom lying on the sidewalk? Oh right, he had been drinking too, had tried to catch her. A fine pair.

And then, her voice. "Tom? Are you okay? I'm so sorry I messed up. I didn't want you to fall. You're going to have some bruise tomorrow. And it's my fault." Her head cleared the slightest bit.

She opened her eyes. Blood pooled under Tom's head, which was bent back like a bird that had flown into the glass pane of a picture window. Nikkie tried to repeat his name, but it froze in her mind, would not move out her lips past her thought. Her head spun worse than the night at the Hollywood Bowl. She felt a sharp pain where she had hit it. Or was it even her own pain she was feeling? Maybe…. She reached over to touch Tom's face…It was his. No response.

She closed her eyes, forced herself to open them again, hoped the vision would change. Her eyelids hurt. The pool of red fanned out around the side of Tom's head on the sidewalk, like the circle the red dress she had worn at the Hollywood Bowl made. It extended toward her, flaring, taunting like the skirt of that dress.

No, she thought. "No," she managed to say out loud. Then blackness filled her field.

Nikkie was whirling on stage but got so dizzy and nauseous she threw up—in front of the whole audience. Shame and panic swept through her, but she made herself look out. Instead of the disgust she expected to see on the people's faces, she saw acceptance, care.

The scene changed. Tom was dressed in a long, white robe. He beckoned to her, but they were separated by a transparent, gelatinous substance. No matter how hard she tried, she could stretch toward him, but not break through. He looked murky, out of focus. Behind him, she made out a blurred view of the woods where they had spent so much time as children. And interwoven, the forest of the vision in Latvia. Tom moved his mouth as if he was calling out, but she could not hear or lip-read his words.

She felt more and more desperate to reach him. Conversely, he seemed calm, relaxed. He opened the robe to reveal his chest. Instead of skin, his chest was orange tree bark, like that of the madrone tree on which they had carved their names as ten-year-olds pretending to be lost in the woods. In fact, their names were there, carved into Tom's chest.

She tried to touch them but could not. The substance stretched, but her hand remained inches away from Tom's torso, sprung back. She began crying, frantic.

In response, Tom placed his hand up against hers on the other side of the transparent barrier, which had now solidified like glass.

He matched her hand, palm to palm, finger to finger. She thought of how prison inmates and their loved ones connected with each other across barriers in this way. Then, the words flashed, "Who's in prison now?"

She looked back up from their hands toward Tom's face again. But it was no longer his. Tom's face had morphed into her own. Her own blue eyes now stared back at her across the obstruction.

Nikkie drifted, the side of her head hurting, neck cramped, her heart pounding. She heard voices, close now. Lights flashed. She tried to ignore them, wanted to sleep. Her mouth tasted like cotton. A light shone in her face. Voices again. Were they talking to her? She squeezed her eyes tighter. *Go away,* she thought, then felt the hard, rough surface below her, the sudden shock of remembering where she was. She reached out to the emptiness in front of her.

"Tom."

No response. She forced her eyes open, reached over to where Tom had been. Then, the voices. Not Tom's.

"Tom," she said once more, panic rising, driving away the lingering haze of alcohol. An unfamiliar man leaned down close to her where Tom had been and touched her arm with compassion she knew she did not deserve.

"*Palīdz man,*" she asked anyway. "*Palīdz mums,*" echoing the words her father had spoken in her vision.

Chapter 21

Nothing could have prepared Nikkie for the shock of seeing her brother, face black and blue, unconscious, connected to tubes. High tech machinery made high-pitched beeps and whirs. Flashing graphs showed the beat of Tom's life force pulsing in his body.

"Coma," the doctor told her, Ellie and Indra in English, without a trace of Latvian accent. She explained Tom's brain was swollen from an injury sustained during the fall. The coma was the body's reaction to allow the brain a chance to rest and heal. They were testing to ascertain the extent of the damage, hopefully not permanent, and what specific treatment steps to take. The good news was nothing was broken.

How could any of this be good news, except that Tom was still alive? Most distressing about Tom's appearance was not the bruising and swelling. Nikkie had expected Tom to look as if he were sleeping, like people she'd seen in comas in movies. Instead, his personality appeared to have dissolved. His expression was flat, devoid of energy, no visible Tom-ness, no sign of the infamous irreverence which could exasperate her so.

"I don't mean to freak you both out, but Tom looks like he's not even in his body. It's like the shell of him." Nikkie's throat constricted and breath shortened.

"But he's still our Tom. The doctor—and nurses—told us it's normal," Indra said.

"Well, having a medical professional tag the word 'normal' to anything so abnormal as a coma is not particularly reassuring," Nikkie said.

"Sit down and talk to him," Ellie encouraged. "That's what I've been doing. You'll feel better. I've read when you talk to people in comas, they can hear you."

"I've read that as well. I've just never had to do it." Nikkie sat down, her mind blank.

"I don't know what to say." She turned to her mother. "Other than to keep repeating how sorry I am. Tom, I'm so sorry you got hurt trying to keep me from hurting myself." Guilt and shame rained in and pooled in the pit of her stomach.

People got drunk every night. Tons drove when they shouldn't, and for most, the most significant consequence was a hangover and some dead brain cells. But no. One time, she drank too much. She acted out. Yes, of course, she acted out. Tom had recognized that, listened like he always did, asked her to take it easy, to slow down on the shots. And now they were in the hospital.

"It was an accident," Ellie said. "Yes, you got high. But no one blames you, except you. I don't."

"I don't either," Indra said. "And Tom wouldn't blame you. It could easily be you lying on that bed after trying to help Tom."

That part was true. The role had been reversed on more than one occasion. Nikkie had sat in a bar while Tom drank and had made sure he got home safely. But now. What if he didn't wake up? What if he had permanent damage? What could they do? "I can't just sit here," she said.

"You're not just sitting here." Ellie came up beside Nikkie and put her hand on her shoulder. "You're loving him. With this face. Hold his hand and be with him. It's okay. I already asked the nurse."

Nikkie lay the weight of Tom's hand on hers. It felt cool to the touch, not corpse cold.

Nikkie closed her eyes and focused on her heart, saw Tom as he had been in her mind's eye. His half smile. His angular face. Then, she felt him, felt the life force in his hand. She extended her fingers toward his wrist. His pulse beat strong and steady. A wave of reassurance and love swept through her.

"Hello, Tom," she said. "I may not be able to see you in your face, but I know you're in there. I can definitely feel you." She squeezed his hand gently. "And your pulse. You'll be glad to know that heart of yours is still pumping."

She gathered her thoughts, leaning into Ellie's touch on her shoulders. She flashed on the photos she had passed in the lobby of Latvian countryside. A stork on a haystack. A creek running in blurred motion over rocks, its water a mix of milky white, the reflected blue of the sky and the green of plant life. Sun filtering through a stand of birch trees.

She wished they were there, smelling the forest, hearing running water, birds and wind. She longed to be anywhere with Tom but in ICU, where a faint scent of antiseptic permeated the air. The main sounds were the pings of elevator doors opening and closing, wheeled things—gurneys, wheelchairs, hospital equipment—rolling across tile floors, hospital staff talking, and the squeaks of nurses' sensible shoes rushing up and down hallways.

When she opened her eyes, she looked around the room, taking it in. She noted with gratitude that Ellie had added personal touches to the sterile environment.

"Tom, Ellie has already redecorated the place." Nikkie scanned his face again for any glimmer of a response. Nothing. She looked over to the bedside table. "She brought photos. Let's see. One shows the whole family in front of the yurt. We're about thirteen. You're wearing a Grateful Dead t-shirt. I'm in purple and pink tie-dye. Our hippy phase. There's one of you up in the maple tree in our yard. The one with the big leaves. And a shot of us in Central Park last year. You'll be happy to know we're dressed in black and looking hip. Oh, and you'll love this. Ellie's draped a rose-colored silk scarf over the bedside lamp—like she always did at home. Trust me, it improves the hospital lights big time."

"The quilt is here too," Indra added. "The hand-crocheted one I made with my mother, Lilija, your great-grandmother. Each square is a unique creation of flowers and leaves, in white and yellow and beige and brown tones. Remember how you hid under it when I wanted you to recite a Latvian poem before you got your Christmas presents?"

When Tom was nine years old, he had wrapped the quilt around his body and head as he sat on the couch, knees drawn up to his chest, waiting for his grandmother to ask for the dreaded annual recitation before she would give him his present. Only his eyes and face peered out.

"You looked like you were in a cocoon, and I asked if you would come out to spread your wings, be a butterfly," Ellie said. "To forget about the Latvian poem if you didn't want to recite it. To recite your own poem if you wanted or nothing at all."

Tom's response had been to withdraw more deeply into his quilt cocoon, so it covered his face and eyes as well. Then, he had emerged and flitted around the room like a butterfly. Arms stretched back, he flared the quilt behind him, flapped his arms like wings. Afterward, he bowed, plopped back onto the couch, pulled the cover over him again, and said, "That's it for this year, folks."

Nikkie longed to be back there now, avoiding the Latvian poem recitation, laughing at Tom's cleverness. The family remained quiet now, staring at Tom. No response to their words. Not a head movement or an eyelid flicker. Not a finger twitch against Nikkie's hand. No telepathic messages. Nothing but her own jumbled thoughts.

Disappointment weighed on her. Her whole life she was used to the ways Tom responded to her. To see a glance pass between them or share words that showed they understood each other when no one else did. Even now, she'd expected some sign of that.

"We could pray for him," Ellie said.

"You know Tom hates when anyone prays for him. He likes to save a prayer for big causes, like world peace."

. "I'm sure he'd make an exception. It's not like he doesn't believe in the power of prayer." Ellie touched Tom's arm. "Tom, you were impressed by that study of AIDS patients in San Francisco. The one where the patients being prayed for had better survival rates and fewer hospitalizations."

Tom's face remained immobile. Nikkie felt his pulse again for reassurance.

"Tom would understand we have to do something besides letting the doctors do their job," Ellie said. "Before you arrived, I visualized him whole and healthy, waking up." She rested her hand on Tom's arm.

Nikkie got up from her chair and pointed at the door, motioning with the other hand for Ellie to follow her outside. "It's okay," Indra said. "You two go. I'll stay with him."

Nikkie stopped in the hallway and waited for Ellie. "I didn't want to say this in front of Tom," Nikkie said. "First off, I've been praying for Tom. But I also think we need to acknowledge he's in trouble here."

Ellie cut back. "Even Tom would want us to do everything alternative we can, not only rely on modern medicine. Why not call on the unlimited healing power of the universe? Prayer and visualization are the best ways I know how."

"I wish there was something more hands-on I could do to help him." Nikkie slipped her arms around Ellie, dove into her mother's embrace for refuge. They hugged in silence. The sounds and smells of the hospital dropped away. Nikkie flashed that Ellie's arms were the first place she'd felt safe and accepted since Tom's accident.

Ellie leaned back first, her arms remaining around Nikkie. "I'm glad you're here—that helps him—and that you didn't get hurt."

"I am too, mom," Nikkie whispered back.

Ellie told Nikkie she needed to take a break and offered to get all three of them glasses of kefir while she was gone. "It's so healthy. I wish we could give Tom some. They serve it in the cafeteria here. Want to come with me?"

She stuck her head back in the room and invited Indra, too. Indra joined them in the hallway.

"You two go on ahead," Nikkie said. "I'll sit with Tom."

Nikkie welcomed the time to be alone with her brother, wondered what he might be thinking, if thought of any kind was part of his coma journey. She wasn't as sure as Ellie that Tom would appreciate being prayed over. "Am I stuck for *No Exit* eternity listening to Ell's prayer drone and Pollyanna visualization?" she imagined him asking. "Whole? Healthy? Hello. I'm in a coma here."

Maybe he'll get so mad, he'd pop back from his coma—to get Ellie to stop. Nikkie smiled.

She stared at Tom to see any glimmer of feistiness cracking through, any indication he was telepathically picking up what she was thinking. Nothing. She held his hand again. Did it feel colder or was it her imagination? She tuned in. Imagination, she decided, relieved.

Still, praying and visualizing was a definite improvement over Nikkie's worrying and self-blame. Lightening up wasn't a bad idea, considering Tom was a master of ironic humor himself, Nikkie mused. She thought for a moment. "Hey Tom, I promise to run interference before Ellie gets overly alternative. How's this for a cut-off point? Hot lava rock massage by a beautiful physical therapist. Yes. Copper pyramid from Mt.

Shasta personally blessed by the Lemurians over the hospital bed. No."

No reaction. *If humor can't get through, what will,* she wondered. *Patience, Nikkie.* But patience had never been her strong suit. Her family may not blame her for Tom's injury, but she wanted to do something more tangible than sit, talk, pray or entertain her brother awake.

A nurse came into the room, moved to Tom's side to start a new IV. "Is it okay if I stay while you're working?" Nikkie asked.

"Yes, this will be quick. Your brother's arm is full of good veins to choose from."

"That makes your job easier." Nikkie focused her attention back on Tom, thought back to when they were children and first experienced telepathic communication if one of them was in trouble or feeling down. She opened her heart fully to the possibility of that happening now, envisioned it, concentrated on the love she felt for her brother, let go into it.

Journey. Turny. Burny.Gourney. Journey. Turny. Burny.Gourney, Nikkie heard in her head.

The ratatat tat lady with the prickly needles. Stop her Nik Nik Nik. Stop chattering long enough to stop. Don't talk. If you gotta talk—and oh you gotta talk, talk talk. Then talk to me me me. Don't go. Don't leave me alone with the Old Gray Mare. She ain't what she used to be. I ain't what I'm used to be be be.

Tom? she asked telepathically. *Is that….*

What did I do do that was so terreebla mon cheri? Ma soeur du coeur. Of the prickly ones. Why do ya have me strapped in like the prisoner of Denda. Da dad a dad a da dadada. Mind moosh. Swoosh. Svoosh mein liebchen. Acht tung. Goddess, do you have to poke me with that armadillo tail. Long. Thin. Prick. Prick. Ouch. Hey, can't a guy sleeeep, sleeeeep. I just neeeed some sum the sum of it all sleeeeeep.

Nikkie's heart leapt. It had to be Tom, even if his words were a jumble, like a variation of his poet voice in a coma. But could she be sure it was Tom and not her own ego playing a trick?

"May I ask you a question?" Nikkie said out loud to the nurse. "Has my brother been saying anything or making sounds while you've been here? I thought I heard…."

"No. But don't worry. It's natural not to. Please know we're doing everything we can to help him come out of this coma." She looked back at Tom's arm, taped the IV in place and adjusted the speed of the drip. "We're giving you more fluids, Tom." She looked over at Nikkie, smiled, then gathered her supplies and exited.

Go go go go. Gone. Safe. Safe. Safe. Am I safe? Can I sleeeep? No. No. Spoke too soon. What now? Who now? Help help. No, it's okay. Okay-Doe-kay. It's twirly girly. The whirly one. Yippee. Thank Goddess you're back, as you've been known ta say. Didja bring? Didja bring? Ya know. Him. Him. Him.

Saaaavvvveee meeee. The Ell is driving me bonkers with her ya-dadayadada. You know. I know that you know. Tell her a person in a coma needs a rest, babe-b-b-b-b-baby.

Will ya stop talkin' back there and listen up? The prickly ones. They keep comin'. Comin'. Comin' round the mountain. Prickin'. I got so many holes. Am I leaking? I feel like I'm leakin'. Drip. Drip. Drip. Did I get busted or something? Am I in jail? Are they messin' with mamamamamy mind?

Nikkie retook Tom's hand. She barely breathed in case she missed anything Tom—she was sure it was Tom—was communicating.

I was almost there, twirly Nik. Close. Close. Almost there. Busted. I knew I shouldn'ta carried cross the border. Thought I'd stopped. Didn't I? Shouldn'ta carried cross the borders of my mamamamama-mymy minda-dind-dind.

Okay, maybe it wasn't all sentences, maybe she didn't understand it on a rational level, but on its own level, it was pure Tom.

And Ell. Sweet Ell. Together again. Mother. Sister. The whole—well, almost—family. Did I give you a bad karma day mamamama-mamamamamom. Mommy. The Ell. Hey, don't bounce the bed. Can't you give a coma a little space? Rant. Rant. Rant. Come back. Come back, Tommee. Where do you think I am, mooommmmeeeeee? Every buddy wants me baaaaack.

Yes, we do, Nikkie concurred. *We want you back, Tom.*

Well, I'm Baaaaack. And who would that be? What ma-ma-ma-ma-monster lies in the hearts of men. What kind of fool am I? Drool. God, how embarrassing. Drooling un-controlla-bubbly in front of my sisisisisisister. I'm not even on anything. Am I? Hey. Whirly one. I thought we were one soul split-sky into two-sky. How come I'm the one drooling in public?

Vood you rub a dub dub my forehead, puh-leese. There is this anvil on it. And if you could just brush it over, I might see. Third eye, the holy grail. So frail.

Nikkie gently stroked Tom's forehead, touched the face that had caused her such dismay at first, but now filled her with compassionate interest. *How quickly we adjust to unfathomable realities,* she thought.

As she stroked Tom, the tightness in her shoulders eased. They had been frozen somewhere up in the vicinity of her mid-neck. Now, they dropped the more she heard his voice in the stream of consciousness.

I hate to be all laid up and nowhere to go. Journeys to take. Nature friends to make. Visions to bake.

I hate to see you go. That's it. You go twirly whirly girl. You go go go. Bring one step. Two-step. Him. Someone to come along for the ride ride ride of the centaury. Wadayasay?

Ya gotta go-ski. Now-ski.

Only first, rub my forehead a little, Nik-sky. Rub it like Aladdin's lamp. There. Get three wishes. Do not pass go. Go Go.

Why doncha go? Can't ya hear? Twirly one. Nik Nik Nik Nik. You used-ta hear so good.

As Nikkie fell into a rhythm rubbing his forehead, she relaxed more, and everything in the room blurred. *If I could just lie down and take a nap,* she thought, her eyelids half closing. Without her doing anything consciously, the boundaries of her own body melted as if turning into liquid light instead of physical flesh and blood. She stopped rubbing Tom's forehead and couldn't feel where her edges ended, and the air or chair she sat on started.

She was going into an altered state. She didn't know how she could remain upright without the edges of her body separating her from her surroundings. Maybe she wasn't sitting anymore but floating above the bed. She was not freaked out though, not like with the visions of the dead. It was the most natural feeling. And she accepted that she did not understand all of Tom's communication or what was happening.

The room, its physical presence and sensations, fell away. The drone of people talking in the distance. The pings and beeps and rolling carts. Tom's expressionless face melted away, leaving only the essence behind it. The wholeness of him Ellie had been visualizing. And the spirit that seemed to be her as much as it was Tom connected her not only to Tom but also to every living thing. An all-encompassing love enfolded her and Tom.

As if on a movie screen in her mind, she saw the Tom from her dream, the madrone tree with their names carved on it as his chest. His face had morphed back into his own. He reached through the gelatinous boundary that had separated them as if it had never existed, extended his arm as if from the screen and gently touched her heart center. His touch magnetized her and carried her onto the screen with him.

"You need to go," Tom said in the vision. Only instead of hearing him speak out loud, Nikkie listened to his words spoken in his voice, but in her head. They filtered in as if from a great distance.

Help. I need some buddy. Not just any boddy. You. Go Nik. Go. Into the woodz. Into the woodz. Find me. You. You. Me.

Ell can protect me. From the prickly Gestapo. From the cadre of ranting chanting ones. Doyaknow.

Sinko. Sinko. Cinquo de Mayo. Bring the Cinquo. Hold the Mayo please. Puh-leese. Can't a guy in a coma get some rest. Rest. Nik. Nik. Nik. Go go sisisisis. No rest for the weary. Into the woodz.

Puh-leeze.

You know. Listen up, twirly girl. Glisten up.

For me. Nik. Into the woodz. Happy camper quester. I caaaannnt anymore. I went whirly twirly. Like you. I went went went. Bye –bye. Crash. Pulverized. Weird. Really weird. Weirder than you. Me. Than any trip pa dip dip. Don't cha know?

In this stage, Nikkie seemed to be able to hold and hear both the Tom in her vision and the one who lay on the bed in a coma. In the vision, Nikkie reached up in slow motion and placed one hand on top of Tom's hand on her heart. Then, she extended the other to touch their names on his wooden madrone chest. She experienced a rush of energy like she and her arm were moving at warp speed, traveling light years across an entire galaxy to touch Tom's chest.

"I was going with you." Nikkie heard Tom's voice speak to her in her head again as she gazed into the Tom-of-her-vision's eyes. "You go."

Nikkie continued to extend her arm, her very being out to touch his chest in her vision.

Pater knows. Him first.

Remember, Nik. Re-member. Re-member the Dis-membered. Re-member me-e-e-e. I re-member you-u-u-u.

"I'll go," Nikkie heard herself say both out loud and in Tom's mind, without hesitation, certainty in her voice.

In her vision, Tom's chest expanded in and out. His shoulders raised and fell slightly in what appeared to be a sign of relief.

"Thank you." He closed his eyes softly and nodded his head toward her in acknowledgment.

When Nikkie's fingers touched Tom's smooth wooden chest, any remnant that separated the twins disappeared. The instant she agreed to go, he vanished. Instead of touching his chest, Nikkie found herself stroking their names on the madrone tree in the woods. Not in their forest in Oregon, but the one in Latvia, even though there were no madrones she knew of in its forests.

But Nikkie wasn't upset. Tom remained with her. Only now he was inside her and every sentient being in the forest that surrounded her—as was she. And she knew that in those woods was where she needed to be. That was where she would be guided in her quest both for Tom in his present state—and to resolve the vision of the dead. She luxuriated, eyes closed in this feeling of oneness with Tom and all beings, in this connection that had so long eluded her. This oneness that had begun in a hospital room and encompassed the vision too.

Peter, Peter, pumpkin-eater—who is that masked man anyway? Do your stuff stuff stuff. Go Johnny go. I mean, go Nik go.

And The Ell. Chatter. Love love love. Light light light. Wants me to stick around. God, help Tom li-i-i-ve. He's gottttttt to l-i-i-i-ve. I got it, moooommmmmmmeeeeee. The first one hundred times. Where's an outta body experience when I need one? Do I haveta die just to get some sleep around here? Can't a guy get some rest? I need some rest. Rest.

Restamylife.

Go Nik go. Go for real. Be a good twin now. Go to sleeeeep. Cantcha hear me? Cant-cha hear anymore? You moosh. Did ya hear? I can't rest. Can't restamy life. You gotta re-member. Palīdz. Palīdz. Palīdz. Me.

Re-member. Me.

Yes, Tom, Nik sent back to her brother. *I heard. I hear. Yes, I'm going, Tom. I'm going.* Nikkie felt herself rushing back now into the confines of her body. She breathed deeply, stroked her own arms, touched the tops of her thighs, rubbed her shoes against the hospital floor, re-oriented herself. The voices and clatter of the hospital filtered back into her awareness. The muted lights invited her to reopen her eyes—the images of the vision, Tom's voice in her head, were gone for now.

Gate gate paragate parasamgate bodhi svaha. "Gone, gone, gone all the way over, everyone gone to the other shore, awakening. Welcome!" The Buddhist Heart Sutra flooded into her, a mantra she returned to again and again for liberation from suffering. It was one that Tom resonated with, too, but it had come in her own voice, not Tom's. She imagined sending it to him telepathically and paused. Or was he the one who had sent it to her first? And was that a patina of a half-smile, hovering above, attempting to merge with Tom's face?

Yes, she would go. She called for the strength needed to do so. She called her own power, the strength of the divine infused in the words of the heart mantra, the strength of the ancestors, the strength of the Latvian goddesses Māra and Laima. She called on them all to come into her heart and fortify her. A woman on a mission. Hail to the go-er. Going to the woods to solve the mystery of the vision. Somewhere. Somehow. All would be revealed. It had to be.

Because Tom needed her to go. And she needed to. For him. For herself. For the dead. And in some way she did not comprehend yet, for Peter. Failure—abort mission—was not an option. Tom's recovery was at stake.

She would go to see Peter first, as planned, but without Tom. Because Tom wanted her to go and somehow, according to the vision on stage—and now her brother, Peter was a link.

Chapter 22

"Let this meeting with Peter be a movement of the soul," Nikkie said, remembering the term Ellie had used about family constellation work. Let her next step bring strength, love and healing for Tom. For Peter. For their lineage.

Nikkie's insides churned, muscles in her arms and legs pulsed with the electricity of fear. Ellie had wanted to come along, but Nikkie declined her offer, insisted her mother stay with Indra at the hospital for Tom. Besides, Nikkie's intuition told her this was her journey alone.

So, here she stood. The time had come for her to be present for her brother in as significant a way as he had been present for her—both growing up as their man-boy of the house and in the last months as her manager.

Telling Peter who they were, bringing their father to Tom had to help Tom's healing. Nikkie hoped, dare she say prayed, it was the tipping point of what was needed for Tom's return to consciousness.

But what if Peter flat out rejected her, refused to come? If she did not deliver one earth-bound solid mass father to Tom's bedside pronto, Tom might not make it.

Stop it. Stay present. Stop futurizing, Nikkie told herself. *None of this mind chatter is real. Why not deal with what is happening? Knock on the door. Do what you came here to do.*

Over these last seconds, any remnants of Nikkie's cool veneer had peeled away, strip by strip, like burned skin, and had uncovered a raw mass of electric quaking she could hardly recognize as her own body. *I need help standing, let alone walking through that door,* she thought.

She called on the Latvian forms of the Divine Mother whom she had grown to love so—Māra. Laima. She called on Dievs, the Divine Father for balance and asked them all to help her get through this conversation she had imagined in countless variations since childhood. Only she had never imagined a scenario where her brother was not also present because he was in a coma. Or that her mother was not with her. She asked her divine helpers to inspire her to speak from her authentic heart, paused for one more deep breath, knocked on the door.

It opened. Peter was dressed to rehearse in black tights and a tight white t-shirt. "You came," Peter said, inviting her in. "I was afraid I scared you away when I asked you to dance with my troupe. I hope it was not too forward."

"No, not too forward," Nikkie said. "I was…am honored." She could barely hear him—or herself. The words sounded muted. Lightheaded, she paused, grounded herself in the doorway. *Not now,* she willed herself to clarity.

"Your apartment is lovely," she said before she even looked. She wanted to change the subject, lighten the tone, stay away from talk of her dancing for now.

Peter's living room was filled with overstuffed furniture, all in burgundy, in the same tone as the deep red of the Latvian flag. Two walls were covered with photographs. One whole wall of Peter as a dancer, posing in the costumes of various ballets, with the corps. In his duet. With the ballet's lead dancer. With Mikhail Baryshnikov. Her heart started. Peter had met Baryshnikov. Or did he know him on a more personal level? Baryshnikov had come from Riga. His parents were Russians who had moved to Latvia.

Nikkie thought of her own photo shoot right before she was fired. That photographer had a photo of Baryshnikov she had taken on her wall, too. Nikkie recalled her own picture again, how her dress unfurled around her, the repetition of her arms around her as she spun.

In the photographer's studio, she had imagined her photo hung up on the wall, fantasized a dancer like Baryshnikov—maybe Baryshnikov himself—seeing it during a photo shoot, wondering who she was.

Then, she had been fired. She did not even know what Tom or Ellie had done with the photo. She did not want to know, but she was sure it was not going to be hanging on the wall at the photographer's studio. That door had closed. Now, she was grateful to be opening another door.

Nikkie planted herself at the doorway, knowing with one small step across this threshold, she was leaving behind the final shred of her—and Tom's—dreams of their imagined father—and in some way the dancer she had been in the U.S. She took her first step into the new reality.

"I thought maybe you would change your mind," Peter said. "I had such a strong feeling we needed to dance together."

"I apologize if it sounded that way," Nikkie said, the warmth of Peter's remarks reaching in to soothe and stimulate her, feeding the part of her who had longed to have this kind of interaction with her father. "It was such an unexpected surprise, that's all."

"I don't mean to go on about it," Peter said. "Only to emphasize I'm glad you came. Your agreement to join with us, at least while you are in Latvia, has already sparked ideas in me for a new dance, new choreography. I'm excited to share them later if you like. I was hoping your brother would hear them as well. Where is he by the way?"

Nikkie felt a stab in her heart. Even the mention of the word, brother, triggered a rise in the trembling inside. *No crying.*

Don't cry, she repeated like a mantra. *That quaking is only the fire of strength inside. Like your ancestors had. Like you have. Let it out.* It was as if Tom's voice was inside her, only now she talked herself down like Tom talked her down before performances. She imagined he was here with her now, knew on some level he was. Maybe those words had come from him.

"Something unexpected came up, and he could not come," Nikkie said, hoping her face did not betray her emotions. She needed to tell Peter why she was there, but the words would not come out yet. She wanted to reestablish her connection to Peter first. "You will see each other again soon." *Very soon,* Nikkie thought. She needed to keep it simple. No long explanations. "Meanwhile, we want you to know how much we appreciate the opportunity for me to work with you—and the opportunity you are creating for dancers in Latvia."

Peter gave a chuckle. "It's something I have been called to do. I don't feel like I have a choice. Since the day I left the Nijinsky Ballet, since the day I consciously chose to fight for personal and artistic freedom, maybe since the day as a boy I decided to become a dancer, I have been moving toward creating *this* company—in *my* homeland."

Peter invited Nikkie to sit down on the couch. She chose the center and placed a big pillow behind her. She visualized Tom and Ellie, spirit guides sitting with her and all around her.

"Please, Peter. I'd love to hear more about your company," Nikkie said, genuinely wanting to know but also seeking the grounding this conversation might offer before she spoke the more difficult words she had come to relate.

"It has been a bumpy path at times. I have lost my way. Or I thought I was not good enough to do such a thing because I had not been the soloist in Moscow. Other times, I was full of pride, like back when I was chosen for the duet, and felt like one of the best because I was with one of the best ballet companies—or later again when I danced with Pina. All of that ego is crazy-making, no?"

Nikkie nodded. "You have to follow your heart, no matter what you have accomplished as a dancer, even if it doesn't work out, even if you or others doubt you," she said. "Even if all the doors seem to shut, and your choices don't make sense to anyone else or at times to you." She felt the passion rise in her for dance again. Images of dancing in the woods, in New York, with Stone Tara flooded her. She flashed through the highs and lows of her own path.

"I like this about you," Peter said. "You have not walked the straight path, even when it was expected of you. You swerved and have now been tumbling for a time. It may be challenging, but you have never lost faith. Like I did not."

"I'm not sure about that," Nikkie said. "I felt pretty low after my experience with Stone Tara." But she felt pleased about what Peter saw in her.

Peter shook his head. "Not where it counts. Because I saw you rise up in Māra's studio when you danced. That takes faith—and courage no matter what happens. I have it as well. Our tumbles build character, test us. Will you go on? Will you give up? You chose to go on. Me, too, and I am pleased to be part of your choice."

And Nikkie sensed the best of her reflected in Peter's words, streaming into and calming her heart. *He sees me,* Nikkie thought, not wanting to say anything to change or dampen the trust inherent in those words, knowing she had to. Oddly, what he was saying made it both easier and harder to tell him why she was here.

"This is what happens when I am around true artists like you." He raised his arms palms up in a "W." "I see their greatness and potential, and I am reminded of what I have learned, what I am still learning, what I have to offer on the creative path."

Peter lowered his arms, walked toward her now, but remained standing a few feet away.

"You are kind," Nikkie said, face hot, sure she was blushing. "It reminds me of all I want for myself, of all I can be as an artist at a time when I need reminding. Thanks."

"I am happy to be able to talk of these things—and even more to be able to act on them—when for the early part of my life, this was forbidden." Peter swept his hand across his neck like he was cutting it, reminding Nikkie of the price a person could pay in the Soviet Union for speaking out. "But maybe I go on too long. I am hungry, and you probably are. I will get some food I have prepared from the kitchen. Then we can talk more."

"Can I help?"

"No. Sit. Look at the photos on the walls if you like. One set is of my dance career. The other, I call my freedom wall. Photos that remind me of my journey, Latvia's journey to freedom. As you can see, both represent a long journey that began in Riga when I saw my first ballet when I was seven. From that moment, I knew. I wanted to fly like that. To leap and turn. I begged my parents to let me dance, and they sacrificed I do not know what to get me lessons. We will talk about the photos later if you want. But now, let me be a proper host to a young dancer who has traveled far on her own journey to freedom, yes?"

And then he did it. Smiled the same poignant, ironic, soulful smile that Tom had. But without Tom's edge. It flooded her with his open heart, like he looked into her eyes and saw her soul, how hard she worked, what she, what they both had sacrificed for the most part with joy, to persist and follow their passion. And Nikkie wished with all her being that she would soon see Tom's smile again—that all three of them would be together, seeing even more deeply. Only this time, they would know they were not only professional colleagues but also family.

Nikkie nodded, holding back tears. "Yes, I have traveled far, and yes, I would love some food. Thank you."

She walked over to the freedom wall. The most recent photos on top showed Peter's dance company performing various pieces, him accepting flowers at the end of a performance. Then came Māra's folk dancers and Peter with Pina's and Olga's companies. Next, the freedom monument overflowed with bouquets of flowers, she assumed after freedom had been assured, people dancing and singing in the plaza.

Photos of Peter himself there. Of Peter bundled in a coat, gloves, scarf and hat, arm in arm with fellow Latvians behind the barricades during the 1991 attempt by Soviets to regain control of Riga. And a copy of the photo Indra had found of him on the barricade. The ache and longing in her mounted. Her own desire to have Peter know and rush with her to Tom's side started to supplant the quaking inside.

Next was a photo of Peter in an office surrounded by phones, desks, fax machines—probably when he was working with the *Tautas Fronte*, the Popular Front. Māra and an older man she recognized as Vilnis, the uncle who had raised her. More photos of crowds protesting.

Her heart swelled with pride, and she inhaled and exhaled with even counts to calm herself, to maintain a semblance of the balance that eluded her so often these days. Then, she moved to images that showed the Singing Revolution, ones Peter might have taken himself. Photos of the Song Festivals and dance performances, she assumed from that era. People filled the plaza of the Freedom Monument. Mouths open. Singing, singing.

An endless line of people holding hands—the Baltic Way protest line that spanned across all three of the Baltic States. Singing. Singing. Peter, Māra and Vilnis, their mouths open, heads held high and back, holding hands with the others. Singing. Singing. Singing life into freedom, to remind themselves of freedom. Hundreds of thousands it had been. Singing away the decaying, crumbling forms of fifty years of Soviet oppression.

Then a photo back in Russia in front of his apartment building, he and another man who Nikkie thought might be his partner in the Duet, the freedom fighter who had been arrested and died. Each one of them had an arm around Alexandra, the opera singer who had helped the twins in Moscow. She stood in the middle. Nikkie smiled remembering that meeting and made a mental note to herself to write to Alexandra and let her know they had found Peter as she and Tom had promised her.

And then her breath stopped. The last photo, bottom right, down low on the wall—at the beginning of what Peter had called his Freedom wall was a Polaroid of him with his arm around a beautiful young woman. The two of them beamed. Nikkie felt her face flush, a pain in her chest. Tears streamed out of control down her face.

It was her mother, Ellie. She was posing with Peter in front of what Nikkie knew to be the Chicago Ballet Theatre. The couple fit together like two pieces of a puzzle matching each together. No spaces between them. Nikkie knew it was the Chicago theater because she and Tom had visited the place where Ellie and Peter had met.

It was Ellie at the same age as one of two photos Nikkie carried in her backpack of her family to show Peter—so she would have some kind of proof she was Ellie's daughter. The other was the photo Ellie had placed at Tom's bedside of the family in front of their yurt.

Peter had a photo of Ellie she didn't know existed. Of all the images of experiences he had in the U.S., the one he had with Ellie was on his wall. Ellie, his meeting her, had instilled some spark of freedom in him, had been significant. Not a meaningless on-the-road affair.

Her heart opened. *Hold it together, Nikkie,* she told herself. *Calm down.* She hugged herself but felt nauseous. The tears continued unabated.

Peter emerged from the kitchen smiling, carrying a tray of meats, smoked salmon, cheeses, rye bread, sliced tomatoes, cucumbers, a pot of hot water and selection of teas. The flow of abundant food Nikkie had seen time and again from her Latvian hosts.

Peter's smile dropped into concern. He looked unsure of what to do, then put the tray down and walked over to her by the photos.

"What happened?" he said. "Come. Sit down." He led her by the arm back to the couch. "Let me get you something." He rushed out and returned with a box of tissues. He lowered himself as if he was going to sit next to her on the couch, then reconsidered. He sat down opposite her on a burgundy arm-chair, waited as Nikkie blew her nose.

"Was it the photographs?" Peter asked. "It is moving, yes, this road to freedom. I also get emotional."

Nikkie opened her mouth, her mind racing. What words to say, how to tell him, but nothing came out except sobs. More tears.

This is not how I had wanted to reveal our identity, she thought, but the more she tried to control her crying, the less she succeeded. She reached into her bag, and her fingers touched her family photos.

Some force stronger than her guided her hand to remove them from her bag, and toward her father. She handed them to Peter and in an instant felt her legs rooting like the trees in her visions into the earth.

He glanced at them. His look of concern turned to confusion.

"It's a photo of the woman you have hanging on the wall," Nikkie said. "Ellie. Elīna. Then one with Ellie, Indra, whom I believe you also met, and of my brother and me. The last is of you, of course."

He looked up at the wall where his own framed photo hung as if to see if it was still there, alarm joining the confusion on his face.

"But how did you get these?" he asked, his own voice catching with emotion.

"My mother and grandmother gave them to me." The words streamed through her as if some being had taken her over and was speaking for her. "*Ellie* gave them to me. The same Ellie you met in Chicago in 1980 on tour. The one who is on your wall here."

"Ellie is your mother?" His voice a whisper, choked. She could almost see his mind racing, trying to make sense of what she was saying. He leaned forward, and Nikkie paused, blew her nose and wiped her eyes.

"Yes, Ellie is Tom's and my mother."

"I don't understand. You can see Ellie was an important person in my life. This is such a shock."

If you think that's a shock. Nikkie's tears subsided now, a surety filled her, willing her forward. If she swerved any way but barreling straight ahead, she would be lost, out of control, running again.

"Ellie is here, but that is only part of what I need to tell you." Nikkie's image of this moment had always been so different. It involved her calmly telling Peter she was his daughter, and Peter embracing her with joy. Sobbing, puffy red eyes had not been part of it.

She took a deeper breath, felt it blast through her feet, shoot deep into the earth and anchor her. *Just do it,* she told herself. And she did.

She faced her father and told him. Told him what had been kept from him for twenty-two years. Told him no matter what the consequences and closing and opening of doors. Told him because she had to do what she could to save her brother. Told him because she wanted him—and Māra—to know.

"I know you two had a brief affair. After you left America, Ellie discovered she was pregnant. By you. You are our father. Tom and I, we're your children."

"No," Peter said. Was that fear she saw in his eyes? His hand lifted as if to block a blow. "This is not possible. If it was so, why is Ellie not telling me herself? Why did she not write to me or come to Russia or Latvia to tell me."

Nikkie thought for a moment. What Ellie had or had not done, what she should do now, did not matter. What most mattered was what Nikkie was doing. She had needed to stop running and stand in front of this man who was her biological father. Who was the only semblance of a father she had, she who had grown up with a mother and a grandmother and a brother, but no father. Only a boy who lay in a coma and more than likely had taken on too much of that role himself, carried too much of it for all of them. Was he paying the price?

"I know we have a lot of explaining to do," Nikkie said. "It was a mistake Ellie kept this from you all these years, but there are extenuating circumstances. I don't blame you if you don't believe me, but I hope you do because it is true. Ellie assured us you were the only man who could be our father. She never wrote to you because she was afraid there would be repercussions for you, your career, your family if the Soviets and ballet knew you had fathered children in the States."

Nikkie related how Ellie feared Peter would lose his job or get arrested and sent to Siberia, how she could not leave the twins to travel to Russia to tell him.

"I deserved to know," he said. "I could have done something, somehow been a part of your lives."

He wanted to be part of our lives. Nikkie let those words sink in, a surge of grief rising and swirling in a sea of missed opportunities.

"I agree," Nikkie said, tightness in the pit of her stomach, disliking this role as middle person defending Ellie's choices. "But she did try to contact you when the Soviet Union was dissolving."

Nikkie explained how they had thought Peter was dead, had only discovered he was alive in April when Indra found the picture. "When we were kids and heard you had died, mom created a memorial for you in the forest near where we lived, telling us you had loved being in the woods as a boy. We sang for you, brought flowers and living things from the forest. Leaves and pinecones. Rocks and stones.

"Ellie told us all she knew about you, what a beautiful dancer and person you were. Inside and out. We cried for your loss and ours. Before that, my brother and I had always fantasized about when we would meet you. Tom learned to speak Latvian.

"I would go back to that tree and ask you questions about life and dancing as if I could talk to you, and you in your spirit form knew who I was. Like you, I knew I wanted to be a dancer from the time I was a child." She paused, "You were my inspiration."

His face softened. Nikkie saw something else. A momentary look of pride?

She chose not to tell him the latest—about the vision of the dead in the forest and his part in it. *I don't want to scare him,* she told herself. *Excess information.* But in truth, she wanted to relish that softening. And going to the woods was the second part of what Tom had asked her to do. The first part was telling Peter and getting him to the hospital.

"Why would you come without your brother or Ellie? Why are they not here?"

Tom. And that's when this momentary reprieve of the joy of the release of telling him, of him knowing, came crashing down. It hit like a mirror falling from a second-floor window, shattering on the sidewalk, shards of glass cutting, drawing blood, piercing her with the thought of Tom lying in a coma.

She explained about Tom's accident and coma. "So besides all I've told you, we need your help in the hospital. We need you to come to the hospital—for Tom."

"I will come," he said, without hesitation. Nikkie's heart eased open, then flooded with tender relief. Peter was going to do what he could. It would help. She was sure of it. "What hospital is your brother in? Who is his doctor? Maybe I can help you with the Latvian hospital system."

Nikkie told him.

"It is a good hospital. I will make calls, make sure your brother has the best doctor," Peter said. "But before anything, I must go to rehearsal, to my dancers. We start in an hour. Before this news, I thought you might already want to join us and dance today. Now." He slowly shook his head, sighed. "I will come when we finish around six."

"Are you sure you can't come immediately. I am so worried. I'm certain you being there would help."

"I am sorry," Peter said. "I will be there in a few hours."

How could she persuade him, Nikkie wondered? "Tom and I have such a close connection as twins that sometimes, we can read each other's thoughts. He communicated to me right before I came here, asked me to get you to the hospital—from his coma state. I heard him. It could be...." She stopped herself. She almost said life and death but did not want to put those words, that possibility, that image out into the universe or into Peter's mind. "I mean, it is so important to act quickly."

Peter closed his eyes for a moment, opened them again. "This is all such a shock. I need to go. I think you can agree it is a lot to find out I might be a father. And one child is in the hospital. I need a moment to take it in. And my company. We have an important performance coming up during the festival."

Nikkie felt the sting of the words, "might be." *Breathe. Breathe.* What he said was true. It was a lot. Tom would hold on. She would hold onto that knowing. She would go back and tell Tom Peter knew and was coming. He cared enough to help them. The rest would come with time.

"Stay here if you like. Eat something. Rest. I will be there. I promise."

"Thank you. But I'm going back. Maybe I'll make a sandwich to take with me if that's all right."

"Please. Take a second one for Ellie," he said, his voice catching as he said her name. He paused, glanced at Ellie's photo again, shook his head. "I loved her, you know." His eyes reached deep into Nikkie's to touch her soul. "I loved Ellie." Then, he turned with a dancer's flourish, without waiting for a response and walked out the door.

Nikkie sat down again, stunned. Her face flushed hot, then an icy chill moved from her head to her feet. She shivered. How could he leave like that? How could he hear he's fathered two children, one of whom is in a coma, and go to a rehearsal? No matter how important. *I'm sorry Tom. I told him. But he'll come. Trust me.* She imagined she sent the message telepathically.

Or would Peter come? He had to. She would return as many times as necessary. She would refuse to leave his apartment or studio, stand outside, camp outside his doorway until he came.

Maybe that's what she could do now. Go to the studio. Stay there. Wait until the rehearsal with his dancers ended. Grab his arm, lead him to the hospital. But she did not want to be away from Tom for that long. Six o'clock—or on the twenty-four-hour clock of Europe—eighteen o'clock. A few hours. Of course, Peter would come. All circumstances considered he had taken in everything she had said and had not denied it—

or them. He had not refused to go to the hospital outright but had offered.

And then the door opened again, and a form come toward her. Real? Or phantom. A ghost. Had her desire been so intense she manifested a mirage? Peter glided toward her. In a daze, she felt his arms around her.

"*Meitiņ. Piedod man,*" Peter said. "*Es jau kautkā zināju bet es nezināju, ka es zināju kad es pirmo reizi tevi un Tomu redzēju.* Daughter. Forgive me. I already knew, but I did not know I knew the first time I saw you and Tom. My heart pounded. I thought I was having a heart attack. When I walked into Māra's studio and saw you dancing, I knew my life had changed forever. How did I know that? I could not name what happened. Now I can. Elīna's children. Our children. *Dvīņi.* Twins. Of course, we need to go to the hospital now. Let's go to Tom—and to Ellie."

CHAPTER 23

When Nikkie and Peter walked into the hospital room, Ellie was sitting alone next to Tom reading from a sheet of paper what sounded like Tom's own poetry to him. She had one of her hands on Tom's heart. She stopped mid-phrase and looked up.

At that moment, Nikkie felt like she was watching a movie, present in the room, but not the scene. Peter and Ellie created such a strong field of energy around them, what Ellie had said happened in Chicago at the reception was happening again. There, Peter's dancer companions had seemed to fall away. Now, Nikkie and Tom seemed to fall apart.

Whatever happened next, Nikkie knew the chemistry the pair had felt for each other twenty-three years earlier remained. It was undeniable. Tangible.

Peter stepped toward her mother. "Elīna," he said. "Ellie."

Ellie placed the poems gently on Tom's chest, rose to her feet and nodded. "Peter, I am so glad you came. Thank you. You're really here."

And simultaneously, the two moved toward each other, Ellie with her arms extended. Peter opened his to receive her. They fell into a long embrace. Then, after a timeless minute, they leaned back without letting go of each other, seemed to drink in every detail of each other's faces to make sure they were real.

"I am glad. To know. We have children," Peter said. "Twins. And to see you. My heart is so full. I'm in shock, but I want to help. Tom. You. Our daughter." He looked over to Nikkie, extended his hand and brought her into his and Ellie's circle, one arm around her and the other remaining around Ellie, whom he did not seem to want to let go.

And whatever fear Nikkie had that Peter would reject them, be angry at Ellie for not telling him about her, that he would not remember Ellie, transformed into relief. Her father was here. His being here would help Tom.

Nikkie, Peter and Ellie sat down next to Tom's hospital bed. Ellie and Peter each held one of Tom's hands.

"When life became hard, and I wanted to lift myself up. I would think about the power and magic of meeting you, how if that could happen, anything was possible," Peter said. "I imagined we had stayed together and lived our lives as artists. In my fantasy, we had a boy and a girl. How astonishing that part was true."

"That's amazing," Nikkie said, feeling goosebumps. "And you were wondering if Peter even remembered you." Nikkie looked at Ellie.

"I'm touched," Ellie said. "And it reaffirms what a poor choice I made not to contact you. You deserved to know you had twins. I am so sorry."

"I wish I had known, but I understand you were making the best decisions you could under difficult circumstances," Peter said. "All I know is, today I am sitting here with my son. And I am holding his hand."

He lifted his hand and extended it toward Nikkie. "And my daughter is also here. Both my children. And Ellie. I am so grateful."

Nikkie placed her hand in Peter's, absorbed the tenderness of his words and touch and let this first three-way physical connection between the twins and their father warm her.

"I am grateful for that, though I will always wish you had gotten to know Tom and Nikkie as children," Ellie said.

"I can picture it. On the way here, I was imagining how it would have been to sit with Tom in the night when he was a child, holding his hand, soothing him while he fell asleep after a bad dream. I envisioned the coma like that—a bad dream from which I would try to help him wake up."

Nikkie also wished Peter had been there soothing Tom back to sleep after a nightmare like Ellie had for both Tom and her. All day, she had been focused on what she needed to do to get her father to the hospital and to help Tom recover consciousness. Now, her father was here expressing thoughts and feelings she recognized not only she, but Tom and Ellie also longed to hear. Her father rose up, put his hand on her back behind her heart. She felt its heat and energy, let herself be held and sourced by the love.

The impact of Ellie's and Peter's words rolled over Nikkie. She shook herself out of her present state long enough to glance at Tom, to see if he was reacting. But he was not.

Peter sat down next to Tom and Ellie again. "After you and I were together for the last time, I have to tell you when I went to bed, I imagined we created a life together. I was embarrassed but also excited to share that with you the next day. I hoped we could talk about what a life might be like if I defected, if I danced in the U.S., what it would be like if you and I did make a commitment."

He reached over to touch Nikkie's arm, looked at her. "That's the story I was going to tell you and Tom today—when I told you I had come this close to defecting while I was on tour. Ellie's and my connection was that strong, despite only knowing each other a few days."

He put his fingers close together again like he had done that day, but now sadness seemed to permeate his being. "When I woke up, practical reality set in. Our lead dancer had already defected. Security clamped down around the remaining dancers and me. I no longer had a moment to myself to think or act on 'what ifs.' You and I had not yet spoken of a long-term commitment, Ellie, nor about the political complications of that choice. But life chose for me at that moment. It separated us. I tried to persuade myself life's choice had been the right one, but I always doubted it."

"I had also been thinking about it," Ellie said. "I was devastated when I didn't get a chance to tell you. I didn't know you had those thoughts." And Nikkie's heart wrenched at the thought of what might have been.

"I did," Peter said. "What if I had been the one to defect first to be free to perform anywhere and to be with Ellie, I wondered? The loss permeated every part of my life, changed something inside me, shut down some indelible life force."

Peter, whose posture was impeccable, slumped. His whole being appeared to collapse under the pressure of an unseen weight. Nikkie sensed a tremulousness in his breath.

"In the aftermath, I rationalized that I had no idea what defection would have meant for my life. No clue if I would have been able to dance again on any stage, let alone a world stage. My family had suffered already, I rationalized—during the war, with the Soviets. What would have happened to them, to their jobs and limited opportunities if I *had* defected in Chicago and was labeled a traitor? Nothing good. The hand of the KGB and Communist Party was unforgiving, reached deep and long and left a permanent mark."

Peter unconsciously rubbed his forearm as if feeling scars of that mark. "I imagined you happy somewhere, a successful potter, even if you weren't with me. That thought of you made me happy." And then he smiled, not a full out smile, but a half smile. And at the same time Nikkie thought it, Ellie said it.

"Tom has your smile, you know," Ellie said. "That one." She pointed at Peter's face. "Kind of a half-smile that seems to see beyond the bullshit of life to the larger perspective. Like you are in on some private joke with the universe."

Nikkie wished she could photograph it. Put it side by side with the countless photos of Tom smiling like that, to show Peter so he would see. And Tom when he woke up. So he would see too.

Ellie rested her hand on Tom's calf now while Peter held his hand. Ellie held Nikkie's gaze and smiled softly, like a flower slowly turning toward the sun.

"I wish I could have helped you and our children through these years," Peter said.

"You did—at least my having known you did."

Peter looked at her quizzically. "How is that?"

"I would contemplate how you had followed your heart and left your family and country behind to go to Moscow. I thought of it often as I built a life for the twins and myself in Oregon—and in building the pottery business. My main job always, however, was to love our children, let them know anything was possible. I know I've blown it repeatedly. But I do believe you know I love you, Nikkie, no matter what. And I hope Tom does."

Nikkie felt into her restless heart and knew Ellie had spoken truth. She did know Ellie loved them, and she had always felt Ellie's support to follow her dreams.

A few hours passed. Peter made calls regarding Tom's care and met with the doctor on the case. Indra, who had left the room to give Peter and his new family time for a private reunion, returned, and she and Peter reconnected, too. She then excused herself again to make her own calls to her connections to make sure Tom had the best doctors.

But so far, nothing had worked to coax Tom out of the coma. Not Peter coming to the hospital or meeting with Ellie.

Not medical care. Peter had even called Māra to let her know what was happening while he sat next to Tom. Still, no squeezing of a hand or flicker of an eyelid indicated Tom heard anything the family said. No more telepathic word streams flooded Nikkie's consciousness.

"I'm so pleased the two of you are going to dance together," Ellie said.

"Yes," Nikkie said. "But I still feel so off course in that regard. I hope I do a good job."

"You will find your way again. Dance is in your bones, even if how you express it changes," Ellie said.

"Dancing with my company can help," Peter said. "And not only while you are visiting here. My invitation extends if you decide to stay in Latvia. Maybe dancing and choreographing with me is your new direction. And Tom could participate with his creative and business skills. But whatever you do, like your mother said, I cannot imagine dance is not a part of it. You are too gifted a dancer for it not to be."

"Thank you," Nikkie said. "Dance has meant everything to me—and I've dreamt so often of dancing with you. But right now, all I want is for Tom to heal and wake up from the coma."

"I had a thought," Ellie said. "Perhaps the coma could be Tom's own wake-up call to meet his destiny. It's one for the rest of us, don't you think? And it has certainly brought us all together again."

Ellie directed her attention toward Tom now, holding his hand with one of her own, placing her second hand on his heart. "Tom, I won't believe your destiny is to stay in a coma or to die on us. Come back to us, and yes, be the caring, supportive human being you are. But also, dear son, please listen—you can bury your words as deeply as you want. But you can't bury your own heart, your own soul. I cannot think of one way it serves to have you deny your gifts of poetry as you have done.

Why hold your creative voice inside? Express yourself first and foremost for yourself. There is meaning enough in that."

"I agree with you there," Nikkie said. "But Tom was, is," she corrected herself, "planning to write again. Before the accident, he told me he wanted to move to Latvia and write in this country where poetry and the arts were valued." *And now he can't,* she thought to herself. An onslaught of guilt rose unbidden, batted at the hope her father's hospital visit and reunion with Ellie had instilled. She willed it away. *Not helpful,* she repeated. *Not helpful.*

"I'm thrilled to hear it. Even Tom moving to Latvia makes sense, though it surprises me," Ellie said. "I never assumed your Latvian ancestry would play such a major role in either of your destinies, other than Peter and me being Latvian. But the more I learn, the more Latvia does seem to be involved. For both of you. And perhaps now for me. I wish I knew more about how."

"Maybe all of us connecting to Peter will reveal more," Nikkie said.

Ellie nodded, reached over and put her hand on Peter's.

He lowered his eyes, then raised them and looked solemn. "I hope so," he said. "I would like that."

"I can't tell you how often I thought about our time together," Peter said, addressing Ellie, but, making eye contact with Nikkie as well. The conversation was moving along on a human level, and Nikkie relaxed into a familiar landscape of emotions. "I wondered, why did I not look for you when Latvia was freed? I have no good reason. I hoped you might look for me."

Ellie smiled in acknowledgment.

"I was sure you had become an artist, married, had children," Peter said. "I did not want to disrupt the full life I imagined you had built for yourself."

"I felt the same way," Ellie said. "You were a good-looking, kind man. I was certain you had a family. When I did check, as you know, I was told you had died. Before that, though, there was one time I read the Nijinsky Ballet was coming back to the States. The twins were three years old. It was before they had asked to know about you. But I checked what dancers were on tour, and your name was not listed."

"I am sad knowing how much I missed of our children's lives," Peter said. "But I understand life is complicated. We tell ourselves stories. When Latvia was freed, I told myself I was a distant memory for you."

He turned back to Nikkie and Tom. "As it turned out, I had not been chosen to be part of that next tour. There was one time though. Right after Latvia was freed. I wrote to you, Ellie, to the address I had for you and your mother in Chicago. But the letter came back. Addressee unknown."

"You did?" Ellie said. "That means a lot. I wish I had known, that I had gotten that letter. Our lives could have been so different. I would have known you were alive. But I don't want to dwell on what might have been any more. Thankfully, all that is in the past. What's most important is this moment, what we do with what we know now."

"The main piece I'd like you all to know from those memories is the knowledge that despite the short time we spent together, I loved you, Ellie," Peter said. "Nikkie—and Tom, the two of you were conceived in love."

"I loved you as well," Ellie said, addressing Peter and including Tom through her touch. "And that love went beyond countries and boundaries, possibilities and impossibilities. On some visceral level, it lives in the cells of these two beautiful beings that came through us, no matter what happens."

Conceived in love. Nikkie had not known she needed to hear that, to know that. Not only a passing passion. But love. Her whole body came alive as she felt that love in her cells.

Undoubtedly, this news would have an impact. She reached over and squeezed Tom's hand, hoping to feel the slightest tightening around her hand in return. Nothing.

Grief gripped at her through the myriad thoughts and feelings the conversation had stirred. It was as if Tom used up all the energy he had in that one coma communication in which he asked her to bring Peter, and he had nothing left. But if this reunion with their father had not brought healing, Tom had requested one more thing. *Go to the woods*, he said, numerous times. *Go to the woods*. But how would that help him heal? And where to begin?

She did know Peter was involved. "Help me," he had said in the last vision, holding the dead girl's body in the forest.

So that was the obvious next step. As difficult as it was, Nikkie would reveal the vision to her father—and to her cousin, Māra. She would ask for their help, trust in the possibility that despite what they thought about her, they could offer up some clue or better yet, know who and what she was talking about and where to find a resolution.

Chapter 24

"*Kuldīga*," Māra said, without hesitation.

"Yes," Peter said. "The forest on our uncle Vilnis' property."

He smiled warmly at Māra, and Nikkie realized he still had a more father-like relationship with Māra than with Tom or her. She ran her hand over her head and hair, lowered her shoulders which had crept up to protect her from the sadness that had slipped in. No time for "what-could-have-been." She had told her new family about the visions of the dead, was eager to hear what insights they might offer.

Māra gave Peter a thumbs-up. "It's possible, Nikkie, the vision you are seeing originated there." Māra sat at the bottom end of Tom's bed, stroking the tops of his feet. She wore a pair of jeans, sandals and a fitted, scoop neck teal top. Around her neck was a narrow black leather choker holding a single piece of amber, also set in black leather. Her blonde hair fell loose around her shoulders.

Nikkie paced, needed to take some action. The early evening sun shone brightly in the window, illuminating Tom's form, casting all their shadows on the floor and wall behind them.

"The forests in Kurzeme—all over Latvia—are full of stories like that," Peter said. "Perhaps Vilnis knows one associated with his forest that we don't."

"You mean you believe what I told you?" Nikkie asked, grateful they had jumped to suggestions without questioning the message. She sat down in a chair against the wall.

Peter and Māra looked at each other with surprise. "Of course," Peter said. "We have a close connection to the dead in our culture –both of us have had experiences that reveal much more goes on in this world than what logic and science can explain, especially in nature."

"What does Vilnis think about that?" Nikkie said. "What if he can't relate to the vision?"

"Even if he can't, he will help," Peter said. "Because you are family. He already can't wait to meet you."

"Are you coming with me to ask him?" Nikkie said. "Given you were in the vision, too, your presence seems crucial."

"Yes," Peter said. "I agree. I have no idea how I am involved, but I want to be there to support you. I'll call Vilnis and tell him we're coming." Relief flooded her knowing her father would be with her.

"I'm so glad you're going to be with Nikkie," Ellie said, explaining she needed to stay behind with Tom.

"I still feel unsettled about leaving Tom," Nikkie said.

"Trust the guidance," Ellie said. "It's what he wants. And trust your own strength and inner knowing. I do. Indra will be here with me."

"Tom wants you to go not only for him but yourself," Peter said. "Your being able to dance again without fear of the vision repeating would bring him as much healing as anything."

Nikkie agreed, and Peter offered to call right away. He assured her Vilnis would want them to stay with him. "You should know about Latvian hospitality by now." He touched Nikkie's shoulder tenderly.

"One more request," Nikkie said, letting the warmth of Peter's touch radiate through her. "Would you tell Vilnis *why* I want to come?"

"That needs to come from you. When he is with you, face to face. Your own wording—not mine—is what could trigger insights for him. No matter what, though, he'll help."

"I agree," Māra said. "Vilnis was like a father to me. I talk to him about everything—even how my dance inspiration comes from tree spirits. He never makes me feel weird. He also has a special relationship with the trees."

"That reassures me. But I would find it helpful to know some more about him," Nikkie said.

"You might recall that he and his wife raised me, when my own parents couldn't," Māra said, straightening up, her hand still resting on Tom's foot. Māra always called him her uncle even though he was her great-uncle. "They—and Peter—rescued me."

"I appreciate him all the more for that," Nikkie said, admiring how despite Māra's challenges as a child, she had such clarity of purpose in her creative expression. But today, Nikkie's path was evident as well. Help Tom. Find the dead. It might not be dance, but she could not imagine doing anything else.

"I was grateful Vilnis—and Peter—gave me a second chance," Māra said. "I also saw the choices my uncles made. During the Singing Revolution, they met violence with nonresistance, even if that meant dying. Standing on the Baltic Way with them and two million Latvians, Lithuanians, Estonians, and others empowered me."

"All of us," said Peter, looking at Māra with pride.

"After Latvia was freed, Vilnis and Peter—like Indra—reclaimed our family's land," Mara said. "I spent my childhood there in the stillness of nature, listening to the trees, dancing in their presence. I danced out the anger and sadness I felt about being abandoned by my parents. I learned to give the pain I felt inside to the trees, and they offered me a never-ending supply of love and healing energy. I still love to create there."

Nikkie realized while she had been dancing in the forest in Oregon, Māra had been dancing in one in Latvia. "I wonder if our spirits were somehow encouraging each other in spirit in ways we did not know while we both danced in the woods."

"Very possibly."

"It would be amazing if the family forest turns out to be the source of my vision," Nikkie said and thanked Māra for sharing more about her background and Vilnis.

"Vilnis is a remarkable man. Like your grandmother, he grew up during World War II," Peter said. "But don't take it personally if he avoids talking about it. Even with us, he won't discuss those experiences."

"But won't I be bringing up the past by sharing my vision?" Nikkie asked.

"It's different," Peter said. "Your vision is yours, not his experience."

"Are you sure?" Nikkie said.

The light began to wane, and Ellie turned on the lamp above Tom's bed. It glowed amber beneath the silk scarf she had draped across it. The family sat in silence, listening to Tom's breath punctuated by pings and whirs of monitoring machines.

"Does anyone have any more thoughts that might help my search?" Nikkie said.

Māra spoke first. "I keep thinking about what Peter said in the vision. 'Help us. Help me.' But in the way we have talked about them, the emphasis has been on how to get rid of them. What if you consider more how you might help not only Tom but them?"

"I don't understand."

"You might ask what the dead need to do or say or have witnessed to move on," Māra said.

"I hear you, but while I feel compassion for them, I still want them to leave," Nikkie said. "It's what I—and Tom—have always wanted."

"But they came to you for help," Māra said. "Across time and space and death and life. To you specifically, Nikkie. More than once."

"It's an interesting idea," Peter said. "When I think of the forests, I am now most aware of nature. But as a Latvian, I also think back to all the people who died in forests. They carry so many secrets and stories. During the war and after. Families trying to escape deportation. Men. Women. Children. The Forest Brothers. They all needed help."

"Maybe you are onto something," Ellie said. "Nikkie, you might have a stronger connection to the spirits you don't comprehend yet. Think of the courage of some of those people. I remember Indra telling me about the Forest Brothers."

"Would you tell me?" Nikkie said.

"I will," Peter said. "They were part of the Baltic resistance after World War II, hiding in the forests to sabotage the Russians until the Allies freed us. Instead, the Allies gave the Baltics to Stalin, the dictator who murdered ten million or more people across Europe. Many of the Forest Brothers were shot in the forests by the Soviets.

"The rest were arrested, even years later. And they were not the only ones who died in the woods. The Germans massacred Jews and Gypsies in Latvia's forests during World War II. Twenty-five thousand Jews in Rumbula Forest alone—outside Riga. Many more were killed throughout the country. In forests, on roads, in their homes. In temples."

"It makes me sad to think of what my family, other Latvians and Jews went through," Nikkie said. "But it still does not explain how I can help the dead."

"I have another idea," Māra said.

Nikkie braced herself.

"Perhaps, given their traumatic deaths, they are stuck between life and death. And they are asking you—and Tom—to help them cross over."

"Whoa," Nikkie said. "I have no idea how to do that—and what could Tom do in a coma?"

"If you like, I'll research it."

"I'd appreciate that. But it doesn't mean I could—or would—help that way. The only spiritual connection between this realm and the next that I work with is through whirling. In the Sufi spiritual tradition, whirling connects Heaven and Earth for the dancer and the audience. But those are live people. Spinning to help spirits cross over permanently is out of my league."

"That gives me another thought," Māra said.

What now? Nikkie wondered. *I plunge into the underworld to bargain for the dead's safe passage?*

"The vision first came while you were dancing, having an experience of being one with everything. Maybe what you said about whirling, connecting heaven and earth, is what attracted them and led to the vision. It may be where their healing lies."

"So, you're saying dancing may not only be the vehicle for the vision to appear but also to resolve it?"

Māra nodded. "Yes, and if we are all one being like spiritual traditions say, each person is an aspect of us here to teach us. The dead of your vision are also part of that oneness, here to teach you something."

"I appreciate the thought," Nikkie said, wondering if she really did. "However, those same spiritual traditions intimate that our path evolves beyond familial and cultural ties—to live in the now, in joy and peace, not mired in the past—ancestral or otherwise."

Rehashing yet again the suffering of ancestors who had died in wars and plagues of this land felt to Nikkie like repeatedly rolling Sisyphus' stone up a hill and watching it roll back down. The practice forever linked present-day descendants to a pain that was not theirs to carry—or resolve. And yet, it, along with the positive, the ancestor's survival instincts and strengths, were passed down energetically in families. Nikkie wanted to find a way to leave the stone behind and focus on their resilience.

"I can see both sides," Ellie said. "But while it's important to stay present and let go of the past, I don't know if you can until you acknowledge it."

"How do you propose I do that?" Nikkie asked.

"Perhaps the dead of your vision simply want to be seen. They want to have you recognize their lives had value—regardless of what they suffered and did or did not accomplish. Maybe they need to reveal their secrets or to know their acts of courage—aren't forgotten."

"I have to admit it has made a huge difference to me knowing about what Indra and our ancestors went through before and during World War II," Nikkie said. "I'm inspired by them and grateful that their courage and choices led not only to the gift of our being born in a free America but also the opportunities of our lives there."

"I remember now how that kind of honoring of what the ancestors went through is part of what takes place in the family constellation therapy I mentioned in Turaida," said Ellie. "This recognition helps to bring healing to you and the ancestral lineage. It frees up the ancestors' strength and love to flow forward unencumbered to present and future generations of family members as well. That way, it can support all of our well-being and the fulfillment of our life's dreams."

"But we don't know that I have an ancestral connection here," Nikkie said.

"Even if the connection does not turn out to be personal, it is part of your ancestral heritage—and part of what all Latvian families have endured," Ellie said. "That counts, too, I think."

Nikkie took in what her mother and Māra said deep into her heart and knew that despite her resistance, the value of their words was worth considering. One thing she knew for sure though. She needed to step out in faith—and seek out the dead without knowing what would happen or what she needed to do if and when she found them.

Chapter 25

Vilnis had left Nikkie and Peter the key to his home and a note. He would be back by morning, he had written. He had an emergency call from a neighboring farm to help birth calves. Meanwhile, a cold dinner waited for them inside—smoked fish and meats, potato and green salad, sliced tomatoes, rye bread. A bowl of fresh strawberries sat on the table with a one-word note: *Ēdi*! Eat!

Nikkie was both disappointed to have to wait and grateful for the opportunity to settle in before her first steps in Kurzeme's forests. She had already been through days of intense revelations. Exhaustion ate at her, made her brain fuzzy, her body heavy. A night's sleep in the country might help. As much as she relished the time to talk to Peter alone, she excused herself and went to bed early.

But despite her enervation, Nikkie could not sleep. The voices of the night vibrated in her being. The trees, the dead, her brother's wandering spirit all called to her. Her own mind and heart called to her.

At the same time, the hardness of the mattress seemed to bore into her bones. The starched bed linens chafed at her skin, and the wool of the blanket made her arms and face itch. She breathed in the lingering scent of detergent. Feeling overheated, she threw the covers off. Then, she felt cold and put them back on. Back and forth. On. Off. On. Off. No blanket. Sheet only. No sheet.

Together, they reminded her how outside the ease of her grandmother's apartment with its soft mattresses and full-featured bathrooms, many living spaces in Latvia still lacked the creature comforts she was accustomed to in the U.S. Even before Tom's accident, life for people she met, for family members, seemed harsher. And whenever they exited her grandmother's building or Riga hotels, they also left the pocketbooks and lifestyles of expats and tourists and ran right into hard edges and rough surfaces.

Interspersed between renovated structures were wrecks of buildings that had not been touched in decades and older buildings sorely in need of repair and updating. More than once, in these buildings, dark stairwells led to apartments with old, lumpy furniture and bathrooms with questionable plumbing.

Outside Riga, Soviet-style brick apartments, eyesores on the landscape still only had five- gallon hot water tanks, barely enough to rinse your hair, let alone bathe. One of her relatives had raised three children with no indoor plumbing or running water. Nikkie thought of families trudging out in the freezing cold of winter snows and rain to go to the bathroom or preparing meals and doing dishes without running water.

What a wimp she sounded like, complaining about a hard mattress with a few bumps. She felt like the princess in *The Princess and the Pea*.

When had she become such a diva? New York? In Oregon, she had slept on the ground many a summer night and for a time, lived in a yurt. Still, surely the second-hand mattresses she and Tom slept on growing up had not even come close to this solid slab.

The bed was narrow. All the single beds Nikkie had encountered seemed to be so, despite how tall young Latvians were. At home, she was used to stretching out the length and width of her plush, queen-size mattress. Here, with every little stretch, a leg or arm fell over the edge of the bed, pulling sheet and blanket along with it and off of her.

Still, Latvians worked hard, had created homes for themselves and their families under challenging circumstances. Even those who had little opened their homes and hearts to visitors with love and generosity. And with new opportunities, for the first time, they could add some of life's comforts. For decades, comfort had not been an option, because none of the goods were available except to the Communist elite.

Home. She was no expert. What was home to her these days anyway? Truth be told, she had no idea if she had ever created one for herself as an adult—with or without comforts. She had left her childhood home in Oregon. When she first moved to New York, she felt like she had come home, but that was not to a place so much as to herself as a dancer and person.

And now? Would she find that kind of home again with her father's dance company?

Or with Māra's? Who knew if dance would ever feel like home again? And if not dance as home, what then?

She had known that as a dancer, at a certain point, she would likely stop performing. She was only twenty-two, but there were already younger dancers who could push their physical edges further than she, though she continued to develop herself. Of course, that physical edge of pre-twenties youth had nothing to do with artistry or bravery, she reminded herself. She was still capable of growing that way, would hopefully always be.

Home, wherever you found it, was shelter, though, and since she was a girl, dance had been her shelter. In a way, it had also sheltered her from having to deal with the real world. It had been a place to hide.

New York as home had been filled with both harsh and magical realities. But in truth, most of her time and energy had been spent in dance studios, rehearsing, taking classes, keeping her body in shape, choreographing. She had not been out on the streets engaging with the city itself or its people. New York was, for the most part, energy more than a place, something she passed through and fed off of on her way to dance.

This dance world and what she had accomplished had done nothing to prepare for and shelter her from the stark reality of a brother in a coma. Nothing in that world had prepared her to spearhead a freedom movement like her father had done.

Home. Nikkie didn't care if she ever landed in a physical home or a soft bed again—as long as her brother would be all right and if she was honest with herself, as long as she knew she could dance again.

She had never thought of where life might take her beyond dance or without Tom at her side helping—until now. What if the unthinkable happened and Tom would not regain consciousness or would come out of the coma with permanent brain injury? She would feel responsible for taking care of him, for creating a home for them. But what could she do to earn money if she wasn't dancing—or if she failed with her father's company? And what would happen to her own future dream of doing a more improvisational spiritual dance?

For now, all these were moot points. Teaching and choreographing required inspired creativity and motivation Nikkie could not sustain right now. She was grateful her father was giving her a chance to dance with his company.

The home she needed to find lived inside of her—regardless of where her physical body landed or what she did in the world. Ellie had sent her a card for her birthday once that said: "Wherever you go, there you are." She needed to develop that strong a core, as her Pilates instructor reminded her. Discover inner peace, any spiritual teacher would stress. From there, she might find and create a home.

Right now, she wanted to stop hurting. And not only from this hard bed. Though it was one challenge she could act on.

I give up, Nikkie got out of bed. The house was still. Peter slept. Vilnis had not returned from helping the neighbor with calving yet. Nikkie grabbed a blue shawl, wrapped it around the shoulders of her white cotton nightgown, and slipped outside.

The air was cool against her skin, and she heard the night sounds of insects around her. She sat down on the damp grass, feeling the earth beneath her.

Peter and Ellie had been right, she thought. She had needed to get away from Riga, away from the hospital and Tom. And not only to meet Vilnis or search for the dead. She couldn't think in Riga, couldn't step back and reflect on all that had happened.

Here, connecting to the earth, the first emotion that beckoned to Nikkie for attention was grief. Grief for the loss of Tom as she knew him, of life as she had known it. She flashed on the dead in the forest. They, too, had lost loved ones and life as they knew it. But most likely, they had not had the luxury of a moment to process that loss before they were dead themselves. No matter what grief she experienced now, at least she was alive. Tom and Peter were alive.

Nikkie pulled the shawl closer around her and laid back on the grass, stretched out her legs, felt the nurturing of the earth beneath her. *Much better than the mattress,* she thought.

She remembered the wrenching grief in her childhood when she thought Peter had died. She had felt a gaping hole inside she imagined only a father's love and acknowledgment could fill and never would. Still, back then, she had believed, as a spirit, he knew he had a son and daughter. She remembered calling on him for support, like a guardian angel.

Now, she had met the man who threw himself into whatever he was into, whether ballet or contemporary dance or freedom. He was creating opportunities for dancers in Latvia and exploring new forms. But would she ever fit into that world in Riga? Could that feel like home? In the U.S., she had left the life of being part of a recognized dance company. What made her think this experience might be different?

She wanted to feel like she could be in partnership with her father, maybe include her form of dance in his roster. But what if the collaboration ended up like the bed she had just left? Her muscles might not be able to breathe in her father's dance company. Her bones. The body might not want to adjust to those shapes, those extensions and foot placements. Her chest might not open. She might feel uncomfortable in her own skin, wanting to contract inside herself and resist rather than extend and expand. His form, as creative and authentic as it was, might not ever be her way.

Stop second-guessing yourself, Nikkie. It's what Tom would have said, had often said to her. Nikkie thought of Tom, miles away in a Riga hospital, lying in his hospital bed and wondered if anything was passing through his mind. Knowing how much Tom loved nature, she imagined sending him the energy of the earth for support on his inner journey.

And dropping below the grief, she moved back to her life and self-expression. She had loved what her dance had become when she first freed herself from the constraints of her dream of working with one of the great dance companies of the world. When she realized that wasn't her dream after all.

But soon she had slipped into another experience, another dream, with Stone Tara. Then, the band had fired her. *Whether I am dancing with others or alone,* Nikkie thought, *I want to be a voice expressing a higher calling through my performance.* She wanted her dance to be like an expression of the Latvian spirituality of seeing the divine in all nature and all beings.

At its purest, this expression was more than her being in the flow, in the zone, inspired by the muse or nature or the collective unconscious. It was not about her at all, but rather about her stepping aside so spirit, so love could move through her. This creative expression was no longer personal, not about feeding her artistic ego, but a gift of grace. That is what she wanted to offer. And if she could not tap that in a professional dance setting, she would rather dance by herself in the woods like when she was a young girl, where no one but the trees and animals—and maybe the dead—could see her.

She still had so much to be grateful for, so much love in her life. She knew her mother, grandmother and brother loved her irrespective of what she did or did not do. All they wanted was for Nikkie to be happy, doing what she loved or not doing anything at all, and to have love in her life. And if no one else gave Nikkie the love, they were going to make sure they gave it—and she gave it to herself. That could be enough. She was enough. She had such bounty, whether or not her father's love or dancing with his company turned out to be lasting or temporary and conditional.

And in any case, the love she most needed to acknowledge was not parental love or sibling love or the love of a partner. Instead, it was God's love for her, the Divine Mother's unconditional love.

That love was without condition and existed for her or anyone whether she was a dancer expressing her highest vision or one of the people who never had a chance to live out their dreams because they had been sent to Siberia or otherwise persecuted during one of the occupations in Latvia. That Divine love existed for everybody, whether they were a world-recognized artist, an unknown dance teacher at a small studio in a small town, or one of the persecutors during the occupations.

That kind of love was challenging to imagine, but she hoped she might bring this message through no matter if she communicated it through dance or any other way. To know that love. To be an expression of it. To see everyone as worthy of receiving it, including the dead of her vision.

CHAPTER 26

Nikkie felt the urge to move. She rose up from where she had been lying in the grass, ran her fingers across the band of lace that gathered the gentle folds at the scooped neckline of her nightgown. The lace felt scratchy, but not nearly as scratchy as the sheets and blanket on Vilnis' bed had been. She left her shawl loosely draped across her shoulders. Her arms looked to her like they had a slightly bluish tinge in the moonlight.

She walked across the grass toward the wall of trees. The forest on Vilnis land. Did it hold the answers she sought? Were the dead there—just beyond reach? A wave of excitement shimmered across her skin. Her hair draped over her shoulders, loose and slightly disheveled from the time she had spent tossing and turning in bed.

As a child, she had always wanted to run through the forest on a moonlit night in her nightgown. Even after the vision of the dead. She wanted to bask in moonglow streaming through trees. But she was not allowed to go alone into the woods at night, not even when her family was camping. "You might get lost or meet up with a mountain lion, a bear and who knows what else," Ellie had warned.

What else, indeed.

Why not do it now? She stroked the soft white cotton of her nightgown. Meet the dead. Don't meet them. Why not run at this moment—without agenda—for herself alone? For that child she had been. That beloved of the Divine. She breathed away the nervousness in her belly and eased on the ballet shoes she used as bedroom slippers. They stuck some to her bare feet, damp from the dewy grass. She stepped forward toward the trees.

The wall of wood and leaves and branches seemed to open for her, then swallow her whole. She ran without looking back. Breezy air moved across her arms and face. Below, it blew up her nightgown, flowed across her naked body, made the cotton material billow around her. Her hair streamed behind her.

Nikkie focused on the ground several steps ahead, running in and around oak and white birch trees as tall and thin as the pine trees that surrounded them. There were others but naming them was not her intention. Being amongst them was. She wanted to make her way home to them and back to what was left of her heart.

The warnings of her childhood flashed in her mind. Leave a trail of cornmeal sprinkled behind you as you go into the woods. Bend a branch. Mark a tree. Something that will lead you out of the woods and home again.

But what if these woods were her home now? These trees.

"I love you," she called out to them. Then words and the boundaries separating her from the trees vanished. She was alone in the one being of the forest, the only sounds her breath heaving as she ran, and a slight hum swirling all around her—in her.

The fear of getting lost disappeared. Nikkie knew these trees even though she had never seen them before. This forest was her friend. She sensed she could always find her way even in the thickest and blackest of woodlands.

She breathed in and out, steady, heart beating faster, lightly pounding. She did not know or care if she had been running for one minute or thirty.

All she had run from flashed before her now, like a mini-life review. The New York dance community. Relationships. Grief. Pain. Heartache. And most definitely—the dead.

But this running in the Latvian forest was not any of that. Not running away. This running had bubbled up inside her. It was her saying yes to being alive in a body that was able to move and express itself. And in that body, she was running toward the dead, no longer away from them.

They were here as well, Nikkie realized as she ran. The dead ones. Somewhere. Though she could not see them. They had to be. And in a flash of insight, she knew that as much as she was now searching for them, they were drawing her to them, too, reeling her in. One step. Two steps. Closer.

Even though weaving in and out of trees, she could not see them, the dead were no longer a breath behind her like she had sensed when connecting with them in the forest in Oregon. The dead had moved up beside her now, in front of her, all around her.

"You are our destiny," she remembered the dead called out to her back then. And now, she accepted she was that destiny, though she still did not know how or what it would be like. "The key is in the forest," the trees had incanted to her. Was that key here in this forest, tonight, within her reach?

Nikkie stretched out her arms. Her feet pounded the earth, and the impact vibrated up her body, her fingers brushing against objects as she passed them. Leaves? Branches? Tree trunks? The key? The extended digits of the dead reaching back to her?

"You are our destiny," they had hummed. And Nikkie wondered if the opposite held true, that they were her destiny as well.

And with that thought, running in her nightgown in the night, her heart was filled with love for these dead. Instead of feeling afraid of them as she had all her life, instead of wanting to push them away, run from them, get on with her "real" life, her heart was filled with compassion for these beings who had haunted her dreams and the quiet of sleepless nights. Love for these beings who had traveled the span of her life with her and led her to this moment in these woods. Love for these beings it made no sense to love.

And then it was as if time slowed, and her pulse slowed, and her running slowed, and she came face to face with a birch tree. Stop, it seemed to say. Be still now. And just like that, she was done running. The urge drained out her feet.

She put out her hand to touch the bark. She turned and leaned back against the tree, let it buoy her up, hold her, infuse her with life. She let out a deep sigh of release.

Her heart, which was pounding from running, slowed, and she felt its steady beat. Boom Boom. Boom Boom. It resonated at an even pace with her breath. Her vision came back into focus taking in the muted shapes and textures of the nighttime forest.

She sensed the soft skin of the birch tree. She felt its branches and its trunk as a sentient being holding her close, ready to listen and soothe without judgment or agenda.

Nikkie turned so that she could put her arms around this birch in a dark forest. Remembering what her grandmother had taught her in Gulbene about giving her pain to the tree, she leaned her forehead against it.

The birch's bark was smooth and papery and reminded her of the madrones of her childhood in Oregon—only the birch's covering was smooth before it peeled, the madrone's afterward. Both trees were like snakes periodically shedding their skins. Their bark served as a dead layer of skin that protected the live wood underneath. For madrones, Tom had told her the process was thought of as evolutionary, the tree shedding the bark that contained lichen, insect eggs, and parasites so disease would not build up and harm the health at the heart of the tree.

She felt the life energy of the tree pouring in through her forehead and pulsing through her body. "Please, blessed tree, take the hurt, the pain and sadness I feel about my brother, my father, my dancing," she said out loud. "Take the loss and pain Tom and I have carried for the dead. Clear their pain. The pain you witnessed."

She felt a shock pulse through her system, jerked her forehead back from the tree. "Is it too much? I don't want to hurt you," she asked the tree, recalling how as children, she and Tom had carved their names into the Oregon madrone. She had felt that tree's scream of pain. Now, her brother was suffering—accident or no accident—and her family was too. She did not want to harm an innocent tree for her own relief, a quick fix.

Perhaps the time had come for her to carry the burden of her pain alone. Or surrender it to the one source she had been contemplating—the divine within and around her.

But this night, this birch tree sighed, like a deep breath of letting go. Nikkie had a sense of it joining with the trees around it. All of them opened to what she was surrendering to the one tree. Serving as a conduit, they let the pain stream through them deep into the center of the earth, deep into the heart of the Divine Mother who could hold it all.

And she remembered Tom saying that the root systems of birch trees were interconnected, each feeding the other, creating a broad support system. The whole gave to and was impacted by each tree. These trees, he had told her, would continue to feed and nurture a tree in their group through their root connection even after it died. Each tree was cared for, held meaning to the whole, was recognized—alive or dead. *I see you,* the trees said to one another. *I see you.*

But instead of the pain and sadness leaving, a voice inside whispered to her, *Go deeper.* And she felt the energy pulling her down the trunk of the tree to the forest floor. She turned and sat on the ground leaning back against the tree. And there in front of her, another tree stood tall. It seemed to have a glow around it, an aura of silver white energy. It was the sacred tree, the oak, Māra had painted on the wall of her dance studio. Nikkie's heart began to pound, but simultaneously, her body calmed down. The oak. The tree associated with the Goddess Māra that Latvians gathered around in ritual when they needed help. "Help," she whispered. *Palīdz man.*

The stories she carried—her own and her brother's—passed before her. Tom's coma. Her guilt at failing herself and her brother. Fear of the dead. Not growing up with a father. The lost opportunities and challenges of being a professional artist. Her successes. The tales of her ancestors. So many more. And below the stories, Nikkie felt as if the wick of a lantern had been lit to reveal a dark tunnel of hollowness she felt inside—beneath the business of her life and mind. The tunnel's air heavy and thick. To exist there was like breathing bricks.

A wave of sadness passed through her again, and she felt the soothing energy of all the trees stream into her shoulders and back. The birch trees and the sacred mother oak.

How long had it been since she had allowed herself to be soothed like this, Nikkie wondered? She thought back to the first time she had seen the dead in the forest. The intensity of that experience had frightened Nikkie to the core. Despite Ellie comforting her afterward, Nikkie had never wanted to feel so afraid again. And hadn't. She had toughened up. Toughened her skin like the bark of a tree. These last months had been a process of shedding that bark to reveal what? Rawness? A new layer of skin? A more profound sense of herself. She hoped so.

All she wanted at this moment was to release whatever remained of that hardened exterior and collapse into some being's arms to be held, rocked against a warm human body. She wanted to be told everything would be all right; it was okay to be vulnerable. Her brother would be all right. And to let herself cry for as long as she needed.

She felt the energy of the trees wrap around her, their branches like arms of light. As she let down, Nikkie felt a primal bellowing build in her. Grief vast enough to sound in a forest of trees. Bottled up, ready to burst, the sorrow and loss she had carried all these years and her ancestors' loss.

She thought she had protected herself from feeling this with the hardened bark she had formed around her heart. But she had not. Instead, the grief had crept in behind the bark and frozen in her, become ice, solid and jagged. Blue ice like a glacier. Ancient water crystalized. She had carried it like a burden bearing down on her heart, so heavy she thought it might burst.

The weight pulled her down, down into what seemed like a never-ending pit of despair. *Open your heart. Feel this,* the trees whispered to her.

"No," she said out loud. "It's too much." She tried to pull away from the trees, to stand up. But the weight bore down all over her now, and she could not move. The fear she had not felt when she ran through the forest caught up to her, floored her. "No no no no," she said. "Yes yes yes yes," the trees answered.

You never carry this weight alone, Nikkie heard inside her. Grounding to the earth, her roots interconnected, entwined with those of the trees, the light of the branches. From within and around the sacred oak, the divine feminine came as the energy of the Latvian Goddess Māra, sending love to thaw love what had frozen inside Nikkie.

A primal keening rose from deep within Nikkie's belly and heart and vibrated through her throat out into the night. Nikkie's cries invited in the pain of the dead in the forest. They were near now. She was sure of it.

Until now, she had sensed if she allowed in their collective loss, she might die as well. She had feared her grip on this life would not be strong enough in the encounter for her to remain embodied here. Unless she resisted, she feared she would be pulled across the veils between life and death. Instead, immersed in Māra's love, she saw that what they offered was not dissolution, but something else. And that would only be revealed when she found them.

Nikkie keened into the night, into the trees and felt the frozen shards that had filled and shielded her heart and gut melting drop by drop —the hardened bark of her shedding away. Nikkie surrendered the rising sea of loss and grief to Māra and remembered that Māra was also the goddess of the waters.

Reaching back to stroke the tree she leaned against, gazing at the Māra oak, she knew with certainty no matter what happened, she was held by the forest, supported by it, by the divine feminine in all its forms, by the stillness of the night air.

Her brother Tom flashed in her mind's eye. Nikkie saw his spirit, the radiance of his being, also held by spirit beings on his journey. She saw him as he was at his core. Whole. Pure. Unencumbered by judgments or misperceptions of who he was.

Nikkie's whole being vibrated with energy, as she imagined taking Tom's hands into her own and the two of them gazing into each other's eyes.

"I love you. I'm sorry, Tom," she whispered. "For any ways I might have taken your support and love for granted. For not seeing and encouraging your own self-expression enough when you gave so much to my dance career. For feeling sorry for myself when I have so much. For not always seeing the love at your core, your true value. Please forgive me."

A moment passed. She felt the forest breathe with her as she waited. Then, she felt Tom forgive her. First in words. "I forgive you. I love you."

Then, it was as if he was a boy again with his knife by the madrone tree in an Oregon forest. Only instead of carving their names into the tree, he was scraping away the bark of her, the dead skin of her old life. He scraped and scraped until the layer of protection was gone, and she was new again. Ready to grow.

Then, held in the broader embrace of the divine mother, she and Tom forgave themselves for their misperceptions of themselves and each other. Nikkie for not living up to what she had hoped for herself as a dancer and in support of her brother. Tom in turning his back on himself and his own creativity. Both of them for not being able to resolve the pain of the dead stuck somewhere in the Latvian forest. And for not recognizing their inherent value no matter what they did or did not do.

Tom also let down and cried, for he had been carrying the dead as much as she had, Nikkie realized with a start. And this night in a forest in Latvia, the moment had come for both of them to put that load down and choose life. Fully. Whether or not she danced again or Tom regained consciousness and wrote as his heart called him to do, whether or not she found and did whatever she was to do to help the dead ones. Whether or not the twins found their deep connection with Peter.

All would be well. Nikkie felt it in her heart, in her bones now. She could not imagine how she could feel or know this with everything that remained unresolved in their lives, but she did and knew what was happening, what would happen, was beyond her human understanding. And she accepted that.

She and Tom were living out their destinies. As much as she wanted Tom to heal, as much as she wanted to dance again, all that could be done now was show up and follow whatever guidance appeared to move towards that goal. But Tom's fate, her own, were out of their hands. The future of the dead ones. Out of her hands.

When she did find the dead again though, she was no longer avoiding, no longer resisting, but actively surrendering to do what was needed, regardless of the outcome, regardless of not knowing what to do or how to do it. And she was not alone in that call to action. She called on Māra to shepherd her through the mystery.

She sensed Laima join Māra now. Laima. The Latvian Goddess of fate, of luck. And Nikkie imagined placing all of them, Tom, the dead, her mother and grandmother, Vilnis, Peter, her cousin Māra, gently in the hands of those two Latvian Goddesses.

Then she heard it. A gentle tinkling all around her. The sounds rose. The forest was singing. A choir of incandescent notes lighting her heart and soul.

This tree song flowed in, filled her. Rising. Falling. Like a choir of angels. Melodious. Sometimes cacophonous but imbuing her with both passion and peace. The tree song vibrated her. And she heard a new resonance. The vibration that remained from the hundreds of thousands, perhaps millions of Latvians who had joined together to sing as one throughout the years, Māra whispered to her.

This song of uniting, this divine song, eased open the remnants of the cells inside her that had crystallized around grief. And she recalled a passage from the Bible: "Let the sea roar, and all it contains; Let the field exult, and all that is in it. Then the trees of the forest will sing for joy before God."

Curled up in the embrace of the sacred trees, exulting in the joy of the forest, Nikkie fell into a dreamless sleep. The first true rest she had had since her vision of the dead on the stage of the Hollywood Bowl.

Nikkie woke up to the morning light, curled around the birch tree. She had no idea if it was 4 a.m. when the sun rose in June or later. Something had shifted inside her. She still might not know who she was without her dance, without her brother.

But now, not knowing who she was or what she wanted was a relief. For the first time, she accepted this murky, not-knowing space. And here, the answer no longer lay in running to fix or improve herself or anyone else. Not even Tom.

She and Tom simply were. And that was enough. No matter what they did or did not do in the world. No matter what healing occurred. Or did not.

Dance may have been her expression all these years, but it was not who she was. Whatever had shifted in the woods that night, dance no longer defined her worth. Her value. It never had. Not even when it touched and moved people or seemed the most profound expression of herself. Nothing she did or did not do was her value. Her value was inherent. The same went for Tom. His worth did not depend on him writing poetry or finding an outer expression. Nikkie's only purpose was to follow the flow of love, of the divine in her life. To be in service of love wherever she was called to do that.

What she needed to do for Tom or the dead would reveal itself. Or it would not. Whatever happened, she had put the burden down. The weight of thinking she had to carry these loads. She had laid down the guilt, shame and need to control her life. Her body. Her dance. Her movement. All of it.

She would surrender each moment to the divine, even if it meant she never danced again. *I don't know who I am anymore,* she said to herself. But instead of terror or resistance, she felt peace. *Thank Goddess. I don't know what I want anymore. Thank God.*

She did know deep in her belly something she had previously known only in her head. That at the root of all, she was love and so was everyone else in her life. Tom. Peter. Ellie. Indra. Māra. Vilnis. Each person she knew. The dead in the forest. Everyone.

Nikkie felt the tree, the earth and the roots beneath her. The embrace of Māra and Laima. She thanked them all, thanked the divine expression around her.

The air was cold, but she was not chilled. Her inner fire burned bright, warming her.

She extended her legs and using her arms for support, raised herself to stand. She hugged the birch and the sacred oak one after the other one, tears of gratitude rising in her eyes. She reached up and tasted one, relishing its saltiness. The body's saltiness. *We are seventy percent water, salt water like the sea*, she said to herself.

The time had come to go back to Vilnis' house. He would have returned by now. As she turned, there, on a leaf within reach, was one perfect drop of water. Like her tear. Had the tree also cried in gratitude? She accepted the gift and anointed her third eye, her throat and heart chakras, touched the remaining dampness with her tongue. Appreciation rose again, filled her with a tingling of life force. She nodded her head once, then slowly walked back through the forest. She followed the rays of the sun filtering through the dark of the shadows, the same sun to which the Latvians had dedicated half their more than one million folksongs.

Chapter 27

After a night in the forest, Nikkie imagined luxuriating in the shower before Peter and Vilnis woke up. Instead, she noted the five-gallon water heater she had seen in many Latvian bathrooms. The tub had only a faucet sprayer for rinsing, no showerhead.

How much I take for granted, Nikkie thought, as she sprayed her hair and body. The water never heated up past lukewarm. She turned it off, soaped up, then rinsed off. She repeated the cycle for her hair, barely making it through the second rinse before the water turned cold. At least its coolness served to bring her more into focus on this day when she would ask Vilnis for his help locating the dead.

By the time Nikkie emerged, Peter sat at a small dining room table drinking coffee. Vilnis was carrying in a platter of traditional Latvian breakfast fare—rye bread, meat, smoked fish, cheese and tomatoes from the nearby kitchen. He was about five foot ten, muscular and trim. Even though he was in his mid-to-late sixties, his hair remained brown. She wondered if he dyed it. He wore a fitted, long-sleeved burgundy shirt and blue jeans. Like Indra, he looked a decade younger than his age.

When he saw Nikkie, he broke into a smile, put down the food and walked over to her. He cupped her hands in his,

leaned back and looked long and hard at her. He nodded, looking from her to Peter and back again. "I see Peter in you. Definitely. And you're tall. Like him. Beautiful. Welcome, Nikola,
Nikkie. To my home. To Kuldiga. I am sad about your brother,
but I am glad you have come."

Vilnis' home was simple and had a lived-in quality. Pillows with designs of Latvian symbols embroidered on them
graced a plush, comfortable brown sofa. Two walls were covered with artwork—paintings and photographs of trees, as
well as a few personal pictures. Another wall was lined with
bookshelves, filled with Latvian and international novels, history, philosophy and books on photography and art. Dance.

As they got to know each other over breakfast, she noticed
the now familiar nervousness edging into her sense of well-
being, the closer she came to telling Vilnis about her experience. She focused on her surroundings to shift her attention to
something concrete that could help center her first.

Her gaze wandered back to Vilnis' personal photos, and
she recognized Peter and Māra at various ages over recent
decades. In others, Vilnis was with an attractive woman with
deep wisdom in her eyes. Nikkie assumed she was his wife,
Lilita. The rest were people she did not know. She asked, and
he filled her in on various family members –including Peter's
parents and Māra's. What was lacking, Nikkie noticed, were
photos of Vilnis own distant past, his childhood and parents,
photos of him and Peter's father as children.

And as warm as his welcome had been, when the three of
them began to talk about people, he became somewhat guarded, seemed to put a check on his emotions and response. Nikkie did not push to delve into what he seemed to want to keep
private. Give it time, she thought to herself. This man had to
monitor what he said for fifty years.

He shifted the focus to the photos of events that had led
to Latvia's freedom, like the Baltic Way and the barricades and

demonstrations, a song festival. "So much has changed in our country since we declared our freedom, but we still have much to learn," he said.

"How so?"

"It's a big topic, but my main lesson has been to discover that freedom needs to be as much inside as out. By declaring Latvia's freedom, we gained the right to move around at will, to choose our work, to buy what we want if we have the money, to speak out. That is all outer. Yet, I, and so many here, do not know how to be free inside. People feel empty like something is missing. But what is on the outside I have found can never fill them up."

"We also see that in America," Nikkie said.

"In what way?" Peter asked.

"What's outside is never enough. I have had to deal with the whole notion of freedom as an artist, in trusting my own creative choices. Or speaking out about or showing what feels vulnerable in my dance. How not to let my fears hold me back from expressing myself. It seems like a lifetime of learning how to be free for all of us."

"Yes, I can see," Vilnis said. "Peter, Māra and I have long discussions about this."

And Nikkie felt excited about the possibility of talking about it with them as well.

"But this is a serious discussion for our first meeting, yes?" Vilnis said.

It's only serious discussion number one, Nikkie thought, wondering if this could be a good jump-off point to tell Vilnis about the vision. Speaking of vulnerable topics, Vilnis....

He mentioned the speeches Nikkie had learned about early in her visit to Latvia where Latvia's president encouraged Latvians to go after their dreams both for their own and for Latvia's good. He explained in many cases, Latvians were learning to think for themselves for the first time and needed that push. For decades, Communists had told them what to think, what they could be.

"Those of us who had dreams learned to squelch them until we were free," Vilnis said. "Now, we learn a new way."

"And not everyone wants to do that," Peter said. "Some Latvians miss having more taken care of by the state. But growing numbers are learning to trust we can have dreams and realize them." Vilnis agreed.

"I feel great potential here," Nikkie said. "You have this chance to create something new in Latvia in some improbably messy, but brilliant kind of way. Latvians have such freshness of ideas."

Nikkie hoped what she witnessed held up a mirror for her own life. She, too, wanted to create something new, outside the mainstream. She yearned to delve into those original forms of dance that reflected her explorations of the inner world and spirituality.

Nikkie may not have feared for her life or imprisonment for artistic expression, but she had known the trepidation that her creative spirit might die in traditional forms.

For a time, her creative center had been lost—even with Stone Tara. Here again, she caught a fleeting glimmer that could not quite be grasped yet that something new might still arise from her, inspire her to create, fill her—in her family's homeland.

She looked forward to talking to Peter about it back in Riga. For now, her focus needed to remain on the prime reason she had come to Kuldiga.

"I would like to show you a place where I am expressing my freedom now," Vilnis said.

"Please do. I'd love to know about it," Nikkie said.

Vilnis pointed to the photos of the trees on the wall and beamed as if he was a proud father sharing his children with someone. All his discomfort and guardedness disappeared when he talked about these photos, which Nikkie discovered he had taken.

"Māra mentioned you used to be a wedding and portrait photographer, right?"

Vilnis shrugged. "It was the only way I was allowed to be a professional photographer in the Soviet system, the only way I was allowed to express myself. But now I take photos of the trees I love. They don't miss appointments, complain about the way they look or refuse to smile." He chuckled.

"And they don't talk back," Peter said, smiling.

"Sometimes they do though," Vilnis said. "If I get quiet enough and fortunate enough, the trees seem to talk to me, even guide me in what images to take."

Nikkie felt a wave of relief. This was a place she knew she could connect with Vilnis—and to Peter. "I've talked to trees since I was a child," she said. "We have that in common."

"It's a very Latvian thing to do," Vilnis said. "It was especially convenient during the occupation when you did not know whom you could trust," and he told Nikkie he used to give his pain to the trees.

Nikkie acknowledged that her grandmother had taught her about that, and she had tried it out on the grandmother oak on the family land. She did not mention her experience with the trees the night before.

"It seems we do have a lot in common," Vilnis said. "Do your brother and mother also talk to trees?"

"Ellie, yes. Tom not so much. He used to make fun of me for believing trees talked."

Should I go for it and tell him about the vision now? Nikkie wondered. Instead, she decided to relish this time of ease between them a little longer. "Do you have any other tree images besides the ones on the wall?"

Vilnis retrieved a portfolio from his bedroom, moved the food off the table and opened it to reveal a series of extraordinary and artistic images of trees. Bark patterns and oozing tree sap that looked like abstract art. Branches and tree trunks that appeared to be dancers with limbs outstretched and in motion. One forest area had light coming through in such a way that the trees formed an outline of what looked like an image of the divine mother, Mother Mary.

"You have a tremendous gift," Nikkie says. "Are these all from this forest?"

Vilnis nodded. Nikkie felt a glimmer of hope that since Vilnis had gone through the woods with an artist's level of attention, he might well have seen the clearing and trees from her vision. She hoped she could describe them in enough detail for him.

"For me, photography is my hobby," Vilnis said.

"If you wanted, these would make a wonderful book or gallery exhibit," Nikkie said and mentioned she would love to share the photos with her friend Mikis in Riga, a photographer for National Geographic.

"See, Nikkie agrees," Peter said and shifted his attention to her. "Vilnis ignores me when I tell him that."

"I'm sure you are both being too kind," Vilnis said. "Taking them is what brings me great joy. And I am happy to share them with the two people here who appreciate them."

There was a moment of silence, and Peter suggested Nikkie bring out the photo album she had brought of Ellie and the twins growing up. And an older one of Indra and her family in Latvia—from before the war and at the DP camp. Nikkie hoped Indra's photos, in particular, might help pave the way to broach WWII as it related to her vision.

They moved over to Vilnis' couch, and Vilnis put the albums in his lap. He asked questions about the twins and Ellie as he flipped through the pages—including Nikkie's dancing. But as Peter had intimated, Vilnis did not volunteer personal details. She told the story of her family escaping from Latvia.

"I'm amazed my great grandparents managed to escape carrying the albums. They are so heavy and bulky."

"That is remarkable," Vilnis said. "This interests me. What people carry when they are forced to leave almost everything and everyone they know behind—and how they survive."

"Vecāmamma doesn't know why her family lived when others did not," Nikkie said. "The bombs were falling all around them. For some unknown reason, it was their destiny. But then, you survived the war as well. Even though your parents remained."

Vilnis sighed heavily. "Yes, me too."

"I'd like to hear more about that," she said. Nikkie sat quietly now, barely breathing, not wanting to interrupt the flow of conversation. Then, to her dismay, her cell phone rang. She had forgotten to turn it off.

"Don't you want to get that?" Vilnis said. Was she making things up or did he seem relieved not to have to answer her question? "It might be important."

Nikkie snapped to attention. Tom.

"I apologize. Excuse me. I'll be back as soon as I can," Nikkie said and got up from the couch to answer the phone.

It was Māra. "Is everything okay?" Nikkie asked, holding the phone to her ear, moving outside into the front yard for privacy. She stopped next to Vilnis' greenhouse made from heavy, clear plastic, where tomatoes, dill, cucumbers, and other summer vegetables were growing.

"No change in Tom's condition," Māra said. "But I did the research I promised you on helping spirits cross over."

"Listen, I'm in the middle of talking to Vilnis," Nikkie said. "I'm about to tell him."

"This won't take long," Māra said. "I found something that might relate to Tom. Greek philosophers called people who could communicate between the afterlife and this one 'walkers between the worlds.' One man, Aithalides, from 600

BCE, was able to pass back and forth at will between the physical world and the afterlife."

"How do you connect that with Tom and my vision."

"Today, this role seems to be played out by people who have near-death experiences. They can serve as mediators and messengers between the living and the dead. I believe Tom's coma would count as that. Tom may be ready to help you."

"I don't know, Māra. All I want is for Tom to get better. I certainly don't want to count on him for help."

"I understand. But what you're doing is not a journey to be taken lightly. You need all the support you can get."

"Now you're scaring me."

"You'll be fine. The dead would not have shown themselves to you if you could not handle this situation. The guides you work with, the nature spirits, the trees, the divine beings will support you."

Nikkie had to tell Vilnis. Now.

Walking back into the house, she saw Vilnis and Peter from behind, their heads bent forward looking at the photographs. But when Peter heard Nikkie, he pushed back the album, sat up straight. "Is everything all right at the hospital?" he asked.

"Yes, that was Māra letting me know nothing had changed," Nikkie said.

"I'm glad," Vilnis said.

"Which brings me to something I need to tell you Vilnis. I'm hoping you can help me."

"Please, sit down." Vilnis lowered his voice in tandem with the gravity of Nikkie's tone. "I will help in any way I can."

And Nikkie told him about her vision, searching his eyes for a response. "I searched the forest near our family land with no success. Then, when I told Māra and Peter we knew it was

Peter in the vision, they both suggested Kuldiga and your forest."

Vilnis let out a deep sigh, lowered his eyes. Nikkie felt like she was spiraling down, losing ground, sinking. "I was hoping you might know of such a clearing, or of a tragedy like this that happened in this forest during World War II."

Vilnis sat in silence. He must not know anything. Maybe she had upset him. He thought she was nuts. But it didn't matter, she reminded herself. What he thought. This property was the logical place. He felt like the logical person, maybe her last hope. She wanted to look at Peter for support but felt compelled to keep her focus on Vilnis.

Vilnis continued to sit. Staring at—what? She was not sure he was even breathing. She felt like she was falling into a deep well, and he was falling back into his own version of a well. Both of them slipping away from the light into the dark waters. She seemed to detect gradations of feelings cracking and crumbling underneath the exterior of Vilnis' face. Or was she projecting her own emotions on him, and she was the one cracking and crumbling as she tumbled in the dark.

"I don't know," he mumbled finally. "I don't know," he said more clearly. He wiped tears filling his eyes with his sleeve, grew pale as if he was in shock. Stunned. "Yes, I do. Wait," he said as if Nikkie could do anything but that. "Please wait." And he rose up, paused for a moment as if testing his ability to stay upright. He walked into his bedroom, closed the door behind him.

Nikkie stared at it, wondering what she was waiting for or if he was coming back. But soon, the bedroom door reopened. Vilnis emerged carrying a photo album under his arm. He sat down on the couch and motioned for Nikkie and Peter to join him. His eyes were red. Part of a handkerchief was visible in his back pants pocket.

What had she released in him, Nikkie wondered.

"I am going to show you something," Vilnis said. "Something not even Peter or Māra have seen. I'm sorry Peter, but I hope you will understand." He opened the album, thumbing through pages. And here were the photos that had been missing from the wall. Old photos. Of what Nikkie assumed was Vilnis' earlier life—before the war. Perhaps during it.

He stopped at a specific page, opened the album flat on his lap. "Here. This. You tell me what you see." He choked on his words as he spoke them, pointed to a lone photo on a page. What looked like a family portrait. A man. A woman. Two children. A boy. And a little girl.

The faces were serious as most pictures from those days were. But there was love there as well. Each adult had a hand on the shoulders of the children. The children sat on a bench, garlanded with flowers, holding hands. They all wore traditional Latvian clothing. The portrait had been taken outside in front of a forest.

Nikkie's gut clenched like she had been punched, and the sinking feeling intensified. She could barely breathe. Her face flushed. She knew these faces, had seen them before.

"It's the girl," she said. "From my vision. And the adults, her parents. It's all of them. Except for the boy."

And as soon as she said "boy," she recognized the resemblance. Faint, but unmistakable. Especially around the eyes and chin. The boy looked like a young Vilnis. "You?" she asked, confused, her mind trying to make sense of the photos. "Were these people related to you?"

Vilnis looked grim, did not answer.

As far as she knew, Vilnis had been raised with Peter's father. They were brothers. No sister that she knew about. And not these adults as parents. Peter had shown her a photo of his grandparents, Vilnis' parents. And Vilnis was Peter's uncle, after all. What was Vilnis doing in a picture with the people from her vision?

"Do you know these people?" Nikkie asked Peter. "These aren't your grandparents, are they?" He shook his head, held her gaze.

Nikkie could hear her heart pounding in her ears, feel it in her chest.

Vilnis sighed again, put his hands on the couch by his knees and pushed off with determination to stand up as if launching himself like a boat from a dock. "Please," he said. "We will go. I will explain there. But it's quite a walk. You will need good walking shoes. And put on long pants and a long-sleeved top. Bring a scarf or a hat. I have extras that might fit if you don't have them. Cover up. The ticks can be bad."

"Are we going into your forest?" Nikkie asked.

"We're going to a forest, but not this one. I will talk as we go." He seemed a man determined now, breathed deeply, closed his eyes. "I have spent much time in hiding. No more. It's time to go."

Chapter 28

In Southern Oregon, the densest of forests had space to walk between the trees, for the sun to shine through and at times dominate the interplay of shadow and light. But in this forest in Kurzeme, the trees grew so close to one another, the ground was so crowded with underbrush, that even in the bright of day, it looked like twilight.

Following Vilnis, Nikkie could not walk with a sense of spaciousness. Instead, she concentrated on carving a narrow path through the dimness and growth. If she looked up, she could make out the muted white of a cloudy sky. But straight ahead, the trees and branches seemed perpetually locked in those moments between day and night, when color drained away, and objects shifted to hues of gray and black.

Many of the trees in this forest were birch. Tall and thin. The contrast of the white skin with black markings looked stark even in the dim light.

But these birch trees were different from those she knew in Oregon. These grew fifty feet high, close together. At home, birch trees were less than half the size and grew individually or in small clusters. In this forest, a young tree did not appear to have a chance unless the older ones were harvested or succumbed to the elements, disease or age, to create enough space and light for the young to thrive.

I could never have navigated these woods without Vilnis, Nikkie thought. No wonder the men in Latvia, who had been at risk for arrest, deportation or execution during the wars, had been able to lose themselves in the country's forests. You could easily disappear here, hide for decades, abiding amongst the wild boars, wolves and other woodland creatures who called the woods home.

She thought about the Forest Brothers again. The post-World War II resisters had survived in these woods until they were caught, or turned themselves in. Most had been betrayed by infiltrators or eventually driven out of the forest by the severe conditions—cold, lack of light and food, illness and isolation. The last of them emerged forty years after the war. She could not fathom living alone in a forest for so many years.

This one, in particular, looked like she imagined an in-between world would look like, a netherworld, not quite in life or in death, but a portal place between the two. One could easily slip between the veils and lose oneself not only in this forest but in another plane of existence. Nikkie felt the tug, knew she could slide into an altered state of consciousness, but firmly intended not to. She wanted to remain in present reality, eyes wide open, for this journey.

The three of them walked silently, holding a sort of unspoken vigil. Nikkie maintained a close watch on Vilnis to make sure she did not lose him. She felt comforted by the sound of underbrush crackling in response to Peter's footsteps behind her, grateful he had come to support her.

Vilnis led her expertly through the trees, oblivious to the branches that scratched at his jacket. She was glad he had told her to wear long sleeves and hats, long pants tucked into thick socks to guard against tick bites. "Ticks not only carry Lyme disease here but also encephalitis," Vilnis cautioned.

Nikkie shuddered. As much as she loved nature, she abhorred ticks. When the twins lived near the wilderness in

Oregon, her mother had checked them for ticks daily. In a way, they reminded her of the dead. Growing up, she had felt like the dead were feeding on her like her lifeblood energy was leaking out to them.

Last night, running in the forest, that sense had changed for her. And today, she was about to find out their story and how Vilnis and perhaps other family members were involved. She wished he would start sharing what he had kept secret for so many years while they walked.

Patience, she told herself. Let it unfold in Vilnis' timing. And she wondered where he was taking them, how he even knew where to go through this densest of forests. He walked with such surety as if he was following a path clearly defined by brightly colored markers on the trees.

Nikkie thought back to the stories Indra had told her about her own family in Latvia when they were escaping the Russians. How her great grandfather led his family over farm-lands, through forests, off-road across Latvia. He had been guided by some inner wisdom as if he had a map and com-pass, a GPS. He relied on instinct, on his deep connection to the land.

Perhaps the trees had guided him. Maybe their inner ra-dar and connection propelled him forward, sending him from one cluster of trees to the next until the family arrived at the shore of Latvia.

Was that happening now? Were the trees guiding Vilnis, this man who talked to them, photographed them with great intimacy, gave his pain to them?

Was he following a trail of the pain people had given to trees? His own pain from childhood? The pain left here by the dead, when they were live beings, people he loved, on the way to their deaths? Not imaginary creatures, not only visions like she had seen. But live people with histories connected to Vilnis —and somehow to Peter—that for them, ended in this forest.

She paused to scan her own mind and intuition about these people who had died and came up blank. She still had no idea what she was supposed to do to help them other than show up. She had no clue how any of this could help Tom.

The energy shifted for Nikkie the more she immersed herself in this place. But rather than feeling invigorated by the excitement of being here, she felt drained again. She wanted to sink to the earth, lay down curled up by a tree like she had the night before, cradled in divine love. But she could not. Because this was the day some sort of healing might take place—where the dead, she and Tom would feel some kind of resolution, and perhaps Vilnis and Peter would too. In an attempt to revitalize herself, she tapped into her memory of the love she had experienced for the dead ones the night before, felt a lifting, drew strength from it to keep moving forward.

"You are our destiny," she heard, and she walked forward with purpose now to meet that destiny, with each step the weight on her lifting a little. She began to pray she would be up to that task. Trust, she told herself, fully believing the dead had come to her for a reason, that the Peter of her vision had asked her for help because she could help. I've got this, she told herself.

And all she knew was that in this precious moment, she only needed to keep placing one foot in front of the other. She just needed to keep saying yes, no matter how futile or frightening the upcoming encounter seemed.

Seeing Vilnis slow down ahead, she sensed in a few more steps she would arrive. She recalled that her childhood vision had been like a rushing river, a torrent of water, shaping her into the curves and forms of a canyon flowing she had known not where. Now she, like her family traversing Latvia during World War II, had come to her own version of the place where canyon and land had come to an end. There was nowhere left to hide. She had reached her destination, her open sea—the clearing.

❧

"We're here," Vilnis said.

Nikkie trembled, her body tingling in recognition. Without a doubt, she had reached the site of her vision. And the eerie twilight of the rest of the forest extended here as well.

While all that physically remained was a gravestone, remnants of flowers, plants, the dead were here. No remains flanked the surface of the ground. But she could see the dead in her mind's eye, feel them buried below her. Their bones. Her stomach gripped, tightened in that recognition. What remained of their decomposing bodies was interred here. Disintegrating in a mass grave. No longer separate carcasses of people who had crossed over. She envisioned the images of people she had seen in her vision. The little girl. The parents. But skulls, pieces of vertebrae disconnected from spines. Arms, hands, digits separated from one set of remains and entwined with another. Leg bones.

The mystics said this reality was only a dream. Well, the one in front of Nikkie was a nightmare. She shuddered. How many men? Women? Children? Unceremoniously shot down, left to decompose in this netherworld. Their collective cry reaching up to her now, enveloping her, ringing in her ears, drowning out the sounds of wind and bird song.

Vilnis had not yet said a word. Peter waited in silence too. She wished Vilnis would begin if only to ease the tension twisting and quaking inside her. This was it. Finally. She and her destiny were meeting face to face.

Vilnis moved closer to Nikkie and spoke his first words since they had left the car. "Is this the clearing you saw?"

Nikkie nodded, overwhelmed with a tumble of emotions.

He turned to face the clearing, knelt down on one knee and made the sign of the cross. Peter automatically raised his own hand and placed it on his heart.

"These are my people," Vilnis said, his voice cracking. "Our people. This is what our people suffered. My mother lies here somewhere. Mana mīļā mammiņa. My dear mother. Mana māsiņa. My sister. Mans tēvs. My father."

Nikkie felt confused. If Vilnis' immediate family was here, who was Peter's family to Vilnis? When she glanced at Peter, his mouth had tensed

Vilnis remained in his private world, fixed on the clearing. "Here is the secret I have kept. From everyone I know and love. From you, Peter. Māra. My own wife. I never wanted to endanger you or them or myself. Having lived most of my life under Communism, I saw what happened to people who spoke out. They were arrested. Their families were stigmatized or arrested with them. But now that Latvia is free, the time has come to speak. Maybe it will help me take a step toward freeing me along with my country. Maybe it will somehow help you also understand Peter. And since you are the one my family called here, Nikkie, I break my silence by telling you. It's time."

A hush fell over the clearing, lay like a haze, a fog ready to be dispelled by the breathing out of Vilnis' words. His story. One of many stories held by people, like him, who had been oppressed around the planet, whose words—if they spoke or wrote them—could mean imprisonment or death. She knew Peter had kept his own silences.

But there were the unspoken stories of people in free nations as well. How many times had Nikkie censored her own voice, gotten smaller, as a result, watched what she said, felt unsafe or anxious speaking out—even with people she cared about and who cared for her in return? At that moment, she sensed the healing power that was released anytime someone spoke out, dispelled secrets and lies, the way Vilnis was about to.

"I remember the night the soldiers came to arrest us," Vilnis said. "The Russians. After Latvia had been occupied by the

Russian army in June of 1940, people, especially landowners and intelligentsia, government officials, Latvian military were being arrested, shot, deported. We called it the Year of Terror that culminated in the mass deportations of fifteen thousand five hundred Latvians on June 14, 1941."

"A terrible time for Latvians," Nikkie said.

"Right, you also had family sent out," Vilnis said. "My own tragedy came not long before the mass deportation. My birth father was not your grandfather, Peter, like you grew up believing, and my birth mother was not your grandmother. Their names were Andrejs and Rasma Kārklis. Rasma was your grandmother's cousin."

Peter let out a long breath. His shoulders relaxed, and he closed his eyes.

"My father had been an officer in the Latvian army, so he was a target when the Russians invaded," Vilnis said. "Like many men during the war, he was hiding from them in the forest with a few soldiers from his troop We did not know where. If our mother knew, she did not tell us."

"And you were still living in your home?" Nikkie asked.

Vilnis nodded. "It wasn't safe, but we did not know where else to go. As a precaution, though, my mother had my sister and me sleep in the barn."

"How old were you?" Nikkie asked.

"I was six. My sister seven. Mama told us if we saw Russians come to our house in the night, we were to run out the back of the barn and into the woods. Don't come for me. Don't look back at all, she said. Run to the cabin of the meža sargs, the forest ranger, Aldis. He was responsible for the well-being of the forest and lived in a cabin there. He was my father's friend. Aldis will help, she said."

Vilnis paused, then almost spit out the words, "Stalin. *Maita.*" He said it softly under his breath. The words held through years of secrecy and repression. *Maita.* Her grandmother had called Stalin the same thing once. The lowest of the low. A scourge. Profanity on the earth.

Maita. Nikkie was sure she would feel the same as Vilnis if her mother lay here, murdered, instead of making pottery in Southern Oregon, her life filled with choices—or if her brother was with them.

"My mother," Vilnis said, his voice cracking with emotion, "was a beautiful woman. Latvians are beautiful people. Your people, Nikkie. Strong. Proud." He looked from the clearing to her, and she felt herself grow taller at the recognition. "She had so much love in her. For my sister and me. For my father. For the land. For Latvia. I wish Peter could have known her."

Nikkie thought of the bones lying in the earth. Which ones? Which ones had been his mother? She knelt down on her knees next to Vilnis, gently put her hand on his right shoulder.

"Our people have endured so much. So much," he said. "I don't know how we have endured."

"But you did," Nikkie said. "What happened, Vilnis? That night."

"I heard the truck drive up. I had been asleep, half buried in the hay. The night was dark, though the days had been growing longer. I heard voices. I was terrified."

"My mother had prepared us for this moment, but I didn't want to go. I wanted to run to the house and into my mother's arms. Protect her somehow, though I knew I could not do that. But if we could get to Aldis, maybe he could do something.

"You have to be the man, my mother had said to me. If anything happens, you have to be strong for you and your sister. It won't last long, this war, she had said. It can't. We'll all be back together again soon."

Vilnis turned his head toward Nikkie, then turned back, looking down at the grave site. "Soon." He snorted in disgust, shook his head in resignation. "How many families?"

"What tremendous pressure for you and your sister," Nikkie said, her voice trembling. "You were both so young."

"I reached over and shook my sister gently," Vilnis said, closing his eyes as if seeing her one more time. "I didn't want her to cry out, so I put my hand on her mouth just in case. Shh, I whispered in her ear. Mama had already told us not to question what we were to do. We were fully dressed and had our shoes on. That night, my own childhood ended."

Vilnis and Kate had run to the edge of the forest, the same woods where many people had fled to hide. But Kate had stopped and told him to go ahead alone, that she was afraid and could not leave her mother. She turned and ran back. Vilnis reached out for her but never had a chance to grab on, to make her go with him. She never slowed down.

"At that moment, I had my own choice," Vilnis said. "How did I manage to make the choice I did when I was only six, and my sister and I were so close?" He shook his head forcefully. "It was more than listening to my mother. On some deeper level, I knew what would happen if I followed my sister. Over the previous months, I had heard my parents whisper to each other of the deaths. The disappearances. I had heard my mother cry when neighbors disappeared. At six, I already knew more about death than many adults. But I also knew the will to live. The will to survive at great cost was strong in me. It carried me that night."

Nikkie could sense that will to live rise in him now and fill him, but something more—a deep inner strength and wisdom.

"I let the darkness of the forest swallow me. Don't look back, mama had said. And I didn't, the instinct to live taking over. Turning away from my sister, I was in shock. If I stopped to think, I would never make it. I would run back with her. Thank God I was physically strong. Raised on a farm. I was like a horse with blinders on. My entire focus was on getting to Aldis' cabin.

"My heart pounded. I couldn't see clearly, but somehow, my feet knew where to take me. I had walked to the cabin many times with my father. It didn't matter that it was dark. The branches scratching at my face and arms did not deter me."

Aldis had hidden the boy in his root cellar amongst the potatoes and turnips. Each day, he would take a chance and let Vilnis come out a few times to stretch his limbs. They had no idea yet what had happened to his mother and sister. And Vilnis, who could usually sense his sister, felt nothing. Aldis was trying to find out without appearing conspicuous. And he did not have a radio or a telephone to help him, let alone the aid of something like a television news program. They held onto the hope that perhaps the Russians would only question Vilnis' mother and let her return and that they had not captured his father in the forest.

Vilnis recounted his story like a Catholic in a confessional. In a quiet voice punctuated by pain as raw as if it had still been that spring day sixty-two years earlier. Many more questions swirled in Nikkie's head—and she imagined in Peter's too, but they did not ask them. Under Vilnis' spell, they did not say a word.

Sitting in the dark of that root cellar, cold even though Aldis had given him wool blankets, Vilnis wondered each day if the Russians would come for Aldis next—or find Vilnis. To calm himself, he thought about times he had sat, leaning up against his mother by the fire, her arms around him.

She would sing him Latvian folk songs, including the country's most famous and favorite song. Pūt, vējiņi. He asked Nikkie if she knew it.

"I know it was the unofficial anthem during the Occupation," Nikkie said. "My mother and grandmother have sung it for me. I hope I will hear the choir sing it at the Song Festival."

"When my mother sang it, I knew it was the soul of the Latvians," Vilnis said. "My soul."

Nikkie thought about the lyrics of this song of unrequited love. Of a man's desire for a woman he is told he can never have as his own. Of promises made and broken. Of human frailty. Of the wind and water and a boat carrying a man to an unknown destiny.

"Since then, whenever I heard choirs sing it, when we held hands and sang it on the Baltic Way, in my mind, I still heard my mother's voice singing it to me," Vilnis said. "While I knew my mother would not see Latvia free again, the song carried other Latvians and me through those years. It was like a secret code that said, You may harm our bodies or brainwash our minds. But you can't own our souls. Our souls are intact. And our hearts. Even as they are broken, even as they are filled with grief for the loss of our land, our dignity, our loved ones, this song heals. It sustains us, bonds us to our strength."

Vilnis sang in a clear haunting tenor.

Pūt, vējiņi, dzen laiviņu,
Aizdzen mani Kurzemē.
Kurzemniece man solīja
Sav' meitiņu malējiņ'.
(Blow, gentle wind,
Drive my boat
Drive me
Back to Kurzeme.
A Kurzeme woman
Promised me
Her daughter would be
My bride.)

Longing permeated the air. Even though she did not know what all the words meant, Nikkie wanted to move to the song, her heart stirred by its feeling. She closed her eyes, felt Peter come up closer behind her left shoulder. His warmth radiated through her, and he put his hand gently against the back of her heart.

Solīt sola, bet nedeva,
Teic man lielu dzērājiņ'
(Promises, promises...
She went back on
Her promise.
Said I'm a drinker)

In her mind's eye, she saw the power of this song to unite, enliven and bolster, when the many voices numbed by oppression came together to give it one voice joined in song. She flashed on the photos of the Baltic Way and the song festivals she had seen on Vilnis' and Peter's walls. She thought back to singing it at the Jāni celebration in Gulbene. People holding hands. People connecting hearts and souls. People singing.

And Nikkie watched in amazement as a tiny ray of light descended into the center of the clearing, almost as if it had been attracted to the song and had floated in from another dimension to brighten the gray.

"I don't know how long I stayed in that cellar," Vilnis said after he finished the song, a determined look on his face. "A few weeks at least. But one day, Aldis brought me upstairs in the night. He told me that my parents, my sister were dead. My father and three other Latvian soldiers, who had been hiding in the forest together, killed a Russian soldier when the soldier had tried to arrest them. Another group of Russian soldiers came after them and found them. They also rounded up their families, brought them to the forest, and condemned all of them as traitors. Enemies of the state. They shot them on the spot.

"My seven-year-old sister. A collaborator," Vilnis said. "An enemy of the state. My mother."

Nikkie remained still, her heart pounding, barely breathing.

"Some days, I wondered why my mother and sister were not sent to Siberia like so many others," Vilnis said. "Why shoot a woman and child? Chances are they would have died there. But maybe they would have survived and returned. Then I would think, maybe they were the lucky ones, after all, to die before they witnessed more of what human beings were capable of doing to one another, before they saw what happened to their beloved country."

"I am so sorry for your loss, Vilnis," Nikkie said. "I cannot even imagine it."

"And I never knew," Peter said. "What a tragedy you suffered. But I also can't help wondering how you survived. How did you end up with our family?"

"It was a miracle."

Aldis knew Vilnis' mother's cousin, who had recently moved to the countryside of a town about seventy kilometers away, Vilnis told her. No one else there had a connection to Vilnis. Just before they had moved, she and her husband had lost a child, a six-year-old boy, like Vilnis, to a virus. It was late June, soon after the mass deportations. Aldis asked them to take Vilnis into their family—and they risked it. The cousins had been close. They let Vilnis take the place of their son.

Vilnis' identity, name, papers and all, was switched with their son's. Vilnis' original name had been Eriks Kārklis. Peter's grandparents became Vilnis' parents. Peter's father, who was two at the time, became Vilnis' brother. In another family resemblance, Vilnis had the same color hair and eyes as their biological child had.

The family knew they could never speak of what had taken place—not amongst family members or with friends. Fortunately, Peter's father, Tālis, was still so young, he had no problem accepting a new brother and, after a time, did not seem to remember the one who was no longer there. It was a grand collusion in his family and by the Latvians who had known them. It worked because people were willing to stay silent to protect one another—and a little boy who deserved to live.

"I am forever in gratitude," Vilnis said. "I missed my family. But my new parents and brother loved me. They kept me safe. I loved them. I was happy my new mother had been so close to my birth mother. I had a life because of them."

But even after Latvia declared its independence, Vilnis did not tell anyone the actual story. At first, he did not trust Latvia would remain free. Then, he did not want to seem ungrateful to the parents who had risked so much for him. "Once they passed away, I don't know," he said. "I had kept the secret for so long. I still remained silent. Many times I thought about telling you, Peter. But I did not, somehow could not bring myself to speak the words."

During the Occupation, Vilnis never tried to find the clearing. But after Latvia was freed, he asked Aldis to take him to the forest grave. The headstone had been placed there by relatives of the other families who had been shot. They did not know about Vilnis. And he did not seek them out to tell them.

"For the last decade, I came back once a year," Vilnis said. "I brought flowers. But every time, I continued to have this fear—what if someone finds out who I am or sees me? I know rationally it makes no sense. I live in a free country. But that is why I said what I did about freedom earlier. I am still not free of the fear and guilt of that boy who lost his parents and sister and does not understand why he survived, and they did not."

Nikkie wished they had brought flowers this time to honor Vilnis' family, the dead of her vision. But she would need more than flowers to calm the spirits of those who had died here. She looked around the clearing and forest for the makings of a natural arrangement of plants and rocks to commemorate them. What was most important, however, was listening to Vilnis' story. That was a significant step in not only honoring the dead, but in opening the path to what she would need to do next.

"It is time to let the secrets go," Vilnis continued. "Coming here with both of you, I take a step out of that fear and bring the light into this darkness. That's what your vision tells me is necessary, for their peace—and for me. I will bring Māra here now. So, she knows who my birth family was—and who I am. And maybe so I know more."

Vilnis' shoulders slumped slightly with unvoiced grief. He was silent now. Nikkie fell into a meditative breath. Seven counts, breathing in. Seven counts, breathing out. In. Out. In. Out.

Thoughts floated through. Nikkie, who for years had emphasized living in the present moment, felt strange immersing herself in the past unfolding before her. Her focus had been to let go of the past, release or block the dead, look toward the future, and move on.

But what had been most alive for her since coming to Latvia, what made her feel most grounded and embodied, was immersing herself in its past. It was embracing her father's and Māra's lives and Indra's stories of growing up in and escaping Latvia, searching for the dead, learning about the country's own distant and recent past—and now Vilnis' story.

All those were what had led them to this moment in the woods. The vision of the past that had first come to her as a ten-year-old girl had led her here to the place where another young girl had lost her life and dreams and her brother had lost the family and life he knew. What could Nikkie now do to acknowledge and affirm the lives of those dead who had summoned her to this place and this man, Vilnis, who despite surviving, had suffered so much because of what had transpired?

Chapter 29

"Did you ever have a ceremony for your family after they died?" Nikkie asked. She thought back to what Indra had shared about Latvian funerals. The bodies of the dead were laid out at home, celebrated with song and stories. Afterward, wrapped in a shroud, they were buried directly in the earth or in a pine box. The process was recognized as a natural part of the cycle of life. But what of unnatural deaths such as these?

Vilnis shook his head. "When the shooting happened, Aldis was doing all he could to take care of me and find me a new home. Besides, going to the site would have been dangerous. But now, I bring flowers," Vilnis said. "I think about them."

"You honored them by surviving," Nikkie said.

Vilnis nodded. "I imagined conversations with them, even the years it was too risky to speak of them out loud."

"You never spoke to Lilita about your birth family?" Peter asked.

"Not even to her," he said. "I couldn't. If I began to talk about it, I knew I would not stop. And I never wanted to do anything that would endanger her or my new family."

"How did you get the photo of them?" Nikkie asked.

"To comfort me, I slept with that picture near me in the barn. I had it when I escaped. It's all that remained from my family except for the clothes on my back. I kept it hidden but would take it out and look at it from time to time."

"I'm glad you had that memory of them," Nikkie felt a fluttering energy stirring in her abdomen, then running through her arms and legs and torso. She focused in on it. This was more than excitement running in her body.

She began to see halos of light around the trees and plants. Instead of whirling on the outside, she felt like she had a spinning top in her belly. Her senses heightened. Sounds amplified and grew more defined. A breeze rustled leaves. Insects buzzed. Vilnis moved over ground cover. She smelled the loamy scent of the earth and compost, the hint of wood and wintergreen from the birch trees, the crisp freshness of the air.

What she had awaited was happening. The dead were stirring. She could see a few human forms with blurred edges and indistinct features in the clearing. She spoke softly, told Vilnis to watch in case he could see the dead.

She began to share the words of the dead as they arose. "Your family and the others want you to know they are here."

Nikkie felt herself more fully easing into a space between the realms of existence of life and death. The forest clearing filled with beings—the dead. Distinct now. Some seemed confused. Others appeared to look at her with pleading eyes or blank expressions. A sadness hung thick in the atmosphere.

So much had shifted for Nikkie concerning the dead since her performance at the Hollywood Bowl and encounter with them in the Oregon wilderness. She was no longer afraid. Any doubt in her ability to help them also fell away, even though she still did not know what to do. Despite years of misgivings, she finally trusted the process, trusted the forces in the universe that had drawn her here.

"The dead need our help," she said. "You telling their story was part of it. But they brought me—and you both—here for a reason. Do you somehow sense the dead?" Peter did not, but Vilnis said he felt a tingling running up his legs and arms, on his cheeks when they came.

Now, Nikkie felt fully aligned with the dead ones before her, consciously opened her heart to receive them. And with that, the scene of their deaths unfolded once more. Only this time, she surrendered to the anguish before her. It was the only choice she had to find her way through and not feel overwhelmed by their pain and suffering.

She merged with all those in her forest vision. She became Vilnis' family being led to the clearing and three more families of the men who had been involved in the death of the Russian soldier. She became Vilnis' sister and the other children holding their mothers' arms for comfort.

Nikkie remained connected to each individual as they crowded together, experienced the fear, indignation, and anger of some, the resignation and bewilderment of others. She stayed as they were gunned down. Men. Women. Children. An excruciating, choreographed ballet of bodies falling this way and that onto the underbrush, into a pile. Her own body falling this way and that, stripped of life, identity again and again. The air vibrated with cries, screams, thuds, cracks, eerie silence.

Vilnis' family had been the last to die. Nikkie dug deep to find the courage she needed not to pull back, to resist, knowing if she did, she might never feel resolved around this destiny with the dead—and with the living. She also wanted to help Vilnis now. She surrendered further and spoke out to him what she was experiencing.

She felt Vilnis' parents' fierce dedication to the cause of Latvia's freedom that had driven them to take risks. But now, they were overcome with grief knowing their daughter would die, not knowing what would happen to Vilnis and feeling powerless to protect either of their children. They prayed for Vilnis to live.

Nikkie experienced Kate's regret at leaving her brother, her confusion as to why anyone would want to harm her or her parents. For this family—and for the others in the forest that day, death brought no peace or release.

Overtaken by weakness, Nikkie, in her human form, sunk to her knees, then further, until she lay curled on the earth, feeling like she was enmeshed with the bodies of the dead. Her soul began to rise up with their souls as they left those bodies.

"Nikkie," Peter called out. "No." Nikkie's forward momentum jolted to a stop when she heard the concern and forcefulness in his voice. He moved toward her, but Vilnis got up and blocked Peter with his arm.

"Don't touch her," Vilnis said. "She knows. She sees. Let her be. They have been waiting for her. Let her do what I could not."

And with that, he went down on one knee, bowed to Nikkie as she lay on the dark earth, extending his arm like he was paying respect to a goddess. Then, he stood, turned and bowed to the death scene before him.

"I also see you," Vilnis said. "Mama. Papa. Kate. Maybe not with my eyes. But always with my heart. And I hear you. I don't know how, but I heard all you endured. I heard your concern for me. I love you."

He raised his head, gazing out, his voice clear, direct. "All my life, I wished I had stayed with you, died with you. I did not understand why I would survive, and you would not. My place had been with you, and I had instead ended up with a new place, new parents, a new home. How could you die? It's crazy, but I felt like you abandoned me. And then, like I had let you down by not doing anything to try to save you. It didn't matter that I was a child. I wish I had done something. I am so sorry, so sorry for what happened to you here and for what happened to other families throughout Latvia, for what we as individuals and as a nation endured."

Nikkie let Vilnis' words dive into her heart and sink below the anguish. There, she had another insight. His parents, the Latvian soldiers, and their families had been good people, their focus on building a future, affirming life. They believed in freedom, peace, connection.

Then, caught in the maelstrom of good and evil that came with war, they found themselves with enemies. They needed to protect their families, their country, to kill or be killed. The enemy was deemed evil. Their own people were deemed good. But then the enemy occupied Latvia and conscripted its own young men for their armies. Who was the enemy now?

Vilnis' parents, Andrejs and Rasma, had not been raised to be killers. No one they knew had. And in secret, they could not help but wonder why they were living out the edicts of leaders, motivated by power, who made decisions apart from the death and destruction those decisions caused, away from the eyes of children and mothers and young men impacted most directly by battle.

"I kill for freedom. I defend and die for my country." For Vilnis' parents, it also meant the death of their daughter, the orphaning of their son. It meant the deaths, displacement and deportation of countless others. Senseless. What humans could do to one another. The way they closed their hearts to one another.

War seemed to be about survival of the fittest, the most strategic, the luckiest, the countries with the most significant populations, the most armaments, the most massive armies.

These were the kinds of thoughts, words, feelings that coursed through the minds of the dead, through Vilnis' parent's minds, in their last moments of life in the woods. This was what weighed on their spirits as human bodies lay in graves in forests all across Latvia and countries like it. Areas where massacres, killings could be hidden away.

But what was it all these beings had in common? What had they all wanted before the war began—those who died that day and the ones who followed the orders and shot them? One answer may have sounded common, simplistic in the gravity of war. But in truth, these people had all wanted to know love—to be loved, to give love. They wanted to be happy. They wanted to create a good life for their families and themselves. They wanted to realize and manifest their hopes and dreams, to share their unique expression.

And Nikkie suddenly got in her gut what she needed to do to support the healing of their spirits so they could move on. It had to do with those dreams. All these people had lost their dreams, their chance. What they needed to heal, at this moment, was to acknowledge those dreams, have them witnessed and honored. By her—in her dancing. By the trees. By the divine beings present. And by Vilnis and Peter. Could it work?

She had only one way to find out. Nikkie's energy began to return to her, to flow like a steady stream, and with it, the urge to dance. Slowly, she stood up and began to turn. Deliberately. She spun, no longer trying to lose herself in movement as she did when she performed on stage. She was already lost. She had been lost before she dissolved in this forest. Until she arrived here, she had hung onto the remnants of her like someone slipping off a cliff, clutching at rocks to regain their grip, about to fall. Now, those remnants lay in the forest grave along with the dead she had felt slip away through her body.

She told Vilnis and Peter her dance honored the dead and their lost dreams so they could move on to take their awaited place in the spirit realm. She danced with the hope Vilnis and

Tom would be freed as well—and somehow perhaps Peter. Perhaps that was the help he had asked for in her vision. And she danced to move on, to reclaim her place amongst the living again. She flashed that when Peter had said, Help us, she had initially thought he meant only him and the dead. Now she intuited that she was part of the "us" who had needed help, too.

She breathed into her heart, remembered what her cousin Māra had said about calling on divine protection. She called on the divine beings she had come to know and love in Latvia, that had guided Latvians, most likely her ancestors for centuries. She called on their Divine Feminine and Masculine. Māra. Laima. Saule, sun. Dievs, God. Auseklis, the morning star Venus. The spirits of the trees. The ancestors. She asked them to support and protect her, to inspire her as she danced, to help her act in service to the dead before her and all others who were to be assisted by this ritual. And then one more connection came.

Not to a Divine being. Nikkie's heart began to race. Heat moved up her body. Not a guide, but a human. The mind of a human. A beloved human. Tom. Her heart exploded with joy, even as she sensed she needed to maintain her grounding and balance, remain silent and listen. So, she listened deeper than she had ever listened, and words flowed through her to join the effortlessness of the guided spin. Tom's words.

"We carry the dreams of the dead ones, lost and battered, yet pure at their core," she sang out, certain Tom was also participating here now in his own way, through these words, his words she sensed, supporting her and the dead. "We speak the dreams of those with stories never told, dreams never lived. Dreams of the ages, of revolution, of joy and longing, arising. Told I am. Not I was, or I will be. But I am. Now I am." Tom's words flowed as Nikkie turned, and the twins joined together in a ritual rising up for the dead, honoring their dreams, the life songs in their hearts.

And one by one, the spirits came forward. They spoke through her now, as Tom had been doing, and Nikkie repeated their words, their dreams, incanted them to the trees, to the sky, to the earth, to the birds, to Vilnis.

"I am Juris," one of the first spirits said. "I was a soldier, called to fight for my country. But I longed to go to Riga after the war and sing. I wanted to be a classical singer. To create harmonies with other singers, never again to participate in the chaos of combat. To express with my art what a rifle could never express."

"We see you," Nikkie incanted, her voice answering like the call and response of a congregation to a minister. "We see you singing, Juris." And an image formed before them of Juris, the singer singing while Nikkie danced, creating a sound and movement duet of beauty and coherence.

"We see you," Vilnis repeated with her, his eyes filling with tears. "We see you," Peter said.

Others came forward, one by one, speaking of those lost hopes and dreams. The Latvian soldiers, young men still, most with wives. Their children. Their parents. They knew their duty to protect their country, but they had aspired to write. To farm. To be engineers. Doctors.

Nikkie was surprised, taken aback to see the next spirit. The Russian soldier whom the Latvians had killed in self-defense came forward. Nikkie hesitated, her own judgment of good and evil rearing, and wondering how Vilnis and Peter would react. But then, she trusted and spoke out her guidance. In the big picture, the larger perspective, this man was also part of the one being, the oneness that encompassed all of them.

In this situation, he had played the part of the enemy. But the Latvians were the ones who had killed him. This young man had also lost his life, his chance to live his dreams at the hands of the soldiers here. He told Nikkie that in Russia, he had studied to be a literature professor, had a university job waiting after the war—and a fiancée. He was hoping to marry, have a family. He had never wanted to go to war.

"Dance for him," Vilnis said. "Dance for him too. It is time to forgive. Even those of us who lost so much. Even me. I want him included." And so, Nikkie's heart opened wider. She felt her energy move deep into the earth, and she danced for the Russian man as well.

More insights came to Nikkie. Of all the spirits here, while alive, many had never spoken of personal aspirations. Focused on day to day survival, they had lacked the luxury of a concept like a personal dream. They were happy to have any job they could, to have food and a home. Only a few decades earlier, Latvians had still lived as serfs of occupying nations' landowners with no chance to live out a personal vision.

Nikkie, who had known what her dream was since she was a child, acknowledged all that in her own heart now. She danced the dead ones' inherent value, beyond whether or not they ever realized a dream.

Her dance honored their suffering, released missed opportunities, dreams ripped away. She spun not only for what the dead had lost personally but also for what the world had missed in not having these souls realize their dreams and share their full potential on the planet. And she danced for Vilnis and Peter, for all those who had had their dreams thwarted or diminished somehow by death, displacement, oppression, or other life trauma.

A new child came forward. Vilnis looked up, started, cried out.

It was his sister, whom he seemed to be able to sense.

"I am Kate," she said, her words dissipating in the wind. "I am young. But I knew I wanted to grow up and see the world. To travel the world outside Latvia. To see the big skyscrapers in New York in America that were taller than the trees in our forest."

"We see you, Kate," Nikkie sang softly. "We see you all grown up and traveling to New York, where I have lived, the buildings I have seen."

"We see your dream, Kate," Vilnis repeated. "Mana mīļā māsina." He paused, placed his hand on his heart. "Maybe I can help. I will dedicate any trip I take to you. I will take you with me in my heart, think of us both there. And I will especially go to New York and see a tall building for you." And Kate smiled and seemed to move over next to her brother, rest her head and shoulder against the side of his body.

"I can feel you, Kate," Vilnis said. "Is she with me?" He looked at Nikkie for confirmation, and Nikkie nodded. "I never thought I would feel her again. I can feel her right here," pointing to the side of the body where Kate was. "Thank you."

After a minute or so of Vilnis and Kate connecting in the silence, Nikkie heard, "I am Rasma. Vilnis' and Kate's mother."

"And I am Andrejs, their father."

Nikkie felt a pain in her heart so great she imagined her own heart might rupture. Vilnis rose up, stepped forward, reached out his hands as if to take his mother's and father's hands in his own.

"Andrejs and I shared a dream," Rasma said. "We wanted to see our children grow up in a free Latvia. We wanted to see our country, and its people free, to work with the government to ensure democracy." Andrejs came up next to his wife, put his arm around her waist.

"We see you Rasma and Andrejs," Nikkie said, turning slowly, back arched, head back, arms flung up in a V-shape. "And today, your country is finally free. And what you taught Vilnis to do the night the Russians came protected him. He was saved. By your beloved cousin. Your son stands before you, a man who not only lived to see Latvia's freedom realized, he participated in it. And your cousin's grandson Peter is here too."

Rasma and Andrejs joined Kate and Vilnis, united with them in a circle of trust. And Vilnis motioned Peter to join them as well. Wave upon wave of energy rippled out from them and over the clearing. Nikkie felt it galvanize her.

"We recognize your sacrifice for your country, your family," Nikkie said. "Please know it was not in vain."

"I see what you gave for me, for Latvia, your gift to our freedom," Vilnis said. "I love you, mama. Papa. Thank you. It makes sense to me now." The family embraced one more time, lingered in this sanctuary of love. Then, expressing their love for Vilnis, their appreciation and gratitude for Peter, his parents and sister moved away, back to the other spirits.

Vilnis fell to his knees again and rocked back and forth, his cries absorbed by the trees. His heart melted and dissolved in the mist.

Turning in silence, Nikkie's own heart pulsed in tune with the rhythm of the universe. Slow. Steady. They continued this way for a time, Nikkie turning, Vilnis bent forward with Peter beside him, Vilnis' tears falling, being absorbed by the Mother of them all, the Earth.

Nikkie spun the light. When she finished honoring the dreams of the dead, she saw a tube of light had formed emanating out from deep in the core of the earth. It encompassed her, spread out to the treetops and heavens beyond, like a spotlight connecting the sacred of mother earth to father sky. Her body served as a conduit, a pure channel for this light, and she felt supported by the divine energy of the forest surrounding her.

All barriers gone between Nikkie and the spirits of the dead, one by one, as if going through the opening of a revolving door, they entered the tube. Vilnis' family. Juris. Andrejs. Kate. Rasma. The Russian soldier. Those who had lost their lives in this place.

They moved in a spiral past Nikkie as she held them in her heart—one human self-acknowledging another human self—love, pain, grief, suffering, joy, self-realization. "The whole catastrophe," as Zorba the Greek called it. A heart nod to all that had been, all that would be and to all that was present in the moment.

And Nikkie got this knowing. The years she had spent dancing, expressing, connecting to an audience, all the spiritual practice she had done to open to the sacred in spinning and dance had been for this moment. The divine forces of the universe had led her to a forest grave in Latvia, to help a man say good-bye to his family and reveal the secrets and pain of many lives. It had prepared her to help these spirits to move past what they had lost into the dimension that awaited them.

Nikkie sensed the appearance of more ancestors, already crossed over, come to greet and guide the dead ones' spirits. And one more being waited for the dead ones at the far end of the cone. The voice inside her head had separated out from her, appeared in spirit form now. Tom stood, arms open, to receive the spirits. He welcomed them and encouraged them up toward a dimension at the top of the tube.

And when they reached the end of all Nikkie could see, Tom was present to usher them through to what lay beyond. Then, when they all had passed over, Tom simply nodded to his sister and vanished with the dead.

He couldn't be dead, Nikkie thought. He wouldn't be. Yet as complete as she felt with the dead, her heart remained uneasy about Tom disappearing with them. *You don't know he is gone for good,* she told herself. But as long as her brother had vanished, she would not feel complete. How could a journey to the forest to heal the dead include losing her brother? She would not accept that healing for Tom and her involved his death.

Her spinning dance slowed, and the tube of light remained. "Walkers between the worlds," her cousin Māra had called people who could move between this life and the afterlife. Surely, Tom was one of them. Surely, his physical body remained alive, in the hospital, would return to consciousness, perhaps already had. And yet, she felt unresolved once more, torn between wanting to follow Tom, make sure he was safe, or stay in the earth realm with Peter and Vilnis.

A lone woman, dressed in white, radiant, emerged from the trees and walked across the clearing to face her. What now, Nikkie wondered. Another spirit left behind? But this being exuded no distress, nothing unfinished. A great silence surrounded her and enveloped Nikkie. Love radiated from the woman's heart straight out to Nikkie's.

No, not a dead one.

"My sister in spirit," the woman said. "You who have helped bring healing to many today. I also bring healing to you."

Now Nikkie knew her. She flashed back to her experience on Vilnis' forest land. This was the Latvian Goddess, Māra, come to her in another form.

Māra stepped closer, extended her hands and reached into Nikkie's chest like a psychic surgeon. She placed her spirit hands around Nikkie's heart and squeezed. Nikkie felt an electric shock. Pain gripped her, stole her breath, left her gasping.

She opened her mouth to cry out, but no sound emanated. She no longer had a voice—or a body for that matter. Free of physical encumbrance, she hovered above the forest scene and gazed down on her bodily form, Vilnis, and Peter. She had stopped moving. They appeared frozen in time.

"Come," Māra said, floating beside her. Māra clasped Nikkie's hand into her own, and leaving her body behind, the two of them ascended up the tube of light.

"Is this a dream," Nikkie asked. "Or, did I die?"

"Your body is suspended outside time," Māra said. "I have come to take you back before time, before destiny, earthly or otherwise. When you knew better, and so did I that generating love was the only purpose in the universe. And doing so was as natural as God's love for every being and Divine Mother's desire to hold all Beloveds in her arms."

Nikkie felt herself basking in that love now, cradled by it as she and Māra continued to move forward. Would she join the dead with Tom?

"We travel to Auseklis, the morning star and beyond.," Māra said. "To the sacred covenant you assigned yourselves before you were born to be in service to love. To recognize the Beloved in each being. In yourself. To know that you are all one. You and Tom went to Latvia to find your roots from this lifetime. But you have never accepted your true roots, beyond country, beyond space and time."

Nikkie thought about the roots she had known and accepted—a mother and brother who loved her, growing up in a mostly safe, beautiful environment in Oregon, support and encouragement to live her dream to dance. If not wealth, she had comfort, a healthy body, friends, a career doing what she loved.

"Yes, you had a life of relative ease this go-around," Māra said, seeming to read Nikkie's thoughts. "You discovered here though in your ancestral roots that your family in Latvia experienced greater struggle. Living through centuries of oppression and the Occupation. The wars. The transition from dictatorship to democracy. But what if you had another choice of perception?"

Māra and Nikkie reached the stars now, and as light streamed around them, they also looked like starlight, only denser, more fluid. They still had a semblance of form.

Nikkie closed her eyes, inhaled and exhaled deeply. When she opened them again, she found herself in a crystal room, with walls of shimmering white light accented with sparks of rainbow colors. How had that happened? Had such a place existed in her subconscious?

And then she saw him. Tom. He sat cross-legged on a cushion floating on starlight at one side of the room. His mouth, rough edges softened, radiated a full, beatific smile. "Like you, I have been finding my way," he said.

Nikkie knelt down next to him and joined hands with him and Māra. Nikkie's heart softened, her eyes softened.

"You will discover life here is poetry in motion, where you can see how you live out all lives, all choices, all dreams concurrently, one big hologram—past, present and future." Māra laughed, and the sound was like the tinkling of hundreds of crystal glasses clinking together in a grand toast. "We've tapped into the origin of your essential truth where all dimensions live as one."

Nikkie gazed into Māra's eyes and saw it—all the lifetimes of joys and sorrows, of paths taken and not taken, of crosses born and laid to rest, of fears tested. She saw lives with Tom and without him. She sensed how she had lost her own way and found it again in her own heart, in Latvia, in the forest.

But most of all, and beyond all of it, she saw the love, felt the love in her heart and the strength that flowed from that love, no matter where she found it in whatever life or with whom.

With that love, she embraced what she and Tom had each borne across generations and lifetimes. And as she received the love, she felt it radiate from her to Tom and Māra and from them back to her.

The love bubbled up in her heart, never-ending, like sacred headwaters on a mountain. It seemed to begin as a pulse from the core of the earth, transformed to a stream, then a river inside her, sometimes gentle, other times chaotic. This cascading river of starlight, divine light, never-ending love carried her like the rapids on the untamed Rogue River, where she and Tom had kayaked and rafted as children.

This river of love carved away residues of earth lives and star lives and lived lives and unlived lives, knowing her and unknowing her. She dissolved, liquefied, became the currents always moving, headed toward the ocean to be freed.

She flashed back on a picture of all the players she had witnessed in the scene in the forest—acting, living out their roles—murderer, victim, nature being, child, adult, parent, survivor. All a Shakespearean drama. Was it an illusion, like the awakened teachers said?

She waited for an answer from Māra, but none came. No matter. Her heart opened to embrace the scene. And, with that action, she saw the spark of love in each being, not only here, but everywhere, even in the soldiers, who held the guns, young men following orders, displacing themselves from the natural order of the universe. They played out dark and light, shadow and consciousness, birth and death, birth and life. And she saw each person, ancestor, event, circumstance, in some inexplicable way led her and the rest of the beings on the planet back to the truth, the one being, no separation, to love.

And now Māra told Nikkie and Tom they each had a choice.

Choice? Māra did not need to speak for Nikkie to know what that choice entailed. Nikkie breathed deep into her belly and felt the "yes" there. She closed her eyes, and when she reopened them, Nikkie found herself back in the forest, minus Māra and Tom. Back in the body she had left behind. Not immobile, not lifeless, but turning. Still turning. She had made her choice.

Vilnis sat against a tree, knees bent, feet on the ground. Peter stood nearby.

She stopped whirling, and the turning inside stopped along with her. Her vision and her mind felt clear. She smiled, and the love she carried always exploded in her chest for these people and the forest beings surrounding them. For all beings.

Then, she heard in her mind.

I return. Fast. Hideous. Gone.
Tremor of butterfly wings carry my heart
Here
Arrived
I arrive carried on butterfly wings
Finding my way home

I have been anon and askance
In the whirlwind dance.
Tussled by the whirl of my mind.
Jostled free of whys and wherefores
Neat packages of what's what

Some call it trauma.
I call it all knowing and unknowing at the same time.
The gift of unknowing myself. Glad to un-meet you.
It's un-been some out of time.

And with those words, Nikkie knew. Tom had made his choice too.

CHAPTER 30

As if choreographed by the divine, Tom had woken up out of the coma the evening after the ritual for the dead in the forest, fully aware and as if he had never had brain trauma. She and Peter would soon return to Riga to greet him.

First though, Nikkie stood on the earth outside Vilnis' house. She felt empty, clear, her being primed to hear the prompting of the universe, of space beyond the heart and voice.

Nikkie sensed a growl rise up from her belly through her torso and hover in her throat. She opened her mouth, and what rumbled out was not a growl, but a warbling, a cry of a hawk, a hoot of an owl, the flap of an eagle's wing.

She moved her finger. It crawled across the air in front of her like an earthworm, stretching and contracting under rich, fertile earth after a spring rain. She felt her face, one of her cheeks, her jaw moving in the same rhythm.

She could create again. She knew it in her body. And while part of her bubbled over with the joy of it, wanted to jump and leap and twirl in gratitude for her artistry returning, the wholeness of her first rested in it. It rested and comprehended she could now dance with a purity of creation. But what it would not include was whirling. The impulse to spin as the centerpiece of her art had stopped.

She paused, surprised, a bit unnerved but excited by the freedom of possibility that afforded. The Nikkie, who lived in New York, danced with Stone Tara, used whirling as a signature move, was gone. The crystallized consciousness had shattered. She sported new skin. Wet. Silky. She dried her dance wings in the sunlight like a butterfly emerged from the cocoon before flying. Was she ready to fly?

Yes, she thought. With her dance for the dead, she sprouted legs and roots, anchored in the earth. Now she grew wings that would carry her aloft rather than wither and dry exposed to the atmosphere.

She stepped forward, felt her feet on the earth. What arose was a cone filled with her inner light like the cone of light through which the dead had passed. It surrounded her, and her body shaped around it, shifted in response to it. But instead of flight, movement appeared in her that thundered like folk dancers' feet stomping the floor, undulated with African rhythms, surprised with the spontaneity of improvisation. Her emerging dance reveled in the spark, the original spark and fire of creation, no beginning and no end, unique to her but not hers. She entered the never-ending stream of life force energy and flowed with it, but ground into the earth at the same time.

When her movement slowed, she looked down. For the first time she could remember, she left footprints on the earth. Body prints. And on her pant legs, her own damp handprints from the moisture on the grass.

She ran her fingers over them, her feet over the prints in the earth, like a blind person using her fingers and feet to sense. Nikkie, a dancer who had been lighter than air, now left a mark when she danced.

"Yes," she said to no one but herself. "Yes," she said to life around her. The pulsing cells. The green leaves. The ground beneath her feet. The chlorophyll. The life force in her.

"Yes," she said to her heart. "I love you. I bless you. I honor you," she said to its beat, pumping strong, its blood circling itself like the earth orbiting the sun. Eye on Venus, Auseklis, the morning star. Lassoing Jupiter, the planet of partnership and expansion and joy. "Come," she said, to all the atoms that made up this new version of herself, recreating itself daily. "I am," she said to the potential to be new, to be present, to know herself again and again and again.

Then she saw him, Peter, watching her from a window. She nodded, and he came outside to her, took her hand in his and bowed, bringing her hand to his forehead as he did. "You are a beautiful dancer Nikkie," he said, standing up straight, still holding her gaze and her hands. "I am so glad I happened to look out the window when I did."

Nikkie wrapped herself in words she had longed to hear, imagined hearing her entire life. She was sure she must be glowing from the inside out.

"Thank you," she said, smiling. "With all that's happened, I do feel freed up creatively again."

"I never had any doubt," Peter said. "And I, too, was deeply affected by what transpired in the forest. I understand better now why I was asking for help in your vision at the Hollywood Bowl."

"Tell me," Nikkie said.

"Until yesterday, this tragedy was like a weight our family carried—not only Vilnis but also those of us who did not consciously know about it. Look at how your vision of the event traveled with you throughout your life and impacted your dancing."

"That's true," Nikkie said.

"Then yesterday, as we witnessed and honored the stories and lost dreams of our family members who were killed, as we experienced them being freed, we were somehow freed with them," Peter said. "And Tom too."

Nikkie flashed back on the power and healing she had felt released as the dead transitioned in the tube of light.

"Today, seeing you dance, I am even more grateful for this opening and cannot wait to see how it will impact our lives and our art as we move forward," Peter said.

"Crazy as it sounds, I did see it all," Tom said. "Lights. Spirit beings. The spirit of that madrone tree we cut our names into. The Goddess Māra. The star place. And while I was in the coma, I was aware of you in my hospital room at times. I heard your conversations, though not with my logical mind. I can't explain how, but I knew my sister and I were communicating. I knew Peter came."

Tom sat cross-legged on a cushion back in Indra's apartment in a way that reminded Nikkie of when she met him with Māra in the star dimension. But whether Tom was in Latvia. In the States. Anywhere. Nikkie did not care, as long as he was alive and well—and conscious. They had brought Tom home the same day Nikkie and Peter returned to Riga, the hospital staff shaking their heads in disbelief about his overnight recovery. They could offer no medical explanation, other than the body's innate healing response.

"So, what was that like?" Nikkie asked. She sat at Indra's dining room table along with Indra. Ellie and Peter sat near one another on the couch. They were drinking black tea in matching white mugs.

"Well, I remember you telling me to come back," Tom said. "Where would I go, I tried to answer. But then I did go— into the darkness where I did not want to communicate with anyone. I wanted to rest."

"It sounds like you stayed conscious," Nikkie said.

Tom nodded. "I hardly know how to express what happened, but I lay in the dark of this kind of void space listening to the drip, drip, drip of time leaking out of whatever remained of me. A string of thoughts leaked out of my head as well, like streamers. I could see them and had not realized how many I carried, how many made up the story of Tom on earth. The string also included everyone else's stories of me. And the ancestors' stories that I carried in my field. I don't know if I was dispersing or coalescing."

"Did you feel afraid? Ellie asked, leaning forward and resting her hand on his knee.

"No," Tom said. "More curious and present. I flashed on the Indian guru you told Nikkie and me about, Ramana Maharshi, and the meditation question he used. The one where you ask yourself, Who am I? And beyond that, who is the I that is asking?

"So, I asked who I was in this new place. Or if that was the right question. And, then questions dripped out. I felt a blankness that eased into peace and spaciousness—like I found an oasis of all I needed which was nothing at all."

"Wow. You seem to have had an awakening experience," Nikkie said.

Tom shrugged. "I did learn some things."

"Like what?" Nikkie asked.

"I want to write it out first now that I'm writing again before I over-talk it. But I know you and Ellie at least will relate to this part. In my gut, I got a knowing that bottom line. I am. We are. One. A mass of humanity recognizing itself. Waking up from the dream and plunging headfirst into God. I plunged into God."

"You sound like mom and me," Nikkie said. "Only more poetic. But truthfully, that's profound. Life-changing." Nikkie felt relief, knowing something positive had emerged from Tom's accident.

"That's quite the spiritual initiation. Bravo," Ellie said. Both she and Nikkie raised their cups in salutation to Tom. Indra and Peter joined in.

"Do you remember how the goddess Māra told us that living in the star energy was poetry in motion?" Tom said, shifting his weight from his right side to his left and stretching out his right leg.

"Yes, I loved that," Nikkie said.

"Get this then. For me, being in a coma was like being in the heart of that poem," Tom said. "It was one long line of metaphor inducting me into god matter. In that state, I learned that everyone matters to the whole, to the divine, including me. We all have value and serve a purpose."

"I gained similar insights, Tom," Nikkie said.

Tom smiled and nodded. "I experienced more fully how our dreams serve a purpose, too," he said. "And mine still includes staying in Latvia, serving however I am able here. I feel lucky to have the choice."

"I'm glad," Peter said. "Besides wanting to know you better, we have much to rebuild, so much new to create."

"It's true," Tom said. "I love that sense of possibility. I differ with the opinions of people in the world who say why waste your time for a tiny population—what difference does a country the size of West Virginia make to the world? Well, we've already seen the difference it makes in the arts throughout the world, in the natural resources it offers, and in the power and magnificence of the mass choirs. But even if those were not obvious, it matters if a language or an individual culture disappears, just like it matters when each animal or plant becomes extinct. Let's not pretend it does not make a difference."

"Do you know how you want to help here?" Indra asked.

"What I know for sure is what I knew before the accident. I want to bring in my business skills to help Peter and Māra if they still want me to. And, for sure, I will write."

"I imagine you got inspiration for what to write during your experience," Peter said.

"Yes," Tom said. "I will begin with the stories and poems about the dead in the forest. I want to honor what they and their families gave up—and so many other families throughout Latvia. But I also want to write about the people who survived and transformed the challenges during the Occupation, like Vilnis, people who choose life and keep creating and expressing."

"I love that idea, and believe Vilnis also will," Peter said. "It gives me a thought. What would you think of collaborating on a piece based on those stories for my dance company? You could do the words. And if Nikkie's willing...."

"I'm willing," Nikkie said. "Whatever it is, I'm in."

"Okay, Nikkie and I could choreograph and dance it," Peter said. "Maybe we could persuade Māra to join us."

"And you could use enlargements or projections of Vilnis' photographs for the sets," Nikkie added. "His beautiful forest photographs. Let's ask him."

"If you like, I could also do fundraising for the production," Indra said. "I'm pretty good at that. And I still have connections to Latvians in the States who like to support the arts in Latvia."

Tom laughed. "Our family creating together. I love the idea."

And Nikkie felt excited as well. The lone wolf had joined her pack.

"I feel funny going back to the U.S. alone," Ellie said. But I have showings of my ceramic art pieces coming up—and orders for pottery. I'll feel happy knowing you are all working together though. I'll return in the fall to join you, and if all goes well, look at the possibility of running my business from Latvia—at least part time."

"Maybe we can persuade you to come back sooner," Peter said.

"I'll certainly be back in time for the premiere of the performance."

For a moment, Nikkie felt sad their dance did not include Ellie, but Nikkie trusted each of their paths had been impacted by the events in Latvia in ways that would continue to unfold. Nikkie never thought she would remain in Latvia, but here she was, here Tom was, and Ellie would soon be back to visit and who knows what else, with a new life and collaboration opening before them.

CHAPTER 31

"Are we there yet?" Nikkie asked Indra. They had been standing stuffed like sprats in a can—sardines in English—for an hour now. Nikkie loathed enclosed, crowded places, avoided the subway and buses during rush hour in New York. But tonight, she had not had a choice and stood with no room to turn around, let alone hold on to the edge of one of the seats. Her top felt damp and sticky from perspiration, and her amber necklace clung to her skin. But her grandmother remained cool and crisp in beige linen pants and a white shirt. How did she do it?

More packed buses and trolleys passed by. Open trucks overflowed with wind musicians and singers. All had one destination. Mežaparks estrāde. The site of the Song Festival's mass choir concert.

"Almost," Indra answered. "It's better than driving and looking for parking." That was what the rest of their family had done though. Vilnis had driven in from Kuldiga and taken the other family members to the venue earlier. Māra's dancers were one of the troupes invited to dance some numbers with the choirs, and Ellie wanted to take any extra travel strain off of Tom. Vilnis had not had room in the car for everyone, so Nikkie and Indra had volunteered to take the bus.

Even though their bus had filled to capacity outside Vecriga, Nikkie watched in disbelief as the driver kept braking at bus stops to let more people in. But then, the focus of much of Latvia was on tonight's concert, and the public transportation system needed to get fifteen thousand singers, hundreds of wind musicians and dancers and twenty-three thousand audience members to the venue in time to see it. Most of the audience would be Latvians like her from other countries here to celebrate song and heritage. For those who couldn't afford to be here themselves—most Latvians—or who had not been fortunate enough to get one of the precious tickets, LTV, the television network, would carry the event so people all over Latvia could watch real time.

When the bus arrived at Mežaparks, people spilled out onto a wide boulevard that led into a forest of tall pine trees. "Where's the stage?" Nikkie asked.

"We have to walk a kilometer or more." Indra slipped her arm around Nikkie's. She guided her granddaughter down the walkway past vendors selling sausages, ice cream, beer, amber jewelry and souvenirs, the trees looming behind them. Many other women walked arm in arm as well, a common practice in the country.

Nikkie thought back to the previous night's dance concert her family had attended. More than anything, she recalled how she wanted to be on the stadium floor, a part of the collective of thousands, like Māra, creating the patterns and sacred geometry visible from above. There had not been enough time for Nikkie to join Māra's group, but Māra outfitted Nikkie in one of her troupe's traditional costumes. She taught her the simple movements of the final dance, then for the last evening performance, one of Māra's dancers graciously volunteered to let Nikkie take her place.

Before that number though, Nikkie watched from the bleachers. She marveled at how one group of fifteen hundred dancers or so danced, then ran off stage so another one thousand could take their place for a new dance. As Māra had told her and Tom when they met, the performances highlighted the four elements: Fire, water, earth and in the end, several numbers for air.

For the final number, all thirteen thousand four hundred dancers came out onto the floor together. Nikkie was one of them, following the music, the dynamism, moving as one organism, in an ocean of energy, a wave in the number called *Debesu Kalejs*—Heaven's Blacksmith.

Her feet drummed the floor to the rhythm of her heartbeat and to the repetition of the powerful drum beat in the music. It resounded like heaven reaching down to pound on the earth. Bagpipes belted out earth music. Heavenly music. Arms waved. Voices around her called out. Some dancers, like her, moved to create squares, then sat still as other dancers streamed by at various angles forming flowing rivers of diamond shapes and triangles crisscrossing the stage. In the end, all of them held up lights that appeared like stars flickering in the night sky.

She felt it. The power of the one. The thousands moving as one being sending its ripples of energy out beyond Riga. Beyond Latvia and the reach of LTV. Beyond Europe. Beyond the earth. Reaching to the stars in sacred communion. And at that moment, she felt herself rise, like a tentative seedling turned into a deeply rooted tree reaching both down into the core of the earth and up to the heavens, buoyed up in the pure love of embodied movement.

Her heart felt the release and joy of reaching that culmination that also pointed to her new direction. After the festival events, she, Peter, Tom, and Māra planned to begin collaborating on their new piece. And they had decided on a second project as well. To continue the healing practice begun for Vilnis, they wanted to perform sacred rituals and dance at other forest and battle sites in Latvia where people had lost their lives as a result of war, resistance or violence. They wanted to do rituals for the Forest Brothers and to go to places where the Germans targeted Jews and Gypsies. Vilnis would photograph the events.

Nikkie brought herself back from her thoughts to the present and the boulevard bordered by the forest of majestic pines she and Indra walked along. Tonight, she no longer feared her visions or what hid in the forest surrounding them. Vilnis' family secrets had been laid bare. The dead of her vision had found their way home. And she and Tom had as well. Now, Nikkie and Indra were on a sacred pilgrimage with thousands of pilgrims come to pay homage to song walking to the center for mass choir singing. What she heard accompanying them on the boulevard that day was the song of the trees around them. Their song for her was always authentic. It told her what resonated with her own heart.

Nikkie had stopped running, but she was not standing still. She walked with her grandmother. She would dance. But the whirling had stopped inside and outside of her. She might turn as part of a dance, but it was no longer the focal point. Life might whirl around her, but she, her own heart and mind, moved freely in whatever direction or manner spirit inspired her.

Large umbrella-like covers on stage rose and revealed the fifteen thousand singers in traditional Latvian costume beneath them. The choir director raised his arms, and the voices rose like a tsunami. The sound rushed forward, sweeping Nikkie and the twenty-three thousand other audience members up and away in a sea of music. They surrendered willingly, joyfully. A hologram of concordance.

"Holy Mother Māra," Nikkie murmured under her breath, tossed and turned, lifted and plummeted by the enormity of the sound and vision.

"I'll second that," Tom whispered in her ear, and she squeezed his hand in response. They watched mesmerized as bobbing bodies of singers in all the colors of the earth, sky, air, and water graced the stage at Mezaparks. Women wore muted red, blue, white, green, purple wool vests and skirts and blouses, and men sported shirts and jackets of grays, whites, browns, and blacks. The women wore flowers, crowns and scarves on their heads.

The earthy tones and melodies of the folk songs, some solemn, others joyful reached straight into her heart, sparking her soul. Songs of the sun. Of thunder. Of nature. Of life and love. Not all the songs were traditional ones. Some had been written by current composers.

She thought back to the last time she was on stage. The Hollywood Bowl. There, no matter how many exercises she did to connect and feel her oneness with the beings and trees in the Hollywood Hills, she stayed separate. She felt like a tree uprooted, toppled over in a storm, not planted firmly enough in the earth. She thought she would leave her mark, but instead, terrified by her vision, barely touched the ground.

Now, she was like, Ground control. We have touchdown. The eagle has landed. Being in Latvia, finding Peter, resolving the vision made it possible for her to launch and land. She would take off and fly again, but this time, she had strong wings and a broad landing base. Her talons could grasp the earth, branches and cliffs. And most important for her, she had a community of support and collaboration.

A flash blinded her. Two more lights came in rapid succession. Mikis. Ever the photographer, he was covering the mother of all Latvian events for the National Geographic piece. Elizabete was somewhere on stage singing. In the moments after one song ended, and the audience erupted, clapping and cheering, Mikis clasped both her hands in his, leaned toward her and said, "You know, Elizabete and my story wouldn't be complete without a photo of the young Latvians we interviewed, celebrating Latvia's freedom through its soul, the singing at its main choir concert."

Nikkie felt her face flush.

"You two may have been born in America," he said. "But right here, right now, in this place, your souls are on your faces. You are home." He kissed her gently on the lips and walked off into the crowd.

Nikkie settled back to listen, the vestige of that kiss warming her face. Some songs that followed were performed by the whole choir, others by segments. Some were fronted by soloists or professional choirs. One soloist captured a drone singing style and sang as if the notes sprung with the earth itself. Her tones vibrated down to Nikkie's core.

Each song was led by a different choir director, who ranged in age from their twenties to their nineties. Respected and adulated, they seemed to have an impact on the audience equivalent to what a rock star would have in the U.S. Two of the best-known were brothers, now into their eighties, Gido and Imants Kokars. They had dedicated their lives to music, taught and directed at song festivals, including the years of the Occupation.

"They're also twins," Indra told them, tapping Nikkie and Tom on their knees.

"I still can't believe all these people spent five years of preparation which culminates in these few hours," Tom said. "That's a lot of dedication."

Then, several hundred dancers, including Māra and her dancers, filed past in a procession down the aisles. They joined the choirs and danced a few numbers. Nikkie listened and watched from a presence in her that lived behind time and place, her skin vibrating.

And then, Imants Kokars, his long white hair swept back, wearing a white suit, climbed up to the raised podium. He swept up his arms, and with a dramatic movement, a song began to end the main program—solemn and beautiful. Evocative. The tenor of the audience shifted. People held hands. Many sang along, tearing up as they did. Those around her seemed to stand a little taller, prouder. Nikkie read the name in her program, *Gaismas Pils* by Jazeps Vitols and the poet Auseklis. "What's happening?" Nikkie asked Indra and Vilnis, as the song ended.

"This song was a standout of the Singing Revolution," Vilnis said. "Its composers were both freedom fighters in the late nineteenth century and early twentieth, another time when Latvians were seeking their freedom from oppression. It's filled with not so subtle double entendre. Latvians knew what it meant when we sang it. *Gaismas Pils* translates to Castle of Light. It speaks of the castle and its light sinking, disappearing, its heroes and freedom lost, but its memory hidden in the scars of the heart. The castle was only revived when it was remembered by the people. Then, light broke through, and the castle rose again. And that's what happened in Latvia. Our light rose again."

With *Gaismas Pils*, the main concert ended. But it was not over. Not until one more special song was sung. After the clapping and cheering, everyone joined hands again to sing the country's unofficial national anthem, *Pūt, vējiņi*. Blow gentle wind. The symbol of the nation in solidarity during the years the Latvians could not sing their own national anthem. The song of longing, hope, obstacles, dreams and great love. Vilnis sang it for them in the forest of the dead, and his mother sang it to comfort him years earlier.

Nikkie closed her eyes to feel the waves of energy, to join the longing for love and freedom the song represented in Latvia and now in her. She opened her eyes to an audience transfixed and transformed. Tears flowed freely down people's faces around her, but they also smiled. The solemnity of the previous song turned transcendent. Their faces, her own family's, and she imagined hers as well, were radiant.

And then, the concert ended. People stirred from their trances, and the audience and choirs began to disperse. Many would stay and sing together until dawn.

Peter and Māra now joined the family, and they walked arm in arm in a row down the road through the forest with tens of thousands of other people toward the waiting buses and trolleys and to where Vilnis' car was parked. Indra and Vilnis walked behind them at a slower pace. They were talking and laughing.

Nikkie began to dance a basic polka. One long step. Two half steps. One two three. One two three. Back and forth. Right. Left. Māra joined her, and they moved to the beat, holding hands as they danced forward on the path. Holding hands, Peter and Ellie came up along Nikkie's right side, grabbed her hand and pulled Nikkie and Māra to create a line weaving up and across the path. They called Tom to join them. The group moved in a circle first to the right for several counts, then to the left.

Peter turned and put his arm around Nikkie's waist, broke her away into a couples' polka. Around and around they spun like she had the first time she performed with Peter in Māra's studio, leaning back, buoyed by Peter's arms. They laughed as they danced, and the crowd near them began to clap a beat for them.

And the trees vibrated with the essence of song. And the trees vibrated, freed at last from the stories they had held, freed to be trees, to dance in the wind to the melody of the rhythm of the earth. The bark of the trees along the promenade was unmarred here. No names carved in them like Nikkie and Tom had cut in the madrone as children. Nikkie and Tom were no longer lost, for real or pretend, but found, found like breezes in the wind.

Acknowledgements

This book birthed its way into being with many helpers and supporters. I thank you all, named and unnamed.

To Robert McDowell, my editor and publisher. You are a true visionary. Thank you for your encouragement, humor, friendship, and editing—and for your own beautiful creative spirit and writing.

To my mother, Vija Miezitis, for sharing her family stories and her love for our Latvian heritage.

To my writer's group for many years: our facilitator—Shoshana Alexander, Jodine Turner, Maggie McLaughlin, Lori Henriksen, Tiziana DellaRovere and Nancy Bloom. Thank you for your encouragement, the gift of reading many drafts and holding the vision of this novel with me. Special thanks to Shoshana for added editorial and publishing input. Thank you to the journal writing group where I discovered pieces of this book: Dami Roelse, Margo Young and Ann Muth. To the writers who have taken part in my writing workshops at Transformational Writers and to the Willamette Writer's organization (and Southern Oregon chapter). Your dedication to writing and craft inspires me.

To my first readers: My Latvian soul sister/friend, Margita LaGrotta Your deep wisdom, insights and attention to detail are much appreciated—for the book and in life. I loved traveling to Latvia with you and my mother. Janet Marie Sola—Your generous comments, suggestions and support went above and beyond and were a true gift of inspired editing. Māris Roze— Your observations and Latvian and personal perspectives added much to finetune and elevate the book. And special thanks for your translation of the Latvian song, *Pūt, vējiņi.*

Thanks to Evy Mcpherson, Susan Hirth, Lawrence Katz, Paula Skuratowicz, Kathleen Conroy, Cori Bishop, Jo Anna Shaw, Karen Joy Turley, Lorena Gonda, Steven Kiralla, Tresha Cuomo, Rob Geier, Michael Arnold, Suzanna Solomon (R.I.P), Dottie Wickmire, Jan Baker, and Mara Owens.

To family and friends in Latvia who took me into their homes and hearts—Rita, Benita, Harolds, Ina, Uldis, Agrita, Silvija, Dagmara, Vesma, Bruno, Birute, Vilnis (R.I.P), Inese, Ziedonis and Inara.

To my muse, divine source, guides, the trees, Lithia Park— thank you for your inspiration, guidance and renewal.

To Charlie, the shaman cat. Thank you for making me smile daily and insuring I take breaks.

To the seven-year-old boy who stopped me in Lithia Park, asked, "Is your name Nikkie and are you lost?" and sparked the idea for the main character for this novel.

And to Jonah Blue: Thank you for your love and belief in me and this novel as we traveled life's path together—and for your inspired editorial and structural suggestions. Journey well, love, on your grand adventure on the other side.

Author's Notes

Latvia

In writing this book, I read books and articles and consulted websites about Latvia's history, nature, folklore, traditions, mass choir singing and the Singing Revolution. I also traveled to Latvia three times, spending time with relatives and my mother's friends in Riga and various communities in Vidzeme and Kurzeme, including Gulbene and Kuldiga. While in Riga, I attended two Latvian Song and Dance Festivals (2003 and 2015) and a Latvian School Youth Song and Dance Celebration.

A first generation American, I also grew up in the Latvian culture, attending Latvian School on weekends to learn the language and history, taking part in Latvian activities and camps, going to Latvian Song and Dance Festivals in the United States and Canada. As part of my research, I attended the 3x3 Latvian Adult Camp in Garezers, Michigan. I speak and write the language and grew up hearing family stories about growing up in Latvia and my family's escape during WWII.

My mother, active in the Chicago Latvian community and at 3x3 in Garezers for many years, befriended Latvian performers, choir directors and folklore experts. I was able to gain added insight into Latvia's politics and arts when we spent time with her connections in Latvia, notably the world-renowned choir director, Māris Sirmais and other song and folklore experts.

A key book I read was Guntis Šmidchens' *The Power of Song: Nonviolent National Culture in the Baltic Singing Revolution (New Directions in Scandinavian Studies)* (The University of Washington Press, 2014) about the power of singing in the Baltic countries. He heads the Baltic Studies Program at the University of Washington in Seattle. It informed and inspired references in the novel to the Singing Revolution, the Baltic Way demonstration and the power of singing and mass choirs in Latvia, Estonia and Lithuania. Another book that offered insight into how Latvians have come to terms with dispossession, exile and ambiguous returns was *The Testimony of Lives: Narrative and memory in post-Soviet Latvia* by Vieda Skultans.

Especially helpful websites were https://www.latvia.eu, https://dziesmusvetki.lv/en/about-the-celebration/the-song-and-dance-celebration/ and https://latviansonline.com

Latvian Song and Dance Festival and Mass Choir Singing

To taste the power of mass choir singing and dancing in Latvia, go to You Tube and search for Latvian Song and Dance Festival. Held every five years, the most recent was in 2018. You can also do searches for the Singing Revolution and the Baltic Way. I've included links here to four songs from the 2018 Latvian Song and Dance Festival, sung by 16,000 singers, to give you an example of the power of the singing soul of Latvia and its connection to nature symbolism:

"Saule Perkons Daugava" (Sun, Thunder, Daugava—main river in Latvia) Written during the Singing Revolution and recently used by Catalonia as their anthem for their split from Spain. Romāns Vanags, a top choir director, directs. Martins Brauns, composer, is the accompanist. https://www.youtube.com/watch?v=Yrug9LApJJs

"Pūt, vējiņi" (Blow Wind)—The most famous folk song in Latvia. It was the secret Latvian anthem sung during the Soviet Occupation when the Latvians were not allowed to sing their own anthem. It is always the last song performed at the Song Festival. https://www.youtube.com/watch?v=pM0ZZ7ogrfo

"Gaismas Pils" (Castle of Light)—The second most famous song from the Singing Revolution directed here by Imants Kokars. He and his twin, who have since died, were the most famous choir directors in Latvia. From 2008. https://www.youtube.com/watch?v=v8tJCv8hwb0

"Lec, Saulīte" (Rise, Sun!) My favorite song at this year's festival from a current composer, Raimonds Tiguls, directed by my mother's and my friend, Māris Sirmais, a world-renowned, award-winning choir director. https://www.youtube.com/watch?v=Yrug9LApJJs

Family Constellation Therapy and Epigenetics

I studied Bert Hellinger's Family Constellation therapy with Stephen Victor and am a certified practitioner. References to it in the novel draw from my training, from setting constellations, and from books written on the subject. A notable reference was *The Art and Practice of Family Constellations : Leading Family Constellations as Developed by Bert Hellinger* by Carl-Auer-Systeme Verlag. Some scenes in the book also have a constellation-like flavor and spirit. The constellation work also informed my understanding of the field of epigenetics as it relates to the passing on of family trauma.

ABOUT THE AUTHOR

Alissa Lukara is a first generation American. Her immediate family escaped Latvia during WWII to avoid deportation to Siberia and were refugees for five years. Many family members remained behind in Latvia and lived through the Soviet occupation. *Secrets of the Trees* is the modern day novel she was called to write that draws on her family history and experiences of ancestral healing. Her memoir, *Riding Grace: A Triumph of the Soul* (Silver Light Publications), was called by the *Midwest Book Review* "a transcendental story about the immeasurable powers of redemption and compassion." She also authored *Night Dancin'* (Ballantine Books). Alissa has been a professional writer for more than thirty years. She guides writers through courses, coaching and editing at Transformational Writers, blogs and speaks on writing and transformation.

Alissa also studied family constellation therapy and was creator, president and editor of Lifechallenges.org, a nonprofit website that for a decade offered self-help tools and inspirational, transformational articles for millions of people facing adversity in 110 countries. She makes her home in Southern Oregon with Charlie the cat and a strong network of "framily."

To find out about upcoming events, read her blogs, view video interviews, performance readings, talks and to sign up for updates, visit Alissa's websites at www.alissalukara.com

and www.transformationalwriters.com. Follow her on Social Media at:

www.facebook.com/AlissaLukaraAuthor
www.facebook.com/transformationalwriters
Twitter: @AlissaLukara
Instagram: @alissa.lukara
YouTube: writerstransform

INTERVIEW WITH THE AUTHOR

Homestead Lighthouse Press: Who or what inspired you to write?

AL: As a child, I wanted to touch people's lives in the ways my own had been touched by the books I read. But I did not begin writing until later. I had been an English major in college, studied journalism in graduate school, then worked at a public relations agency in New York City. In my heart, though, I longed to write creative nonfiction and fiction. I signed up for Elaine Sorel's workshop for creative people, described by The New York Times as "the Shape Up or Ship Out or Get Off the Dime clinic" for creative people struggling with some aspect of their creative expression. Elaine had been an artist's and photographer's representative and had worked with many well-known writers as well. During our introductory meeting, I brought out a poem I had written for it, and she asked me to read it out loud to her. She responded with one word, "More." Four months later, I quit my job and become a freelance writer. Four months after that, I had a contract for a nonfiction book with Ballantine Books.

HLP: Are you spiritual or religious? If you are, how does that enter your fiction & non-fiction?

AL: Spirituality is central in my life and, as such, makes its way into my writing. To me, life is one long lesson from the divine opening us to the love at our core. I included spiritual experiences that refected that in my memoir about a transformational healing.

When the character of Nikkie emerged, I knew her dancing would be an embodiment of her spirituality. Throughout her transformation, Nikkie deepens her recognition of the divine in herself and in all creation, most notably nature and trees, a concept which is central to Latvian spirituality. Nikkie also strengthens her connection to the divine feminine in the form of the main Latvian goddesses Māra and Laima, who support and guide her.

HLP: What led to your creation of this novel?

AL: I had a strong calling to write a novel set in Latvia that would touch on both my ancestry and family history and this deep connection I felt to them growing up. But I did not only want the novel to retell my family's story of living in or escaping from Latvia. After completing my memoir, I was hiking in a local park, longing to find inspiration for the new book, when a young boy ran up to me. He asked me if my name was Nikkie and if I was lost in the woods. Nikkie had carved her name into a tree, he said, and he was looking for her with his father and sister. They had made a game of it, his father told me.

That encounter sparked the idea for the novel and the main character, named Nikkie. But I did not know how or if the book would tie into Latvia until scenes set in Latvia began to emerge two years into the writing. I had recently traveled to Latvia and spent time with relatives and my mother's friends, including several involved in the arts and folklore. These Latvians were now experiencing freedom of choice and living in a democracy for the first time.

HLP: Share with us your deep and wide connection to Latvia.

AL: I am a first generation American with several generations of Latvian ancestry. My parents and maternal family escaped Latvia during WWII and were refugees and lived in a Displaced Persons camp in Würzburg, Bavaria, Germany for five years before emigrating to the U.S. My relatives in Latvia lived through the Soviet Occupation. Others had been arrested and sent to Siberia, where most died. This family history has struck a deep chord in me.

Growing up, I was active in the Latvian culture and community in Cleveland, Ohio, learning to speak, read and write Latvian, speaking it at home, attending Latvian school, events and camps. Since the Soviet Union was trying to destroy the culture in Latvia itself, my parents and many other Latvian parents taught their children that it was up to the Latvian diaspora to carry forth the culture so it would not die. I participated in Latvian Song and Dance festivals in the U.S. and Canada and as a young adult was part of the Latvian community in New York City. I get teary when I sing the Latvian national anthem or it's unofficial anthem, *Pūt, vējiņi* in a way that makes no logical sense, given I have always lived in the U.S.

I pulled away from the Latvian community as an adult in order to find myself and my artistic voice outside my ancestral heritage. But starting in 2003, I traveled to Latvia three times and became a dual citizen. In researching *Secrets of the Trees* there, in meeting my family, in attending its song and dance festival, I realized that much of what was important to me as an individual in fact had its roots in my Latvian heritage and its land: my love of the arts and nature, spirituality that sees the divine in nature, poetry, dance, a longing for freedom, my resilience.

HLP: What is the novel's place in culture and society?

AL: This novel explores themes of home, homeland, and the impact of displacement during a time when the refugee and immigrant crisis is prominent. It looks at the impact of war, oppression, displacement and trauma not only on present, but also future generations. The field of epigenetics reveals how the effects of these are actually passed on in our DNA. The novel considers in what form present generation and ancestral healing are possible for traumas suffered in the past. This applies not only to Latvians but to all countries. I think part of the fascination with genealogy is that we are hoping to understand how our roots and what our ancestors faced impacts us today, who we really are in relation to the ancestors and cultural influences that subconsciously informed aspects of our lives.

In addition, Latvia is a country most people know little about. Yet, its culture is rich. Too often, our world seems to value only the accomplishments of the super powers while ignoring or discounting what smaller countries have to teach us. The novel offers a look at what Latvians have to share globally through the filter of what has most touched me about it. For instance, they have managed to create and preserve their cultural identity and identification as a singing nation despite living through centuries of oppression and serfdom. During Glasnost and Atmoda, Latvians' conscious decision to stage a nonviolent Singing Revolution led to the dissolution of fifty years of Soviet Oppression. They continue to hold a Latvian song and dance festival, as they have since 1873, that is on the UNESCO Masterpieces of the Oral and Intangible Heritage of Humanity list. It involves mass choir and dance events of forty thousand plus participants (fifteen thousand singers, fifteen thousand dancers) from a country with a population of two million. And only the top choirs and dance groups in the country participate.

Numerous Latvian classical music and opera stars grace the top opera houses and symphony halls in the world and the country's choirs repeatedly win gold medals in world competitions. The country also maintains a deep connection to and respect for nature, the land and its forests.

HLP: Do you enjoy teaching? How does teaching co-exist with fiction?

AL: Yes, I do enjoy it. I teach and coach mostly adult writers in person and using online workshops, webinars and other technologies. I find that helping other writers hone their craft hones my own. I feel inspired and excited by the voices, stories and creative dreams of those writers and enjoy creating communities of writers.

HLP: What are your thoughts regarding the public performance of fiction?

AL: I love doing readings of my fiction and hearing other fiction writers read and perform their work. I feel transported by the rhythm of words, the poetic elements, the unique voices and styles, the dramatic impact – and enjoy sharing all that.

HLP: Is there perhaps a sequel in the works?

AL: In writing the first draft of *Secrets of the Trees*, several chapters of Nikkie in Egypt crept in that I cut but thought might turn into a sequel. I also wrote chapters in the voice and point of view of Tom, Nikkie's twin brother. His poetic voice intrigued me. At the same time, I feel like I'm on a whole new journey in my life and in my writing and can't wait to see what emerges from that